A LOVE BEYOND TIME

"Michel, you may tell me I have no right to speak on this subject, but surely you have not given up all hope of recalling your identity?"

"In fact, I *have* given up hope," he informed Danise. "It's best to get on with the business of living."

"But you don't know if you have a family." Danise could not say what she wanted, could not speak the word wife to him.

"What can I do about it?" he asked. "I cannot force my memory to return."

"You have changed overnight," she accused him. "You are so reserved, so closed upon yourself. There is a deep difference in you."

"Of course there is. You see before you a man who has accepted his lot and who has found a place for himself."

"But just a few days ago you told me—" She broke off, recalling in vivid detail what he had said, what he had done to her. "Michel, I do not understand."

A LOVE BEYOND TIME

FLORA SPEER

LOVE SPELL ◆ NEW YORK CITY

LOVE SPELL®

July 1999

Published by

Dorchester Publishing Co., Inc.
276 Fifth Avenue
New York, NY 10001

ISBN 0-505-52326-4

The name "Love Spell" and its logo are trademarks of Dorchester Publishing Co., Inc.

Printed in the United States of America.

Chapter 1

"Has anyone ever told you that you are crazy?"

"All the time. But I never pay any attention, because I know I'm right." Henry Adelbert Marsh regarded his visitor with cool arrogance. The man facing him was of average height, with dark hair and nondescript features except for the startling blue eyes that lifted his appearance far out of the ordinary. Hank Marsh wasn't one to be unduly impressed by a person's looks—he wasn't all that handsome himself—but he was annoyed with this man, and he was curious. He met the blue gaze with open defiance. "What I want to know is how you found me. I covered my tracks pretty damned well."

7

"You did. I'll give you that much. I lost you for a long time. It took me months of searching and a lot of trouble to discover just where you were hiding." Ignoring the woman who was the third person in the room, Bradford Michael Bailey moved a little farther into the back bedroom of the house, his eyes on the computer that filled the better part of the space. There could be absolutely no doubt; he had found his quarry at last, and Hank was up to his old tricks again. "As it happens, I am something of a detective. An historical detective, since I'm an archaeologist. I enjoy the challenge of a difficult search. And I was given a few clues to help me find you. Do you remember Mark Brant? Or India Baldwin?"

"India sent you after me?" Hank's arrogant mask slipped a bit. "I never thought she'd talk. She was so adamant about forgetting what happened last Christmastime."

"You mean about you accidentally sending her far back in time? How could anyone ever forget living through such an experience? No, India didn't talk. My friend, Mark, figured out what had happened. He's the one who sent me after you."

"I knew that guy was trouble the first time I saw him," Hank muttered. "O.K., now you've found me. What do you want with me, Bailey?"

"The name's Mike. I've learned enough about you during the last ten months to put us on a first-name basis. I assume this is your latest machine." Mike took a couple of steps toward the computer, noting the additional components and the power enhancers. He was no stranger to computers. Archaeologists found them remarkably useful. "You have made some interesting changes to this thing, haven't you? Are you hoping to prove some wild new theory, or are you still working on the old one?"

At this point, the young woman who had let Mike into her house when he claimed to be Hank's friend inserted herself between Mike and the computer. From his investigations into Hank's whereabouts, Mike knew her name was Alice. She was small and thin, with dark hair scraped back into a tight ponytail. She wore no makeup and her expression was grimly intense. It occurred to Mike that she would be a lot prettier if she would lighten up a little. But perhaps her interest in Hank was more scientific than romantic. It certainly seemed that way.

"Leave Hank alone," Alice ordered. "And you stay away from his computer, too. Our theories and what we are doing are none of your business. You don't have any right to intrude on our privacy."

"Did you know your friend here is a thief?" Mike said to her. When Alice glanced toward Hank, Mike took another step in the direction of the computer. "Hank has stolen the property of this India Baldwin we've just mentioned. I have been sent to collect and return that property."

"Hank is no thief," Alice protested. "He's a great and misunderstood scientist."

"He broke into India Baldwin's house and

took two floppy disks and a notebook that belonged to her. Then Hank left town with those disks and the notebook. If that's not stealing, I don't know what is. But if he'll return her property, India has promised she won't press charges against him."

"You can't interfere with important scientific work," Alice cried, apparently oblivious to the legal implications of what Hank had done. Mike decided he wasn't going to get anywhere with her. Alice was on Hank's side, and she probably wouldn't budge from her position without a good scare.

"Hand over the disks, Hank. And the notebook." Mike put out his hand, waiting. "If you give them to me, I won't call the police. Refuse, and you are going to be prosecuted for possession of stolen property and for trying to recreate a dangerous accident. That is what you are trying to do here, isn't it? You want to repeat the accident that happened to India. You intend to try to send someone else back to the eighth century. Are you going to use your friend Alice as the guinea pig, or are you planning to go yourself this time?"

"He knows, Hank." Suddenly, Alice looked frightened. "I don't want to go to jail."

"Shut up, Alice," Hank ordered. "He doesn't know anything. He's bluffing."

"Wrong," Mike informed him. "I know everything about your theories and your experiments. Now, ask yourself where I got the money to trail you across the country for all these months. Does it begin to dawn on you that I'm not acting solely on my own initiative? There are some very important people who are determined to stop what you are trying to do, Hank. After I leave here, you may have some other visitors, whom I don't think will be as pleasant as I am, or as patient with you. Now, come on, hand over the evidence and you'll be in the clear when other people come searching."

"Are you saying the federal government is after him?" Alice squeaked, backing away from Hank. "I didn't ask for this kind of trouble."

"Last chance, Hank. Hand over the disks." Mike paused for a moment, watching Hank, who stood unmoving and glaring at him. "All right, time's up. If you aren't going to give me the disks, then I'll just have to take them. Here's one. I guess the other's in the machine, isn't it? Now, where have you hidden the notebook?" As he spoke, Mike picked up one floppy disk from the shelf beside the computer and pocketed it. He reached toward the computer to remove the second disk.

"Don't touch that thing!" Hank yelled. "It's all set up and ready to go."

"Then turn it off and give me the disk," Mike demanded. "The notebook, too."

"No way!" Hank shoved at Mike, trying to get him away from the computer, but Mike caught his arm in a tight grip.

"Knock it off, Hank. I don't want to hurt you. Just hand over the disk and I'll leave." Knowing he was the stronger man, Mike released the furious scientist. Doing so was a mistake.

11

"You aren't going to stop me," Hank declared.
"Not you or anyone else, including the government. I can just imagine what the Feds would
do with my material. Damn it, I'm sick and tired
of uninformed idiots trying to interfere with my
work!" With that, he clenched his fist and took
a wild swing at Mike, who ducked. Hank was
not a fighting man. The punch missed Mike's
chin with plenty of room to spare, and Hank's
fist slammed into the computer.

"Ow!" Hank cried, nursing his aching hand.
"Get out of here. Just leave me alone."

"I can't do that." When Mike did not move,
Hank and Alice came at him at the same
time, but from different directions. Mike was
concentrating on what Hank might do, so he
wasn't expecting Alice's attack, and he didn't
want to hit a woman. He tried to sidestep
Alice while at the same time fending off
Hank. As a result of his misplaced chivalry,
he was pushed backward until he was up
against the computer. He put out a hand to
steady himself.

His hand went through the computer screen,
vanishing into the solid surface. The computer
screen appeared to be undamaged, but Mike
could no longer see his own hand and arm.

"Hey! Come back here. You're not the one
who's supposed to go," Hank shouted.

But Bradford Michael Bailey was beyond
stopping what was happening. He could not
believe what was happening, so at first he did
nothing to help himself. Within half a second it
was impossible for him to do anything anyway,

because his own body would not follow his commands. Incredibly, he was being pulled into the computer. He saw an orange blur first, then an odd blackness with bright-colored numbers whizzing through it. His head ached and his ears popped as if he were falling fast. Which he was.

He came out of the blackness into empty air. Then he was tumbling downward through tree branches. He grabbed at them to try to stop his precipitous fall, but some of the branches broke and his hands slipped off others as he plummeted toward the ground.

He knew he was going to die. Oddly, his life did not pass before his eyes. All he saw was tree leaves and branches, a few rocks below awaiting him, and the too-solid earth on which those rocks were resting.

He hit the ground hard, knocking all the air out of his lungs. His head cracked against one of the waiting rocks. Unable to move or breathe, Mike fell into blackness again, a different kind of blackness this time, a sucking, greedy darkness that engulfed him in an instant, snuffing out his consciousness.

Chapter 2

Francia
Spring, A.D. 779

At first Danise thought the man was dead.
He lay perfectly still, prone on a pile of
leaves and branches, and when she turned
him over she saw that his face was swollen
beyond recognition.

Not that she would have recognized him if he
had been in the best of health. She had never
seen anyone wearing such strange clothing. His
breeches, made of the common dark blue fabric
woven in Nimes, had been worn and washed
until they were threadbare and faded to near
whiteness in places. The knees were torn and
bloodstained. She would have thought him a
peasant save for the stitching. Danise, no mean

needlewoman herself, had never encountered stitches so even or so close together—two rows of them at each seam—and there were little pouches set into the garment near the waist, perhaps to hold the man's personal belongings. His upper body was covered by a short tunic of matching fabric, open down the front. Beneath it he wore a round-necked blue shirt of some soft material. His hair was black and straight. All this she saw in a moment, before her servant Clothilde spoke.

"Is he breathing?" Clothilde knelt in the leaves beside her mistress and pressed a hand against the man's chest. "His heart is beating. He is warm."

"Poor man." Danise let her fingers touch his face softly, so as not to hurt him further. She could see that his nose had been bleeding, but the blood had stopped. In addition to his scraped knees he had scratches on his face and hands and a nasty lump on the left side of his head. Danise could find no open wounds to require immediate stanching of blood. If he had any more serious injuries, they must be internal.

"How could a stranger come so close to the royal camp and not be stopped by Charles's guards?" asked Clothilde.

"I don't know," Danise said, "but he fell from a tree. Those are fresh spring leaves he's lying on, on top of the old leaves from last autumn. Look up, Clothilde. You can see from the broken branches up there the path by which he came to this spot."

15

"He was in the treetop, spying on us?" Clothilde gasped. "We must alert the guards at once."

"No." Danise spoke sharply. "We don't know that he was spying. He may have thought *we* would do *him* harm. We can't call the guards. They would think as you do, and be rough with him. He looks too badly hurt to endure such treatment. Clothilde, I think by the fine seams on his clothing that he must be a nobleman. Look at them. No peasant woman could make stitches so small or so straight. I believe he has been traveling for a long time, if such sturdy fabric is so badly worn. Therefore, until he can tell us who he is, we would be wise to treat him as a visiting noble.

"I will stay here to watch over him," Danise went on. "You must find my father or Guntram, who will know where my father is. We will need a litter to take him back to the camp."

"Savarec would not want me to leave you alone," Clothilde protested.

"One of us must go, for we cannot leave him by himself," Danise pointed out. "And, Clothilde, be discreet. Don't talk to anyone but my father or Guntram. Be careful to avoid Sister Gertrude. You know how she loves to make a fuss."

"How am I to do that?" Clothilde demanded, standing and planting her hands on her wide hips. "That nun has eyes like an eagle."

"You and I together have avoided her eagle eye often enough," Danise responded. "I know you can do it, Clothilde. Just be quick. I fear he must be badly injured, or he would have wakened by now."

Left alone with the stranger, Danise took off her light spring cloak and used it to cover him. Then she sat beside him, gently stroking his hair.

"Why did you climb so high in the trees?" she murmured to him. "Was it to look over the landscape and thus find your way? Were you intending to come to Duren to meet with Charles?"

Since the man remained unresponsive, Danise settled herself more comfortably to await the arrival of help. Despite Clothilde's qualms, she was not the least bit frightened to be alone in the forest. There could be no danger to her there, so close to the Frankish encampment.

Charles, king of the Franks, had called the Mayfield, the great spring assembly of Frankish nobles, to meet at Duren on the River Rur, about two days' journey east of Aachen. The choice of place was deliberate, to demonstrate just how powerful the Franks were to the ever-restless Saxon tribes who lived on the eastern borders of Francia. Still, Duren and the forests surrounding it were safe. If they were not, Charles would never have allowed his beloved queen to accompany him there, for Hildegarde was seven months gone with her sixth pregnancy in eight years of marriage, and she was not at all well.

Nor, if Duren were unsafe, would Savarec have summoned his daughter Danise to meet him at the royal court. Danise had made the journey from the convent school at Chelles, near Paris, to Duren in the company of her usual chaperon, Sister Gertrude, her personal maidservant Clothilde, and two men-at-arms whom her father had sent to protect her along the way. She had seen her father only briefly on her arrival the prèvious night, before retiring to the tent Savarec had provided for his womenfolk next to his own tent.

Duren was but a small settlement, so the Franks had established a town of tents on a broad space cleared between river and forest. There they would live during the weeks of Mayfield, feasting out-of-doors in the fine spring weather, and enjoying the contests of skill in wrestling, weaponry, and riding put on by the younger warriors. Meanwhile, in the huge royal tent or on the open field, the nobles would meet with Charles to decide whether another campaign was necessary against the Saxons. While the men conferred, the women, too, would meet, renewing old friendships and making new ones.

The annual assembly was also the time when Frankish nobles traditionally arranged marriages for their children, and Danise very much feared this was why Savarec had called her to Duren. At nearly eighteen, she was almost too old to be wed.

The man beside her moaned, diverting her thoughts from herself to him. He raised one hand to his face, then moaned again.

"It will be all right," she told him, catching

his hand. "Help is coming soon. We will take good care of you."

He grew still at the sound of her voice, and she thought he was trying to frown. It was hard to tell for sure, since his face was so swollen, but his expression seemed to change and he winced.

"Just lie still," she advised.

He muttered a few words in a language she could not understand, then said a word she did know.

"Angel?"

"*Ange?*" she repeated. "Oh, I comprehend. You think you are dead and I am an angel? I'm afraid not. I am far from being an angel."

He grew still again—listening to her, she was sure—and then he opened his eyes.

They were blue, the deepest, purest, most heart-stopping blue she had ever seen. In his sorely damaged face, swollen and bruised and streaked with dirt and scratches, and smeared with blood from his injured nose, those eyes were like torches in a dark forest. Not even the famous piercing blue gaze of Charles, king of the Franks, had ever affected Danise the way this unknown man's eyes did.

"Who are you?" she whispered, caught and held by light and color and unmistakable intelligence. When she saw the puzzled expression invading the blue depths, she repeated her question, speaking slowly and carefully, hoping he would understand her.

He said something and started to shake his head. The movement elicited a groan of pain.

The blue eyes closed and he slipped away from her, back into unconsciousness. Only then did Danise realize she was still holding his hand, clutching it in both of hers, pressing it against her bosom. She let it go, laying it upon his chest and stroking the limp and dirty fingers with her own white ones.

"Don't die," she whispered. "Please don't die. I want to know you. I want to hear you speak again in that strange language."

It seemed a long time before Clothilde returned, leading Savarec, his man-at-arms Guntram, and a third man whom Danise did not know. The black-bearded Guntram carried a rolled-up litter made of two wooden poles thrust through the hems of a length of strong fabric.

"Clothilde has explained what happened." Savarec knelt beside his daughter. "Is he still alive?"

"Yes, he's breathing, and now and then he moans." Danise met her father's level gaze. "He opened his eyes for a moment or two, and he tried to speak, but I could not understand him."

"If he wakened, it's a good sign." It was the third man who spoke, a golden-haired fellow with a pleasant face. He went to his knees and put out a hand, feeling the unconscious man's head and apparently coming to the same conclusion as Danise. "He has a lump here, beneath his hair. From the blood on this rock beside him, I'd guess he hit his head on it when he fell."

"Danise," said Savarec, noting his daughter's questioning look, "this is Count Redmond. I had planned for you to meet him under more agreeable circumstances, but this moment must do."

"On the contrary, Savarec," said Count Redmond, "these *are* agreeable circumstances, for your daughter has shown herself to be both intelligent and discreet. Another maiden might have run into the camp crying to anyone she met that a strange man had been found in the forest, thus leading everyone gathered at Mayfield to imagine we faced a Saxon attack."

"This man is no Saxon," Danise said, certainty in her voice. "I have seen Saxon prisoners and heard them speak. He is unlike any of them. His speech, his clothing, his hair, his clean-shaven face—"

"As I said, Savarec," Redmond interrupted, "an intelligent young woman."

"Father, he will need good care," Danise said. "Will you have him taken to your tent? Clothilde and I can nurse him, and if you think it's necessary, you can easily set a guard there to watch him."

"Yes," said Savarec, "that's what we'll do. We'll keep your cloak over him, Danise, to hide his strange clothing, and if anyone asks who we are carrying on the litter, we'll say he's one of my men-at-arms who met with an accident. That way, we'll cause no alarm. But I will tell Charles in private what has happened, in case he wants to post more guards around the camp."

Guntram unrolled the litter, and he, Savarec, and Redmond lifted the unconscious man onto it. With Savarec and Danise leading the way and Clothilde walking beside the litter, Redmond and Guntram carried it out of the forest and into the Frankish camp. They were not stopped. Savarec was well-known, and his story of an injured man-at-arms was at once accepted.

Inside Savarec's tent, a folding camp bed was quickly set up and the stranger laid on it. Danise sent Clothilde for hot water and cloths so they could bathe the man, and while she was gone, Danise began to undress him. She was not so involved with her patient, however, that she did not hear her father and Count Redmond talking just outside the tent.

"A lovely maiden," Redmond said. "Your daughter is all you claimed her to be, Savarec."

"I knew you would be pleased," Savarec said.

"We will talk again soon, my friend."

"You understand," Savarec said, "she must agree."

"I would not agree myself if Danise did not," Count Redmond responded.

A moment later, Savarec entered his tent and stood behind Danise, watching while she worked.

"Where is Sister Gertrude?" Savarec asked. "Why is she not with you?"

"She has gone to the queen," Danise responded. "Sister Gertrude was of help to Hildegarde during her last pregnancy, while

22

we were in Agen, so Hildegarde asked to see her as soon as we arrived in Duren."

"Which is why you took the opportunity to go off by yourself into the forest?" demanded Savarec.

"I was not alone. Clothilde was with me. I thought it would be peaceful amongst the trees."

"Peaceful?" To Danise's surprise, considering Savarec's overly protective attitude toward her, her father chuckled. "On occasion I have myself wanted to escape to some peaceful place far from Sister Gertrude's sharp tongue. But she does mean well, Danise, and she has your welfare always at heart."

"I know. It's why I am so patient with her. Father, look at this. I found it tucked into a pouch inside his tunic. What could it be?" Danise held up a flat, square object contained in a parchment-like cover.

"I have no idea what it might be. I've never seen anything like this before." Savarec took the floppy disk, looked at it in perplexity, then handed it back. "Keep it with his other belongings until he is well enough to tell us what it is."

"And this? What could this be?" Danise held up a leather object. Again, Savarec took it to examine.

"It appears to be a folding purse of some kind. These green and white parchments have lettering and numbers on them. Perhaps this man is carrying a message. Now, that is a very strange way to fasten breeches."

23

Savarec bent to help Danise, who was struggling with the unfamiliar fastenings, and soon their patient lay naked. At once Savarec pulled a quilt over the man's exposed torso and then together they examined his arms, legs, ribs, skull, cheekbones and jaw, noting the many bruises and scrapes he had sustained.

"He appears to have no broken bones and no serious injuries other than the blow to his head," Savarec said. "His body beneath the clothing is surprisingly clean, which suggests you were right to assume he is a nobleman. Here is Clothilde with the water. Bathe his injuries and cover him quickly so he doesn't catch a chill. I am going now to report to Charles what has happened." Savarec paused at the tent flap. "I have posted Guntram just outside. Call him if our guest gives you any trouble. If he wakens, have Guntram send someone to me at once."

The two women worked quickly as Savarec had bidden them, but not so quickly that Danise did not have time to note how well made the stranger was. He was not as heavily muscled as most Frankish warriors, but there could be no discounting the potential strength in his long legs, or in his shoulders and arms. His hands were long, with tapered fingers, and his nails were well shaped, though several had been broken as a result of his fall from the tree.

Clothilde, after an exclamation of annoyance that a young man should be lying almost naked to her mistress's view, made a point of covering his manly parts with a cloth, but not before Danise had rested fascinated eyes on him. She had lived a protected life since her mother's death a few years ago, but her earliest youth had been spent in a freer way, so the sight of unclothed male babies or little boys had been common. She had also, on several occasions, helped wounded men. This unknown man's body should have been no different from any other. But it was. Danise glanced at the cloth over his groin and blushed.

"Be particularly careful when you wash his face," Clothilde advised. "Those scratches must be painful. I wonder if his nose is broken?"

"My father thinks not, but we won't know for certain until the swelling subsides." Gently Danise wiped dirt and pieces of leaves off the man's hair, taking special care around the lump on the left side of his head. Then, after rinsing the cloth first in warm water, she began to work on his face. He muttered a string of unintelligible words and groaned, but did not rouse from his stupor. When he lay clean and well-covered, Danise turned to Clothilde.

"You will have to ask Guntram to find clothes for him," she said. "He cannot go about in his own clothing. He will attract too much unwanted attention."

"I'll see what I can do," Clothilde replied, "but from the look of him, don't expect him to waken soon, if ever. I think Savarec ought to have the physicians look at him, and then the priest."

"We will leave those decisions to my father."

25

Flora Speer

Danise pulled up a stool and sat down beside
the bed. She smoothed back the man's damp
hair, sighing at the condition of his face, which
was turning blue and purple where the bruises
were darkening. He was not a pleasant sight,
yet in his very strangeness, in his battered form
and his helplessness lay a peculiar attraction,
while the mystery of his presence alone and
unattended in the forest intrigued her.

"You cannot be a Frank," she murmured.
"You are from a land far away. When you
can speak again, will you tell me about your
home?"

"He may never speak again," Clothilde
warned. "I'll get rid of this dirty water and
wash out the cloths we used on him."

The tent flap had barely closed on Clothilde
when the man opened his eyes. Twin pools of
brilliant blue regarded Danise with an intensity
strong enough to make her hold her breath. He
did not speak. When she could bear the silent
scrutiny no longer, Danise asked, "Can you tell
me your name?"

Still that intent stare, clouded now by a
growing anxiety. He moistened his dry lips.

"Je ne sais pas," he whispered.

It took her a moment or two to understand
what he was trying to say. The language he used
was not Frankish, though it was somewhat
similar.

"You don't know your own name?" Thinking she might have misunderstood him, she
touched her bosom. "Danise. I am Danise. And
you?" She laid her hand on his chest.

26

"No!" He nearly knocked her over when he tried to get out of bed. "No!"

"Guntram!" Danise did not need to call him; Guntram was with her before the word was out of her mouth. He forced the stranger back onto the bed and kept him there. The stranger put both hands up to his head, holding it tight and groaning.

"He's in pain," Guntram said. "It's the head wound. Stay there!" he shouted at the man on the bed and shook his finger for emphasis. The man stared back at him, then nodded to show he understood. Guntram released his hold on the man and stood watching him, ready to prevent any threat against Danise.

"He can't remember his name," Danise explained. "My asking upset him."

"His confusion will end when the swelling is gone," Guntram replied. "Don't give him anything to eat or drink until tomorrow. If you do feed him, he may vomit and choke to death."

At that moment Savarec returned with a black-robed physician and the physician's assistant, who carried a basket filled with supplies.

"Charles has sent us the royal physician," Savarec explained. "He said his physician may as well practice on this man, since *he* is never sick enough to give the doctors employment." Guntram and Savarec exchanged manly grins at this statement, acknowledging Charles's famous good health and vitality.

"You must leave," the physician announced,

waving them toward the tent opening. His assistant took a pottery jar out of the basket.

"What are you going to do?" asked Danise, unwilling to turn her patient over to anyone else, even the king's own physician.

"Why, I'll put leeches around his head wound to reduce the swelling," the physician replied. "It's the best treatment. He will awaken sooner with my help."

"When he did wake for a moment or two, he seemed to have no memory," Guntram said.

"Then he is in dire need of my treatment, and the sooner, the better." The physician waved again. "Go, please, all of you."

"You may need someone to hold him down," Guntram said.

"My assistant is stronger than he looks." The physician turned his back on them and lifted the lid off the jar of leeches that the assistant held out to him.

"He's quite right," Savarec said. "Physician, I'll leave my man Guntram outside the tent in case you need him. Danise, come with me. It's time I spoke with you about my reason for ordering you to join me here at Duren."

Danise knew well that particular note in her father's voice. She made no objection. After a backward glance toward the bed and the physician bending over it, she followed Savarec out of his tent.

"Here is Sister Gertrude, come from the queen," said Savarec, pausing to let a tall, thin nun join them. "How does Hildegarde? Better today, I hope."

"She is as well as any woman can be who is forced to bear child after child with only a few months of rest between each pregnancy," Sister Gertrude told him tartly.

"Hildegarde is not forced." Savarec's method of dealing with Sister Gertrude was always to speak mildly and calmly in response to her verbal provocations, and he did so now. "Hildegarde loves Charles deeply and truly, as he loves her. Their affection for each other is beautiful to see."

"The problem of loving between men and women," said Sister Gertrude with no diminution of sharpness, "is that for the men it is all loving and pleasure, while for the women there is the burden of childbearing and the ills that go with it. Not to mention the trials of motherhood for a woman whose husband is away fighting for half the year, leaving her to attend to his lands as well as his children."

"Sister Gertrude," Savarec warned, "you will turn Danise away from a woman's natural desire to be a wife and mother."

"So I hope to do, and thus prolong her life and her happiness," responded the nun, meeting Savarec's glance with glittering eyes.

"Both of you, please come into your tent," Savarec bid them. "I will not discuss my daughter's future here in public."

"There is precious little privacy in a tent," Sister Gertrude told him. "All the way here from seeing Hildegarde I could not avoid noticing what people were saying and doing in their tents. It is disgraceful the activities supposedly decent folk will resort to in the middle of the day." But she did follow Savarec into the undyed woolen tent she shared with Danise and Clothilde.

Savarec pulled the entrance flaps closed, then turned to face the two women. The tent was small, with barely space enough for three narrow folding cots and a couple of clothes chests. There was no other furniture.

"Sit down, Father." Danise motioned him to one of the beds, then sat facing him, with Sister Gertrude beside her. "I am curious, since you have been content to let me stay at Chelles undisturbed since last autumn. Why did you want to see me now?"

"The time has come," Savarec informed her, "for us to discuss your marriage."

"Marriage?" Danise repeated, looking distressed. "This is what I feared. Father, you promised me you would not force me. You gave me your word."

"And I will not break it. I was too happy with your mother ever to insist that our daughter should wed a man she does not like. But, Danise, if you are to marry at all, it must be soon, before you are too old. Over the past winter I received several offers for your hand. I thought it would be a good idea for you to meet the men who are interested in you, so you will be better able to decide if any of them pleases you."

"What will you do if none of them pleases her?" Sister Gertrude asked. "If Danise decides she wants to return to Chelles to live, rather than marry, what will your response to her be, Savarec?"

"Danise, I will never force you into a decision that will make you unhappy. Because you are so dear to me, I will allow you to decide for yourself whether to marry or to devote yourself to the religious life."

"You know what I will advise," Sister Gertrude said to Danise. "Spend your life safe and comfortable at Chelles, and thus avoid all the problems and heartbreak of marriage to a Frankish warrior. You have heard the story of my youth, Danise, of how I was betrothed to a man who, against all my pleas, left me to go to war, and how he died in battle. He claimed to love me, but he left me. The same fate, the same bitter grief, could easily befall you if you marry."

"No man worthy of the name of warrior would heed a woman's tears and entreaties to stay at home when his honor and loyalty to his king required him to go to war," Savarec said sternly.

"Father." Danise looked at her parent with troubled eyes. "There is something you do not know, which I now must tell you. Last year, when the queen requested my presence at court and you sent me to Agen with Sister Gertrude here, under the protection of Count Theuderic and his men—during our long journey across Francia I became fond of one of those men." She stopped, trying to think how to explain to her father what it had been like during those enchanted spring weeks of riding through the countryside with a man she had loved from their very first meeting.

"Hugo was good and kind and a most honorable man," Danise went on. "When we reached Agen, he told Charles boldly that he wanted to marry me and begged Charles's permission to ask my hand of you. Charles promised he might, when the Spanish campaign was completed, after Hugo had earned rewards to make him wealthy. Charles all but promised him a great estate and a title." Again Danise stopped, this time choked by tears.

"He knows, child." Sister Gertrude's hand touched Danise's. "I wrote to Savarec soon after Charles and his army returned to Agen from Spain. Charles sent my letter along with his own message to Savarec. Your father knows your affection for Hugo was both true and innocent. He knows you did not lie with Hugo. At least my watchfulness was able to save you from that much grief after Hugo's death at Roncevaux. Your body remains untouched, and I believe your heart will heal in time, for you are still young, and there was nothing formal between you, no betrothal vows."

"You knew, all these months, and you never mentioned it in any of your letters to me?" Danise looked at her father. "Is that why you let me stay at Chelles so long?"

"Sister Gertrude thought it would be best for you, and I agreed," Savarec said. "But you cannot dwell forever in the past. Eventually, as I had to do after your sweet mother died, you must make your peace with what has happened and go on with the remainder of your life. I will leave the choice of wedlock or the religious life to you as I have promised, Danise, but I would not have you remain at Chelles solely because you are afraid to face the world again after Hugo's death. You have had more than nine months in which to mourn him. For the weeks of this Mayfield at Duren and the coming summer at Deutz with me, I ask you to consider what good you may do in the world if you marry and have children and make some noble Frank happy—for any man married to you must be a happy man."

"I need not repeat my opinion on this proposal," Sister Gertrude said.

"Indeed not," said Savarec with unusual asperity. "We know your thoughts on marriage all too well."

"You will give me until the end of summer to decide?" Danise asked.

"I will." Savarec smiled at her. "I have no doubt you would like to hear the names of the men who have offered for you."

"The choice of possible husbands might sway my decision," Danise admitted, smiling back at him. How dear and kind he was. How much she loved him. She knew her happiness was important to him.

"You have three suitors," Savarec said. "First, there is Count Clodion."

"An ancient ogre!" cried Sister Gertrude. "The man has had three wives already and has killed all of them with constant childbearing. He even offered for me when I was younger.

That would be thirty years ago at least. I suppose he wants someone young and strong to nurse him in his dotage, though with his history he may yet hope to get more children on a young wife."

"Clodion's offer was honestly made," Savarec said patiently. "Therefore, we will consider it with equal honesty. He is an important nobleman. However, I must admit, I would prefer to see Danise wed to someone closer to her own age."

"Who else asked for me, Father?" It was so strange to sit here in her tent and discuss in this detached way the qualities of men she did not know, one of whom, before the summer was over, might be her husband. Did she want to marry? Danise could not deny to herself certain stirrings of her body, urgings not completely quelled by the tragic loss of her beloved Hugo. He had scarcely touched her and had kissed her only a few times, but his affection for her had been deep and enduring. She would have married Hugo gladly and given him all her heart and soul until she died. But he had died first, while she was young and healthy and of a disposition to embrace life. Chelles had been a safe place to which she had retreated after Hugo's death to nurse her aching heart and her disappointed hopes. Danise did not think she had a vocation strong enough to keep her contentedly at Chelles until she was an old woman. Still, she was wise enough to know she ought not to close the door on a religious life before she had definitely made up her mind. As for possible husbands, Count Clodion seemed to be favored by neither her father nor Sister Gertrude. "Tell me about the other men, Father."

"There is Autichar, who is a Bavarian nobleman of great note, and who holds lands as vast as Clodion's." Savarec was but a minor member of the nobility and he was perhaps too easily impressed by rank and wealth. Danise could tell he held Autichar in great esteem and had been honored by the offer for her hand.

"Autichar's loyalty to Charles has come into question," noted Sister Gertrude. "Autichar is a known companion of Duke Tassilo of Bavaria, who is no friend to Charles, though the two are close cousins. If a dispute arises between Charles and Tassilo, and from what I have heard of Tassilo's character it is inevitable, on whose side will Autichar fight? Do you want to oppose your son-in-law on a battlefield, Savarec?"

"Is there no man on earth of whom you approve?" Savarec's face was growing red with suppressed anger.

"I want Danise to be happy just as much as you do," Sister Gertrude told him. "But I do not think marriage will make her happy."

"If you will let me finish," said Savarec between clenched teeth, "perhaps you can find one good thing to say about the third man who is interested in my daughter."

"Who is he, Father?" Trying to avert one of Savarec's rare outbursts of temper, Danise said, "I promise I will most seriously consider all of these men, and if they are here at Duren, I will ask you to present me to them, so I can be at least somewhat familiar with all of them before I decide."

"You always were a sensible girl." Savarec appeared to be mollified by his daughter's words. "The third man you have already met, and he is the one I most favor. A man of honorable lineage, with lands near Tournai and also other estates in Burgundy. He is Count Redmond."

"The pleasant man who helped us with the stranger?" Danise tried in vain to recall Count Redmond's face. All she could bring to memory was a thick crop of golden hair and a pair of pale eyes. Was he tall or short, handsome or not? She could not remember. When she thought about the incident in the forest, what stayed in her mind was an instant of shock brought on by the penetrating blue gaze of a sadly injured, unknown man.

"Well, Danise?" Savarec looked at her expectantly. "What is your opinion of Count Redmond?"

"As I said, he seemed pleasant, but I scarcely had a chance to note him," Danise responded.

"You will have ample time to know him," Savarec told her. "And Clodion and Autichar, too, since all of them are gathered here at Duren. You have my permission to speak to any of them when and as you wish, so long as Sister Gertrude or Clothilde is with you. I do not think any of them will make improper advances to you, but it is always best for a young woman to have a chaperon."

"In so much at least, we are agreed," said Sister Gertrude.

Chapter 3

He did not know where he was. Worse, he did not know *who* he was. His head ached without letup, and his eyesight was totally undependable, ranging from a complete blur to abnormal clarity. Every time he tried to sit up he was overcome by nausea so severe he had to lie down again at once.

People came and went. He knew the man in dusty black robes was a doctor. He knew the leeches the doctor periodically placed at the most painful spot on his head really would help him. Their sucking would diminish the swelling and make his headache go away. How he knew these things he could not recall, but know them he did.

Lying flat on his back, unable to move for nausea, with the repellent leeches working away at him, he went over the faces he had recently seen, seeking in those faces some clue to his own identity.

There was the portly middle-aged man with gray-streaked dark hair who slept in the other bed in the tent and snored away the long and lonely nights. The others called this man *Savarec*, but to his confused tentmate the name meant nothing.

There was Guntram of the bristling black beard and mustache. He had a fierce expression and wild eyes, but could be gentle enough to turn a patient or attend to his personal needs without causing increased pain. Guntram was Savarec's man, and he loved and respected his master.

A motherly, middle-aged woman, brown of hair and eye and thick of waist, came frequently to change his linen or wash his face and hands. A scrawny, sour-looking nun occasionally glared down at him along her elegant nose.

And then there was the angel, who drifted into and out of his consciousness like a vision. But she was real. She touched his forehead or his cheeks with tender hands and coaxed him to swallow the food she spooned into his mouth, even when he feared it would only come back up again. When the angel fed him, the food stayed down, perhaps because she did not rush him as the others did, but sat patiently waiting until he opened his mouth for the next spoonful.

Her face was a perfect oval, her hair was

so pale it was almost silver. She wore it in twin braids tied with green ribbons to match her deep green wool gown. Her eyes were a soft gray-green, shadowed by some undefined sorrow. She was small and shapely and her voice was like heavenly music. Unfortunately, he could not understand what she said.

She tried to make him understand and he struggled to remember the words she spoke, but his head ached so badly that he could make no sense of her language. It ought to be easy for him. He was fluent in several languages and had the ear to learn new ones quickly.

How did he know that?

As time passed and the pain in his head eased, fragments of memory drifted into and out of his thoughts. Glimpses of scenes bedeviled him . . . a skinny young man throwing a punch at him and missing . . . blinking lights . . . numbers . . . the green leaves of springtime slapping against his face . . . falling . . . falling. . . . Where? When? What had happened to him?

What was his name?

"He is much improved." The royal physician regarded his sleeping patient with considerable satisfaction before turning his attention to Danise and Savarec. "My treatments have been successful. All he needs now is rest and time, until he is himself once more."

"He still doesn't know his own name," Danise said. "The poor man is so bewildered."

"Only time can cure the loss of memory."

A Love Beyond Time

The physician had told her this repeatedly over the last three days. "When he can rise without pain or dizziness, let him do so. Allow him to walk about and see familiar sights, for they will speed his final recovery. Feed him well. I can give you no further advice, nor can I do anything more for him, unless he suffers a relapse. If he does, it will be necessary to bleed him, or perhaps to administer a series of clysters."

"Thank you for the help you have given him." Savarec pressed a purse into the physician's hands. "If we find we need you again, rest assured we will call upon you at once." But as soon as the physician was out of earshot, Savarec snorted in derision. "I have as little use for physicians as Charles himself has. Clysters, indeed! Those idiots delight in ramming a funnel into a man and filling his innards with foul-smelling potions and then letting him spend the rest of the day at the latrine until there is nothing left inside him and he can't walk without help. Then they prate of the good they do for their patients."

"I am so glad you were able to convince Charles to give this man over to your keeping, instead of letting the physicians have him," Danise said.

"See that your charitable concern for him does not keep you from your other duties. Attend the queen when it is your turn to do so," Savarec admonished her. Looking at the stranger, he shook his head sadly. "I wish I knew who he is. His family may be praying for

41

news of him. If we only knew where to send a message, we could relieve their anxiety."

"I confess, I had not thought of his family." Danise sighed, wondering if there were a wife somewhere, worrying about him. With a guilty pang, she hoped he was neither wed nor betrothed. "The next time he wakens, I will try again to teach him a few words of Frankish, so he can begin to speak to us and tell us about himself. It seems his head has ached too badly for him to think clearly, but now the physician has turned him over to us, he surely will soon be well enough to talk and to begin to move about."

"It would be a kindness to him." Savarec patted her shoulder. "I'm off now to attend Charles. Don't be late for the midday meal. It's time you met all of your suitors."

"Yes, Father. I'll be there." But her eyes and her thoughts were on the unknown man. He had a habit of waking whenever she was left alone in the tent with him. She drew up a stool and took her usual place beside his bed. His eyes opened at once. "Oh, yes, you are clever. Always you wait until the others have gone.

"But, sir, if you are aware enough of your surroundings to know who is here and who is absent, then you are well on your way to recovery, and thus you should not be allowed to lie here idling away your days and nights. You, sir, are about to begin your schooling."

The blue eyes stared into hers with such intensity that Danise had to look away or lose her ability to reason. Reaching across his narrow bed, she touched the rough wool fabric of the tent wall.

"Tent," she said, indicating the entire structure with an expressive wave of her hand. "Tent."

He continued to stare at her.

"Say it!" she demanded, and made the gesture again. "Tent. *Tent.*"

"Tent." There was a change in his expression, a stirring of interest, a glimmer of hope.

"Good. Tent," she repeated. She slapped a hand against the side of his cot. "Bed. Bed."

"Bed." His hand moved toward hers, but she had already picked up a corner of the coverlet.

"Quilt," she said.

"Quilt." He was smiling at her. Danise caught her breath. Most of the swelling in his face had subsided, but the bruises remained. Over the past three days they had slowly turned from blue and purple to gray and yellow. She suspected that even at his best this man was no handsome young warrior, yet there was something compelling about him, a strength and intelligence she had seldom encountered before.

"Face." She touched her cheeks. When he repeated the word she went on to name nose, eyes, ears, hands, and as many other body parts as she decently could, until he caught her hands, stopping her excited flow of words.

"Speak—to—me," he said very carefully. "Make—sentences." That last word was spoken in a foreign tongue, but she understood what he meant.

"You have been listening to us," she cried. "These past days, you have been soaking up our words as cloth soaks up moisture. You know more than I realized, perhaps more than *you* realize."

"I—speak—easily," he said. "I learn—learn languages—quickly."

"Indeed you do. I am so happy for you. Now you need not be so isolated. You can talk to my father and to Guntram."

"And—to—you." Still he spoke slowly, feeling his way through the Frankish language. "If we talk more, I learn—will learn—more fast. No—I will learn *faster*."

"Then we will talk until you are tired. Tell me how you came to be in the forest?"

"Forest?" He frowned. "Trees. I was falling. Tried to stop—to catch branches."

"That is why your face and hands were scratched," Danise told him. "But what were you doing in the tree?"

He released her hands. Danise watched him grow perfectly still, as if he were listening to a voice inside his own mind.

"I don't know," he said at last. "I can't remember. Just the trees, and falling."

"The physician says your memory will come back to you as you recover," she assured him. "Since he is the royal physician, he must be right."

"Royal? What king are we talking about? Where am I, anyway?"

"You did not say that last sentence correctly," she informed him, after a pause while she

44

interpreted his words to herself.

"To hell with grammar," he said. "Where am I?"

"At Duren, in Francia. It is the Mayfield."

If he had been still before, now he was like a statue. Danise waited to hear what his next question would be.

"Francia," he repeated. "Land of the Franks. Who is this king who keeps a physician?"

"He doesn't really need one, though Hildegarde too often does. Our king is Charles."

"What year is this?"

"Ah, you are truly lost, aren't you? I am so sorry."

"Just answer my question."

"It is spring in the Year of Our Lord 779."

"Oh, my God!" He sat up so suddenly that Danise feared he would faint. Swinging bare legs over the edge of his bed, he sat with his head in his hands. Guntram had found a linen shirt for him, which covered him to his thighs, but still Danise averted her gaze. However, she did not move from the stool where she had been sitting throughout their conversation.

"What am I doing here?" he asked. The question was directed more toward himself than to her, but she answered it anyway.

"I have told you, we found you in the forest and brought you here to my father's tent."

"That's not what I meant. Something is dreadfully wrong. I know it. I'm in the wrong place. I should be—be—somewhere else."

"Where?" she asked.

"I don't know, damn it! I don't know!" He

added more calmly, "I shouldn't yell at you. It's not your fault. Tell me, is it permitted to get myself up?" He was still uncertain about some of the words he needed and the exact sentence construction of the Frankish language, but Danise could understand what he wanted.

"If you feel well enough, you may rise. But before you go outside the tent, I would advise you to dress. Guntram has located a tunic and breeches for you, and shoes that ought to fit."

"Don't I have clothing of my own? Did I come here naked?"

"Your own garments are so unusual that we feared they would cause much comment, and thus we assumed you would prefer to wear Frankish garb. But your clothes are here, in my father's clothes chest. Clothilde washed them for you." She opened the lid of the wooden chest to show him. "Here are some coins Clothilde found in your breeches. She put them into this little pouch so they would not be lost. My father says this object must be your purse. Perhaps there is something in it to answer your questions."

He took the folded brown leather wallet and flipped it open to rifle through the contents. Danise gave a cry of surprise when he held up a stiff card.

"It is your image, as you must appear without these unattractive bruises. How clever the artists of your land are, to capture your likeness so closely. Is that writing on it? I cannot make out the unfamiliar letters."

"If this is my face," he said, "then this must be my name, too. 'Bailey, Bradford Michael. Expiration date, 3/31/95.' I have no idea what those numbers mean. Nor these words. 'Connecticut Motor Vehicle Operator's License.'" He turned the card over, squinting at the tiny blue letters on the other side, shaking his head because they meant nothing to him.

"How well you read," Danise said. "Could you be a scholar?"

"I don't know." He sank back onto the cot, staring at the card in his hand.

"Bail—ley," she said. "Bailey."

"No," he corrected, still looking at the photograph of himself. "That's not right. It doesn't *feel* right."

"What shall I call you, then? Perhaps 'Bailey' is your title. Is your name Bradford?" she asked. "Or is it *Michel,* like the archangel?"

"*Michel,*" he repeated. "Yes, that's better. Not exactly right, but better than Bailey or Bradford."

"Now you have your name." She smiled at him. "Michel. *Michel.* I like it. It suits you."

"How can you possibly know such a thing?" he demanded. "I may have a label, but we still don't know who I am, or why I am here." He watched her mouth the word *label* and think about it.

"I believe I understand," she said. "In your language, the word for *name* is *label.*" When he did not answer, she put her hand over his, enclosing both his fingers and the driver's license. "Michel, I think you must learn to be more patient. Your memory will return to you in time. The king's own physician has said so, and my father and Guntram, also."

They remained thus for a while, Michel seated on the bed, Danise crouched before him with her hand over his, each looking deep into the other's eyes, Danise longing to unlock the secrets of his mysterious mind, aching to help him and knowing only time could cure his affliction. Then, at a sound by the tent entrance, they pulled apart, not with a guilty start but with a slow and reluctant motion.

"Danise," said Sister Gertrude, "you should not be alone with a man."

"My father knows I am here," Danise said.

"Whether Savarec knows where you are or not, it is time for you to wait upon the queen." Sister Gertrude cast a scornful glance at the man sitting on the cot, who now rose respectfully. "If he is well enough to be out of bed, then he is well enough to be left alone for a short time. Come along, Danise, you are already late."

"So, he has a name now, has he?" Michel heard the nun say as Danise followed her out of the tent.

"Midday meal," he muttered, reaching for his clothing. He would go to this midday meal himself and see what it was all about. But when he bent over Savarec's clothes chest, he was assailed by a wave of dizziness and by a pain in his head so severe it drove him to his knees. Feeling weak and nauseated, he groped his way back to his bed and got into it. With his head on the pillow once more, the pain eased enough to allow him to think.

"Not today, then," he told himself. "Perhaps tomorrow I'll be steady enough on my feet to get dressed and then I'll find out what is going on here."

Danise was so delighted to know Michel's name and to be able to talk with him that she almost floated across the crowded meadow to the royal tents. When she saw her father coming toward her with an elderly gentleman, she wanted to tell him her news at once. But the proprieties meant much to Savarec, so they must be observed. With Sister Gertrude beside her, Danise paused a short distance from the queen's tent, unaware of the effect her glowing expression and bubbling good spirits were having on the men and women gathering for that day's outdoor feast. More than one young noble looked at her with admiration, and the white-haired man with Savarec nodded enthusiastically.

"So, this is your Danise. I'd wed her this very day if she would have me."

"Humph," snorted Sister Gertrude, unimpressed by this declaration. "You said much the same thing to me more than thirty years ago."

"Forgive me, sister, but I do not remember you," said the elderly man. "There have been so very many women in my life."

"So I've heard." Sister Gertrude put all her disapproval into her voice.

"Danise," Savarec told his daughter, "if you

have not yet guessed, this is Count Clodion, one of the men who has asked for your hand."

"Good day to you, sir." Danise inclined her head and gave her hand into Count Clodion's bony fingers.

"Delicious," said the count, smacking his lips as though he would like to have Danise for his next meal. "A beauty, Savarec. A rare jewel, and one I would like to add to my possessions."

"I have no desire to become a possession, Count Clodion." Danise tried to withdraw her hand from his. He would not let her go.

"All wives are possessions, my dear." The count bared discolored teeth in a mirthless grin. "Were you mine, I would be kind, and bind you with ropes of softest silk."

"No innocent maiden ought to be forced to listen to such disgusting talk," snapped Sister Gertrude. "Clodion, you have not changed one bit since I was a girl—save, perhaps, to grow even more lecherous."

"And all the more appreciative of youthful beauty with the passing years." Clodion was not the least abashed by Sister Gertrude's scolding. He tucked the hand of the unwilling Danise into his elbow and held it there while he led her toward the tables set up before the royal tents. "Danise, you lovely girl, you must sit beside me this afternoon."

"I believe my father wanted me to meet another suitor, Count Clodion." Danise finally succeeded in getting her hand free of Clodion's clutching fingers. "Also, I must pay my respects to the queen, whom I have neglected these past few days."

"By all means, you must remember your duty to dear Hildegarde." Clodion stayed by her side when Danise began to move toward the queen's tent. "I shall accompany you."

"It won't be necessary," Sister Gertrude told him. "Here comes the queen now. Charles is with her, and from the look of him, he wants to speak with you."

"So he does. Danise, I will rejoin you later." Count Clodion hurried off in the direction of the royal pair.

"Stay here a moment, Danise," Sister Gertrude instructed. "You don't want to appear before Charles and Hildegarde with that creature by your side. They might imagine you have decided to accept Clodion's suit. Really, Savarec, how could you even think of handing Danise over to that dreadful man?"

"He was a great warrior in his youth," said Savarec.

"Yes, forty years ago in Charles Martel's time," Sister Gertrude snapped. "With his teeth rotting and his muscles grown stringy with age, Clodion has nothing to recommend him now."

"For his courage in battle Clodion was awarded an important title," Savarec responded with his usual patience. "He was also given large estates, which he has managed well. He is one of the richest men in all of Francia. If Danise were to marry him, Clodion has promised she would never want for anything."

"What nonsense!" declared Sister Gertrude.

"Clodion was known for a miser forty years ago; I doubt if he has changed in his old age. Furthermore, he has at least a dozen children by his previous wives and uncounted brats by his concubines. Several of those women are still living. Women and children alike, they will all expect Clodion's lands to be divided among them when he dies. No, Danise would not be welcome in Clodion's family, nor would any children she might bear to him. Tell me, Savarec, do you really want your daughter in that disgusting man's bed?"

"Now, see here," Savarec began, losing his patience at last.

"Please, please," Danise begged. "Do not quarrel on my account. I have not yet decided to marry anyone. I haven't even met Autichar of Bavaria."

"Another prize specimen," muttered Sister Gertrude, fortunately speaking too low for Savarec to hear her. "Are there no decent men in Francia who are looking for wives?"

"Count Redmond seemed very nice," Danise remarked, hoping to calm the nun's rising irritation.

"That young fool? He'll wear you out in bed. If you were to marry him, you would have a child every year." Laying a hand on her arm, Sister Gertrude stopped Danise in her forward progress toward Charles and Hildegarde. "My dear girl, I am only trying to protect you. A man can break a woman's heart. A man can be the death of a woman, either because she loves him and he will not love her, or because

52

he loves her too well and too often, and thus gives her too many babies."

"Would you have me avoid all men?" cried Danise. "I am not sure I want to do that."

"Oh, child, child, if only I could make you understand the heartaches and the loneliness that lie in wait for the woman who gives her life into the keeping of a mere mortal man. How much better to give yourself to God."

"Yet I am but a mortal, too," Danise said. Impulsively, she put an arm across the nun's back, hugging her. Sister Gertrude was usually too rigid to accept such an affectionate gesture, but this time she not only accepted it, she returned it, clinging to Danise as if she could by sheer physical strength save her young charge from all the dangers and pitfalls of a woman's life.

"I do promise you," Danise said, "that I will consider your warning carefully before I finally decide what to do. Whether I wed or become a nun, I will not do either without much thought and prayer. Now, dear Sister Gertrude, I must speak to Hildegarde. Come with me, for you know she is fond of you."

Hildegarde was also fond of Danise. But, except for a brief greeting the day after Danise's arrival at Duren, the two had not had a chance to talk together since the previous autumn, shortly after Hildegarde's twin sons had been born at Agen. The smaller of those babies had since died, and now Hildegarde was large with the burden of another pregnancy. In the queen's life Danise could see an example of the hazards that fueled Sister Gertrude's concern for her own future.

Hildegarde took her seat in a large wooden chair padded with thick cushions. The queen's sweet face was pale, her light brown hair hung in lusterless braids, while her swollen abdomen only accentuated her overall thinness. Her ladies and her children clustered about her. Baby Ludwig, just nine months old, and two-year-old Carloman were in the arms of their nurses, four-year-old Rotrud was playing at her mother's feet, and seven-year-old Charlot was strutting about with his toy sword as if he were already a grown man and a warrior.

Off to one side Charles stood talking to several of his nobles, with his uncle, Duke Bernard, and Count Clodion among them. Looking at those men, Danise sighed. So many of Charles's closest companions of the previous summer, men who should have been in the group about him now, instead lay dead in Spain, or in the treacherous pass at Roncevaux, or buried at Agen, like her dearest Hugo. In the sad aftermath of the Spanish campaign, Charles was much changed. He refused to speak about the tragedy at Roncevaux, he would not even mention Spain, and he seemed to Danise to be sadly aged and careworn.

Savarec had told Danise that Charles's present most pressing woes concerned the Saxons, who repeatedly rose in revolt against their

Frankish rulers, looting and burning and killing wherever they found the opportunity, for the Saxons were determined to remain independent and heathen. Since they had a habit of torturing and killing any Christian missionaries who ventured beyond Frankish territory, and since they often made unprovoked attacks on Frankish lands east of the Rhine, Charles had decided Saxony needed to be subdued and converted to the True Faith. Savarec believed the task would be a long and daunting one, in which he would be deeply involved, for the fortress he commanded was situated on the eastern bank of the Rhine.

"I'll speak to you again later, Danise." When Savarec left his daughter to join Charles and his male friends, Hildegarde gestured to Danise to come closer.

"How does your injured guest?" asked the queen, who had been kept fully informed by both Charles and Sister Gertrude.

"He is much better today. We have discovered his name." Danise went on to describe her most recent visit with her patient.

"Michel," mused Hildegarde. "Named for the warrior archangel. Is this Michel also a warrior?"

"At the moment, he's too weak to be anything," Sister Gertrude answered for Danise. "Though he has a tough and wiry look to him, he is not at all well-muscled. Danise, here comes your father and it seems he has found the rest of your suitors."

Hildegarde laughed at the nun's disgruntled

Flora Speer

expression as Savarec and two men drew near. The golden-haired Count Redmond came forward at once to greet first the queen and then Danise. He also made a polite bow to Sister Gertrude, who favored him with a nod of her head before glaring at Savarec.

"I have found Autichar," Savarec announced, and presented him to Danise.

Count Autichar of Bavaria was not much taller than Danise. He was thickly made, with massive shoulders and arms. By contrast his short legs appeared underdeveloped, as though he spent more time on horseback than walking or standing on his own feet. His hair was orange-red, his eyes gray, and his snub-nosed face was sunburned and peeling. His bright red tunic and cloak clashed with the color of his hair. Danise would have dismissed his lack of physical attractiveness as unimportant if only Autichar had been a pleasant man, but she quickly learned that his personality matched his appearance. He scarcely looked at the queen, whom he ought to have acknowledged first, instead examining Danise as if she were a horse he was thinking of buying.

"She doesn't look big enough to produce healthy sons," Autichar said. "But then, Hildegarde isn't much larger and she has borne several male children, so perhaps this girl will, too. All right, Savarec, if you will promise to come to my aid with fighting men if I should need them, and swear never to fight in any battle against me, then I'll take your girl and get my heir on her."

56

"I have promised Danise the choice shall be hers," Savarec said.

"A foolish thing to do," Autichar told him. "Women don't know what they want until a man shows them."

"Nor can I make promises to you that might interfere with my first loyalty to Charles," Savarec went on. "Any agreement of mutual aid between us must be subject to Charles's approval first."

"Well spoken, my friend." Charles, his uncle and his companions now joined the group around his queen. He towered above them all, his pale gold hair glinting in the May sunshine, his blue wool cloak carelessly draped across his broad shoulders. Autichar had to look upward more than a foot to meet Charles's eyes.

One of Charles's feet, Danise told herself with some amusement, for the size of the royal extremities had been used to determine the new official measurement of a *foot*.

"Autichar," Charles said in a deceptively quiet voice, "I do not think I can approve of your suit for Danise's hand. You are too fond of my cousin, Duke Tassilo of Bavaria. Your insistence that Savarec ought never to fight against you makes me wonder what you and my cousin are planning."

There was an uneasy silence when Charles stopped speaking. Years before, while Charles's father, Pepin, was still alive and king of the Franks, there had been a war in Aquitaine. Duke Tassilo had taken his troops there to fight for Pepin, as he was obliged to do, having pledged his loyalty to Pepin. But before the battle was joined, Tassilo deliberately quarreled with Pepin and then took his men and departed the field. This *herisliz*, this act of treachery and desertion, was the most serious crime a Frankish noble could commit. It was punishable by death, though for family reasons neither Pepin nor, later, his son Charles, demanded that ultimate penalty of Tassilo. As a result of Tassilo's actions in Aquitaine, relations between the Frankish kings and their cousin the Duke of Bavaria had been strained for years.

"Last summer Tassilo sent troops for your Spanish campaign," Autichar reminded Charles.

"Only a small contingent," Charles replied, smiling a little. "And Tassilo himself did not join me. Perhaps he feared I would have him arrested."

"Are you accusing Tassilo and me of plotting against you?" demanded Autichar.

"Certainly not," Charles said. "Not without clear evidence. However, you and Tassilo are not only related to each other by marriage, you are also close friends. And now I find you trying to subvert Savarec's primary allegiance to me."

"You heard him," said Autichar. "Savarec wouldn't agree to defend me should I become his son-in-law." Turning to Savarec, Autichar added, "Savarec, I formally withdraw my request for your daughter's hand in marriage. Nor will I remain where my loyalty and my honesty are in question. I will take my men and leave Duren for Bavaria this very day."

"God speed you on your way," Charles said, the smile still playing about his lips. He watched as Autichar stalked away. "You and that small army you brought to Duren," Charles added thoughtfully.

"Do you think that was entirely wise?" asked Savarec. "He will go home to Bavaria and tell Duke Tassilo what you have said."

"Which was my intent," Charles informed him. "Let Autichar remind my cousin Tassilo that I have not forgotten what he once did to my father. There will be a reckoning between us. Perhaps not for years, but it will come. I foresee Tassilo ending his days in a secure, well-guarded monastery."

"Meanwhile," Sister Gertrude said, "Danise is rid of at least one unwelcome suitor."

"Here is an added advantage to my decision to convince Autichar to go home." Charles was grinning now. "Danise, you deserve a husband far better than Autichar."

"So I had already decided." Danise met Charles's sparkling eyes with laughter. "But I do thank you, sir, for sparing me the trouble of sending him away rejected."

"And I," said Savarec. "I admit, I was in awe of his lands and his titles, but he would have made a poor husband for my girl."

"Now, if we could just rid ourselves of Danise's other suitors," Sister Gertrude said.

"Oh, no." Hildegarde burst into laughter. "Sister Gertrude, do not deny Danise the joys

59

of wedded life, for they are sweet indeed. Even the discomforts are but trivial when one has married the right husband."

"Thank you for those words, dearest wife." Charles beamed at his queen. Catching her hand, he raised it to his lips and kissed it.

To this testimony to marriage Sister Gertrude dared make no critical response. Not with Hildegarde smiling at her husband and Charles watching his wife with a tender gaze. But when Charles turned his attention elsewhere, the nun did have a few choice words for Savarec.

"You claim to love Danise, yet the quality I would expect to see in her possible husbands is sorely lacking, Savarec."

"I am not so rich or so powerful that I can afford to ignore the proposals of such men," Savarec responded. "In fact, Clodion earlier today all but accused me of outright trickery because he has discovered that Danise's dowry is much smaller than he expected it to be."

"In that case, let us hope Clodion will decide not to pursue her."

"He made his suit contingent upon his meeting with Danise," Savarec said, somewhat uneasily. "You heard him. He is enthusiastic about the prospect of marriage to her. I am not unwise enough to refuse him."

"Unwise?" scoffed Sister Gertrude. "Say rather, you have no wits at all in such matters. If you had, you would not trust Clodion for a moment."

Savarec's face turned red, and it seemed to Danise that he was preparing a sharp retort to Sister Gertrude's scathing comments on his intelligence. Tired of their bickering, she moved away from them. When she did so, Count Redmond fell into step beside her.

"I hope you do not find me as unacceptable as Count Autichar," he said.

"Compared to Autichar, you are the most charming of men," she teased.

"I do hope so. May I tell you about my home, and why I believe you would be an excellent wife for me?"

To this suggestion Danise assented, so while they walked along the riverbank in the golden midday sunshine, Redmond set forth all the sensible reasons why they should marry. She thought he was an honest man, and his person was clean and comely. He provided a humorous description of life on his estates, making her laugh several times. Danise felt completely at ease with him.

"I have spoken enough about myself," Redmond said at last. "Tell me how the stranger fares."

When Danise revealed the man's name and described his improved condition, Redmond had another question for her.

"May I visit him? He might like to talk with a man close to his own age, which I think I am. Michel may be lonely, or feeling apprehensive among people he does not know. By providing instruction in the ways of our menfolk, I might be able to ease his anxiety until his memory returns."

"How good of you," Danise cried, liking

Redmond even more for his generous concern over a man who was never completely out of her own thoughts. Neither Clodion nor Autichar could begin to capture her interest the way Michel had done. But Redmond? She regarded her third suitor with true warmth and a bright smile.

"I believe we will become good friends," she told him.

"I would wish for more than friendship from you," Redmond replied, "but it is a fair beginning. Now, when may I see Michel?"

"I will take you to him immediately after the midday meal," Danise promised.

Chapter 4

"We are agreed, then." Redmond rose from his seat beside Michel's bed. "As soon as you are well enough, I will introduce you to the other young men and teach you how to use Frankish weapons."

"The *fransisca*," Michel replied, the image of the deadly short-handled throwing ax clear in his mind.

"The *fransisca* is an older weapon, used in the time of the Merovingian kings and seldom seen in these days," said Redmond, looking surprised. "Under King Pepin, and now under Charles, we have new and better arms."

"But, I thought—" Michel stopped, shaking his head. "Obviously, I am mistaken. What weapons will I learn to use?"

"The *scramasax*, our dagger, though sometimes it is as long as a sword," Redmond
replied. "Also the spear and, most important,
the sword. We Franks are famous for our fine
sword blades. They are so envied that Charles
has made a law forbidding them to be taken
out of Francia, so our enemies cannot buy them
and thus use Frankish-made weapons against
us in battle."

"I look forward to the lessons," Michel told
him. "It is boring to be so confined, to be dizzy
each time I try to stand and move. I long for
activity."

"There speaks the true warrior." Redmond
nodded his understanding. "From whatever
country you come, we are brothers in heart,
I think. Nor, after talking with you, have I any
doubt that you are noble."

But I have doubts, Michel thought when he
was alone again. Impatient as he was to be out
of bed and moving about without feeling weak
or light-headed, he was even more impatient
to have his memory return. Too often Danise
or Savarec, or now Redmond, used words that
brought distinct images into his mind, but
when he described those images he was told
they were long out of date.

"Mystery upon mystery," he said to himself,
swinging his feet to the ground. He sat on the
edge of his bed, waiting for the dizziness to
subside. When he felt steady enough to stand
he went to Savarec's wooden chest and lifted
the lid. He knew by now that Danise was
right when she said his own clothing would

make him conspicuous in the Frankish camp and thus raise questions he was unable to answer. When he finally was well enough to don clothing and leave Savarec's tent it would be in the wooden tunic and breeches Guntram had given him. But the clues to his identity lay in the belongings with which he had come to this place. He picked up the pouch of coins that Clothilde had saved for him and took it back to the bed. There he opened it, letting the coins spill out across the quilt. They were in various sizes, most silver, a few of copper.

"How finely they are made," Danise said from just inside the tent entrance.

"I didn't hear you come in." As always when she was with him, she captured his full attention. She sat at the foot of his bed, the folds of her green wool gown graceful about her. When she leaned forward to pick up a coin one of her thick braids fell over her shoulder, swinging between them, a rope of pale gold bound at its end with green ribbon.

"Well?" she asked, and he realized that while he was absorbed in contemplating her hair and the delicate peach glow in her cheeks, she had been examining the coins and asking questions he had not heard. "Michel, have you discovered anything in these coins to tell you who you are?"

"Not yet." He was not looking at the coins. He was still looking at her. Nature had given her light brown brows and lashes several shades darker than her silvery hair, and her eyes were gray-green. Soft, trusting eyes, meeting his with perfect honesty, yet with a peculiar haunted quality. Michel put out a hand to stroke her smooth cheek and run his finger across the curve of her jaw to the tip of her chin. She sat still, not pulling away, allowing his caress while not encouraging it. He longed to touch her lips with his finger. He did not do what he wanted. The shadow in her eyes stopped him. He let his hand stray to her braid instead. He felt its silken smoothness sliding through his fingers and heard her catch her breath, a quiet sound, quickly smothered. Her glance did not forsake his, but the haunted expression deepened.

"Why are you so sad?" At once he wished he had not asked. By the immediate withdrawal in her lovely face he knew he had trespassed into a personal domain where he had no right to go.

"You are too perceptive." With an irritated gesture she tossed the coin she was holding onto the little collection of silver and copper spread upon the quilt. "I cannot answer you. It is not your affair."

"I am not deaf, Danise, and I have begun to understand your language rather well. I hear what the people around me are saying. Are you unhappy because your father hopes you will soon agree to marry?" He stopped there, not telling her what it was on the tip of his tongue to say, that the thought of her marriage to anyone, even to a man as good-hearted and decent as Redmond, was as unpleasant to him as it apparently was to her.

"You do not understand." Danise rose, turning her back on him. She did not look at him when she spoke again.

"Since you feel well enough to leave your bed," she told him in tones reminiscent of Sister Gertrude, "you plainly do not need my nursing care any longer. I leave you to the men, Michel. I wish you the best of luck at weapons practice." With that, she was out of the tent, the entrance flap swinging shut behind her.

Michel shook his head in wonder at his own ineptness. No need to ask what had annoyed her. He had blundered into her private life and she did not want him there. He thought about the way her expression closed so quickly against him, recalled the rigidly straight line of her back as she left the tent. He groaned in frustration.

From the first moment when he had glimpsed Danise's face through pain-blurred, unfocused eyes, he had been aware of a peculiar connection to her. For days after that initial sight of her, Danise had been a near-angelic presence, drawing him back to consciousness when it would have been easier to slip away into painless darkness. Now that he was almost well again common sense told him this mysterious bond was an illusion created by his helplessness and nurtured by his continuing lack of memory. Common sense told him so but his heart, or some other buried part of himself that believed in miracles, insisted that there was more to his presence at Duren than mere chance. And though he thought she would have denied it if he asked her, he believed Danise also felt the connection between them.

But what did he want from her? Did he have the right to ask anything at all of her? Or, as Savarec had once suggested to him, did he have a family and friends somewhere else who were even now wondering where he was and if he yet lived? There was no way to answer any of those questions until his memory returned.

He went back to the coins still spread out upon his bed, seeking in them some information about himself. He picked up one of the larger coins to examine it, turning it over, frowning while a chill slid down his spine. He picked up another coin, and then another, until he had looked closely at all of them. Certain numbers on the coins were dates and all of them fell within a twenty-year period. The dates represented an impossibility. But they were accurate. He knew it in his heart as well as in his mind. Furthermore, these were not ancient coins of the kind he was accustomed to finding in his work. This was recently minted money.

His work? How in heaven's name did he know about ancient coins?

"Hold your arm so," Redmond instructed. "Slash like this. Auggh! Do you want to kill me? Gently, my friend, gently, please." He drew back, grinning at Michel. "You are not new at this. You have used a sword before."

"So it would seem. I regret that I cannot recall the circumstances."

"You will, soon enough. Just be patient for a while longer." Redmond lifted his broadsword again, ready to continue this first lesson in the use of Frankish weapons.

Michel was not paying attention to his new friend. Lowering his own blade, Michel looked around the practice yard. Bounded on two sides by forest, this warriors' territory opened on its third side to the roped-off corral where the horses were kept, and on its fourth side to meadow and river. Within the practice yard several groups of men were testing their skill in friendly combat. One of those men was strikingly tall and obviously had the strength to match his height, for he was holding off a cluster of young warriors, doing it easily and with much laughter on both sides.

"Pay attention," Redmond ordered, touching Michel's side with the point of his sword. "Were I an enemy, I could have killed you just then. You must concentrate."

"Like this?" Michel met Redmond's blade with a movement familiar to his hand and arm if not to his conscious mind. At once Redmond countered the attack and the two of them moved back and forth through a long series of blows and feints until both were drenched with sweat and Redmond called a halt.

"Well done," cried a cheerful voice. The tall man whom Michel had noticed earlier came up to them, putting out a huge fist to grip first Redmond's offered hand and then Michel's. "I am Charles. You can only be the stranger I have heard so much about. Welcome to Duren."

"Thank you, sir." Michel was taller than all of the Frankish men he had met, but Charles was a good five inches taller still. Like most of the men at weapons practice on this warm May morning, Charles had stripped to the waist, exposing massive arms and a broad chest covered with golden hair. His shrewd blue eyes searched Michel's face. Apparently approving of what he saw there, Charles nodded, then swept out an arm to indicate the encampment with its tents arranged in haphazard rows.

"Let our temporary home be your home, too, Michel, for as long as you wish," he said. Lifting his face and drawing in a deep breath, Charles continued, "I smell our next meal in the making. Join us at table, Michel. The hunting has been good today, so we will be eating spitted game birds, my favorite dish. I also smell newly baked bread, and onions and cabbage. Hildegarde mentioned fresh greens. After the efforts of this last hour, I am hungry. And hot," he added.

"So am I." Redmond grinned at his king with easy familiarity. "And you, Michel? Has your appetite returned now that you have had some exercise?" Redmond slung a friendly arm across Michel's shoulders.

"There is nothing like good food eaten in the open air among friends," Charles put in. "I much prefer such a meal to a boring official banquet."

They stood together, all three of them bare chested, Michel and Redmond still holding their swords in their hands. All of them looked with interest toward the open space before the royal tents at the center of the meadow, where they could see servants setting up trestle tables. The odors of roasting birds and simmering vegetables and herbs drifted their way from the fires where the cooks were hard at work preparing the meal. The companionable moment among the three men was interrupted when one of Charles's servants came up to speak to him and, after a word to excuse himself, the king turned aside from Michel and Redmond.

"Why don't we swim before we eat?" Michel suggested. "We can wash the sweat away in the river."

"You are cleaner than a woman." Redmond chuckled, slapping Michel on the back. "Let us swim, by all means. If I am freshly bathed and sweet-smelling, perhaps Danise will like me better. She spent too much time with Count Clodion last evening." Redmond's smile turned into a scowl. "I do not like that man, and not only because he and I are rivals for Danise's hand."

"I met him only briefly yesterday when he stopped at Savarec's tent, but I don't like him, either," Michel said. "There is something shifty about Count Clodion."

"Shifty?" Redmond asked, puzzled by the unfamiliar term. "Do you mean unfirm, like shifting sands on a beach? Not to be depended upon? Untrustworthy?"

"All of those things," Michel responded, recalling with distaste and anger the way in

71

which Clodion looked at Danise.

"You have made an accurate assessment of Clodion's character for such a short acquaintance," Redmond said. "I have my own criticism of him. Clodion is known to be a miser, and a lecher, too, in spite of his advanced age. I do not understand why Savarec allows him to press his suit for Danise. I fear if Clodion were to marry her, he would not treat Danise as she ought to be treated."

"And you would?" Michel could not keep the edge out of his voice. Redmond gave him a curious glance before answering.

"I would always treat Danise with respect and affection. I would give the care of my estates into her keeping while I am away at war and entrust the raising of our children to her."

"Do you love her?" The question was abrupt, even rude, but Redmond, having sheathed his sword, was occupied in gathering up his folded tunic and cloak from the bench where he had left them and he did not seem to notice Michel's sudden tension. He responded with measured thoughtfulness.

"After a man and woman have been married for years," Redmond said, "after they have endured life's trials together and learned to know each other well, then comes a deep and abiding affection. I saw this between my own parents and have noted it in other long-married couples. If that is what you mean by love then, yes, I expect to feel it for Danise, in time. Until then, I find her desirable, and I do need to marry and get an heir. I like Danise very much, and the bedding of a pretty and willing young woman is always a pleasant business. Do you not find it so?"

Redmond said all of this in such a matter-of-fact way that Michel could not take offense for Danise's sake. But neither could he stay where he was and listen to Redmond talk of bedding Danise.

"Michel?" Redmond touched his shoulder. "Is something wrong?"

"My head has begun to ache again," Michel lied. "I think it's because of the bright sun and the heat. A swim will help."

They reached the river, where they discarded their weapons and stripped off their clothes before plunging naked into the cool water. Feeling the need of a few minutes alone, Michel struck out toward deeper water, leaving Redmond behind.

He was determined not to quarrel with Redmond over Danise. Damn it, the man was his friend! Improbably, over the past few days and mostly out of the goodness of Redmond's heart, they had become friends. Redmond had introduced Michel to many of the young nobles, who accepted him because of Redmond's sponsorship. Michel knew Savarec was pleased by the way he was fitting into this group of young men, and he vowed he would repay the debt of gratitude he owed to Savarec by not causing any trouble for his host. No, he would start no arguments with Redmond.

Michel turned over on his back, floating with the current, thinking about Danise. She seemed

Flora Speer

to have lost all interest in him since he was
up and about, and could communicate in the
Frankish language. Her nursing duties toward
him completed, she had turned him over to
Redmond and then occupied herself so completely with her attendance on the queen that
for the last day or so Michel had seldom seen
her. And never alone. She was avoiding him.

He missed her. He began to devise a plan
to convince her to spend at least a little time
alone with him. If he used that time well, other
opportunities to be with her might follow.

His musings were interrupted by a shout
from some distance away. Treading water now,
Michel looked toward shore. The current had
carried him downstream until he had floated
well past the spot where he and Redmond
had first entered the water. Redmond stood
hip-deep, waving to him to return. Standing
beside Redmond, Charles also beckoned, and
Michel could sense their concern for him. With
a wave of one hand to show he understood,
Michel began to swim back to them.

The current was not particularly strong, and
he was an accomplished swimmer. His long,
measured strokes soon took him close to the
place where Redmond and Charles were waiting for him. Charles swam out to meet him.

"I have never seen anyone swim like that,"
said the king of the Franks with great admiration. "How is it done?"

"You are using the breast stroke," Michel
replied, "while I was doing the crawl. Like this."
He demonstrated, while Charles watched.

"I must learn this," Charles said. "It is faster."

"I just assumed that everyone knew how." Michel stopped, wondering about that.

"Perhaps everyone in your land swims that way," Charles said. "When your memory returns, I believe there will be much for us to learn from you."

"If it ever does return." Michel headed for shore, leading the king and Redmond out of the water.

By the time the midday meal was over Michel's head was in truth aching again and he was seething with frustration. Flashes of memory tormented him, moments when he felt completely disoriented, knowing with absolute certainty that he should not be where he was, yet not at all sure where he did belong. His cordial hosts accepted him as a nobleman, but Michel believed in his heart that he was no such thing.

As far as surface appearances were concerned, he experienced no difficulty. After several days of intense practice he could converse in the Frankish tongue without any great effort, and in the relaxed royal court, protocol and table manners were simple. He did find it odd to sit down to a meal eaten with fingers, knife and spoon. It seemed to him that some important implement was absent, but since he could not think what the missing object might be, he soon adapted.

On this bright afternoon, like the other young

men among whom he was sitting, he began to tear apart with his hands the small roasted fowl that was served to him. He found the bird's legs particularly tasty and gnawed the meat off right down to the bone. He was about to begin on the breast meat when he saw Danise talking to Clodion.

Michel told himself there could be no harm in such a conversation, not in the open air with so many other people nearby, not with Charles and Hildegarde, Savarec and Sister Gertrude all sitting close enough to observe what was happening. Clodion was one of Danise's acknowledged suitors. And yet Michel found something sinister in the way Clodion clutched at Danise with his long, clawlike fingers. Michel thought he saw his own apprehension reflected in Danise's face.

He knew he ought to express his concern to Redmond rather than take matters into his own hands. Redmond was, after all, Danise's second official suitor. But Redmond was engaged in a boisterous discussion with two other young men. Interrupting them would require an explanation that might result in embarrassment for Danise if Redmond decided to make an angry protest about the way Clodion had just put his arm around Danise's waist and attempted to kiss her. A more subtle diversion than Redmond's anger was required, some clever means of separating Danise from her lecherous suitor.

Michel knew just how to do it. It was time to put into effect the plan he had concocted earlier while swimming. Rising from his seat he began to wend his way among the laughing, talking Franks, who thought nothing of moving from table to table carrying their meat and their flagons of wine or beer with them as they conversed with their friends. Michel paid little attention to the men and women he passed. His eyes were on Danise.

"Surely you would not deny me a kiss," Clodion said to Danise. "Yesterday I saw you kiss Count Redmond on the cheek."

"It was purely out of gratitude," Danise replied. "Redmond has been so kind to Michel."

"Ah, yes, your mysterious guest. Does he also claim your kisses, while you deny me?" Clodion's lip curled scornfully, revealing a glimpse of his discolored teeth. His arm slipped around her waist and he bent his face to hers.

"I kiss no man as a lover," Danise cried, trying to pull away from him. Where was her father when she needed him? Where was Sister Gertrude? Did they imagine this odious man could not seriously harass her in the midst of a crowd? She saw her father talking with the scholar Alcuin and one of his clerks, noticed Sister Gertrude with Hildegarde. Both were too far away for her to attract the attention of either without causing a scene. She did not like Clodion and had quickly decided she could never marry him, but he was too important a noble to offend in public. With a sinking heart Danise realized she alone would have to find a way to free herself from Clodion's attentions and his clutching hands. She began by trying to reason with him. "Let me go, sir. I wish to return to my chaperon's side."

"I remember Gertrude when she was not so strict as she is now," Clodion said, still holding Danise. "She may protest, but I believe she would understand a man's eager desire to kiss his betrothed."

"I am not yet betrothed to anyone." Danise pushed hard against Clodion's chest. "I do not want to kiss you."

Her protest had no effect on Clodion. He lowered his face until his mouth was almost on hers. She turned her head, trying to twist away from him. Just as she feared she would be kissed in spite of her best efforts to prevent it, she heard a familiar and most welcome voice.

"There you are, Danise. I've been looking for you." Michel strolled up to them, the very picture of a relaxed young noble. "Good day to you, Count Clodion."

"What do you want?" Clodion demanded with a notable lack of courtesy.

"Danise has been helping me in my attempts to regain my memory," Michel informed him. "Since I want to return to my own land as soon as possible, I am understandably eager to continue our efforts."

Danise stared at him, amazed to hear him dissemble so easily. She had done nothing at all to help Michel regain his memory. To her great relief, Clodion removed his hands from her arm and waist. At once she stepped away from him.

"So you intend to leave Francia?" Clodion gave Michel his full attention. "Might you take Count Redmond with you?"

"I have thought most seriously of inviting him to accompany me when I go," Michel replied. The gravity of his expression gave no indication of his thoughts, but Danise was certain that Michel was secretly laughing at her disagreeable suitor.

"By all means, regain your memory," Clodion said. "I would do nothing to prevent you—or your friend Redmond—from returning to your home."

"I thank you for your good wishes." Michel made a deep bow. Danise saw the gesture as mocking; Clodion appeared to accept it as evidence of respect.

"You and I will speak again later, Danise." Clodion moved off into the throng of nobles near Charles and his queen.

"Is aught amiss here?" Savarec approached his daughter and Michel. "Danise, I saw Clodion with his arm about you. You should not allow such familiarity in public unless you intend to accept his suit."

"I did not allow it," Danise began, hurt that her father could think she would be so careless with her reputation. Michel interrupted her protest.

"It was a minor misunderstanding," he told Savarec, and then changed the subject before Danise's father could ask what the misunderstanding was. "Savarec, I would like your permission to go alone with Danise into the

79

Flora Speer

forest. I want her to take me to the exact spot where she found me. Perhaps something there will stir my memory."

"Alone?" Savarec considered this proposal. "For appearance's sake I should go with you. Or Sister Gertrude."

"Neither of you was present when Danise found me," Michel said. "I would like to repeat exactly what happened when I was first discovered."

"Then you should have Clothilde with you," said Savarec.

"It is my understanding that Danise sent Clothilde away at once, to find you," Michel replied. "I don't think it will take long, Savarec. If I am to remember anything, I believe it will happen at once. This request is vitally important to me, so I ask your indulgence. I promise to return Danise to you unharmed."

"My daughter is precious to me," Savarec began.

"I know it," Michel told him. "I honor Danise as my rescuer. You have my solemn word, I will not harm her."

"Well," Savarec wavered.

"Will no one ask my opinion?" Danise looked from her father to Michel. "I will help you. I know how much it will mean to you to have your memories back again." She did not add what she was thinking, that it was just as important to her to know who he really was, to know if he was married or if he had children.

"Very well, then," Savarec said. "Do what you can for him, Danise. However, you must not

80

stay in the forest too long. You and I may know that Michel is an honorable man who will keep his word, but if Clodion realizes you are gone and becomes annoyed, he may impugn your virtue, and some folk here at Duren will listen to him. Not to mention what Sister Gertrude will say to me if she hears of this project."

"Thank you, Father." Danise looked at Michel. "Let us go at once, so we can return before we are missed."

"Lead the way and I will follow," he responded.

Danise did not hesitate. She walked first to Savarec's tents and then began to retrace the path she had taken into the forest on the day when she had found Michel. It was not long before they were enclosed by trees and underbrush, sheltered by the canopy of newly unfurled leaves. The sound of voices from the camp was but a distant murmur muffled by the foliage. Nearer were the pleasant sounds of occasional bird calls and of water trickling along over stones and exposed tree roots.

"This way," Danise said. "Clothilde and I followed this little stream."

"Wait a moment, please."

"Michel, are you in pain again?" Seeing him with both hands at his head, Danise stopped walking. "Perhaps you should rest. We can do this another day."

"We'll do it now. I can't rest until I know who I am." He took his hands from his forehead to look at her, weariness etched on his face. "The bright sunshine and the reflections from the river hurt my eyes. The noise made by so many people talking all at once, the smells of the food, the strangeness of it all—sometimes it's overwhelming."

"You are not completely well yet."

"If I am not well, why did you desert me?" he burst out. "Why do you refuse to talk to me?"

"I am talking to you now. I am trying to help you."

"I know. I do know." He gripped her shoulders, hurting her. "I have been experiencing moments when I remember—*something*. Unfortunately, those moments never last long enough for me to make any sense of them. It's unsettling."

"I am sure it is. Come now, the spot you want to see is only a short distance away." Her heart pounding, her own thoughts awhirl, Danise moved out of his restraining hands to lead the way along the path taken by the stream until they reached a clearing.

"Is this it?" Michel looked around as if he could not believe he had ever been in that place before.

"You were lying there when I found you." Danise pointed to a rock half buried in dry leaves. "We decided you must have hit your head on that stone. We thought you were in the tree just above before you fell."

He looked up into the green height of the tree in question, then down at the rock. He dropped to his knees in the pile of leaves. Shaking his head, he looked at her.

"I was so sure coming here would jog my memory, but I recognize nothing I see, and I feel nothing unusual," he said. Grasping her hand he pulled her downward. "Show me exactly how I was lying when you first saw me."

To do as he wanted it was necessary for her to push his arms and legs into the position she remembered. She also remembered bathing those same limbs while he lay naked and helpless beneath her ministering hands, and while she tried unsuccessfully to convince herself it was his very helplessness that tugged at her heart.

"Where were you when you found me?" he asked, his voice somewhat muffled because he was lying face downward. "What was the first thing you did?"

"I was here." She sat beside him. "I turned you over, this way." And there he was again, lying on the ground, gazing up at her from unbelievably blue eyes just as he had done on the first day she had ever seen him. The man before her now was anything but helpless. Her reaction to him was far more intense than on their first meeting, and the strength of it frightened her. She knew only as much about him as he knew about himself, which was little, indeed. Who he really was did not matter. Her heart recognized him. Having loved once, she could not be unaware of her feelings now. She ought not to let him affect her this way. Her father would not approve and worse— oh, far worse than Savarec's opinion—what she was beginning to feel toward Michel was disloyal to . . .

"Danise." He was holding her hand, drawing her closer. When she put out her free hand to keep them apart, she rested her palm on his chest, where she could feel his warmth and the beating of his heart.

"I am dislocated," he said. "Only when I am with you does any of this make sense. Only when I see you do I feel as if I am in the right place. Everything else is confusion and frustration."

"Do you feel that here you are where you should be? Here, where I found you?"

"Only because you are here, too." He let go of the hand he was holding, to catch the back of her head. He pulled her downward, his other arm around her waist as Clodion had held her just a short time ago. How different Michel's embrace was from Clodion's, how warm and strong and tempting. The hand with which she had been pushing against his chest was now trapped between their bodies. Though her knees were still folded up beneath her, she was all but lying in his arms and she found it altogether too pleasant an experience. His mouth brushed across hers.

"No, Michel, please." If he heard her, he paid no attention to her feebly whispered protest. He held her firmly and kissed her hard. Danise found herself succumbing to the heated delight of his lips on hers, letting him do what he wanted and responding to him as though she had no obligation to anyone but herself and him. She felt his tongue against her mouth. When she parted her lips in surprise at this pressure, he thrust into her.

All her thoughts fled away. Danise wanted only to stretch out beside Michel and feel the length of his manly frame along her body. She wanted him to go on kissing her, and kissing her, and then . . .

"Danise." Michel sat up, still holding her in his arms. His lips caressed her forehead. His arms tightened again. She knew he would kiss her once more.

"No." She began to struggle, pushing at him. He let her go at once. She faced him with an anger made all the stronger because she knew she wanted that next kiss. "Michel, you have broken your word to my father. You promised him no harm would come to me."

"I have not harmed you. You did not fight me," he said. "It was only one kiss."

"Not one kiss. Two kisses. How could you do this to me?" Shame and remorse flooded over her. "How could you make me forget? Make me disloyal?"

"Disloyal to whom?" he asked. "To your suitors? To Clodion? I don't think so. To Redmond? Do you love him? Is he the one you want?"

"No, no, you don't understand." *Oh, Hugo, how could I kiss another man? How could I betray you so easily?*

"Perhaps I could understand if you would explain," Michel said. "I honestly thought you wanted me to kiss you. I thought you enjoyed it as much as I did. You seemed to enjoy it."

"Stop it!" She was on her feet, her hands over her ears to shut out his words. It was true, she had welcomed his kisses, but her pleasure only made things worse, only made her feel more guilty and more disloyal to Hugo. She could not stay where she was, not with Michel's blue gaze probing into her heart until she believed he must see what a callous, dishonest woman she was.

Danise began to run, dodging among the trees, tripping, then catching herself so she could run on, run anywhere, so long as it was away from Michel and the temptation he represented.

He followed her. She could hear him crashing along behind her. And because he was stronger and faster it was not long before he caught her. He grabbed her by the shoulders once more and pushed her against a tree trunk and held her there.

"Now," he said, "you are going to tell me what is wrong. You are too sensible a woman to carry on like this without a good reason. You know we both wanted that kiss. Why are you so upset about it?"

"Not one kiss," she said again, sniffing to hold back incipient tears. "Two." She saw laughter in his eyes at her insistence on the exact number.

"All right, two kisses. The first scarcely counted. It was only to test if you wanted a real one." As quickly as it had come, the flicker of amusement vanished from his face. "Your eyes are haunted, Danise. You speak of disloyalty because you enjoyed my kiss—sorry, my *kisses*. Both of them. A few days ago you refused to tell me why you are sad. I have a right to know."

"What right?" She made the mistake of looking into his eyes and found she could not look away. She could feel her will bending to his.

"You know what right," he said. "You know why I kissed you. Answer me, Danise."

Still she was captured by his eyes as firmly as she was by his hands. She knew he would not let her go until he had the answer he sought. She had to speak.

"Hugo loved me," she whispered, "and I loved him. We hoped to marry. You are the first man to kiss me since—since he died."

"I am sorry. I didn't know." Suddenly she was no longer pressed against the tree. His arms were gentle, holding her, and she did not protest the embrace. "How did he die? How long has it been?"

"He marched into Spain in May of last year and died in August, at Roncevaux, on his way home to Francia. Many others died there, too."

"Last August?" he repeated. "And it's May again now? Then it has been an entire year since you've seen him. There's no reason for you to feel guilty, Danise. Many women do not mourn their lovers for so long a time." She thought he could feel the way she stiffened in resistance to that idea, for he released her and stepped back a pace. Danise leaned against the tree trunk, not sure she would be able to stand without its support.

87

"Do you feel disloyal when either of your suitors kiss you?" he asked. "Or is it only with me?"

"They have not kissed me, not the way you did. I just told you, you are the first since Hugo."

"Do you intend to refuse to marry both Redmond and Clodion out of loyalty to Hugo? If so, you ought to tell them now and not keep them dangling in suspense. Clodion, especially. I have a feeling the man could turn nasty if he's thwarted."

"I have not decided yet whether to marry or not." She wished he had not asked those questions. Michel was forcing her to think about a subject she had avoided since learning of her father's wish that she should decide whether to marry or become a nun. She thought about it now.

She would never willingly marry Clodion. Of that much she was certain. She found Clodion repulsive. But she could marry Redmond or return to Chelles to live with no disloyalty to Hugo's memory in either case. At Chelles she would remain a virgin all her life and dedicate herself to good works in service to God. She did not think Hugo would have objected to such a decision. If she married Redmond, Danise could still remain loyal to Hugo, for Redmond, much as she liked him, did not and never could engage her heart as Hugo had done.

As for the man standing before her here in the forest, he was a dire threat to her love for Hugo. Danise sensed that if she allowed her reactions to Michel to guide her, he would soon eclipse Hugo in her thoughts. She could not allow that to happen. Hugo had loved her with a deep and tender devotion. He had died a hero, doing his duty for his king. She had a duty, too, a duty to keep Hugo's image bright in her memory for as long as she lived. However compelling Michel's attentions to her might be, she could not allow him to take Hugo's place.

"Danise." She tried to look at him without being captured by his brilliant eyes, but it was an impossible task. "If I can learn my true identity, and if I prove to be the nobleman your father and all the others I have met here at Duren seem to think I am, or if I am in some other way a worthy person, would Savarec accept me as one of your suitors? Would you?"

She could only stare at him, unable to speak. Thrilled and terrified at the same time by his suggestion, she began to shake her head, to reject his idea.

"Answer me," he prodded gently. "Tell me what you are thinking."

"I do not know what my father would say," she whispered.

"And you? What would you say?"

"That you disturb me. That you make me feel things I ought not to feel. That you threaten to turn my life upside down until I do not know what to say to you, or how to act."

"As soon as I was well enough to think about it," he said, "I wondered if my attraction to you was just a classic case of a patient becoming attached to his nurse."

"Perhaps it is." Eagerly she grasped at the possibility he offered. "I was the person who was with you most often during the time when you were terribly confused and ill, so it would be natural for you to begin to depend upon me, rather than upon my father, or Guntram, or even Clothilde. I have heard of this sort of thing before. It is not unusual for wounded warriors to think they care about the women who nurse them back to health. It happens all the time, even when the attachments are most unsuitable. When the men are well and back in armed service once more, they sometimes joke about their former emotions. So I have heard."

"This is no joke," he said, stopping the nearly desperate flow of her words. "I cannot believe that what I am feeling is no more than an injured man's dependency."

"Yet it must be so," she insisted. "As your body recovers from your injuries, so will your emotions."

"What if I don't want to recover?" he demanded. "Through all the confusion and the uncertainty since I came here, the one thing I know is that I want to hold you in my arms. I keep telling myself it's crazy to feel this way, but I can't stop wanting you."

She stared back at him, unable to tear her eyes away from his intense face.

"Danise, you can't be seriously thinking of

going into a convent. You are too young, too intelligent, and far too beautiful to give up on life."

"I have not given up, I am merely undecided," she replied. "Sister Gertrude would tell you that a decision to enter a convent is not a rejection of life but a positive act."

"It would be a rejection of your womanhood. Would Hugo want you to be lonely and unfulfilled? If he was the kind of man you could love so deeply, then I think he must have been unselfish enough to want you to be happy. So, I ask you again, if I can discover who I am, will you accept me as one of your suitors?"

Danise felt weakened, her maidenly defenses battered by Michel's tenacity of purpose. Could he be right? Would Hugo, if he could speak to her, tell her to let another man share the innermost space in her heart where until now only he had lived? As was her custom, she took refuge in honesty.

"I am as confused as you were when first I met you," she said to Michel. "You use incomprehensible words and your foreign ideas disturb me. But I ought to be as fair to you as I would be to any other man who offered for me. If my father has no objection to your suit, then neither will I object. Beyond that, I can promise nothing."

"It's enough for now. We'll have to take it one step at a time," he said. "The first step was getting your agreement. The second step will be finding my identity and my memory. After that, we'll decide what to do next. In the meantime, may I ask one favor of you?"

"What is it?"

"One kiss more, so you'll know what you will be getting in me."

"You have already kissed me twice," she protested. "Neither Redmond nor Clodion has yet kissed me on the lips. Nor would I allow it if they tried," she added, thinking of Clodion with a shudder.

"Grant me this favor and in the future I will behave with the utmost propriety. I swear it." He smiled at her, his rather plain features coming alight with humor and warmth, his remarkable eyes sparkling. "It will be hard, but I will keep my word. I warn you, if you refuse this one request, I'll pursue you relentlessly and kiss you more than once, when and where I find an opportunity. Public or private places will be all the same to me."

"You are threatening me." She did not sound as severe as she wanted to sound. His smile was too contagious for her to remain shocked or angry for more than a moment.

"Are you afraid?" The laughter lines at the corners of his eyes crinkled more deeply.

"Certainly not." Instantly she rose to his mocking challenge. She was usually a person of some spirit, and she was chagrined by how cowardly she had appeared to be during this trying afternoon. She *was* afraid of his effect on her, but she did not want him to know it.

"You may kiss me, Michel. But only once."

"A kiss cheerfully given by me and willingly received by you," he murmured, reaching for her. "Let's not delay. I don't want you to change your mind."

"I am not a woman who breaks her word. It will be an honest kiss." She went into his arms willingly, as he had asked of her, and lifted her face. His mouth touched hers, withdrew, then pressed hard. His arms caught her, holding her tight, while her hands crept upward around his neck. Danise stood on tiptoe, opening her lips to his thrusting tongue, responding honestly as she had promised.

There was sweetness in Michel's kiss, and warmth and tenderness, too, but no terrifying passion and no demands she could not accept. In some deeply buried segment of her mind she understood that he was skilled in romantic matters and was taking care not to frighten her. Part of her was grateful for his consideration, but another part of her, a rebellious, treacherous, well-hidden part, wondered what it would be like to be kissed by him when he was not being so careful. And because she was entirely too aware of that most unmaidenly bit of her own character, she reacted to his kiss by scolding him when it was over.

"You promised to take but one kiss," she told him. "Once again, you have taken two kisses. You count poorly, Michel."

"Ah, Danise, Danise." He held her lightly now, resting his cheek against hers. Thus, she could not see his face, but when he spoke again she knew he understood and forgave her inner turmoil and her fears. "How I wish we could have met when my memory was clear, and your heart was whole."

Chapter 5

"Savarec, bring your friends and join us," called Charles from his place at the trestle table set in front of his tent. "We are discussing plans for the building of my new palace at Aachen. I want the site of my old hunting lodge to become a great and beautiful capital."

"With an important church at its heart," added the tall, stoop-shouldered man in cleric's robes who sat beside Charles.

"Of course," Charles responded. "We must create the finest place of worship to be found anywhere in Francia. I saw a church in Lombardy during my campaign there a few years ago. Beautiful columns. Lovely marble. If I could but bring those columns to Francia . . . hmmm." He paused, his thoughts on a building far to the south, on the other side of the Alps.

Flora Speer

In her chair set on her husband's right hand, Hildegarde stirred uneasily. Danise bent to adjust a pillow for the queen, and Hildegarde smiled up at her.

"Always Charles talks about this new palace," Hildegarde murmured. "It will take so long to build that I wonder if any of us will live to see Aachen completed."

"We can at least be grateful," said Sister Gertrude, "that when men speak of building, they are not discussing the possibility of going to war."

"Yet I do believe there will be a short campaign against the Saxons this summer," Hildegarde said.

Michel was aware of what the women were saying, but most of his attention was fixed on Danise. This morning she had wrapped her braids into a silver halo about her head, and her green gown clung to her softly rounded figure. Her mouth curved into a smile as she looked from her father to Redmond to Michel, greeting each of them in turn. Michel was stung by a vivid memory of kissing those richly tinted lips. He grew warm just looking at Danise. She met his eyes briefly before she glanced away, blushing a little. He wondered if she was also recalling with pleasure the way he had kissed her. He hoped she was.

"Must we endure the presence of that dreadful man?" Sister Gertrude demanded of Savarec.

Thinking she meant him, Michel regarded the nun with some surprise, unaware of having

96

done anything to offend her, unless Danise had felt a need to confess that they had kissed in the forest on the previous day. Somehow, he did not think Danise would talk about their tender embraces. He quickly realized that Sister Gertrude was not referring to him at all, but to Count Clodion, who was approaching the group surrounding the king.

"I believe Clodion intends to speak to Charles, not to Danise," Savarec said with his usual patience when dealing with Sister Gertrude. "You cannot banish him entirely from this gathering, so I must beg you to treat him with the respect due to his title."

"Respect must be earned," Sister Gertrude retorted. When Savarec moved on to intercept Clodion and direct him toward Charles, she muttered, "I would banish Clodion from Francia if I could."

"I perceive that you like him no better than I do," Michel said to her in a low voice.

"I like Clodion not at all," Sister Gertrude told him. "Nor did I like Count Autichar any better."

"Redmond has told me how Autichar left Duren in a huff," Michel said. "I cannot imagine any man willingly walking away from the possibility of marriage to Danise."

Sister Gertrude regarded him with the same puzzled expression he was growing used to seeing on the faces of other Franks to whom he used words or phrases perfectly natural to him but foreign to them. Michel smiled to himself, imagining he could see her thinking through and interpreting what he had just said.

"I also find it difficult to believe that Autichar would leave Duren so easily," Sister Gertrude said. "I would not be at all surprised to learn that we have not seen the last of him. I cannot understand why Savarec, who loves his daughter so dearly, would allow either Autichar or Clodion to court her. He cannot wish to see one or the other as his son-in-law."

"Perhaps Savarec thought Autichar and Clodion would make Redmond look more attractive by comparison," Michel said.

"A clever idea on your part," Sister Gertrude responded after taking a moment to interpret the meaning of his words. "However, Savarec is a straightforward man who does not think in such devious ways. No, I believe he was more interested in the titles and the lands that Autichar or Clodion could bring to a marriage. But neither man would make Danise happy. Why must men be such fools?"

"Perhaps because we do not think like women." When the nun's dark eyes opened wide at this statement, Michel smiled at her. "You love Danise as if she were your own daughter."

"I will admit to a certain fondness for her. Danise has been an excellent student. Still, she can be willful, and at such times she must be sternly admonished for her own benefit."

"You love her," Michel repeated, still smiling. "More important, you understand the pain she has endured since Hugo's death. You see Danise's life mirroring your own."

"How can you know about my life?" Sister Gertrude demanded.

"From Savarec. I asked him. Danise herself told me about Hugo."

"I am astonished. She has scarcely mentioned Hugo's name since the day of the funeral service at Agen." Sister Gertrude looked hard at Michel. "Why would she reveal her deepest pain to you?"

"Tell me," said Michel, deliberately not answering the question asked of him, "do you think Danise would be happy with Redmond?"

"Do you?" Sister Gertrude gave him such a searching look that words failed him. She did not comment on it, but he knew she had not missed his remark about not knowing how any man could walk away from marriage to Danise. This tough, outspoken woman was too intelligent not to take note of his words. In spite of her sharp tongue he liked Sister Gertrude and he shared her disgust for Clodion. Unquestionably, Redmond would be the better husband for Danise, but, much as Michel liked Redmond, he could not bear to think of Danise in Redmond's arms. He had a feeling he and Sister Gertrude were in agreement on that, too.

"Michel, come here," Savarec called to him. Michel excused himself to Sister Gertrude and went to join the other men. He could feel her probing eyes on him until he had to force himself not to turn around and look at her again.

Nor would he permit his glance to stray toward Danise, who stood just a few feet away from him at Hildegarde's side. He knew if he did, he would not be able to look away from her. But while he greeted Charles, or talked with Redmond and Savarec, or exclaimed with honest interest over the drawings on parchment that were the plans for Charles's new palace, Danise remained in his thoughts.

"You have not yet met my friend, Alcuin," Charles said, "though he has heard much about you."

"I've heard a lot about you, too," Michel said to the cleric who sat beside the king, "and all of it good."

Alcuin frowned as if struck by some peculiarity in Michel, and looked more closely at him. Michel was growing used to this kind of response. Charles having asked shortly after his appearance at Duren if anyone there knew of a missing man, or if anyone meeting Michel could recognize him, his situation was common knowledge. Most of the warriors and their womenfolk knew of men who suffered confusion after a hard knock or a wound to the head, though seldom did anyone survive for more than a week without recovering from the condition. Thus, Michel was looked upon as something of a curiosity.

"Is anything wrong? Do you know me?" Michel asked Alcuin. With his intense awareness of Danise's presence, he sensed it when she stepped away from Hildegarde's side to move nearer to him. She touched his arm as if to offer comfort or encouragement. He was grateful for the contact, but he kept his primary attention on Alcuin, hoping to hear from the great scholar something that would provide a clue to his identity.

"Nothing wrong," Alcuin said, "only that I see in you a likeness to a woman I met last year at Agen. It is not a physical resemblance. The similarity is more in the way you act with others. There is in you the same independence of spirit. Danise, does Michel remind you of India?"

"Alcuin, you are right," Danise exclaimed. "I did not see it before, but now that you mention it, yes, it is so. There is something in Michel which is very similar to India."

"Who is this woman?" Michel asked. "Is she here at Duren? Can I meet her?"

"Her lover, Count Theuderic, died at Roncevaux with my Hugo," Danise said, so low that Michel had to bend down to hear her. "Afterward, she returned to her own home. Michel, could you be from her land?"

"I won't know till I remember who I am." Michel looked over Danise's bowed head toward Alcuin, who still sat beside Charles. The other men stood or sat about, talking among themselves—Duke Bernard, Savarec, Redmond, Clodion, and others whom Michel had met in recent days. He saw none of them. He gazed straight at Alcuin, sharing a long, deep look that told Michel the scholar knew, or suspected, far more than he had revealed.

"We must talk," Michel said to him. "Later, perhaps." Alcuin nodded and then, breaking their intense eye contact, returned his attention to the plans for Charles's palace.

"Perhaps he can help you," Danise murmured, her hand still on Michel's arm. "How wonderful it would be for you if Alcuin can offer some clue to open your memory."

There was one in that gathering of men and women near to the king and queen who was mightily displeased by what he had just seen.

"Savarec," demanded Clodion, "do you always permit your daughter such familiarities with men whose origins are unknown?"

"Danise meant her sympathy for me in a kindly way and nothing more," Michel spoke up before Savarec could answer. Clodion would not be silenced.

"Has this unknown man become another suitor for your daughter's hand, Savarec?" Clodion's voice dripped contempt for Michel. "If he has, I consider his suit an insult to me and to Redmond. I warn you, Savarec, to guard Danise more closely or I will withdraw as Autichar did."

"It would be a blessing if you were to do so." Sister Gertrude moved to stand next to Danise and Michel. "Danise has done nothing wrong, nothing that any honest woman would not do for a man who has been ill and in her care."

"Indeed, Count Clodion." Hildegarde now spoke from her chair. Looking over her shoulder toward where Danise and Michel were standing with Sister Gertrude, she went on, "I find no fault in Danise's actions, nor in Sister Gertrude's guarding of her. Be patient, Clodion, and press your own suit for Danise with the polite consideration that is the only way to win a lady's heart."

It was plain to see in Clodion's face what his opinion of this sentiment was, but he did not respond to the queen's gentle scolding.

"There, do you hear that?" said Charles, laughing away the dispute. "As usual, my wife shows more wisdom than most men. Treat Danise kindly, Clodion, and when the time is right, she will make her choice. Now, let us return to consideration of my palace. Clodion, will you look at these plans and tell me as a devoted hunter, what do you think of the size and placement of the stables?"

"Come, Danise." Sister Gertrude shepherded her charge along the few steps back to the queen's side.

Michel's head had begun to ache again. He stood alone, rubbing at his temples until Redmond joined him.

"Is it true?" Redmond asked. "Do you also want to wed Danise?"

"That was Clodion's spite talking, not truth," Michel ground out, wishing the pain in his head would stop. "How could I ask for Danise, when, for all I know, I may already have a wife?" The very thought of it made his head ache still more.

"I thought you'd say something like that. No one ought to listen to anything Clodion says." Redmond paused, looking at his friend with a worried expression. "Michel, are you ill again?"

"My head is throbbing. My eyes ache." Michel gritted his teeth against a wave of nausea. "I need to find a quiet place, somewhere out of the sun."

"I'll help you back to Savarec's tent. It will be the best place for you." Redmond took his arm, guiding him in that direction.

"What's wrong?" Danise had seen them. She came to Michel and took his hand. "Can I help? Is there something you need?"

You, he wanted to say, *I need you.* He tightened his fingers over hers. The desire to put his arms around her, to kiss her beautiful, trembling mouth was nearly overpowering. And the pain in his head grew worse, until it brought tears to his eyes. Swaying on his feet, he clung to Danise's hand.

"He needs to lie down." Sister Gertrude's voice was sharp, bracing Michel, directing him through yet another wave of nearly unbearable pain. "Leave him to Redmond, Danise. Redmond will see him safe to his bed. Your place today is with the queen."

"Michel?" She was worried about him. He could see it in her eyes when he forced his own eyes open to look at her. He knew she would not leave him unless he told her to. Much as he wanted her with him, he knew Sister Gertrude was right. Clodion would be watching this little scene and might cause trouble for her or for Savarec if he thought Danise was showing too much favor to a stranger. He owed Savarec— he owed . . .

"I'll be fine with Redmond," he managed to say. He glanced toward Sister Gertrude and saw her approving nod as she turned Danise away from him.

"Why is everything so damned complicated?" he groaned to Redmond as, with his friend supporting him, he made his stumbling way toward Savarec's tent.

"I have lately begun to ask the same question," Redmond replied. "Here we are. Guntram, he's sick again and he needs to lie down. Watch over him, will you? I cannot stay, I am expected by Charles. We are to discuss our situation against the Saxons this afternoon, so I cannot be absent."

Scarcely had Redmond left them than Michel became violently ill, losing everything he had eaten that day. Guntram found a bucket and stayed with him, supplying wine to rinse out his mouth afterward and a cool damp cloth so he could wipe his face.

"Your tunic is soiled. I'll give it to Clothilde to wash," Guntram said, adding in his rough way, "You stay in bed."

"Feeling the way I do, I can't do anything else." Clad only in his long-sleeved linen undershirt, Michel lay back on his narrow bed. At first he felt as if the top of his head would burst open, but he soon discovered that if he lay very still with his eyes closed and the cloth Guntram had given him laid across his eyes to shut out all the light, then the pain would begin to ease. After a while, he slept.

He wakened to midnight darkness. In the other bed Savarec snored softly. From outside the tent came the muffled sounds of a large camp at rest. He could hear the sentries talking softly together, could hear a woman's husky laugh, while some distance away a man sang a plaintive song.

He knew exactly where he was. His head was perfectly clear, all trace of pain gone.

And he was stricken with terror such as he had never known before—no, not even when he had fallen into the tomb of an early Merovingian queen and the walls had caved in around him and he had thought they would not dig him out in time and he would die there, curled up beside the queen's bones with his head pillowed on her golden serving tray. This was a thousand times worse than being buried alive.

For Bradford Michael Bailey had recovered his memory.

Chapter 6

He did not sleep at all during the remainder of that night. Fearing to waken Savarec or Guntram, either of whom would be sure to ask questions he did not want to answer, Mike made himself stay quietly in his bed when he would rather have gone for a long walk while he thought through the implications of his situation. Because he was so horrified by what had happened to him, he deliberately tried to be methodical and as unemotional as he could. From past experience he knew this was the best way to stave off panic.

The first item for consideration was whether he had any hope of returning to his own time. The possibility of such a resolution seemed remote. Mike believed that Hank would be glad to be rid of someone who was bent on

Flora Speer

interfering with his work on the space-time continuum. Hank would probably make no attempt at all to get him back. With grim humor Mike thought that his removal to the eighth century could be classed as a perfect crime. As far as the twentieth century was concerned he was as good as dead, yet Hank had no inconvenient body to dispose of and if anyone should inquire of Hank or his friend Alice, they could honestly say they had no idea where Bradford Michael Bailey might be.

For one angry, crazed minute Mike wondered what the two of them would do with his much-loved car, which he had left parked in the driveway of Alice's house, but he quickly dismissed the question as irrelevant under the present circumstances. The fact that he thought of the car at all indicated how close to cracking he was. He could not afford to give way to fear. He had to get hold of himself. He would do what he had done when he was accidentally buried in that ancient queen's grave. He would stay calm and he would use his brain, for muscle alone would not help him here.

Having reached this point in his reasoning, Mike next tried to accept what he saw as reality. The chances were good that he would have to spend the rest of his life in the eighth century. He would have to get used to that fact as soon as possible.

Fortunately, he was not without knowledge of the time in which he found himself. In the twentieth century he had been a noted archaeologist specializing in the violent Merovingian era, a period of intrigues and murders within the Frankish royal family, and of ruinous local wars between nobles. At the end of that period the Carolingians, the dynasty of which Charles was the most famous member, seized power and then brought order to a land in sad need of strong rulers. Charles, known to the twentieth century as Charlemagne, was one of the few kings in history whom Mike admired. Having met the man, Mike liked him as a person and, while generally not in favor of kings, he thought he could live under Charles's rule.

With the return of his memory Mike now had an explanation for many of the mysterious mistakes he had made since his arrival at Duren. He had been experiencing flashes of recall, but his knowledge of Frankish weapons, coins, and customs was a hundred years or so out of date. Using the information amassed through his studies and his work at archaeological digs, he felt confident of his ability to catch up easily.

To begin with, he knew how to use Frankish weapons. In the twentieth century, he and a colleague had supervised the forging of replicas of both *scramasax* and *fransisca*, and then had practiced using them. This was why he had learned to wield a broadsword so quickly under Redmond's tutoring. In addition, he could ride a horse well. For the rest, he could learn what he needed to know by watching other people and by listening. It was a great advantage that he was able to pick up new languages with little effort. With the skills he already possessed, he believed he could make his way in Frankish society without serious difficulty. He would not starve or go homeless.

However, looming beyond the questions of everyday life was one major problem. *Danise.* While his memory was gone he had forgotten all the reasons why he did not trust women, so he had left himself wide open to her and thus learned to care for her with a tenderness that shook the worldly, cynical twentieth century man to his roots.

Danise was different from other women he had known. She would not lie to him, or keep important information from him, or betray him with another man. Not honest Danise, whom he loved beyond hope of ever being cured of that sweet affliction. But in the time in which he now found himself, Mike had no property, no family connections, no chance of winning her.

Unless he could earn by his personal valor enough wealth to convince Savarec to consider him as one of Danise's suitors.

It was what he had told Danise he would do. Other men in Frankish times won wealth and title and wellborn wives by the clever use of their swords. But Mike knew now that he was not a Frank, was not trained from childhood to the hardships and dangers of battle. If he was going to succeed it would take every ounce of focused determination and willpower he possessed, along with more bravery than he had ever displayed in his former life, and a fair amount of sheer luck.

He was going to try. More than try, he was

going to do it, he was going to turn himself into a Frankish nobleman, because if he did not, he was going to have to adjust to a loveless existence twelve hundred years before he had been born.

When Savarec rose from his bed, Mike got up, too, and went outside the tent. On this morning, with his mind clear at last and the headache completely gone, he looked about as if for the first time. Through the trees to his right and down a gentle slope, the River Rur sparkled dark blue and silver. Before him and to his left lay the Frankish camp, with the two bright blue royal tents at its center, where Charles and Hildegarde and their children were staying. Most of the other tents were of beige or brown or gray undyed wool, though here and there a green or blue tent made a spot of clear color against the general drabness. The green tops of the trees bordering the camp were gilded by the rising sun. Overhead the dawn sky arched pure and cloudless, with a flush of gold and pink in the east. From what he had seen of it so far, Francia was a beautiful place.

"O.K., Mike, you aren't Mike anymore," he said to himself. "*Michel.* That's your name from now on. To coin a cliché that's not even a phrase yet, this is the first day of the rest of your life. Make the best of it."

"A fine morning," said Savarec. Having finished washing his face and hands, he tossed river water out of a basin and handed the basin to Michel. "Use this if you like. You are welcome to my towel, too. Here's a bucket of clean, fresh water. Take what you need." Savarec inspected Michel's appearance with a kindly eye. "Guntram said you were sick last night."

"I am much improved today." For the last time Michel met Savarec's eyes with openness and honesty. Now the lies must begin, and he would have to make them sound like the truth. Breaking eye contact with Savarec, he looked away toward the forest before speaking again. "You know, Savarec, I have begun to believe that my memory will never return. I feel wonderfully well today, healed by the good care I have received in your tent. But there is still a high wall in my mind separating me from my past life. No matter how hard I try, I cannot break through that wall, so I have decided to stop trying. If Charles has no objections, I will stay here in Francia and offer my services as a fighting man to you if you will have me, for I owe my life to you and your daughter. If you have no use for me, I will offer myself to Charles."

"On the eastern bank of the Rhine where I command a fort," Savarec said, "the Saxons remain a constant threat in spite of all the lands we Franks have conquered in Saxony. I can always use another man who is as handy with a sword as Redmond claims you to be. When Mayfield is over, go home with me to Deutz. You will be welcome there."

"Thank you. Until this moment, I had no home in this world. Savarec, is there some ceremony required of me, perhaps an oath I ought to take?"

"A handclasp will be sufficient." Savarec put out his right hand and Michel took it. "Unlike you, I do not entirely despair of your memory's return. Let me say now that if at some time yet to come you discover that you have to leave my service to return to your home, I will understand. Until that moment arrives, if it ever does, I think you are wise to try to make a useful life for yourself."

"I will gladly serve under your command," Michel said, much relieved to find that in those words at least, he could be truthful.

Danise noticed the change in Michel as soon as she emerged from her tent that morning. He was talking with her father and Guntram, and there was something about the way he stood, a new confidence, a jauntiness she had not seen in him before. She went at once to greet her father, kissing his cheek and wishing him good day.

"And to you, too, Guntram," she said. "Michel, you appear to be much improved after your long sleep." Before speaking to him she braced herself to withstand the impact of his burning gaze. She was disappointed when he did not look directly at her. Instead, he smiled at her father.

"Michel is in such good health that he has just pledged himself as my man-at-arms," Savarec told her.

"But why?" She could not understand his

motives for such a decision. "Michel, you must have a home somewhere. Don't you want to find it?"

"I cannot find it until I remember where it is," he said, still looking at Savarec. "I doubt if I will ever remember."

"Today he begins a new life." Guntram slapped Michel on the back in hearty welcome. "We start with a hunting party. You will need a horse. Savarec, what think you of the dapple gray for Michel?"

"A good choice." Savarec gave Danise a quick pat on her shoulder before turning his attention to masculine affairs. "Michel, we ought to find Charles. He hasn't heard your news yet. He will be glad of your decision." The men moved away, leaving Danise staring after them.

"Sister Gertrude," she said to the nun who now joined her in front of Savarec's tents, "he is going hunting."

"I heard them talking," Sister Gertrude replied. "It's time Michel did something other than lie about all day and complain of an aching head."

"But he has been injured!"

"And has been restored to health, in part thanks to you. Still, you cannot expect a man to be forever grateful, nor can you continue to treat a grown man as though he were a mere child."

"I never thought he was a child." At a searching look from Sister Gertrude, Danise closed her mouth on any further comment.

She did not see Michel or her father again

until well after midday, when the men and the ladies who had chosen to go with them returned from hunting. Danise and Sister Gertrude had spent the morning inside the queen's tent with Hildegarde, who was again feeling unwell. But Hildegarde insisted on greeting Charles on his return and on sitting with him during the midday meal. Hearing the laughter and the loud talk of the hunters, the women left the blue dimness of the tent for the bright afternoon sunshine. Charles received his wife with a warm embrace, then led her to the chair drawn up for her at the table. Hildegarde's ladies followed her, Danise looking around for Michel. She saw Redmond first.

"We brought down a deer," Redmond announced, "and enough birds to keep Charles eating happily for several days."

"I do not see my father or Michel," she noted.

"They are helping to bring in the game. They'll be along soon." Redmond looked closely at her. "If you have been worrying about Michel, I can tell you he easily kept up with the rest of us. He's a fine rider, and from what I've seen of him today, I believe his health is completely restored."

"I'm glad to hear it," she replied absently, still watching the men returning to the open space in front of Charles's tents.

"Danise." Redmond touched her arm. She turned to him, meeting his pale eyes, seeing in them sincerity and a warmth that disturbed her, for she knew she could not return his feelings. "Since Michel has recovered, his place is with the men now."

"His memory is not recovered."

"He says he will disregard his lack of memory, and I think he is right to do so. Now that you are no longer so occupied in caring for him, may I hope you will find more time to spend with me?" When she did not answer, Redmond went on, "How can you decide if you want to marry me if we do not know each other? Will you spend an hour with me this afternoon? We could walk by the river, or in the forest if you prefer, and talk. If you want Sister Gertrude to go with us, I will understand, though I would like to have a little time alone with you. I promise not to importune you for favors you may not wish to grant just yet."

"Oh, Redmond, I don't know." She wasn't really paying attention to Redmond. She was looking for Michel and wondering why he had not returned to camp. Searching among the familiar faces for the one person she longed to see, Danise did not notice the man she wanted to avoid. Count Clodion joined Redmond and herself, and quickly captured her full interest.

"So, Redmond, you think you are the favored suitor, the one who will win Danise," Clodion snarled at the young man. "I say you will have to deal with me before you wed her."

"Are you challenging me?" Redmond's tone of voice dared Clodion to say he was.

"Count Clodion," Danise said, hoping to put an end to any chance of a contest of weapons between the two, "I am flattered by your great interest in me, but I must tell you again that I have not yet decided if I will marry at all."

"I blame your father for setting up this ridiculous competition," Clodion told her. "No woman should be allowed to make such an important decision. Savarec should have made the choice for you and then informed you of it."

"It is because the choice is so important to my happiness that my father gave me a voice in it," Danise declared. "I insist that you treat Count Redmond with the respect due to his title and his fine character."

"You insist?" Clodion glared at her. "You, a foolish girl, would tell me how to behave? You have spent too much time in the company of Sister Gertrude."

"Count Clodion, I must ask you to be silent. I will not allow you to insult my dear friend," Danise told him. "Since you find me both foolish and rude, perhaps you would like to withdraw your suit, as Count Autichar has done."

"Withdraw?" Clodion's face went hard and white. "No, I will not. You will pay dearly for your insolence. I'll have you yet, Danise, and when I have tamed you, I promise you will become completely biddable to my every wish." With that, Clodion stalked off.

"Is he mad?" asked Redmond, looking after him. "How can he imagine you would ever agree to marry him when he speaks to you in that way?"

"I hope he is not angry enough to cause

Flora Speer

trouble for my father," Danise murmured.

"It's not likely. Your father has the respect of more men than Clodion will ever have, and Charles's abiding friendship besides. Clodion cannot harm Savarec," Redmond concluded.

"I hope you are right," Danise said.

After his kind words about her father, Danise felt she ought to grant the request Redmond had made of her, and so she spent an hour with him after they finished eating. They walked to the riverbank, where Redmond spread out his cloak so they could sit upon it and talk. She found it easy to be with Redmond. There was in her relationship with him none of the tension she felt when she was with Michel. Redmond spoke of ordinary things, told her about the morning's hunt, described his principal home near Tournai, asked her opinion on his new green tunic, informed her about his favorite foods. He was polite and agreeable and unquestionably a good man. Danise was bored to the brink of tears. When Redmond excused himself to go to the practice yard and work with his weapons, she was grateful to see him go. She headed toward Hildegarde's tent.

"Danise." She spun around, her heart thumping, to meet the piercing blue eyes of the man she had longed to see all day. Weary of the polite conversation she had endured for the last hour, she did not give Michel a chance to tell her what he wanted to say, but went straight to the subject that interested her most.

"I do not understand why you were so quick to become my father's man," she blurted.

"Michel, you may tell me I have no right to speak on this subject, but surely you have not given up all hope of recalling your identity?"

"In fact, I have given up hope," he informed her. "It's best to get on with the business of living."

"But you don't know if you have a family." She could not say what she wanted, could not speak the word *wife* to him.

"What can I do about it?" he asked. "I cannot force my memory to return."

"You have changed overnight," she accused him. "You are so reserved, so closed upon yourself."

"Apparently, this is the way I always am when I am in good health," he replied.

"No." She shook her head. "No. There is a deep difference in you."

"Of course there is. You see before you a man who has accepted his lot and who has found a place for himself."

"But just a few days ago you told me—" She broke off, recalling in vivid detail what he had said, and what he had done to her. "Michel, I do not understand."

"There is no need for you to understand."

"Do not speak to me in such a brutal way. I have during this afternoon endured Clodion's threats and insults, and then Redmond's endless politeness. I thought you and I were friends. No, more than friends, for I told you about Hugo and I allowed you to kiss me." She clamped her lips shut, refusing to remind him that he had declared his wish to become one of her suitors. Obviously, he had changed his mind. But why? Seeing a familiar figure in clerical garb approaching, Danise made another attempt to convince Michel to explain his actions. "Here is Alcuin. I believe he has come for that discussion you agreed to have. Perhaps Alcuin can help you."

"I don't need help." Michel flung away from her, and then stopped short, staring not at Alcuin but at the slender young cleric with him. "*Hank?* Is that really you?"

"It is not," said the young man. "I am Adelbert."

"But I thought—I hoped—oh, hell and damnation, I imagined you might have a conscience after all."

"I assure you, I have," the young man said. "Though why the state of my conscience should interest you, I do not know."

"There has been a mistake made here," Alcuin said. "Adelbert, I have no further need of you just now. You may leave me and do whatever you wish for the remainder of the day."

With a fearful backward glance toward Michel, Adelbert sped away.

"I am free for the next hour or two," Alcuin said to Michel and looked at him expectantly, waiting for his response.

"I find I have no need to talk," Michel said. "You may have heard of the decision I made this morning to join Savarec's men-at-arms. I am content with my choice, and have no questions left."

"I doubt if any thoughtful man has no questions at all about his life," Alcuin said, "but I shall not press you to speak when you would prefer to be silent. However, where Charles is, there am I also. If you should change your mind while we are still at Duren, you have only to ask for me."

"Excuse me," Michel said. "I have an appointment to meet Redmond."

"He has no appointment, or Redmond would have mentioned it to me," Danise murmured, gazing after Michel's departing figure. "Master Alcuin, what is wrong with him? Has some new ailment come upon him? He is so unlike himself."

"I think it is rather the end of an ailment," Alcuin replied. When Danise looked at him in surprise, he went on, "In Agen last year, when our friend India first met Adelbert, her reaction to him was the same as Michel's just now. Astonishment, a hint of anger, then embarrassment and, in India's case, an attempt to pretend she had made a foolish mistake."

"What are you saying?"

"That India and Michel both know someone who closely resembles Adelbert, a fact which suggests to me that they both come from the same country."

"We can't know that. Michel doesn't remember—" Danise stopped, one hand at her mouth. "He could only think he recognized Adelbert if he *does* remember. Master Alcuin, Michel's memory has returned! But why did he not tell us?"

"For some deep reason of his own," Alcuin said. "I sense no more evil in Michel than I ever did in India. Rather, Michel is confused and unhappy—and angry with this *Ahnk* person for whom he mistook Adelbert. Danise, I believe we ought to remain silent about Michel's recovery of his memory. When he is ready to announce it, he will. Noblemen have their reasons for what they do, and women and clerics should not interfere."

"Do you believe he is a noble?" Danise asked, hoping it was true, and that Michel was unmarried as well. It would make such a difference if he were not wed. She pushed away that thought because it made her feel guilty and uneasy. She had no right to feel about another woman's husband the way she felt about Michel.

"I believe Michel has a noble heart," Alcuin responded to her question, rather evasively. "Let us trust him until he can make a full explanation."

In the days that followed Danise began to fear that Michel would never provide her, or Alcuin, with an explanation for his sudden change in behavior toward both of them. He spent most of his time with the men, a fact that was not particularly notable. At gatherings such as Mayfield, Frankish men tended to congregate together, leaving the women to their own devices.

Thus it was that Danise stood a little apart with Hildegarde and the other women during the sporting contests, watching Michel reach the finish line first in a horse race against Redmond. Later, again from a distance, she saw him wrestling with various young men. Frequently he lost in that particular sport, but twice he did win. He laughed with carefree pleasure when Redmond clapped him on his bare shoulder. He accepted the congratulations of the other men and acknowledged the applause of the queen, but he did not once look toward Danise.

From comments made by her father and Guntram, and from Danise's own observations, Michel seemed to her to be growing steadily tougher and more daring. The man who had once been her helpless patient, the would-be lover with whom she had shared an intimate and revealing afternoon, was now an intimidating person whom she seldom dared approach.

Sometimes she found Michel almost frightening, as on the day when, having wandered away from the royal tents to the far side of the encampment where the horses were penned and where the men gathered to practice with their weapons, she saw him riding out of the camp with Savarec and Redmond. All three of them wore chain-mail *brunias* and were armed with broadswords. The troop of twenty men who followed them were also armed and wore chain mail or heavily padded woolen tunics.

Danise did not know that Michel had acquired chain mail. No one had bothered to tell her and she had not thought to ask.

She stared at him, marveling at the hard set of his face, noticing that he looked as ready for battle as any of the other men. She could see no softness or gentleness in him.

"Why are they all garbed for war?" she asked of no one in particular. She did not expect an answer from the men on foot who hurried by her on their own errands, but she quickly received a response from a surprising source.

"They are looking for Autichar."

"Master Alcuin, what are you doing in this part of the camp?" cried Danise.

"I came bearing a final instruction from Charles to Savarec," the scholar replied. "When Charles thought of it, there was no one else immediately available, so I offered to carry the message. It is a pleasant morning for a walk." Alcuin paused beside Danise, both of them watching the men on horseback who were heading into the forest.

"I thought Autichar had gone home to Bavaria," Danise murmured.

"So did we all, until Charles received word that your erstwhile suitor was seen not far from Duren. Charles thought it wise to investigate the rumor."

"My father told me only that he would be gone for two or three days on a mission for Charles," said Danise. "Now I think I should be worried about them."

"They are warriors all. Even Michel sits his horse like a man well used to riding. They will know how to deal with Autichar if they find him. There may be nothing in the story of his presence in the vicinity." Alcuin began to walk back toward the royal tents and Danise went with him. "Danise, I hope you will join in our discussion again this evening. The remarks you contributed last night were most intelligent."

"Thank you, Master Alcuin. I plan to be there." Danise was flattered to be included in the learned group of men and women who, each evening, gathered about Charles and Alcuin for lively talk on a variety of subjects. Sometimes Alcuin or one of the other clerics would read aloud from a book Charles had chosen. Most often it was Saint Augustine's *The City Of God*, but whenever Charles gave them the choice, the clerics voted for the lighter works of the Roman poet, Virgil. Some of them could recite verse upon Latin verse from memory, and they had a habit of choosing the most romantic poems. Danise especially liked the nights when they all watched the stars come out while Alcuin explained the circular motions of the heavenly bodies as set forth centuries earlier by the great Egyptian astronomer, Claudius Ptolemy. These informal meetings were pleasant endings to busy days, and ordinarily Danise could turn her full attention to what was being discussed. But in recent days there lurked in her bosom a growing discontent.

If Savarec imagined that exposing his daughter to the life of the Frankish court would turn her away from any inclination toward a religious vocation, then his plan was succeeding. With each day that passed since her coming to Duren, Danise was more certain that she could not return to Chelles to live. She thrived upon the new responsibilities that had fallen to her, first to the care of the injured Michel and now to the queen and the royal babies. She was deeply fond of Charles and Hildegarde and of their children. She yearned to enjoy the same kind of happy family life they did. Therein lay the source of her discontent, for every time she admitted her true wishes to herself, Danise suffered severe pangs of guilt for betraying Hugo and the dream they had once shared. This inner conflict cast its shadow over the sunny warmth of mid-May. Danise knew she could not long avoid making several important decisions, and it seemed to her that whatever choices she might make, she would be unhappy.

The continued importunities of Count Clodion only added to her concerns. With her father away on the mission for Charles, leaving Guntram in charge of Savarec's men-at-arms who remained at camp, and with Sister Gertrude spending much of her time with the queen, Danise too often had to fend off Clodion's romantic advances on her own. Clodion was annoyingly persistent.

"There you are," he said one afternoon when Danise was returning to her tent after a morning spent with Hildegarde. "I have been waiting for you, my dear."

"I cannot stop to talk with you now," Danise responded. "I am tired and I have a headache."

126

"Of course you have. A young woman is often bothered by such trifling infirmities. It is a sign that you ought to be married. A good husband would know how to cure your headache in a most agreeable way."

"I do not think so." Danise tried to continue along the path to her tent, but Clodion stepped in front of her. She moved to one side. He blocked her way again. Danise stepped to the other side. Clodion was there, too. "Kindly let me pass, Count Clodion!"

"If you want to reach your tent, I will require a toll from you," Clodion told her. "A kiss, or perhaps several kisses, will do nicely."

"I do not wish to kiss you."

"You pretend to be shy now, but once you are in my arms you will soon begin to moan in ecstasy. Come, Danise." Clodion stretched out his arms. "Come to my bosom and let me tutor you in the pleasures of the body." He appeared to be blissfully unaware of the shudder this image evoked in Danise, and of the anger that quickly followed upon her revulsion.

"Count Clodion, if you do not stand aside and let me pass, I will scream. Guntram is nearby. He will hear me and come to my rescue."

"That black-bearded barbarian?" Clodion sneered. "No doubt he lusts after you, too. How many other men trail in your sweet-scented wake, Danise? Do you take pleasure in discovering just how many of us you can torment?"

"If you suffer torment, Count Clodion, it is of your own making. I have never encouraged you

127

to believe I care for you. Surely you can find some other woman who will happily receive your lustful attentions. I do not find your suggestions pleasing."

"I know the kind of woman you are," Clodion said with a self-assured smirk. "You delight in driving a man mad with cruel words and repeated refusals, while all the time your own lust is rising in response to your chosen victim's discomfort. Women like you want to be conquered, not wooed. You need to be bound and gagged and beaten. Only then can you find the true ecstasy of roughly joined bodies and the gasping release of fearful, driving passion." Clodion was breathing hard.

"You are disgusting." Danise backed away from him. "I tell you now, Count Clodion, that I want nothing more to do with you. I will not speak to you again, and when my father returns, I will tell him that I will never marry you. And, I will tell him why!"

"How cleverly you play your little game," Clodion said. "How angry you look, how dark and dangerous are your eyes. You will say nothing to Savarec, my dear. Your father's righteous anger would only spoil your passionate anticipation of the rapture you will find in my bed. One day soon, you will be mine."

"Never! I will live the rest of my life at Chelles rather than marry you. Now, if you do not go away at once, I will tell Charles that you have been bothering me."

"More threats. How delightful. How stimulating." Clodion did not move. Danise seriously contemplated trying to run around him and back to the royal tents. Only her fear that he might capture her and actually embrace her kept her standing where she was. The thought of Clodion touching her made her feel ill.

At that instant of indecision she saw two groups of men approaching. A trio of nobles walked along the path, heading for the tents just beyond Savarec's, while from behind her father's tent came Guntram and one of the men-at-arms. Guntram saw her and hastened forward just as the nobles reached them.

"Clodion," said one of the nobles, "join us. We plan an afternoon of gaming, not to mention drinking some fine wine and enjoying the company of a couple of willing camp followers. What say you to a wager or two?"

By this time Guntram and the man-at-arms had positioned themselves on either side of Danise. Guntram fixed a fierce glare upon Clodion.

"I would be delighted," Clodion said to the noblemen. "Danise, my dear, I fear you must excuse me. Our conversation has been most pleasant. We will speak again soon. Good day to you." And off he went with the nobles as though he and Danise had been discussing nothing more serious than the unusually hot weather.

"Beware of that man," said Guntram. "His soul is sadly twisted toward forms of cruelty you are too innocent to understand, Danise."

"Aye," agreed the man-at-arms. "I've heard stories about Count Clodion. Mistress, you

129

should never be alone with him."

"He pursued me," Danise said, "though I swear to you, I don't know why he persists. He must know I dislike him. In the future, I will stay as far away from him as I can," she vowed.

Oddly, after that incident Clodion kept his own distance from her, and she soon pushed his outrageous suggestions to the back of her mind in order to concentrate on her duties to the queen. Hildegarde's current pregnancy was a difficult one and was not made any easier by a series of overly warm, humid days when there was no breeze at all. The sun beamed down as if it were already midsummer, and inside the royal tents the air was stifling. Only within the shade of the forest was there any relief to be found from the oppressive heat. Danise and the other ladies piled up mattresses beneath the trees so Hildegarde and her children could rest there.

On an unbearably hot afternoon, with the queen and her children napping in the shade and Sister Gertrude and several other women sitting near her, Danise was given some free time. Feeling restless she made her way to the riverbank not far from her father's tents. There she stood beneath an ancient oak, staring at the water without seeing it. Half formed images floated through her mind. Recollections of Hugo, grown dim and soft with the passage of time, were quickly replaced by more recent memories of Michel sorely injured as she had first seen him, and then of Michel returned to health, clad in chain mail and sitting upon his gray horse. She recalled his kisses and the way he had embraced her with a firm yet gentle strength. She remembered his hands upon her body. And she wondered again why he was now treating her so coolly.

"It is too hot to think on such serious subjects," she muttered, pushing back a loose piece of hair and tucking it behind her ear. "The river will cool me."

She looked around to be sure there was no one to see her. Apparently anyone who did not have a pressing duty had gone off to seek the green shade of the forest. Convinced that she was completely alone, Danise pulled off her dress, shoes and stockings. After a moment's hesitation, she removed her shift, too. Then she stepped away from the oak tree and into the water.

It was as cool as she had imagined it would be, a lovely refreshment from the heat of the day. Danise waded out from the riverbank until she was waist deep before she began to splash water onto her breasts and shoulders and arms. Because of the heat she was wearing her hair pinned up in a topknot to keep it off her neck, so she did not need to worry about it getting wet. After rinsing her face she sank into the water until it reached her chin. There she floated, drifting a bit with the current, but never moving far from the place where her clothes were folded at the base of the oak tree. Knowing it would only lead to useless confusion, she tried not to think about her personal dilemma over the choices she would soon have to make. This was an hour in which to relax and think about nothing at all.

When she was sufficiently cooled, she lazily worked her way back to shore. She stood on the riverbank for a moment, rubbing the excess moisture off her body with her hands, before she picked up her shift and put it on. She was still damp, so the garment clung to her, revealing the high, pointed tips of her breasts and the curving lines of hip and thigh. She did not care if her undergarment was wet. Perhaps the dampness would help to keep her cool. Her dress was blue silk, light in weight and loose in style. She was just reaching for it when she heard a sound. She looked up to see a man coming down the sloping ground toward her.

"Michel, I did not know you had returned. Where is my father?" Then, blushing, she added, "Have you been watching me?"

"I didn't know you were here," he said. "I was planning to bathe, myself. We've had a long, hot ride." His chest was bare. The tunic he had just pulled off was slung over one shoulder.

"You are staring at me," she accused.

"Who wouldn't?" He did stare then, letting his glance roam slowly from her flushed cheeks to her parted lips, to her slender shoulders and throat and then on to the figure so clearly revealed by the inadequate linen shift, and finally to her legs and bare feet below the hem of the shift. For a moment or two longing was written clearly upon his face, before he pulled cool distain across his features like a veil hiding his true emotions. "If you don't want people to look at you, then wear more clothing."

"I was here first," she declared, her nervous embarrassment giving way to irritation. "When you saw me, you should have gone away at once, instead of remaining to spy on me."

"I wasn't spying," he said wearily. He tossed his tunic onto the ground and tugged off his shoes, unfastening the leather strips that bound shoes and hose to his lower legs. "Is this the way you treat all your suitors, by snarling like an angry tigress when they speak to you?"

"Since you make a habit of avoiding me," she snapped, "I did not know you still meant to be a suitor."

"Danise, I am hot and tired," he began, but she cut him short.

"I remind you that you intruded on me," she said, bending to gather up her clothing. "I leave the river to you. Perhaps it will wash away your ill humor."

"Aren't you going to dress? You can't go back to the camp wearing only that—that invisible *thing!*" When she would have brushed by him, he caught her upper arms, keeping her where she was. "Are you insane, to walk around like that?" he demanded.

"Not at all," she replied with admirable coolness considering how upset she was by his sudden unexpected appearance and by his manner. "I will dress there, in that clump of bushes where no one, including you, will be able to see me. I assure you, I will not look toward the river to see you unclothed, so you need have no concern about revealing too much to me. I have recently learned how little you like to reveal of yourself, or of your intentions."

"You already know what my intentions are. Damn it, Danise, why are you doing this to me?" Jerking her roughly forward, he held her tightly against him while he planted a hard, angry kiss on her half opened mouth. Danise's damp shift was scant protection against the prickly sensation caused on her breasts by the dark hair of his chest, or against the warmth of his body pressed close to hers from waist to shoulder.

After a moment the kiss changed. His lips on hers ceased to demand and instead began to coax and tease until Danise granted him free access to the inner moistness of her mouth. Michel's arms went around her, and her hands worked their way about his waist. Her silk dress slid unnoticed from her fingers to the ground. Slowly Danise became aware of a hardness against her thigh. She knew what it was. She reveled in this evidence of his desire for her and sensed a fluid heat beginning in her own body in response to his masculine assertiveness.

"We can't. We can't do this." Too soon he was pushing her away. She raised heavy lids to meet his gaze. For all the delicious surge of desire between them, it seemed he was still annoyed with her. Or perhaps he was hurt by the sharp words she had spoken. "I thought you would understand that I have been trying to prove my worth to Savarec before I approach him about you. And that you would realize we cannot be alone like this until Savarec gives his approval."

"Then you do want me?" she whispered. "I feared you might have changed your mind since that day in the forest."

"Oh, yes, I want you. So much that if I don't take my hands off you right now, I won't be responsible for my actions." He released her and stepped away. Casting a rueful look toward the river, he said, "I ought to throw myself in there and swim to the other side. I'm not sure even that would cool me off, not with you standing there as good as naked at the edge of the water like some alluring river sprite."

"You are quite right, Michel. I ought to dress at once." But she made no move to pick up the dress she had dropped. "You do intend to speak to my father then, about becoming one of my suitors? Or have you already done so? Perhaps I ought not to be so insistent on knowing, but it is my future we are considering as well as yours."

"I have made a good start with Savarec," Michel said. "I think I have made a favorable impression on him during the last few days. But I need more time. I need a chance to win wealth and perhaps even a title by my sword. I hoped to have a chance to begin earning those prizes by fighting against Autichar, but that was not to be."

Danise bit her lip, trying to repress a cry of fear. This was the way Hugo had once talked, so sure of gaining all he wanted by proving his valor. Hugo was dead—and she had just besmirched his tender memory by embracing a half unclothed man while she herself was barely covered. Worse, she had let Michel believe she would seriously consider marrying him. How could she think of marrying anyone but Hugo, to whom she had promised her heart for all time? How could she feel such a flood of desire for another man? Why was she so unable to control her feelings for Michel? To hide her shame at her own wanton behavior, Danise spoke coldly.

"I assume you did not find Autichar?" Michel gave her a puzzled look before answering.

"We located a deserted camp where he and his men may have stopped for a night, but we never saw a soul from his troop. It's too bad we didn't catch him in some mischief. From what your father says about him, I wouldn't be surprised if Autichar were up to something devious."

"Is there anything else you want to tell me, Michel?" She hoped he would reveal that his memory had returned. She was sadly disappointed by his casual answer to her question.

"Only that Savarec ought to be in his tent by now, if you would like to welcome him back in private," he said.

"Is that all you will say to me?"

"I've said all that I decently can," he replied, "and done more than I should have done by kissing you. I understand that there are certain customs I will have to follow. I need your father's approval to officially become your suitor. Trust me, Danise. It'll work out, I promise."

How could she trust him when he kept something so important from her? Not telling her that his memory had returned was like lying to her, for the omission was meant to lead her to believe an untruth. But she knew about his memory, and his refusal to tell her made his promises worthless.

And how could she trust herself and her own emotions when she gladly returned the embraces of such a man? Sighing, Danise retrieved her garments and began to trudge up the slope toward the bushes she had earlier pointed out to Michel.

"Danise?"

"Yes?" She waited, praying he would say what she wanted to hear, hoping he would trust her enough to tell her everything.

"I do promise," he said again. "You'll see, it will be all right."

"You ought not to make promises you cannot keep," she replied, and turned her back on him.

Chapter 7

The river was cool, but not cold enough to ease the throbbing at Michel's groin or calm the disorder of his thoughts. It had taken all of his willpower to keep from pushing Danise down onto the soft grass to make passionate love to her. There had been a moment when he sensed that she would allow it, that she wanted him as much as he wanted her. But he owed a great debt to Savarec and he was determined not to do anything to harm either his benefactor or that benefactor's daughter. If Danise was to be his, he would win her openly and fairly. As for Danise herself, he could not understand the way she could change in an instant from warm and willing to cool and distant. She should have understood without being told that a man in his position would have to be careful when dealing

138

with his commander's daughter.

As Michel waded out of the river he noticed Count Clodion waiting for him. Clodion sauntered forward, looking with open interest at Michel's naked form.

"You are remarkably well-endowed, aren't you?" Clodion drawled, letting his eyes rest boldly on Michel's private parts. "Now I begin to understand."

"Why are you here, Clodion?" With sudden chilling comprehension of how a woman must feel when ogled by a man with sex on his mind, Michel grabbed his tunic and pulled it over his head, tugging it downward to his thighs as quickly as he could.

"Why cover it when it's so large and handsome?" Clodion leered at him.

"How long have you been here?" Michel demanded.

"Long enough to watch Danise trying to cool her own lust in the river," Clodion answered. "I was about to reveal myself to her when you appeared. Why, after kissing her so passionately, did you also resort to the water? Why didn't you sate yourself on her? I would willingly have joined you, you know. Three is always such an interesting grouping."

"You were hiding so you could watch Danise? Why, you filthy-minded—!" Michel doubled his fist and drew back his arm. Clodion's self protective reflexes were remarkable. He sprang lightly up the slope, putting himself out of reach before Michel could hit him.

"I must confess, I judged her wrongly,"

Clodion said. "I believed for a time that Danise's favorite was that young fool, Redmond. That I could have borne; Redmond would be easy for me to best in this contest Savarec has set up for us. I have more land than Redmond, a better title, and years more practice in the art of seducing innocent young creatures both male and female. But that Danise's fancy should light on you, a man with no lands, no title, and as everyone here at Duren knows, no past, is insulting to me. Of course, if you have shown her the marvelous equipment I have just seen, it's no wonder she has lost her wits over you."

"Shut up, Clodion!" Michel found himself at a serious disadvantage. He could not run up the slope to where Clodion now stood and throttle the man as he wanted to do, because Michel was still wearing only his short tunic. It took time to pull on breeches and shoes, and to fasten the leather strips around his calves. Meanwhile, Clodion was moving farther away, up the slope and toward the camp where, since the return of Savarec's troop, there were plenty of men around. Michel knew he would look like an idiot if he went charging after Clodion while only half dressed. He did not want Savarec to think he had no brains, or that he could not control his anger. In this strange time and place, Michel knew his future depended on his ability to think before he acted.

"Do not imagine," Clodion taunted from his higher vantage point, "that you can win Danise. You will not, I tell you. Not while I am alive."

"Your death can be arranged if that's what's

necessary to keep Danise safe from you," Michel growled, taking a purposeful step toward the man in spite of his inadequate clothing.

"You would not dare. You are trying too hard to make yourself acceptable to Charles and to Savarec." Clodion's perfect confidence and his shrewd assessment of Michel's thoughts infuriated Michel.

"Why the hell does a decent man like Charles keep someone like you in his company?" Michel shouted.

"Out of gratitude." Clodion's mouth curved into a mirthless smile. "In my youth I fought bravely for his father. I have a large contingent of well-trained warriors whom I place at Charles's disposal whenever he needs to put down another Saxon revolt. A fair number of my men died for him in Spain last year. I do assure you, Charles would not like to see me harmed." With a jaunty wave of his hand, Clodion marched away.

Michel dressed as quickly as he could, then went in search of Danise.

"She is with the queen," said the first lady he encountered. "They are there, beneath the trees at the edge of the forest."

"You may not disturb Hildegarde," Sister Gertrude warned when Michel approached the gathering of ladies. "She has finally fallen asleep. She needs to rest. This heat wearies her."

"It was Danise I wanted to see, but you may be a better person to hear what I have to say." Michel took the nun's arm, drawing her aside.

"Please keep a close watch on Danise. I have just exchanged angry words with Clodion and I believe he means some harm to her. He is determined to make her his prize."

"I told Savarec no good would come of allowing that man to ask for Danise's hand, but he would not listen to me, and I don't think he will listen to you, either. In Savarec's eyes, a fine title eclipses all personal faults." Sister Gertrude looked sterner than usual. "Were it not for Clodion's military skills and his complete loyalty to Charles, I believe he would have been banished from court years ago. Not all of our Frankish nobles are good Christian men, Michel, least of all where women are concerned. In my opinion, Charles is much too tolerant of such disgraceful fellows. And about Clodion, Savarec is a blind fool. Thank you for the warning. I will speak to Danise. I cannot always keep her within eyesight, but I will do my best to protect her."

But it seemed no warning was needed. Clodion did not appear for the evening meal, and the following morning his servant informed Charles that Clodion was ailing and would keep to his bed that day.

"I will gladly send one of my physicians to attend him," offered Charles, always ready to assign his own doctors to someone else so they could not annoy him with their concerns for his health.

"Count Clodion bid me tell you he needs only to rest. He is not the youngest of men, you know." The servant looked distinctly nervous over Charles's proposal. "My master begs you to allow him to sleep uninterrupted by well-intentioned physicians who will only poke and prod him and make him more uncomfortable."

"I can understand his feelings," said Charles, eyeing his physicians with some humor. "Tell Clodion we will respect his wishes."

"From the guilty look of his servant, I think Clodion may not be sick after all," Redmond murmured to Michel. "He may have some camp follower in his tent and not want to leave."

"Let's hope he sticks to camp followers," Michel responded.

When Clodion did not leave his tent for a second day, Michel began to relax his vigilance a bit. Mayfield would end in three more days and Danise would be safely removed from Clodion's vicinity, returning with Savarec to his fortress at Deutz to stay there until summer's end while she decided whether to marry or to return to Chelles with Sister Gertrude.

Michel knew he did not have much more time in which to prove himself to Savarec so he could compete for Danise's hand. Secretly he began to wish for some minor skirmish, perhaps with a few Saxons, in which he could display his skill with weapons.

As a result of her interlude with Michel beside the river, Danise decided the time had come for her to take her future into her own hands. She was tired of the questions and the uncertainty within her own mind. When she saw Michel leave the table at the end of the midday meal, she hurried after him, calling out his name. He stopped, waiting until she caught up with him.

"You shouldn't be wandering around alone," he said. "Didn't Sister Gertrude pass on my warning about Clodion?"

"Clodion isn't here. He's still sick and hasn't left his tent for two days. Michel, if we do not talk, I think I will go mad."

"Talk about what?" He headed toward the trees. Danise went with him.

"Do you know a woman named India?"

He stopped walking to stare at her for a long, assessing moment. She sensed a strange tension in him, as if he were waiting for something terrible to happen.

"India was my dear friend," Danise went on. "I miss her. I wish she and I could speak together now, so she could advise me. Do you know her, Michel?"

"We've never actually met. We have a mutual friend, that's all." Still tense and wary, he frowned at her. "How much do you know, Danise?"

"Only what Alcuin understood. He said when India first met his assistant Adelbert, she mistook him for someone else, a man called *Ahnk*. You also thought Adelbert was *Ahnk*. Since you know the same person, Alcuin concluded that you and India must have come from the same country. We both realized that if you can remember this *Ahnk* person, then your memory has returned."

"Clever fellow, Alcuin," Michel muttered. "You're pretty sharp yourself, Danise."

"Is it true, then?" she asked. "Do you know who you are?"

"It's true," he said after some hesitation.

"Why didn't you tell me at once?" she cried.

"It's complicated."

"Are you married? Have you family? A wife? Children? You are no young boy. It would be strange if you were not wed." Danise held her breath, waiting for him to speak.

"My family consists of a couple of cousins whom I seldom see," he said. "I was married once. I am divorced now. I really don't want to talk about that. Let's just say I wasn't home often enough to have a good marriage. My work keeps me in northern France and Belgium. Your ancestors built villages in the weirdest places."

"My ancestors?"

"I shouldn't have said that. There's no way to explain to you or to anyone in your world what my work is. God, this gets harder every day. Danise, I don't *want* to keep things from you, but I have to, for your sake."

Danise was so moved by his painful intensity that she spoke her thoughts without concern for maidenly modesty. But then, when had she ever been modest in her dealings with this man?

"Michel, you have caused me so much distress. Since the day I found you, my heart has been torn between you and my pledge to Hugo. You have said you want to earn the right to become one of my suitors, you have embraced me more intimately than any other man has ever done, including Hugo, yet you are still concealing an important truth from me. Don't deny it; I can tell it is so by the way you treat me. You alternate between rudeness and an almost overwhelming affection."

"Leave it alone, Danise."

"I cannot leave it alone. Your secret, whatever it is, stands between us."

"I can't talk about it."

"You must. There is no hope for us otherwise." As she spoke those words, Danise knew why his recent treatment of her had hurt her so badly. Her first feelings for him had been a mixture of pity and fascination, but she had quickly passed beyond those emotions to something more. He had led her to believe that he felt the same way.

"You wouldn't understand." His voice was low and sad. "The whole story would only frighten you."

"Do you think me a coward, then? I assure you, I am not." When he did not speak, she regarded him from tear-filled eyes. "Your continuing silence means you do not trust me enough to confide in me."

"It means I want to protect you," he said.

"From what? I can bear any truth. I bore the news of Hugo's death, and though it brought me low, it did not break me. I thought that was the most terrible news I would ever hear, but this is worse, for you are still alive, yet you are separating yourself from me as if you were dead, or at a distance so great that I cannot reach you." She paused, swallowing hard to keep herself from weeping, before she went on. "Is that it? Are you planning to return to your own country and leave me behind? But if so, why did you place yourself under my father's command? Michel, neither your actions nor your words make any sense to me; they contradict each other. It's no wonder I am confused, no wonder I cannot decide between you in the present and Hugo in the past."

"I never intended to hurt you. Danise, you are the loveliest woman I've ever seen, you are intelligent, you have a kind heart. I even like your father," he ended on a wry note.

"You are not telling me what I need to know."

"You wouldn't believe me."

"How can you know that until you tell me?"

"You are also the most persistent woman I've ever met," he said. "You aren't going to stop, are you? You are going to keep asking questions until you get the information you want."

"If you do not want anyone else to know, I can keep a secret," she promised. He regarded her in tense silence for so long that she began to wonder if he would ever speak to her again. But it seemed he was wrestling with the decision whether or not to do as she wanted.

"I hope you meant what you just said," he told her, "because you are going to have to keep this secret for the rest of your life."

"I swear," she promised, "that I will never

reveal what you say to me unless you release me from this vow."

"I believe you." He touched her cheek for an instant, before he spoke again. "Is there some place where we can talk and be absolutely certain we won't be overheard?"

"In the place where I found you," she suggested.

He led the way. It was cooler beneath the trees, and the hot glare of the open meadow faded as they moved farther into the forest. In just a few minutes they reached the tree that marked his entry into Francia.

"In a way, I'm glad you insisted on this," Michel said, seating himself on the ground. "I need to talk to someone, to make all of it more real to me."

"Tell me everything," she invited. She sat beside him, hands clasped in her lap, her eyes fixed on his. When Michel began to speak she did not exclaim in disbelief, she simply listened. He had been right to warn her that she would be frightened by what he said. What she did not understand was why he had not gone mad from terror over what had been done to him. Since he appeared to be in complete possession of his reason and in control of his emotions, she did her best to hide her own fear.

"Your story is beyond comprehension," she said when he was finished. "Yet I believe you would not lie to me about something so amazing, so magical. You are right when you say that all we can do is accept what has happened to you, and be glad that you were not more seriously injured when your journey to Duren came to such an abrupt end. Michel, I believe there is a heavenly purpose to everything that occurs on this earth, so I know there is a reason for your arrival here. In time, we will learn what it is. However, I do have a few questions."

"Ask away," he said. "I'm just glad you aren't calling me a liar, or crazy."

"You say that my friend, India, also came to Francia from your time? And later returned home again?"

"That's right."

"Is she well?"

"She married the brother of our mutual friend who sent me to see Hank. I hear she's very happy."

"But she loved a man in this time. He died with my Hugo."

"Then, she learned to love again." He smiled at her. "Some people do love more than once, you know. I asked you this before, Danise, but I am going to ask again. Do you think Hugo would want you to be lonely for the rest of your life? If he would, then his was a poor, selfish kind of love."

"Hugo was not selfish. He always thought of me. It's why we never lay together." She blushed a little at the intimate confession, but did not lower her eyes from his.

"Don't you think it's time you stopped dreaming about the past and started living in the present?"

"As you have done? Except that you have

been forced to put aside the future in order to live in the present in which you find yourself. Michel, I marvel at your courage."

"You've taken all this very well yourself," he said. "I was afraid you wouldn't believe me."

"A story so strange must be true. No one could invent such a tale. It's also true that your explanation has answered most of my questions about you, and has laid to rest some lingering concerns about the happiness of my dear friend, India. Do you think we should tell Alcuin? He was fond of India."

"The fewer people who know about this, the better," he said, lacing his fingers through hers. "You did promise to keep the secret."

"I will do so." She sat silent for a while, staring at their linked hands and thinking that their futures were linked together, too. Michel's honesty had forged a new bond between them to strengthen the connection she had always felt to him. "Shall I tell you a secret of my own?"

"Must I swear to keep it to myself before I hear it?" he asked lightly.

"You may do what you like with it. It is only a simple secret, not a great and terrible one like yours. You advised me to stop dreaming of the past. I have stopped. Here, now, in this present moment with you, I am happy."

"So am I, because of you. You make all of this bearable." He drew her into his arms. She went willingly, and rested her head on his shoulder. He kissed her brow, her cheek, her ear, then lifted her chin to kiss her soft lips.

A Love Beyond Time

When his hand drifted downward to caress her
breast she did not protest, but leaned into his
palm, letting him feel the delicate roundness,
murmuring softly when her breast tightened
and grew hard at his stroking touch. He eased
her backward onto the ground, half covering
her body with his so he could more easily
scatter heated kisses onto her throat and face.
Danise now lay with her head on his arm and
one of his legs thrown across hers, letting him
explore the supple curves of her body.

"We belong together," Michel whispered.
"I've known it since the first time I saw you.
There is something binding me to you."

"I feel it, too," she admitted. She raised one
hand to skim tender fingers over his face and
then to smooth back his dark hair. "When you
touch me as you are doing, when you kiss me,
my blood begins to stir and I do not want you
to stop."

"I don't want to stop, either. But we must."
He drew away from her. "I owe it to you, and
to your father, to treat you with some respect.
We have to face the truth, Danise. My future
is highly uncertain."

"Do you think there is a chance that you will
be taken home again?" She clutched at his arms
as if she would keep him with her by force of
will and sheer physical strength.

"Nothing in life is certain, least of all in my
life," he said roughly. "But, as I explained to
you, I don't think Hank will make any effort
to return me to the twentieth century. I was
talking about my lack of property. In my own

time, there would be no problem. I had a career I enjoyed and I had been honored for my work. I had saved a fair amount of money. But none of that means anything here in Francia, in this time. I came to Duren with only the clothes I was wearing. My Frankish clothes, my armor, even the horse I ride, are gifts from your father. I have nothing to offer you, Danise. If I tell Savarec how I feel about you, he will refuse to accept me as one of your suitors, and I couldn't blame him. I wouldn't want a daughter of mine to marry an unknown, penniless man."

"Then, what are we to do?" she cried.

"Unless a war erupts in the next week or so, to provide me with a chance to prove what I can do, I don't know," he said. "I just don't know."

Charles arranged a large hunting party for the last day but one of Mayfield. Hunting was his favorite sport and he urged anyone who was physically able to take part in the day's activities.

"We will have a great final feast tomorrow," he declared. "We'll eat the game we bag today and give the leftovers to the folk who make their permanent home here at Duren. Clodion, I'm glad to see you have recovered from your indisposition. I hope you feel well enough to join us."

"How could I miss such an event? I am eager to start," said Clodion.

Danise was sorry to hear this. She had been hoping that Clodion would keep to his tent until

Mayfield ended. She was not fond of hunting, but when Charles personally asked her to be there, she did not want to refuse him, not even if her presence meant she could not avoid speaking to Clodion. Gowned in sturdy brown wool, with the hunting knife all ladies wore at such times belted at her waist, she sat upon her horse, waiting until Charles, his uncle Bernard, and the huntmaster together decided how to organize the large group of participants. Redmond rode up to join her, but she did not see Michel.

" 'Twill only take a short time until they are ready," Redmond informed her. "Over the past days, they have grown used to dividing us into smaller groups."

Danise gave him only a distracted smile in answer because she was still looking for Michel.

"Ah, there is the signal," Redmond said, craning his neck to see what was happening. "We are to leave in the next group. Come this way, Danise. And there is Michel. Michel, will you join us?" Redmond shouted. He waved an arm in the air.

"Where is Michel? I can't see him." Even as she spoke, Danise was separated from Redmond as the other hunters began to move forward, heading toward the forest. Eager men and women streamed past her on both sides.

"Danise." Savarec drew abreast of her. "Clodion has asked my permission to ride next to you today."

"No, Father. I do not like Clodion. I would

153

much prefer to ride with Redmond and Michel."

"Humor me, my dear." Savarec leaned across the space separating their horses to touch her hand and speak to her in a quieter tone. "I am not completely blind. I have noticed the way you try to avoid Clodion. I know now that you will not marry him. It may be that Clodion knows it, too. But this kindness from you will make him believe that you are seriously considering his suit, so that when you do finally refuse him, he will be less likely to claim the contest between him and Redmond was unfair."

"Father, I wish you would not insist on this." Danise knew her father could not afford to have so important a nobleman as Clodion angry with him. Perhaps she could agree to do as Savarec wanted and then lose Clodion during the heat of the hunt. At Clodion's age and having recently been ill, he might well find it difficult to keep up with the rest of the hunters. Besides, what real harm could he do to her while they were both mounted and while there were so many other people, including her father, around them? It would not be the entirely pleasant morning she had envisioned, but she would refuse to listen to any salacious remarks Clodion might make.

"Very well, Father," she said, intending to separate herself from Clodion as soon as possible in order to join Michel and Redmond. Turning in her saddle she looked for them, but she could see neither man.

"You will be surprised by how well Clodion rides," Savarec said to her. "He is a famous horseman."

"Really? How interesting." Danise groaned inwardly, suddenly fearing she would not be able to escape Clodion's presence as easily as she had hoped.

At Savarec's sign to him, Clodion, who had been waiting off to one side, quickly joined them, moving through the crowd of horsemen with a deftness Danise found dismaying in view of her plans. With Savarec present, Clodion was on his best behavior.

"I thank you for allowing me to spend this time with you," he said to Danise. "I fear that Count Redmond has had the better opportunity to win your approval, since my recent illness has kept me away from you. I hope to rectify that unhappy omission today, and make you realize what a fine husband I will be for you."

"My father must have told you, Count Clodion, that I still have not decided whether to marry at all. But you are welcome to ride with us." It was all she could do to get the words out. She despised the man, could scarcely bear to look at his smug face, and she wished he were at the uttermost end of the world. And, like Sister Gertrude, she wished her father had exercised better judgment when choosing her suitors.

"Danise, perhaps I did not explain that I will not be riding with you after all," said Savarec, looking embarrassed. "There is a certain lady who asked me to ride with her today. You must excuse me."

"Father!" Danise was appalled. "I have told you about Clodion. Please don't leave me with him." But Savarec had kicked his horse's flanks and moved out of hearing. "Father, how could you!"

"The lady who wants to ride with him is a friend of mine," Clodion informed her, "a wealthy widow, and still surprisingly attractive. I suspect your father of lusting after her. He will not be disappointed. I doubt if anyone will see Savarec again before nightfall."

"Did you arrange this—this—?" Danise was so angry she could not complete the sentence.

"Assignation?" Clodion supplied the missing word. "Your father is usually so protective of you that I had to think of some clever means of getting you to myself. Isn't it amazing the way any man will rise to the bait of a charming woman who pretends to be interested in him, even to the point of neglecting his beloved daughter? Foolish Savarec."

"I will not ride with you!"

By now the hunt had begun in earnest, with riders moving quickly into the nearby trees. Danise's mount was caught in the midst of this rush of horses. Savarec was gone from sight, and Danise could not find Michel or Redmond. Nor could she turn her horse and return to camp. There were simply too many horses, too many people, and all heading in a direction opposite from where she wanted to go. The best Danise could do was try to work her way to one side, away from the other riders, hoping to find a place where

156

she could turn. She did her best, but she was not an expert horsewoman, being accustomed only to the gentle palfreys provided at Chelles. The horse she was riding on this morning was a more restive beast and difficult to control. Unfortunately for her, Clodion was every bit as good on a horse as Savarec had claimed he was. Through every movement Danise attempted in her efforts to get away from him, Clodion stayed with her. In fact, she had the feeling at times that he was directing her progress by the way he rode his horse next to hers.

"Do you like your new mount?" he asked. "It's a gift from me, Danise. I trained it myself and gave it to your father for you to ride today."

She hadn't paid much attention to the horse, except to note that it was not the one on which she had ridden from Chelles. She had been so busy looking for Michel that she just assumed her father would choose from among the horses he owned the right animal for her to ride in a hunt.

Clodion moved closer, until his leg brushed against hers. Before she could protest the familiarity, he seized the reins from her.

Danise reached for the knife she wore at her belt. It was long and sharp and would make an admirable weapon of defense against her unwanted companion. Before she could pull it out of its sheath, Clodion struck her hand away and took the knife from her, tucking the blade into his belt.

"Let me go!" Danise cried, trying to wrench the reins out of his hands. "Give me back my knife. Let me go, Clodion."

"You are coming with me, Danise." With unerring skill Clodion worked his way out of the press of riders.

"Help!" Danise shouted. "Someone, help me!"

No one heard her screams or paid any attention to what was happening to her. There were horns blowing, dogs barking, people calling to one another, men and women shouting and laughing, and now the hunt picked up speed. Charles and his friends burst out of the forest into a wide meadow, where almost everyone broke into a full gallop. Danise continued her struggle with Clodion for the reins until he swerved his horse and she was compelled to grasp her own horse's mane with both hands if she wanted to stay in the saddle. Wildly she looked around, praying she would see Michel.

"Clodion, stop this! Someone, help! Help! Oh, Redmond! *Redmond!*" From across the field she saw his face momentarily turned toward her. Letting go of the horse's mane she waved frantically. "Redmond! Help me!"

Clodion caught her arm, pulling it down so she could not wave again.

"You are mad!" Danise screamed at him. "You cannot hope to carry me away. There are too many people here. They will not allow it."

"It's as good as done," Clodion said. "They are all too intent on the hunt to see what is happening here at the side of the field. If they note us at all, they will only think your horse has gone lame and that I am helping you. Now,

Danise, we go back into the forest on this side of the meadow."

"I won't go with you," she declared.

"What do you plan to do instead?" he asked, laughing at her. "If you throw yourself off your horse, you risk serious injury. How far do you think you could run with a broken leg or a sprained ankle or worse?"

"I'd rather die than go anywhere with you, Clodion!"

He did not bother to answer her. Instead, he drew back his right hand and slapped her hard. Danise was so stunned she could not move at first. While she sat staring at him Clodion caught one of her long braids, pulling it hard, ignoring her cry of pain as he twisted it around his fist.

"You *will* come with me," he said. "You will obey me in everything."

"Where are you taking me?" she gasped.

"To our bridal bed," he replied.

Chapter 8

They rode until Danise thought she would faint from weariness. She did not ask Clodion to stop and let her rest. She was too proud to ask Clodion for any favors, and she feared the conditions he might place upon such a rest period.

Clodion soon discovered that keeping her bound to him by holding on to her braid limited his own movements, so he released her hair, but he still kept the reins of her horse in his hands. Danise considered leaping from the horse in a desperate bid for freedom, even though she knew Clodion was right when he warned her of injury if she tried it.

Nor did she know where they were or how to get back to Duren if she should escape. She had not been so far from camp before. The prospect of wandering about the forest on foot with Clodion tracking her on horseback was most unappealing. She decided the wisest thing for her to do was to appear to be completely passive while staying alert for a chance to get away from her captor with her horse. Since Clodion was on the brink of old age, he might need to stop soon. Then again, he did seem remarkably active for a man of his years who had recently been ill.

She expected that when he finally did decide to stop he would try to rape her. Once he had done so he could insist that she marry him, if marriage was what he truly wanted of her. Forcing back the bile that rose to her throat at the possibility of Clodion touching her in any way at all, Danise made herself think about what he might do and how he would do it, until in her innocence she thought she knew a way to stop him. He could not rape her on horseback. He would have to dismount and make her do the same. He would have to make at least some adjustments to his clothing, and to hers. If he tried to prevent her from resisting by holding his knife in one hand and threatening her with it, that would leave him with only the other hand free for whatever needed to be done. Knowing of only one way in which a man might use a woman, she thought if she kept her wits about her and did not give way to fear, she would be able to wait until Clodion was thoroughly distracted but had not yet harmed her. She might then be able to get away from him and escape. Perhaps she could mount one

horse and take the other one with her, leaving
Clodion stranded. He deserved to be left alone
in the forest. She began to consider the various
things she might do or say to make him drop
his guard.

As they rode along she tried to find distin-
guishing characteristics of the landscape that
would help her to retrace her route once she
was free, but the forest did not vary. Danise was
so frightened that she no longer cared whether
she could find her way back to Duren or not.
It would be far better to be lost in the forest
forever than to be raped by Clodion.

They rode on and on through unending trees
and occasionally thick undergrowth. The land
was relatively flat, with no notable hills or
valleys. Nowhere was there a sign of human
habitation. Clodion seemed to know where he
was going, but Danise could see no track nor
any marking that might have been set out
to guide him. The shadows were lengthening
when Clodion drew up and looked around. He
sniffed the air, then turned the horses toward
the setting sun and moved forward again.

Danise could smell what Clodion had
smelled. The scent of burning firewood and
roasting meat hung on the humid air. They
had not gone much farther before she saw
smoke drifting through the trees and heard
men talking. They came out of the trees into
a small clearing by a pool of water, and there
Danise's fantasies of escape vanished like wood
smoke in a high wind.

There were a dozen or so men in the clearing,

all of them drawn up facing the newcomers and all clearly prepared to do battle if necessary. Each man wore armor and held a sword or a spear in one hand and a dagger in the other.

"You are late, Clodion." A broad-shouldered man whose deep red cloak and ornately decorated metal helmet marked him as the leader of the warriors stepped forward. "I expected you at midafternoon."

"The hunt was delayed in starting," Clodion explained. Dismounting, he gave the reins of Danise's horse to one of the armed men. "I had to wait until there was enough confusion to hide the sight and sounds of our departure. Danise made a lot of noise, as I was certain she would."

"I don't care to hear about your cleverness, Clodion. I wanted to be away from here before sunset. Now it's almost dark. We will have to wait until morning, and by then the alarm will be out."

"It can't be helped." Clodion's tone of voice suggested that he did not much like the man standing before him. "Where is the rest of your army?"

"They are camped a safe distance away, near the Rhine," said the leader. "It is easier for me to hide here with only a few men."

"The days are so long at this time of year that if you leave at dawn, you shouldn't have any difficulty in reaching your army in keeping with our original schedule," Clodion said. "You need have no concern for what Charles will do. Before he discovers where Danise has been taken, you will be long gone from this place."

"Perhaps you are right, but I don't like having to change my plans once I have made them, not even for a single night. Since you are here at last, I suppose we need not worry about a surprise attack from Charles." The leader lifted both hands to his head to remove his helmet.

Danise had been watching the two men and listening to them with a growing certainty as to the identity of the leader. She bit back a cry of dismay as her fears were confirmed by the sight of the red hair and sunburned face of Count Autichar.

"So," she said, putting all the cold contempt she could into her words, "the rumors were true after all. You did not return to Bavaria."

"Why should I, when the things I most desire remain here in Francia?" demanded Autichar. "Dismount, Lady Danise, and surrender yourself to my hospitality."

With four men standing around her with their weapons pointed at her and another man holding her horse so it could not move, Danise could see that she would have to obey Autichar's command. She got off her horse and stood glaring at her host. Autichar burst into laughter.

"I am glad to know you have more spirit than you showed to me at Duren," he said. "Has Clodion treated you well? Has he kept his lascivious hands off you?"

"I would not call it treating me well to abduct me," Danise responded. "You cannot think to harm me in any way and go unpunished by

Charles. My father and I are his guests at Duren, and Charles insists that all maidens be treated with respect." She fell silent only when Autichar's continued laughter drowned out her words. She could not comprehend what was happening or why Autichar and Clodion would cooperate to take her away from Duren. What she did understand was that she would never be able to escape with Autichar's men guarding her so closely.

What Autichar referred to as his hospitality was rough indeed. Their evening meal consisted of stale bread, beer, and the few wild birds Autichar's men had killed and which they roasted on a makeshift spit over the fire. Their only water came from the stagnant pool next to which they were camped. Autichar assigned two men to Danise and they never left her side. Even when she went into a thicket of nearby bushes to relieve herself, the guards stood one on each side of the bushes until she was finished. When they all returned to the clearing, Autichar and Clodion were arguing.

"I want Danise tonight. I have waited long enough," Clodion said, his words freezing Danise into immobility from fear. She could do nothing but stand between her guards and listen while her fate was decided.

"I cannot allow it," Autichar told Clodion. "I will have discipline in my camp. If my men see you or hear you with Danise, they will want to enjoy her themselves. Then who will guard this camp? If you had met us earlier, as you were pledged to do, we might have reached a safer place before dark and you could have done what you want with her before you leave us. As it is, you will have to wait until our plan is closer to completion."

"I want her now!" Clodion sounded like an overaged child who has been denied a promised treat.

"If you touch her, I will have you tied up for the night," Autichar warned. "What you do with yourself is your own business, but you will leave Danise alone until I say you may have her, which will not be until I am certain we will not be attacked while you are in the midst of your sensual transports—nor while my men are occupied with her. I have not lived so long by being careless about security."

Clodion looked at Danise. His face was flushed, his eyes narrowed, his gaze intense. After a few moments he stalked away into the darkness and Danise began to breathe again. She fell to her knees beside the campfire. Autichar sat next to her.

"Thank you," Danise whispered.

"Clodion is a fool. The thing that hangs between his legs governs his every action," Autichar said. "Don't think for a moment that I care what happens to you, Danise. It's only a matter of discipline among my men. When we all reach our destination safely, and Clodion rejoins us, he can have you. In the meantime, we carry out our plan as he and I originally agreed."

"What plan, Autichar?" Danise told herself she had to stay calm and she had to learn as much as she could about Clodion's dealings with Autichar. She wondered what the final destination Autichar had mentioned could be, and where Clodion was going, since Autichar had just said he would be rejoining them there.

"Clodion was not really sick, you know. He only pretended illness to disguise his absence from Duren while he and I met in secret to make our arrangements." Autichar tore a chunk of bread apart and offered a piece of it to Danise. His hands were dirty and he smelled as if he had not bathed for days. Danise did not want to make Autichar angry. She took the crust of bread and pretended to gnaw on it.

"I am surprised to find you and Clodion friends," she told him, "because you are so unalike."

"Whoever said we are friends?" Autichar's voice was soft. "I merely pointed out to Clodion that we could help each other, so that both of us could achieve our fondest desires."

"I know what Clodion wants," Danise said with a shiver. She was about to ask Autichar what he wanted when he spoke again.

"You are too inexperienced to know anything at all about a man like Clodion," he said, still in that same quiet, insinuating voice. "You imagine he would have married you."

"He has repeatedly told me that is what he wants," Danise cried, exasperated by Autichar's superior attitude. "What you are saying makes no sense."

"I assure you, everything Clodion has done

makes perfect sense to him. The first thing you must learn about Clodion," Autichar went on, "is never to trust him, never believe anything he says. Clodion's life is dedicated solely to the satisfaction of his lust. Unfortunately, lust has its consequences. In Clodion's case, the consequences are several wives, all now dead and their dowries long ago dissipated, half a dozen concubines who brought him nothing but themselves, and far too many children. All of them, concubines and children alike, expect to be fed, clothed, and housed by Clodion. A life like his can make the richest man into a pauper."

"Then he needs a wife with a larger dowry than mine," said Danise. Before she could say anything more, Autichar interrupted her.

"I told you, he no longer intends to marry you," Autichar said. "At first Clodion believed your father had amassed great riches from his many battles with the Saxons, and at that time, Clodion might have wed you. But Savarec is an honest man who turns the Saxon loot over to the royal treasury as he is obligated to do. Not that the Saxons have ever provided much in the way of useful goods. A few furs, amber, a little gold, the occasional slave—it's hardly worth fighting them at all. Clodion was furious with Savarec when he discovered the true size of your dowry. I believe he expressed his feelings to your father. He certainly told me how he felt, and that was the end of his intention to wed you."

"Then why," cried Danise, "has Clodion continued to pursue me, knowing my father is not a wealthy man? It cannot have been for my person. I am not a great beauty and I made it clear to him how much I dislike him."

"Your dislike in itself would be enough to pique Clodion's lust," Autichar said. "He enjoys subduing unwilling women. He will have you before he's done with this plan of ours. It's a pity, because whether you think so or not, you are a beauty. I would have relished taking you myself. But I cannot, I have given my word. You are part of the bargain, a small portion of Clodion's payment."

"What bargain?" Danise asked, curiosity warring with her intense fears for her own safety. "What payment?"

"Clodion needs gold," Autichar said. "Gold in huge amounts such as only an important ruler could provide."

To Danise's knowledge there was only one man besides Charles who could have a large supply of gold in his treasury, and that man was a friend to Autichar.

"Duke Tassilo is going to give Clodion gold," she whispered.

"You are intelligent as well as beautiful." Autichar gave her an approving glance. "There you have it. We all know how little Duke Tassilo loves his cousin Charles. Tassilo was delighted to learn that he has his own devoted man in Charles's camp."

"Why would Clodion betray Charles to Duke Tassilo?" Danise was left almost breathless

169

by the audacity of this idea. "Charles treats Clodion with respect and honors him for his lifetime of loyalty to Charles and his father."

"For some men, respect and loyalty mean little when there is no gold in the family coffers," Autichar said. "You are indeed an innocent if you think otherwise."

"What is your part in this scheme?" Danise asked, trying her best to sound impressed by what she had just been told. Her determination to free herself had bloomed anew during Autichar's revelations, which had shown her that more than her own safety was at stake. If she could manage to escape and find her way back to Duren, she could warn Charles about Clodion's treachery. She tried to flatter Autichar in the hope that he would reveal more of the plan between Clodion and Duke Tassilo. "Autichar, you are too clever not to have helped in the devising of this plan. You are a Bavarian, so Tassilo is your overlord, and I have heard he is also your close friend. He and Clodion must have needed your help. From what I've seen of Clodion in recent days, I believe everything you said of him earlier is true. He thinks only of his lust and the women he is going to use to satisfy it."

"Not only women," Autichar told her. "Clodion likes little boys, too. And older women, young men, whores of every kind, and I have no doubt, he also eyes the occasional sheep."

"Oh! I pity any girl who marries him."

"I've seen his future wife," Autichar said. "She's a thirteen-year-old virgin, pretty as a spring morning, with hair even paler than yours. I feel a bit sorry for her myself, but it can't be helped. She and her enormous dowry of land and gold will go to Clodion in return for his assistance to Tassilo. Then, of course, there is the direct payment of gold that will be made from Tassilo to Clodion on the success of our plan."

"Just exactly what is it that Clodion is going to do to help Duke Tassilo?" Danise asked.

"He has already done it," Autichar responded. "He abducted you."

"Me? But I am no one of importance."

"There you are wrong," Autichar said. "You are of great importance, if only for a few days. Then you will have no further value to us. That is why I will let Clodion have you after he rejoins us at a place where his ravishing of you will in no way imperil myself, my men, or our arrangements with Tassilo. What happens to you after Clodion is finished is of no interest to me, though I suppose you will want to know, won't you? Clodion will probably hand you over to my troops, so I doubt if you will live to see the end of this, but if you do, you will be free to go where you want."

There would be no place for her to go save to some obscure convent where no one would recognize her. Danise could not bear to think about what Clodion would do to her—or Autichar's men, either. Worse even than her defilement at their hands would be the disgust and pity she would see on Michel's face, or on her father's, or Redmond's. She could never see any of them again. If she lived, she would have to let them believe she was dead so they would never learn of her shame.

"But why?" Danise cried, not ready yet to accept the terrible fate awaiting her. "What have I to do with all of this?"

"You are the excuse, the maiden whose cruel abduction will infuriate Charles. He and your father are friends. Charles's queen is fond of you. All of them will want vengeance for your sake. Charles will gather his army together and march against Duke Tassilo."

"I have been abducted to provoke a war between Charles and Tassilo? Charles will crush Tassilo," Danise said scornfully. "The Frankish army far outnumbers Tassilo's Bavarian followers."

"Not if the Frankish army is divided." Autichar grinned, his eyes shining in the firelight. "Tassilo has been negotiating in secret with the Saxon leaders. As soon as Charles marches into Bavaria, the Saxons will attack outposts on the border between Francia and Saxony. To put down those revolts Charles will have to divide his army in two. Tassilo's own army will then be the larger, and it will easily defeat the Franks who remain in Bavaria. Once that victory is accomplished, Tassilo will march to Saxony to join his allies there, and together Saxons and Bavarians will destroy what remains of the Frankish army."

"The Saxons are untrustworthy. They will turn on Tassilo," Danise declared.

"He and the Saxons have already come to an

agreement on the division of Frankish lands."
Autichar spoke with perfect confidence. "Is it
not a clever plan, Danise?"

"A diabolical plan," Danise said, appalled
that Autichar could be so openly proud to be
involved in such treachery, "except for the fact
that Tassilo will never defeat Charles."

"Charles is not invincible. We know it well
after last year's disaster in Spain. And Charles
knows it, too."

"Why do you hate Charles so much?" Danise
asked.

"I don't hate him. But Tassilo is my true overlord and he despises your Frankish king. Therefore, I fight with Tassilo against Charles."

"If Tassilo hates Charles, it's because he suffers from a guilty conscience for deserting the
Frankish cause in time of war," Danise declared
angrily.

"That may be so," Autichar agreed. "Guilt is
often a reason for hatred. Whatever the cause,
I do not question that Tassilo will be the victor
in the coming war."

Danise did not know enough about military
matters to determine whether Duke Tassilo's
treacherous plan could succeed. She feared it
might. After listening to Autichar she was more
frightened than ever. Autichar would not have
spoken so freely to her if he expected her to
survive her captivity. It was a chilling realization, but not only her virtue and life were in
danger. Michel, her father, Charles, Redmond,
perhaps even Hildegarde and the royal children, Alcuin—all those she held dear—could be

Flora Speer

mistreated, imprisoned, killed, by these wicked men. When she thought of so many lives senselessly destroyed, her own fate seemed almost unimportant.

While Danise considered what she had just learned and tried to think of a way to free herself and warn Charles, Clodion reappeared and sat down across the fire from Autichar and his prisoner.

"Well, Clodion," said Autichar with a malicious glance at his partner's disheveled clothing, "did you enjoy yourself by yourself?"

"You'll pay for keeping the girl from me," Clodion muttered.

"Speak kindly to me," Autichar warned, "or I will advise Tassilo not to give you your next bride after all."

"You do, and I'll tell Charles what you plan," snarled Clodion.

"Warn him," said Autichar, not at all concerned by this threat, "and I will free Danise and give her safe conduct back to Charles so she can tell him about your part in this scheme. This is another reason for me to keep her away from you, Clodion. I can always send her back to Duren unharmed."

"And ruin your own plans?" Clodion was shouting now, while Autichar maintained his calm and humorous outward appearance.

"When he learns from Danise of my part in that plan, Charles will still chase me into Bavaria, where he will find Tassilo waiting to do battle with him. You see, Clodion, now that you have delivered Danise to me, I don't really need you any more. Perhaps I ought to kill you now and be done with it." He chuckled when Clodion made a strangled sound in his throat.

"What villains you are," Danise cried. "No one ought to trust either of you, and you cannot trust each other."

"You, be quiet," Autichar ordered, still smiling. "Actually, I rather like the next step in our original plan, so we will carry it through after all. Clodion, you ought to find it perversely stimulating."

"It was my idea," Clodion said.

"I do remember." Autichar's smile now was not pleasant.

"You need me alive to carry it through," Clodion said. "I can delay Charles in his search for Danise, giving you time to move on toward the Bavarian mountains unimpeded. You need me," Clodion said again.

"What are you going to do?" Danise asked, half expecting to see murder committed before her eyes if Clodion and Autichar continued to quarrel.

"To you, for the moment, nothing," Autichar responded. "You, Danise, have just become our security for Clodion's part in this plan. If he wants you, he will have to return to me, and he knows I will kill him if he plays me false. Nor will Clodion get his Bavarian bride and all her wealth without my personal recommendation to Tassilo. Which ought to guarantee my own safety. It's checkmate, Clodion," he ended with a nasty grin.

Danise could see flaws in the plan concocted

by these men, but she would not point them out to Autichar or Clodion. A great many things could go wrong for them. For herself, she could see no future unless she could manage to escape. She realized that she could not do so that night. After a word from Autichar to one of his men, she was led to the side of the camp, given a blanket, and told to lie down and sleep. Her two guards remained with her. They did not sleep at all that night and neither did she. Nor did Autichar and Clodion sleep. They sat together by the fire, talking and occasionally arguing. Danise could not hear what they were saying, but she was certain they were still plotting against Charles and the Franks.

Toward dawn two of Autichar's men rose and began to saddle horses.

"Give Clodion the same mount he rode yesterday," Autichar commanded. "Someone is sure to remember his horse."

After a hasty meal Clodion and the two men mounted and rode away together through the trees. When Autichar paused to look down on Danise on his way back to the fire after seeing them off, she hastily closed her eyes and pretended to sleep.

Chapter 9

In the forest near Duren it was so uncomfortably hot even in the shade that Charles's great hunting party ended early. It had been successful, with many birds and rabbits brought down, and in spite of the heat most of the hunters were cheerful as they headed back toward the campsite.

"Redmond, have you seen Danise?" Michel called to his friend. "I have been looking for her all morning."

"I have not seen her since the hunt began," Redmond answered, glancing around in search of Danise. "She was with Savarec and Clodion. I don't see them, either."

"Clodion?" Michel reined in his horse next to Redmond. Riding with Michel was Guntram, who also halted. "Savarec knows Danise doesn't like Clodion. Why would they all ride together?"

"Perhaps Savarec thought to soothe Clodion's injured pride," Redmond suggested. He frowned. "Now that I think on it, the last glimpse I had of Danise, I did not see Savarec with her, but only Clodion. Danise waved to me."

"Was she beckoning? Did she want you to join her?" Michel asked in sudden concern.

"She called something to me, but I could not hear what she said. There was so much crowding and everyone was in such a rush that it was more like a race than a hunt. But if Savarec was near, and so many ladies were present, what harm can there be if Danise rode beside Clodion? We'll find her soon enough."

"Are you out of your mind?" Michel demanded, his concern for Danise becoming certainty that her absence meant something was amiss. "How can you be so complaisant with Clodion wandering around looking for opportunities to get Danise alone? My God, Redmond, just the other day, he was spying on her while she bathed in the river!"

"That is disgraceful. It is unworthy of a nobleman to behave in such a way. But, as I said, Savarec was with her today," Redmond assured Michel. "Clodion would not dare to say or do anything offensive toward Danise if her father is present."

"No," Guntram interrupted the heated retort Michel was about to make. "Savarec was not with Danise, not after the hunt advanced into the forest."

"Where was he, then?" Michel turned his full attention to Guntram.

"Savarec ordered me not to say," Guntram replied. He got no further in any explanation he might have made because Michel leaned over and grabbed the front of his tunic, nearly pulling Guntram out of his saddle.

"Damn it, Guntram, Danise is missing and no one has seen Clodion recently! What do you think that means? *Where is Savarec?* He must be told."

"He had an assignation," Guntram revealed, most unwillingly.

"*What?* Savarec?" cried Redmond in disbelief.

"A certain lady invited him to her tent. He was to meet her there while most folk were absent in the forest. Don't look so angry, Michel. Savarec is a healthy man and needs his recreation."

"It's not Guntram's fault." Redmond put a restraining hand on Michel's arm and kept it there until Michel released Guntram. "If something terrible has happened to Danise, we are all equally to blame. You, Michel, myself, Savarec, and you, Guntram—all of us know what Clodion is. We should have been more protective of Danise. She should have had a guard with her at all times."

"Hindsight won't help Danise now," Michel said, his expression grim. "We have to find her as soon as possible."

"First find Savarec," said Guntram. "He may be able to tell us more. I'll look in his tent in

179

case he has returned there, and then I'll ask the lady."

"Who is she?" Michel demanded.

"Savarec ordered me not to tell, but you are right, Michel, this is not a time to blindly obey Savarec's orders. It is Lady Ingeborg. She's a widow of Savarec's age. When he told me about their meeting for today, I suspected Lady Ingeborg was looking for a good second husband. It may be as I thought, but still, I begin to wonder now."

"Well you should wonder about her intentions," Redmond told them. "I know Lady Ingeborg. You wouldn't want Savarec to marry her, Guntram. She is circumspect enough here at court, because Hildegarde insists on discretion in all her attendants. Away from court, Lady Ingeborg's reputation is none too savory among certain of our nobles. Furthermore, she is a friend of Clodion's—another person who keeps his private affairs well hidden from Charles and Hildegarde."

A moment of tense silence followed this revelation with the three men looking at each other until Michel began to issue orders.

"There is no time to waste," he said. "Danise is in danger. I feel it in my bones. Redmond, ask among the rest of the nobles, particularly the ladies. Perhaps one of them has seen Danise recently, or someone may have noticed in which direction she was heading. Guntram, you check Lady Ingeborg's tent, and Savarec's as you suggested. Find Savarec."

"What will you do?" Redmond asked.

"I'm going to talk to Sister Gertrude," Michel said. "She's a sensible woman and she has known Clodion for years. She may have some ideas that would help us. We will meet at Savarec's tent."

They separated, Redmond to mingle among the nobles, Michel and Guntram to ride ahead of them back to camp. Near the royal tents Michel dismounted, turning his horse over to Guntram. Then he hurried to the queen's tent. Only a serving maid was there.

"The women have gone to the edge of the forest again, to rest beneath the trees," the maid said in answer to Michel's agitated questions.

He found Hildegarde lying on a mattress in the shade while her ladies fanned her. One glance at the queen's pale, wan face and Michel knew he could not raise the alarm over Danise until he had more information. Hildegarde would be terribly upset at the news that Danise was missing, and being so disturbed might well complicate her pregnancy. He would have to depend upon Sister Gertrude's sharp eyes and swift comprehension. He was not disappointed in the nun. She came to him at once, and drew him aside so they could speak in private.

"What has happened?" she asked.

"Have you seen Danise recently?"

"No. She's at the hunt. Hasn't she returned?"

"Do you know a Lady Ingeborg?" Michel asked.

"That one." Sister Gertrude's voice conveyed her opinion of Lady Ingeborg. "She was late in joining us this morning."

"Is she here now?"

"She's over there." Sister Gertrude pointed to a plump, middle-aged lady in a dark red gown that was too tight for her ample curves.

"I don't want to alarm the queen unnecessarily," Michel said. "Can you coax Lady Ingeborg into strolling to Savarec's tent with you?"

"No need to coax," replied Sister Gertrude. "I'll order her and she will obey or I will tell Hildegarde a few interesting facts about dear Lady Ingeborg. Michel," Sister Gertrude's eyes were dark with worry, "where is Danise?"

"That's what we are trying to discover," he said.

"And you think Lady Ingeborg may know something? She is one of Clodion's oldest friends. Oh, dear saints in heaven!" Sister Gertrude's voice sank to a harsh whisper. "You believe Clodion has captured Danise."

"Exactly," said Michel, not troubling to hide his own concern from her. "Bring Lady Ingeborg along as fast as you can, will you?"

He found Guntram in front of Savarec's tent, supporting a dazed, soaking wet Savarec.

"I found him in his bed in a stupor," Guntram said, "so I dragged him out here and dumped a bucket of cold water over his head. He'll wake up soon enough."

"Wine did it," Savarec muttered in a thick, slurred voice. "Herbs."

Michel caught Savarec by the hair, pulling his head upward. Savarec winced as the sun fell full on his face.

"Are you saying that Lady Ingeborg drugged

your wine?" Michel demanded.

"Couldn't stay awake," Savarec said. "Why here? I was—her tent—her bed."

"She probably had her servants carry you back here," Michel observed. "I believe this is the lady herself, come to apologize to you. Good afternoon, Lady Ingeborg."

"I have nothing to say to Savarec. He was a great disappointment to me." After a scathing look in Savarec's direction Lady Ingeborg started to leave. She was prevented by Sister Gertrude, who took her arm in a tight grip and turned her around again to face the three men.

"You will answer Michel's questions honestly," Sister Gertrude instructed, "or I will speak to the queen about you. I know a great deal about your activities, alone and in concert with Clodion. I can have you banished from court forever."

"I do not want that. I love being so close to the power and the excitement that swirls around Charles. Life on my late husband's estates is so boring." Lady Ingeborg's resistance wilted. "Very well. What do you want to know?"

"Let's begin with Savarec's condition," said Michel. "Why did you put sleeping herbs in his wine?"

"It was the only way I could think of to fend him off," Lady Ingeborg protested. "He insisted on meeting me in my tent, and I—I was afraid of him. I feared he would ravish me."

"Rubbish," said Sister Gertrude. "Ingeborg, you are not afraid of anyone, including the devil himself. I point out to you that you have just contradicted yourself. If Savarec was disappointing in the way you implied, then you had no need to fear ravishment at his hands."

"*She* suggested the meeting," said Savarec, apparently more recovered from the drugged wine with every moment that passed. "When I got to her tent, she gave me wine to drink. I remember nothing after that, until Guntram doused me with water."

"Sex had nothing to do with your part in today's events, nor had fear," Michel said to Lady Ingeborg. "You invited Savarec to your tent and gave him drugged wine to keep him out of the way while Clodion abducted Danise."

"What?" cried Savarec. "Danise, abducted? I'll kill Clodion for this! And you, you conniving witch!" He would have attacked Lady Ingeborg if Guntram had not restrained him.

"Do not trouble yourself to punish her," Sister Gertrude advised. "In due time heaven will see to Ingeborg. Her life is not worth what it would cost you to take it from her, Savarec."

"You all do insult me." Lady Ingeborg was the picture of offended innocence. "Even if this preposterous story were true, what would the removal of Savarec from today's hunt accomplish? You would still be there, Michel, along with Count Redmond and Guntram here. Any of you could easily protect Danise, if she needed protection. Don't blame me if she is missing. If she is really with Clodion, she may have gone along with him willingly. Clodion can be most persuasive."

"Danise loathes the man," Sister Gertrude declared, her eyes flashing angry fire. "She would never have gone anywhere with him. Savarec, at root this is all your fault, since you allowed Clodion to become Danise's suitor."

"I did not know he would harm her. I hoped to secure a luxurious life for her as the wife of an honored nobleman." Savarec moaned, his hands at his head. "You are right, old friend, this is as much my doing as Clodion's. Oh, my poor, poor Danise, my baby, my little girl." Tears streamed down Savarec's face.

"It's my fault, too," Michel said, moved by Savarec's open grief. "I should have been more alert to Clodion's actions. Guntram and I rode with Charles this morning at Clodion's suggestion. Charles told me so after I complained that I couldn't find Danise in that mob on horseback. Charles sent Guntram and me to look for her. At least he had sense enough to be worried right away."

"You are wasting time," snapped Sister Gertrude. "You must find Danise at once. We do not need to ask what Clodion will do to her if he has indeed abducted her." At these words Savarec moaned again.

"You are absolutely right," Michel said to Sister Gertrude. "I think we would do well to assume that Danise *has* been abducted. I will go to Charles and ask for his help to find her. And you, Lady Ingeborg, are going with me, to provide whatever information Charles asks of you."

"I'll go, too," Sister Gertrude volunteered, still holding tightly to Lady Ingeborg's arm.

"I know nothing about any of this," Lady Ingeborg cried.

"After what you did to me, do not expect anyone to believe you again," warned Savarec, his grief over Danise rapidly changing to anger. He wiped his eyes and straightened his shoulders. "I'll see you severely punished for this, Ingeborg," he promised.

"Here comes Redmond," said Guntram. "He may know something."

"I do not," said Redmond. "No one I have spoken to has seen Danise or Clodion since immediately after the hunt began. Michel, we must inform Charles at once."

They found the king of the Franks just dismounting before his tent. It took only a few minutes to tell him what little they knew and what they had deduced.

"I do not want Hildegarde overly distressed," Charles said. "We will organize a search, but we will do it quietly. Give out only the news that Danise has not returned from the hunt and may be lost in the forest. That's bad enough, but not as bad as the truth. Lady Ingeborg, you will remain in your tent, under guard, so you cannot communicate with Clodion. Redmond, I want you to use your own men-at-arms to set a watch on the men Clodion brought to Duren. Give orders that none of them is to leave camp. Discover if any are already missing, and if so, report it to me at once. Return as quickly as you can; I want you to join in the search. Sister Gertrude, I depend upon you to keep Hildegarde quiet and unaffected by this."

"I want to go with the search party," Sister Gertrude replied. "When you find her, Danise will need me."

"You can do more good here," Charles told her. "When we find Danise—and I promise you, we *will* find her—we will treat her with every kindness and promptly bring her back to you."

"I pray you will not be too late," said Sister Gertrude.

"So do we all pray," Charles responded. His face was grave, his voice solemn.

Willing searchers were quickly recruited. Fresh horses were saddled. Men weary after a day of riding in humid heat paused only to refresh themselves with a little bread and cheese and wine before returning to the forest. There, at the place where Redmond had last seen Danise, Charles divided them into several parties and sent them off in different directions. Charles and Savarec rode with Michel, Redmond, and Guntram, the five of them spread out among the trees, moving along slowly, watching the ground for any trace of Danise or Clodion. They did not stop until it was too dark to see.

"We will begin again at dawn," Charles said. "Savarec, I swear to you, I will not leave Duren or end Mayfield until we know where Danise is."

"Knowing where she is does not mean she will be safe." Savarec had dark circles under his eyes and his face was set into strained lines as he looked toward Charles. "All the same, I thank you, my friend."

Savarec did not sleep that night. Michel and Guntram insisted he must eat something and then lie down to rest, but the worried father only tossed upon his bed, cursing himself for his foolishness in underestimating Clodion's determination to have Danise.

Michel was not in much better condition. Left to himself, he would have continued the search in the dark. Only Charles's direct command prevented him from doing so. The thought of Danise struggling in Clodion's embrace nearly drove him mad. Lady Ingeborg's luring of Savarec, and the way Michel and Guntram had been maneuvered into riding with Charles so neither of them could protect Danise, suggested careful plotting on Clodion's part.

The sun was not yet above the horizon when the search for Danise was resumed. By noon Michel had begun to lose hope, and he was growing worried about Savarec.

"The man is driving himself to the limits of his strength," Michel said to Charles. "He is ready to drop from exhaustion and from this miserable heat." Michel's own woolen tunic and linen undershirt were saturated with perspiration.

"I would order him to return to camp," Charles said, "but I believe he would disobey me for the first time in his life. No, Michel, if one of my daughters were missing, I would not stop until I found her or I died. Let Savarec follow his heart. It will help to relieve the burden of guilt he feels." Charles did call a brief halt for their little group of men and he insisted that Savarec must take off his tunic and bathe in a nearby stream to cool himself. Such was Savarec's impatience that they did not stop for long.

It was some time after midday when they heard a cry from a short distance away. Immediately Savarec kicked his horse's flanks, hastening ahead of his companions. A few seconds later Michel heard Savarec's angry shout and then a scream of terror. Michel and Charles urged their horses through the trees to the spot from where the noises were coming. Redmond and Guntram followed close behind them.

And there, stripped naked and tied to a tree, was Clodion. And there was Savarec, tumbling off his horse, his knife in his hand, and no question in Michel's mind just what Savarec meant to do.

"Stop!" Charles's voice rang out, stopping Savarec in midstep. "Do not harm him, Savarec. Clodion has much to tell us."

"Thanks be to heaven, it is you," Clodion cried. "Savarec, release me. I know where they have taken Danise."

"They?" Michel got off his horse. "What *they?* It's you who took Danise away."

"She agreed to ride with me for a while," Clodion insisted, "to hear my pleas that she should marry me."

Flora Speer

"I find it difficult to believe that Danise would go anywhere with you." Redmond was on the ground now, too, and his face was a study in barely controlled fury.

"Try, *impossible*," Michel said to him.

"I'm telling the truth," Clodion screamed. "We were set upon by Autichar and his men. They left me like this and took Danise away with them. It was Autichar who abducted Danise, not me."

"So, the rumors were true. Autichar was in the neighborhood." Charles came forward to stand with a fist planted on each hip, regarding Clodion with a sharp eye. "Where did they go?"

"Autichar spoke of carrying Danise home to Bavaria," said Clodion. "I do not know if he means to wed her or to ravish her. Autichar was greatly angered by the way he was treated at Duren. Charles, he said he would take his complaint of you to Duke Tassilo. Mayhap he intends to use Danise as a witness to his story."

"Mayhap, trees can fly," muttered Guntram. "Don't believe a word this man says."

"You can see what they did to me," screeched Clodion. "They took away all my clothes, they tied me to this tree, and then they abused me most grievously."

"I'll wager he enjoyed it," said Guntram beneath his breath.

"Which way did they go?" Michel demanded of Clodion. "You must have seen them leave."

"They were headed toward the Rhine,"

190

Clodion answered. "Autichar did say that the rest of his men were camped there until he rejoined them. He had but a small band with him here. Autichar planned to travel as fast as he could until he is safe in Bavaria."

"You are right, Guntram." Michel scowled at Clodion. "We can't believe this man. He may have hidden Danise somewhere."

"Clodion had more than enough time to ravish her," Guntram agreed. "Or to kill her. If he did either, I want a chance at him with my own knife. I'll see to it that he is made incapable of ever harming another woman."

"You'll have to stand in line and wait your turn," Michel said, "behind Savarec and me."

"And me," Redmond added.

Clodion whimpered in fear before their threatening faces, struggling against the hide ropes that bound him. Now Charles moved forward another step or two.

"Surely you do understand," he said to Clodion, "how little these good men trust your word."

"I would never," Clodion gasped, looking from Savarec, still with knife in hand, to Michel, to Redmond and Guntram. "Charles— I'm loyal—always—your father—and you."

"For the sake of your years of service to my father and to me," Charles said, "I will not allow them to harm you. But I warn you, Clodion, if we find proof of your culpability, then I will see you severely punished."

"What more proof do you need?" Savarec objected. "Clodion admits he brought Danise

191

into the forest. For what reason, it is not hard to guess."

"Charles is right." Michel laid a restraining hand on Savarec's shoulder. He sent an admiring glance toward the king of the Franks, who stood tall and calm in the midst of so much anger and fear. "I'd enjoy carving this subhuman creature into pieces just as much as you would, Savarec. But killing him won't help Danise. Charles has made laws to protect women from being carried off and raped, and those laws ought to be obeyed. What we want here is justice, not revenge."

"My friends, I will give you justice," Charles promised. "Before we leave Duren, Clodion will be convicted, or acquitted, in the matter of Danise's disappearance. At the moment, I will have him returned to camp and there kept under strict guard.

"Guntram, I will not order you to blow your horn, for I do not want the search stopped. You have but to ride northward a short distance to meet another search party. Find it and bring the men here. Redmond, do the same in a southerly direction. That will add nearly a dozen other men to our group." At once Redmond and Guntram leapt onto their horses to obey his command.

"Aren't you going to set me free?" cried Clodion.

"Why, as to that," said Charles, a slight smile playing upon his lips, "if we leave you as you are, we need not worry that you will wander away and become lost among the trees. If that should happen, we'd have to search for two people instead of one. Considering the mood of these men with me, I'd say you are safer where we found you."

"We can't break off the search for Danise," Michel said.

"Certainly not," Charles agreed. "Once the men Redmond and Guntram are summoning have arrived, I will send out word to the remaining search parties to work their way south and eastward, toward the Rhine. I must return to Duren, to alert the men there to the possibility of an attack by Autichar."

"He won't attack Duren," Clodion insisted. "Autichar is headed toward Bavaria."

"How can you be so sure?" Charles contemplated Clodion's face for a long moment before he spoke again. "How can you know if what Autichar said in your hearing was true? Perhaps he intended to mislead you, knowing you would convey to us what he said."

"He—" Clodion clamped his mouth shut on the words he had been about to speak. With a barely perceptible nod of satisfaction Charles turned away from him.

"There is more to Clodion's story than he's telling," Michel said, too low for Clodion to hear.

"Agreed." Charles paused, thinking. "Savarec, I want you to return to Duren with me. If we should be attacked, I will need you there."

"But, Danise," Savarec protested.

"Michel and Redmond will continue to direct the search for her," Charles decided. "You

193

may allow Guntram to remain with them if you wish."

To this Savarec assented.

"Thank you," Michel said to Charles, still in the same low voice. "The man needs food and rest. He's so worn out with worry over Danise that he'd be more a problem than a help to us."

"So I thought," Charles replied.

The bands of searchers contacted by Redmond and Guntram soon assembled. There was some amusement displayed over Clodion's situation, but at Charles's order he was released from his bonds, covered with a cloak someone lent to him, and mounted upon his own horse, which Guntram discovered wandering loose among the trees. Then, taking three men along for guards, Charles led Savarec and Clodion back toward Duren, leaving the other men with Michel, Redmond, and Guntram.

"We ought to spread out as before," Michel suggested, "and head in the general direction of the Rhine."

"And pray that Clodion was telling the truth," Redmond added.

They moved out at once, not wanting to waste the remaining hours of daylight. Having agreed not to call out to one another or use their hunting horns until they found Danise so as not to alert any lurking enemies, they resumed the search.

Danise did everything she could think of to delay Autichar. She pretended to be ill, saying she would lose the bread and rancid cheese she had eaten if she were forced to ride immediately after breaking her nightlong fast. In truth, the cheese was enough to make anyone sick, but she had eaten as much of it as she could, knowing she would need the nourishment it would provide.

Next, she dawdled among the bushes, claiming her bowels were greatly disturbed. Finally, when Autichar ordered her to mount her horse, she feigned dizziness until Autichar told her he would tie her onto the horse if she could not sit in the saddle unaided. After that, all she could do was protest that they were riding too fast for the peace of her delicate stomach.

During the morning the oppressive heat increased until soon it was easy to pretend that she did not feel well. The part of the forest through which they were now traveling was dense, with heavy underbrush to slow their progress. After midday the heat grew worse. By midafternoon, when his men began to grumble, Autichar called a halt beside a stream that flowed down the side of a hill into a shallow pool. Here there was a general relaxation of the tight control Autichar had so far maintained over his men.

"We'll rest and cool ourselves in the water," Autichar decided. "By now, we are far beyond pursuit from Duren, so there's time to stop for an hour."

His casual remarks plunged Danise into despair. If they were so far from Charles's camp, then there was little chance that she could escape and find friendly assistance.

She was going to attempt to escape anyway, for if she did not, her future was unthinkably horrible. If Autichar and his men killed her while she was trying to get away from them, it would still be a better fate than the one they planned for her. On the other hand, there was no point in arranging for her own death if she could possibly devise a better chance for herself.

On her knees by the stream, she splashed water onto her face and the back of her neck, wishing she could remove her clothing to wash all over as some of the men were doing. She turned her head so she would not have to see the naked, laughing Bavarians. And there, just a few paces from where she sat, was the opportunity for which she had been praying. The entrance to the cave was half hidden by bushes, but to Danise it was unmistakable. More bushes extended from the hillside back into the forest, where they merged with the general greenness.

The plan formed in her mind within a moment or two. At once Danise began to take action to save herself. Being careful that no one saw what she was doing, she removed from one of her braids the green and brown embroidered ribbon that bound the end of it. Concealing the ribbon in one hand, which she clutched over her stomach, she rose to her feet.

"What are you doing?" asked the man next to her.

"Sick," she muttered. Still clutching at her

stomach, she raised her other hand to her mouth. "Oh—oh! I'm going to be sick again." She stumbled toward the bushes at the side of the cave entrance.

"Let her go," said a second man when the first would have climbed out of the stream to follow Danise. "She can't escape. There's nowhere for her to hide, and I'm tired of guarding her while she pukes, or squats in the bushes and groans. After listening to her this morning, I'd rather kill her than guard her. I don't know what Autichar is keeping her for."

"I know. And so does Clodion," said his fellow with a loud, suggestive guffaw.

Danise had by now reached the bushes near to the cave entrance. With a moan and a gasp as realistic as she could make them, she plunged behind the concealing leaves. Getting down on her knees she crawled toward the cave opening and tossed her hair ribbon inside. If Autichar's men found it when they began to search for her, they might waste precious time looking through the cave, believing she had foolishly fled into it. Praying that the cave would prove to be long and deep, Danise moved back into the bushes, pausing to moan and gag again in case anyone was listening. Then, carefully, she worked her way around the side of the hill, trying to stay within the shelter of the bushes.

That morning she had heard Autichar say he would head south and east toward the Rhine, which meant she would have to flee northwestward. The only way she could keep herself on course was to head into the path of the sun, which was beginning to move lower in the sky. It was not an easy thing to do there beneath the trees, with their leaves hiding most of the sky and with the need to stay hidden in the underbrush. After a while, hearing no sounds of pursuit behind her, Danise forsook caution. She stood up and began to run.

Chapter 10

It had been too easy. She should have known they were only playing with her, letting her believe she had escaped, letting her run herself into exhaustion before they began the chase.

Perhaps, Danise thought as she dodged the scratching branches of yet another bush, *perhaps Autichar never intended to take me to Bavaria at all, never meant for Clodion to have me. And when they catch me, after they finish what they—what they will do—they will kill me.*

Pain stabbed at her side, taking her breath away. She tripped over a tree root, but she caught herself before she hit the ground. Terrified of spraining an ankle and being forced to stop, she pressed onward. She could not afford to slow down or try to be more careful where she stepped. There was no time or energy left for thought now, nor for lofty notions about warning Charles of Autichar's plan or Clodion's treason. She was reduced to the mere desire for survival, to the necessity of taking one more step away from her pursuers, and then one more step . . . and just one more . . . over and over again. Behind her Autichar's men called to her, laughing, mocking, making obscene promises. She scarcely heard them.

Gradually, another noise came to her ears, and it came from the wrong direction. Danise did not pause in her flight, but she did change course, instinctively heading toward the new sound. Fear drove her onward, adding speed. She ran until she saw movement ahead.

Someone was there, coming toward her through the trees. Fragments of sight and sound drifted across her consciousness. Horses. Men on foot. The blast of a hunting horn. Shouts. Loud voices, calling words she was too weary to comprehend.

Still not knowing toward what she ran, only aware that it was something different from the impending horror that followed her, Danise moved forward on aching, heavy legs, gasping for every breath. During her desperate flight the hair had begun to pull out of the unbound braid from which she had taken the ribbon. Branches projecting from bushes or low trees had finished the job of undoing the neat braid until now long silver-gold locks blew across her face with every step she took, obscuring her vision.

Danise could not stop to brush the hair out of her eyes, for the enemy was closer now. She could hear hoofbeats. They came not from directly in front of her, where the hunting horn still sounded, nor from behind, where Autichar and his men were, but from the side. A horse suddenly appeared off to her right. She saw it out of the corner of her eye. Before she could so much as turn her head to see what was happening, the horse's rider bent out of his saddle to reach toward her. An arm came down and scooped Danise off her feet. She was thrown across the saddle, where she hung face downward, too weak and out of breath to protest this rough treatment.

She did not know if it was Autichar or one of his men who had taken her up onto his horse, or if it was someone else entirely. The horn was still blaring. Men were shouting. She heard the unmistakable clash of steel upon steel.

Strong hands lifted her, twisting her around until she could see the face of the man who had caught her. Blue eyes more intense than the deepest summer sky burned into hers. Still out of breath, Danise could not speak, she could only clutch at him before she fell against his chest and felt his arms enclose her.

"It's all right," Michel told her. "You're safe now, Danise. We'll keep you safe."

Next Danise recognized Redmond's voice, giving firm orders to the man who held her.

"Get her out of here, Michel. We'll stop Autichar. Take Danise and escape back to Duren."

The hunting horn sounded again. Lifting her head from Michel's chest, Danise watched Guntram blow a mighty blast, summoning more men. One by one Frankish warriors rode out of the forest shadows to join the fray under Redmond's command.

"Go on," Redmond urged Michel. "A battle-field is no place for Danise. Do you want a guard?"

"You'll need every man you have," Michel replied, hesitating. "I ought to stay."

"If you do, who will keep Danise safe from Autichar?" Redmond demanded. "Get her away from here *now!* That's an order, Michel. If you value our friendship, obey it."

"Redmond." Danise had recovered enough to speak. "Take care. And thank you for coming after me."

"Keep Autichar alive if you can," Michel said. "Charles will want to talk to him."

"I know. It won't take long to disperse these few weak Bavarians, not when they're fighting against Franks. We won't be far behind you. Now, ride!"

Michel pulled his horse around and headed away. Looking over his shoulder Danise could see more Franks arriving with swords and spears at the ready. She caught a glimpse of Autichar's metal helmet and red cloak.

"Don't look," Michel said, pulling her closer to him. "Just rest. It's going to take us a while to get back to Duren. It's a long way home."

"I tried to delay them, hoping someone would be tracking us." Suddenly she began to shake.

Afraid she would start to cry if she tried to say anything more, she turned her face into his shoulder.

"You've done very well." His arms tightened. "We'll talk about it later. For now, don't think about anything at all."

"I must, I have to tell someone. It's a treason plot, Michel. Clodion—you must find Clodion and take him to Charles. I will accuse him."

"Hush, my sweet. It's done. We've found Clodion. I think Charles suspects there is more behind your disappearance than Clodion's lust."

"I must tell you." Danise took a long, shuddering breath. "If I die, someone else should know what they plan."

"You aren't going to die." His arms held her securely against his solid strength. "I plan to keep you alive for a long, long time. For now, just relax. I'll have to stop in a little while to rest the horse, and we can talk then."

Danise stifled a sob and tried to still the trembling of her limbs. Though the heat of the day was nearly unbearable, she was chilled at the memory of what she had so narrowly escaped. But she was safe at last and no longer alone. Michel would protect her. Slowly the tremors eased. The steady gait of Michel's horse, the comfort of his arms, and the certainty that Autichar and his men could not harm her while they were busy fighting Redmond and the other Franks, all combined to lull her into a state between sleep and waking, in which she was completely at peace while at the same time intensely aware of her companion's nearness. She did not know how long she traveled in that blissful condition before Michel pulled on the reins.

"We have to stop," he said. "This seems to be as good a place as any."

Lifting her head from his shoulder, Danise looked around. Her senses were not at their sharpest, so it took her a few moments to identify where they were.

"It's a charcoal makers' settlement," she murmured.

"There's no one here now," Michel replied, "and hasn't been for years. Look at all this new growth. If people were working here, they'd keep this area clean."

It had once been a wide clearing in the forest, the older trees almost certainly cut down and used to build the rude huts in which the charcoal makers would have lived while they plied their craft. To one side of the clearing and apart from the huts stood three beehive-shaped brick kilns, located where they were for safety's sake, so their heat would not burn the huts. Danise could see where the kilns had been patched with clay which was now cracked and showing holes in places. They were overgrown with weeds and vines. There was, as Michel had noted, a fair amount of new growth, bushes mostly, and the absence of any tall trees in the immediate vicinity of this tiny settlement gave them a clear view of the sky. Angry gray clouds blocked the sun, cutting off most of the late afternoon light. As Danise looked upward, a gust of wind caught the treetops, shaking them. In the distance thunder rumbled.

"It will rain soon," Danise said. "An early season thunderstorm to end this unnatural heat."

"All the more reason for us to stop here." Michel dismounted, then lifted Danise off the horse and lowered her to stand beside him. "I don't know much about charcoal making, but wherever people live and work there has to be a source of water. We won't suffer from thirst."

"They would have cut down the hardwood trees in the nearby forest to turn the wood into charcoal in those kilns," Danise said. "I wonder why they left? The kilns look to me as though they could be repaired and used again, and there is no shortage of wood."

"They could have been driven out by warfare or disease," Michel noted. "Stay here with the horse, Danise. I'm going to look around."

She watched him move from hut to hut until a crash of thunder made him glance skyward. The treetops were tossing about and down at ground level a sudden wind lifted a strand of Danise's hair, whipping it across her face. Michel's horse shifted uneasily. Danise caught its reins, holding it steady.

"It looks to me as if they packed up and left in an orderly fashion." Michel returned to Danise's side. "The largest of the huts is fairly clean. We can shelter there. The hut next to it will be fine for the horse. I found the water; there's a stream off to the side of the clearing."

He led the horse to the water while Danise

went to see the hut he had chosen. It was made of crudely dressed logs, with a firepit in the center of the tramped earth floor and openings at the gable ends of the roof to let out the smoke. The roof looked to be intact and would keep them dry until the coming storm had passed. A worn-down broom stood propped in one corner of the hut next to a wooden bucket, gifts left by the last housewife to live there. Danise took up the broom and began to sweep out the dusty floor.

"If you can find some branches or small logs, we could start a fire," she said to Michel when he appeared at the door with his saddlebag and a wineskin slung over one arm. "We don't need the heat, but the light will be cheerful and it will help to rid the hut of dampness. Do you have a flint in your saddlebag?"

"I do. There's plenty of wood near the kilns. There is even a little charcoal." While he brought the supplies for the fire, Danise took the bucket to the stream to wash it out and fill it. The leather handle broke as soon as she picked it up, so she carried the bucket in her arms.

"How I would like a bath," she said, looking down at her soiled dress. The brown wool was torn around the hem and at one arm, where a tree branch had snagged the cloth while she fled from Autichar.

"So would I." Michel held out grubby hands, his fingers blackened from charcoal. "We left Duren this morning prepared to sleep in the forest tonight. I have food for the horse, a blanket for him and one for us, my cloak, food and wine, even an extra linen shirt and wool tunic. But no soap, I'm afraid."

"There is sand in the stream bed. You could scrub your hands with that."

"It will be better than nothing," he decided. "We ought to hurry, though. The thunderstorm is ready to break at any minute."

They washed as best they could with only the sand and the cool stream water. Danise dried her hands on her skirt and began to rebraid her tangled hair.

"Leave that until later," Michel advised, slanting a glance toward the sky as lightning flashed. He caught her hand. "Come on, let's get inside." His words were punctuated by an ominous rumble of thunder.

They did not make it to the hut before the skies opened and rain poured down as though buckets of water had been thrown over them. They were immediately drenched. Michel pulled Danise into the hut and slammed the door on the pounding, wind-driven rain. Above, the thunder rolled, peal after peal of it, and flashes of lightning showed around the edges of the ill-fitting door. Michel went to the firepit and began to work with his flint and a bit of woolen lint.

"We were fortunate to find this place," Danise said. Picking up a few dried leaves from the pile of fire supplies, she held them out to the sparks Michel was striking into the wool. She tried to speak naturally, as though being alone like this were an ordinary occurrence, but she was painfully sensitive to Michel's presence and to the fact that the raging storm enclosed them in a private haven of warmth and security. Michel blew on the fire, encouraging it to burn. Danise fed it a few small twigs. Together they nursed the flames until the logs he had brought in were crackling merrily. Danise held out her hands to the blaze.

"You're shaking again." Michel ran his hands along her arms to her shoulders, apparently unaware of the effect his touch had upon her. "After what you've been through during the last couple of days, you have to be exhausted. If you get chilled now, you'll probably develop pneumonia and you won't have the strength to fight it. I don't want to lose you, Danise." His hands grew still on her upper arms. His eyes burned into hers.

"Take off those wet clothes," he ordered. "I'll give you the choice of my extra undershirt, or the tunic. They are dry."

Danise's teeth were chattering and water was streaming off her wet hair. She knew Michel was right. This was not the time for excessive modesty.

"I'll take your undershirt," she said, "and if you will allow me, I'll wrap up in your cloak until I am warmer."

"Sensible girl." Kneeling, he began to unpack his saddlebag. "I'm glad I carried in extra firewood. That storm sounds as though it's going to last all night. Here you are."

The linen shirt he handed to her was thick enough not to be transparent, made with short sleeves and a round neck. Turning her back to him, Danise pulled off her sodden dress and shift and quickly donned the shirt. She used her shift to towel her hair until it was no longer dripping water, and then hung shift and dress on a pair of pegs she found driven into the narrow spaces between the logs of the wall. Her shoes were so muddy that she took them off, too, and her stockings as well. Lastly, she braided her hair into a semblance of neatness. When she finally turned around again she almost bumped into Michel.

"Whoever lived here must have been a decent housewife," he remarked, brushing past her to hang his tunic and breeches from two more pegs. "I can imagine her telling her menfolk to hang up their clothes."

He now wore a light brown tunic, and like Danise, his legs and feet were bare.

"Help me with the blanket, will you?"

Danise thought he was trying as hard as she was to pretend that these were normal circumstances in which they found themselves. He did not look directly at her, which made her feel a little less exposed. She grasped one end of his brown blanket and together they unrolled it and spread it out upon the dirt floor near the fire.

"Here." He pulled his cloak out of the saddlebag and gave it to her. She recognized it as her father's old one. It was blue, though not as blue as Michel's eyes, and it was worn until it was smooth and soft to the touch. She wrapped it around her shoulders and sat on the blanket while he produced the food he had packed in the saddlebag.

"Here's bread, the ever-present cheese, my knife to cut it with. And here's the skin of wine," he said. "We won't starve overnight."

"Must we stay until morning?" she asked. "I am certain my father will worry until he sees me again."

"Do you really want to go out in that?" He cocked his head, listening to the latest clap of thunder. "Would Savarec want you to travel in this kind of weather?"

"No, I suppose not. Michel, do you think Redmond and the others will find us soon?"

"I would expect them to look for shelter where they are," he said. He cut a wedge of cheese and offered it to her. Danise stared at it. "Eat, Danise. I'd be willing to bet you haven't got much in your stomach. Your blood sugar is probably way down."

"My what?" She looked at him in bewilderment at the unfamiliar term until he smiled.

"It's a current saying in my country," he informed her. "It means you are close to fainting from lack of nourishment. Even if you don't feel hungry, eat what I give you."

She nibbled at the cheese, discovered to her surprise that she was hungry after all, and reached for the bread. Michel handed the flat loaf to her, and when he did, their fingers touched. Danise looked at his hand, tanned, long-fingered, newly callused from days spent handling weapons in his attempt to reach the same proficiency as Frankish men. Shaken by the sudden realization that she wanted to feel those hands on her body, she let go of the bread. Michel took it and broke the loaf in half.

"We ought to save some of it for the morning," he admonished.

"I have been half asleep until this moment," she murmured, wondering how she was going to control her unruly emotions.

"I would say you have been in a state of shock. It's perfectly natural, considering what you've been through. The food will help to bring you out of it. Have some more cheese." He watched her eat for a while. "Do you feel like talking about it now? You said something earlier about Clodion and Autichar hatching treason between them."

"Hatching?" She smiled briefly at his choice of words. "They intended to use my abduction to cause a war between Charles and Duke Tassilo." She told him everything that had happened since she had been taken from Duren, and all that she had been able to learn from Autichar.

"This is serious business," he said. "It really is treason those two have been plotting. Danise, did Clodion harm you in any way? If he laid a hand on you, I'll personally tear him into pieces, though I may have to fight Guntram for the honor. Guntram threatened to castrate Clodion."

"I'm not surprised. Guntram's fierceness is legendary. Still, there's no need to do it in punishment for anything Clodion did to me during these last few days, though I am sure there are

211

women in Francia who would applaud the act as vengeance for their own wrongs at Clodion's hands."

"Your father and Redmond were ready to help Guntram," Michel said, "but Charles insisted on justice. When he hears what you have to say, I wouldn't be surprised if Clodion receives the worst punishment possible under Frankish law. In Merovingian times, the method of execution for treason was to tie each of the offender's arms and legs to one of four horses, and have the horses whipped into running in four different directions. Queen Brunhilde was executed that way back in the early seventh century. The same punishment would serve Clodion right for what he did to you, and for what he was planning to do."

Danise watched him staring into the fire as he spoke, his face hard as any Frankish warrior's. He was so deep in his thoughts of male vengeance that he did not notice the effect his words were having on her. She gulped back tears, brushing at her eyes.

"I can't," she whispered, and he turned to her, startled out of his bloody reverie. "Michel, I can't make light of what has happened, or talk about bloodshed and punishment. When Clodion took me away from the hunt, I was terrified. Autichar said he would let Clodion have me and then give me to his men. He said that afterward, if I still lived, I could go where I wanted, but what would there be for me after such shame? I feared I would never see you, or my father, again—or anyone else I love."

"I'm sorry. Danise, I am sorry." He seized her, holding her tightly. "I've been thinking about my own anger at Clodion and forgetting how you must have felt. Your abduction never should have happened. We should have protected you far better than we did."

She clung to him, and the tears would not stop no matter how hard she tried to get them under control.

"I am such a coward," she sobbed. "I was afraid from the moment Clodion captured my horse's reins until you took me onto your horse today."

"Anyone with any brains at all would have been afraid," he said. "You had wit enough to stay alive and unharmed, and courage enough to escape. You got away from them on your own, Danise. You found us. You can be proud of that."

"But I can't stop weeping!"

"It's a delayed reaction. Cry all you want. Soak my tunic. I don't care. I'm so happy to have you safe in my arms that you can saturate every piece of clothing I own. Work on the cloak for a while if you like."

"Oh, Michel." Poised between renewed sobs and laughter at his words, she looked into his eyes—and found she could not look away.

Gently he wiped the moisture off her cheeks. When he was done, he did not remove his hand. He cupped her face, holding it steady while he kissed her. Danise made a soft sound, part whimper, part laugh, part cry of surprise. And then he was crushing her to him and his mouth was hard on hers. She felt his tongue and parted her lips to give him access, pressing herself against him while he searched out every sensitive corner of her mouth. She was dimly aware of the pounding noise of rain upon the roof of the little hut where they sheltered. She was more conscious of the warmth and dryness of the interior of the hut. And at the heart of that warmth, that shelter and safety, was Michel. He was the heart and center of everything.

"I mustn't do this." He was pushing her away and Danise, half drowning in sensual pleasure, caught at his arms to keep him close.

Michel knelt on the brown blanket, his features now softened by desire. Danise sat facing him, her legs drawn up beneath her, hands wrapped around his forearms, not willing to let him go.

"I was sent to rescue you, not to violate you," he said. "How can I return you to Savarec after taking you, when I would have killed Clodion or Autichar for doing the same thing? Worse, how can I take away your freedom to choose the life you want or the husband you prefer?"

"You will not take anything away from me, you will give to me," she cried. "I know you, Michel. You would not touch me if I did not want you also."

"You're overwrought, you don't know what you are saying. It's a natural reaction to nearly losing your life." But he did not move, he put no further distance between them while Danise spoke.

"I did not have my time with Hugo. We denied ourselves in hope of greater joy at some later time. Will you also be taken from me, Michel? I know you believe it will not happen, but what if you are removed to your own time and I never see you again?"

"All the more reason not to take advantage of you now," he said.

"What if Autichar has bested Redmond and his men? We do not know the outcome of that battle, Michel. Suppose Autichar should track us to this place and take us prisoner. I know what Autichar will do to me after I have escaped him once. He will not give me the chance to escape a second time. He will watch while his men make sport of me, and he will make you watch, too. And then he will kill us both, and what will your forbearance matter then?"

"It won't happen," he said. "Redmond has twice the men that Autichar has."

"The lesson I learned from Hugo's death almost a year ago," she said, "and learned again in these last days, is that life is brief and most uncertain."

"That's not reason enough for me to break faith with your father," he declared. "I promised to return you to him unharmed."

"And what of me?" she whispered. "Can't you think of what I want? I am a woman grown, Michel. My father gave me free choice in this matter. And you—you all but asked me to marry you. Have you changed your mind?"

Flora Speer

"Never. But I still don't have anything to offer you, or your father."

"Honesty," she whispered, nearly overcome by her longing to be held by this man. "Loyalty. Friendship. A good heart. I have recently learned how rare these qualities are. And how valuable."

"Danise." Still he hesitated.

"Have you changed your mind?" she asked again. "Don't you want me?"

"I'm dying for you," he said with a groan.

"And I for you. I have been since the first moment I saw you. Knowing that, will you lie beside me all this night and never touch me? Or do you plan to stand outside in the rain until dawn, guarding my virtue and your own?"

His eyes grew dark, his face intent and serious.

"I've never known a woman like you before," he said, "never anyone so honest and open. Danise, are you absolutely certain this is what you want?"

"Yes." Looking into his eyes she knew her long time of mourning, and of longing for something she had believed lost to her forever, was over at last. "I would lie with you, Michel. I would have you make love to me."

"God knows, it's what I want myself," he said.

"Then I am yours."

It was as though they were entering upon some solemn ritual. In silence he moved the food and the wineskin to a far corner of the blanket, then smoothed out the woolen folds until the blanket was perfectly neat. Kneeling beside her again, he unfastened the hair she had tried to make tidy, unbraiding it until it hung in long, shimmering strands of pale gold. Once or twice during this slow process he touched her lips with his, very lightly, but they were not real kisses, they were promises of kisses to come. When he was finished and her hair was loose, he sat back on his heels, watching her breasts rise and fall beneath the linen of his undershirt. As slowly as he had dealt with her hair, he now put out his hands to cover both of her breasts at once. Danise kept her eyes on his face, memorizing the play of emotion upon his features. He rubbed a thumb across each nipple and she caught her breath. She knew her nipples were hardening at his touch. She could feel it happening. There was a warmth far inside her that grew in response to his caresses. When he bent his head to nibble at her through the borrowed shirt, she changed position restlessly, moving upward onto her knees and thrusting her breast against his mouth. There was no shame in anything they did. It was all natural, all meant to be. It seemed to Danise that their coming together had been fated long before they ever met.

He caught the hem of her shirt, which lay upon her knees, and pushed it upward, his hands sliding along her thighs and then her hips. She raised her arms so he could draw the shirt over her head. For a moment she covered her nakedness with one hand and arm across her breasts, the other hand hiding the place

Flora Speer

where her thighs joined. Then she moved her
hands aside, to let him look at her.

She had been told by older women that she
possessed a nicely rounded figure, but secretly
she thought her breasts were too large. Michel
did not seem to think so. He touched her again,
without the linen to separate his hands from
her sensitive skin. When he began to lick
around the tip of one breast she cried out in
shock at what the moist heat of his tongue did
to her. The warmth inside her burned brighter
still when he attacked her other breast in the
same way. And all the while his hands caressed
her spine, her hips, her shoulders.

Danise's heart was pounding, her head was
spinning, she could barely breathe for choking
emotion. Surely she would die soon if he did
not—did not . . . She whimpered with aching,
as yet unfocused desire.

"You are still dressed," she whispered, trying
to break the intensity of what she was feeling.
Girls and new wives often talked, and Danise
had many friends at school and at Duren. She
knew she ought to be apprehensive at what
was about to happen. She was not. She trusted
Michel and she wanted him to be close to
her. She wanted it more with every struggling
breath she took, with every touch of his hands
upon her burning skin. But when, in answer
to her complaint, he removed his tunic, she
recoiled for an instant, her desire checked by
the burgeoning evidence of his need for her.
Now she understood the whispers of the other
women. Michel had never been so large while

218

she tended him when he was injured. She was not a very big girl and he was so huge. Surely that enormous, rigid part of him would split her asunder. Or would it fill her with unexpected pleasure, as Hildegarde had once hinted could happen? She stared at it, fascinated.

"Are you afraid, Danise? You needn't be."

"I am not afraid." Miraculously, she was not. To prove it, she put out a tentative finger and touched the very tip of him. He caught his breath, but she was too entranced by the velvety feel of him to pay attention just then to his response. She ran her fingers down the length of him, curled her hand around him. Desire flared in her anew, bright and free from apprehension. On an irresistible impulse, she leaned down to kiss him. That was when he caught her shoulders, pulling her upward.

"Was it wrong to do that?" she asked, not at all sorry for what she had done.

"Not wrong," he said. "Delightful. But you will drive me mad if you keep on like that. I need to be in control of myself, Danise. I don't want to hurt or frighten you."

"You would never hurt me. Your very words prove you would not. Even large as you are, you will have a care for me and be gentle."

"You do know, don't you, that the first time, just for a minute—?"

"I know. I have been told." She stopped his words with a finger at his lips. "I thought, when the time came, I would be afraid, but I am not. You have eased my concern. That first moment you spoke of is simply a part of our coming together, and since I want to be one with you, how could I fear it?" They were still kneeling, facing each other. Danise put a hand on each of Michel's shoulders and edged closer to him.

"May I kiss you again, on the lips this time?" she whispered. "I do like to kiss you, Michel."

"You are the most amazing woman." He put an arm around her waist, pulling her closer still. With his other hand he moved her legs apart until she was straddling his thighs and her bare breasts were rubbing against the hair on his chest. With her eyes closed and Michel's mouth on hers, she became intensely aware of the way he was holding her. She could feel the hard part of him caught between her belly and his. He loosened his hold on her and drew back a bit to watch her face as she wriggled around, not quite sure what it was she was searching for. Michel gave her time to find her own way. She knew he was observing her, knew he knew what it was she wanted. There was a hot burning between her thighs. She needed something to press against it, to ease her growing discomfort.

She found it. The tip of his hardness slid into hot wetness. Never had Danise known such a sensation. She closed her eyes more tightly and threw back her head, the better to relish this new experience. Michel's mouth seared across her throat. Every bit of her body came vibrantly alive. She pushed more firmly against his hardness, wanting more of him inside her. She felt a faint stretching sensation. Abruptly, Michel withdrew from her.

"No," she protested. "Don't go away. Come back to me."

"I couldn't leave you now." Though his movements were gentle, his voice was harsh with tension. He eased her down onto the blanket. His hands were on her thighs, separating them. He was pushing himself into her, pushing farther than he had been just a moment or two before, and she felt the stretching begin once more. He went slowly, and she helped him, she lifted herself to meet him. She wanted him inside of her, all of him deep and hot inside her, but still the stretching was uncomfortable. Just when it threatened to become outright pain her body gave way and accommodated him so that he was buried in her.

At that very instant there was an explosion of thunder above them so loud and terrifying that Danise cried out and jumped, wrapping her arms around Michel and holding on tight to him. She heard his gasp and then his low laugh in her ear.

"That was for dramatic effect," he whispered, kissing her. "Are you all right?"

"How can you speak? How can you think? I can only—only—oh, Michel, what are you doing?"

"Loving you." He was moving inside her, carrying her to a state of ecstasy beyond anything she had ever dared to dream. And she, without thought or will of her own, was moving with him, wanting everything he cared to give her, moaning and calling out his name until his mouth silenced her wild cries and she could scarcely breathe and there was nothing in the world but his strong, demanding body and her eager, receptive one.

Only gradually did she become aware once more of the drumming rain on the roof, or the rattle of thunder or, most important, Michel's form sprawled atop her. She held him in her arms, loving the weight of him, loving everything they had done together.

"If I am made yours by this," she whispered, "then you are made mine as well."

"Always and forever," he murmured.

She had not been sure he would hear her. She had thought he was asleep. He moved to one side, taking his weight off her and she regretted the loss. He reached out an arm to pull the blue cloak over them, tucking it in around her. She lay contentedly in his arms while he kissed her face and her hair and told her how wonderful she was and how happy she made him.

"It did not hurt," she whispered in answer to his concerned question. "It was beautiful."

"I'm glad." His lips brushed hers. "You are beautiful, Danise. You are all any man could ever want."

She fell asleep with his voice in her ears and the sound of the rain in the background.

Danise woke to the crash of the door swinging open at a blast of wind. Rain blew into the hut, dampening the lovers upon the floor. Michel leapt up to close and relatch the door. Danise turned her head to watch him.

As he reached the door there came a near-blinding flash of lightning. In that long, sustained burst of blue-white light, Danise saw Michel clearly outlined—and saw, superimposed upon his being, Hugo's face and form. The apparition lasted for only the blink of an eye, until the lightning was gone and darkness came again. The sight shook Danise to her very soul.

In a blaze of comprehension akin to that lightning bolt she understood the meaning of what she had seen. Michel was not Hugo; they were two very different men, but some portion of Hugo's spirit dwelt in Michel. It was what had drawn her to him, the reason she had been unable to resist Michel since their first meeting. It was also the reason for Michel's immediate and unwavering desire for her.

It was beyond understanding. Still, Danise was certain that Hugo's boundless love for her had survived the centuries and had found a way to join with her so that, in Michel, she could discover the happiness she had for so many long, lonely months believed must be denied to her because of Hugo's death.

Very little time had passed since Michel had risen to close the door. He lay down beside her again. At some time in the future she would tell him about her astounding discovery. But not now, not just yet. For this moment it was enough that she loved him and was certain of his love. She opened her arms to him and drew him closer, holding him while he rested his head on her bosom and drifted into sleep once more.

"My love," she whispered softly, her heart filled to overflowing with peace and joy. "My dear, dear love."

Chapter 11

Danise wakened to a morning of dazzling sunshine, to tree leaves glittering with the last, lingering droplets left by the previous night's storm. The air was cool and dry, the breeze gentle. Clad only in Michel's linen undershirt and his blue cloak, she stood in the door of the hut, looking out upon the sparkling day and recalling the events of the night. All of those events.

The slight tenderness between her thighs reminded her of the momentous change in her body, and the man who lay still sleeping within the hut provided proof of that other amazing discovery of her mind and heart. In loving Michel, she did not have to forsake Hugo's memory or be disloyal to him. In the one man, she could love both. A smile curved her lips, happiness filled her being.

Michel stirred, stretching, and turned over. A tiny spot of blood upon the blanket next to him was evidence of their first joining. A second loving, near dawn, had caused Danise only the faintest twinge before passion overtook her. Michel had promised her that never again would there be discomfort. Henceforth, only pleasure would attend their lovemaking.

He was looking at her, his eyes shining with love. Danise went to him and knelt, holding out her arms with the cloak caught in her hands. When she dropped over him, his arms went around her and the cloak covered both of them.

"What a way to wake up," he said, laughing.

"I do perceive that you are entirely roused from sleep and eager for the morning's first activity," she murmured.

"I am, but I'm going to restrain myself. After last night you ought to be sore and I don't want to make matters worse for you."

"You are much too considerate."

"Don't complain or I'll forget my good intentions," he teased. Then, sobering, he asked, "I hope you have no regrets about what we did?"

"I am too happy for regrets."

"So am I. You are the woman I have wanted all my life and never found until now."

"I know it. And you are the man for me. The only man."

He looked a little puzzled by her words, but he did not mention Hugo. She was glad of his silence. She wanted more time to consider her new knowledge before she tried to explain it to him.

"Will we be able to reach Duren today?" she asked. "It is our duty to warn Charles as soon as we can about the scheme Clodion and Autichar have devised."

"Not to mention relieving your father's mind about your safety," he added. "Or discovering what has happened to Redmond and Guntram and the rest of the men. We ought to leave here at once, but I hate to go. I will always think of this as a special place." His arms tightened around her briefly, before he released her.

"There is just one problem," Michel confessed later, after they were finished eating and dressing. "I'm not sure exactly where we are. So, let's follow the stream and hope it spills into the Rur. If it does, we can use the river to guide us back to Duren."

"How clever of you," she said, and added, smiling at him, "I would have suggested the same course myself."

"Imp." He was laughing when he lifted her onto his horse. "I'll have you know I learned that bit of wilderness lore in the Boy Scouts." Seeing her raised eyebrows, he laughed again. Mounting the horse, he took up the reins and put a steadying arm around Danise. "I'll tell you all about the Boy Scouts some day," he promised.

"There are surprising things for me to tell you, too," she murmured.

"I look forward to it." He paused to kiss her

before urging his horse away from the charcoal makers' settlement.

With a well-rested mount and weather that made action a delight instead of an overheated trial, they made good time, reaching Duren shortly after midday. Michel rode past the sentries, right through the camp, and up to the royal tents. Their passage created an outcry of relief and curiosity, so that by the time Michel let Danise down into Savarec's waiting arms, the open space at the center of the Frankish camp was filled with people.

"My little girl, my dear daughter," Savarec cried, embracing Danise over and over.

"In the name of heaven, Savarec," said Sister Gertrude, "let the girl catch her breath before she faints from lack of air."

"Michel." Charles drew him aside. "Where are the others who were with you?"

"Redmond ordered me to carry Danise to safety," Michel said. "I thought it best to obey him. I left him and the other men in combat with Autichar, who I believe had less than a dozen warriors to Redmond's twenty or so. I would expect them to arrive with their prisoners before this day's end. We agreed they would try to keep Autichar alive so he can talk to you, but Danise was clever enough to coax much of Autichar's plan from him, and she'll be happy to tell you about it."

"Then I will see both of you in private at once. It would be well for me to have as much information as I can before I meet Autichar." Raising his voice to be heard over the excited conversation of the Franks, Charles called out, "Savarec, will you bring your daughter and join me in my tent?"

"After such an ordeal, Danise needs to rest," Sister Gertrude objected. Charles fixed her with a wise and knowing eye.

"You may come with us," he said, "so Danise will need to tell the tale but once. Alcuin, you come, too." He led the way into his tent, Alcuin close behind him, Savarec following with a protective arm around Danise. When Michel would have gone with them, Sister Gertrude stopped him, placing a hand on his shoulder.

"Is she truly unharmed?" the nun asked. "I want to have the right words prepared to say to her if Clodion—if he—"

"Save for the abduction itself, Clodion did not hurt her. Nor did Autichar." Michel's eyes were on Danise's back as her father escorted her into the royal tent.

"And you?" Sister Gertrude's voice was sharper than usual. She moved in front of Michel, thus forcing him to take his gaze from Danise and look at her. Sister Gertrude regarded him in silence for a while, her expression gradually changing to one of disgust. When she spoke again her voice matched her face. "So, after all, you are like every other man."

"I love her with all my heart," he said. "It's as though I have loved her since the beginning of time."

"Which is what every man says to an innocent young woman when he is at the promising stage. Later, he forgets those promises and leaves her, as you will do."

"I did not force her," he said, beginning to be angry, "and I will not leave her." He would have added that what he and Danise did in private was none of her business. Sister Gertrude did not give him the chance. She turned her back on him and stalked into Charles's tent. Michel could only follow.

While Savarec interrupted frequently with exclamations of rage and dire threats against Clodion and Autichar, Charles listened in ominous silence to Danise's story and to Michel's report of the search for Danise and how they had found her.

"I do not know which angers me more," Charles said when the tale was finished, "the treachery of a man I trusted for years, or the use of a maiden as a pawn in the plot. Danise, I commend your courage. Michel, I thank you, as I am sure Savarec also does, for your part in rescuing Danise. I do promise, you will be well rewarded for what you have done."

"I didn't do it for reward," Michel said. "I did it for Danise. And for Savarec, who has been my friend since my first day at Duren."

Sister Gertrude greeted these remarks with a derisive snort, and for a moment Michel feared she would announce that he had proven himself no true friend to Savarec when he made love to Savarec's innocent daughter. It was Alcuin who prevented Sister Gertrude from saying anything.

"It seems to me that Danise is weary and would like to rest," Alcuin said. "Perhaps our good Sister Gertrude would carry these happy tidings to Hildegarde. Later, Danise may wait upon the queen to recount her adventures."

"An excellent idea," said Charles, whose sharp eyes did not miss the way Sister Gertrude was looking at Michel. "Sister Gertrude, you are the one person who could speak to Hildegarde without overly distressing her for Danise's sake."

"I will go to her at once." Sister Gertrude rose, adding in a stern voice, "I will speak to you later, Danise. You will find Clothilde at our tent, where she is doing the laundry."

Scarcely had Sister Gertrude left Charles's tent for the queen's tent next to it, than there began a fresh noise of cheering and happy shouts of welcome. Those in Charles's tent stepped outside to see what had caused the noise just as Redmond and the men he commanded arrived. Riding proudly by Redmond's side was Guntram. In the middle of the company, surrounded by guards, was Autichar, his hands bound behind him, his feet fastened together by a rope drawn beneath his horse's belly. His fanciful metal helmet was gone, but the red cloak still lay about his shoulders and his head was held high.

"I am mightily sorry to see you in such condition," Charles said to him. "That a fine warrior like you should be brought to shame distresses me."

"I have done nothing wrong," Autichar replied.

Danise thought he must have seen her standing behind Charles, and known that she would tell Charles all she could about his plans, but Autichar gave no sign that he recognized her.

"Put him in a tent as distant from Clodion's as you can," Charles said to Redmond. "Let there be no message carried between them. Allow him no visitors. Keep Autichar well guarded, so he cannot escape. On the morrow, I will hear the case against him and his friend, Clodion."

"Come, Danise," said Savarec. "Come to our tents. Let me talk quietly with you. Assure me that you are indeed unharmed."

"Thanks to Michel, I am," she said. "Thanks to Redmond and Guntram, too, and all the others who searched for me."

"To think that I could have been such a fool," Savarec cried, "that I believed Lady Ingeborg. Ah, Danise, your father is not worthy of you."

"It was not your fault," she said, hugging him. "They are wicked schemers all, and you are an honest man. They took advantage of your trust."

It took her quite a while to calm him down, to convince him she was unhurt by her experience, and by then Redmond had claimed Michel and borne him off to join the other young men who planned to spend the rest of that day exchanging their various versions of recent events while they celebrated the successful conclusion of the battle with Autichar. Saying he wanted personally to thank Michel, Savarec finally left Danise alone in the tent she shared with Sister Gertrude and Clothilde.

"Come down to the river," said Clothilde, looking in at her. "I have kept two buckets of clean hot water after the laundry was done, and there is a bowl of fresh soap. I am going to scrub you clean, Danise, and then I am going to put you to bed. After such an ordeal, you will want to rest."

"Not at all," said Danise. "Why does everyone expect me to want to sleep? But I would like a bath and fresh clothes."

Clothilde's reaction to her discovery that Danise was wearing a man's undershirt was almost comical.

"We were drenched in the rain," Danise explained. "Michel had an extra shirt and it was dry." She did not add that she had used her own shift to wash herself on the morning after she and Michel first made love, or that she had left the shift behind because in the cold stream she could not get it entirely clean of the blood then staining it.

"Of course," said Clothilde, blandly ignoring the fact that in order to put on a dry undershirt, Danise would have to remove her dress. "Anyone would do the same. I will just wash the shirt and give it back to Michel when it is dry. And I won't say a word about this to Sister Gertrude." When Danise did not respond to her provocative comment, Clothilde said with a sly smile, "If ever I needed to be rescued when I was a younger woman, I would have wanted it to be done by a fine, strong man like Michel. He likes you, Danise. I have seen him looking at you. If you want to meet him later, I can distract Sister Gertrude's attention."

"You ought to be ashamed of yourself." Danise was not scolding her servant. As she said the words, she returned Clothilde's smile.

"I am not the least bit ashamed of what I am thinking," Clothilde declared, "nor should you be. I am not so old that I cannot recall what it was to be young. A man like Michel will make you happy."

Danise smiled again and said nothing more. Nor, later, did she answer Sister Gertrude's persistent questions. But she was grateful when Clothilde drew the nun aside to voice her concerns over Savarec's health and ask Sister Gertrude's advice on whether he ought to have some medicine to calm him after so much excitement and worry. Danise had by this time reached a point where she did not want to make explanations or relive her frightening abduction. What she wanted as evening drew on, was to find Michel and go into his arms and be held by him. But there was no sign of Michel. He was still with his male friends.

Danise was wanted for a similar occasion among the women. She was obliged to pay a visit to the queen. Hildegarde was a kind lady, so though she made it clear to Danise that she had been deeply concerned for her safe return, she did not press Danise for every detail. Some of the women in attendance on the queen were not so polite. Before long Danise was heartily sick of pretending to answer probing questions while not actually saying much at all. Finally, pleading a headache, she asked Hildegarde for and received her release from the queen's tent. Once outside it, Danise made her way to the riverbank, there to sit beneath the great oak tree in undisturbed peace at last.

"I thought I'd find you here." Michel dropped down beside her. "If it were still daylight, I'd have gone to that place in the forest, but I was pretty sure you wouldn't be allowed to go anywhere very far from the camp without a guard of some kind." His hand found and held hers.

"I am so weary of people asking me if I am truly unhurt," Danise said, "or if I want to rest."

"I know. I faced a barrage of questions, too. I guess it's to be expected, after what happened." He paused, then spoke again. "Sister Gertrude knows we made love. She guessed."

"I thought as much, from the questions she asked me. Which I did not answer." Danise sighed. "I will have to tell Redmond that I cannot think of marrying him. It would be unfair to let him go on believing that I am still considering his suit when all I can think of is you. We must also tell my father. He deserves an explanation."

"Let's wait until Charles decides what to do with Clodion and Autichar," Michel suggested. "Tomorrow's trial is what is first on everyone's mind just now."

"Very well," Danise agreed, glad to have an excuse to postpone telling her father or Redmond truths they would not be happy to hear. "After tomorrow, then."

"Those two traitors aren't the only ones who can make clever plans," Michel confided. "I have a few schemes of my own to try."

"I do hope one of them includes devising a way for us to escape the fond concerns of relatives and friends," she murmured.

"You can be sure of it. For the moment, I think I ought to deliver you to your tent and say a proper good night." He stood and offered a hand to help her rise. Before Danise knew what was happening, she was locked in his arms and his mouth was on hers. She knew then that just as she had been yearning to embrace him, so he had wanted to hold her during the hours when they were apart. She let herself dissolve into the sweetness of his kiss.

"That's all I dare to steal tonight," he whispered. "But soon, I promise you, we will be together again. Even Sister Gertrude won't be able to stop us."

From Sister Gertrude's attitude when Michel said his proper good night at her tent entrance, Danise thought the nun's future goal in life might well be to keep the lovers sternly separated. But Danise had her own private reasons for believing that nothing could keep her apart from Michel for long. He had been sent to her across the centuries. He would not be taken from her now.

At mid-morning Charles took his seat on a foot-high wooden dais built just outside the entrance to his tent. Ordinarily, he moved among his nobles without any special designation of his royal state, and when he sat it was in a chair placed at ground level just like everyone else's chair. On those daily occasions only his strong character and the respect in which he was held indicated that he was the elected king of the Franks. On this particular day Charles knew that all those assembled at Duren would want to see him clearly so they could observe for themselves how their king would dispense justice to the accused men. Thus, he ordered the construction of the dais on which he would sit elevated above the others who attended, with only a few of his closest advisers standing around him.

That this would be a momentous morning no one present could doubt, and no one, including the queen, wanted to miss the excitement. Ignoring her unwell condition, Hildegarde insisted on joining her husband on the dais, saying it was her duty to be in her rightful place beside him. Alcuin was there, too, standing on the dais behind Charles and next to Charles's uncle, Duke Bernard. At Charles's command Savarec, along with all of the men who had taken part in the search for Danise, were given places close to the dais. Off to one side Adelbert and a second clerk sat at a table, inkpots and quill pens at the ready, prepared to record the proceedings and Charles's decisions.

When everyone was in place, Autichar and Clodion were brought forth from the tents where they had been held. Blinking in the bright sunshine they were marched to low stools set facing the dais and far enough apart from each other to keep the two from conversing without their words being overheard. Lastly, Lady Ingeborg arrived in the custody of Sister Gertrude and was given her own stool.

"Danise," Charles said as soon as all was in readiness, "I will have you speak first. When you have finished, stand here beside Hildegarde, where you can hear all that is said, and where I can ask further questions of you if it proves necessary. Do not be nervous, just tell us what was done to you."

Danise stepped into the open space before the dais and began to speak.

"I thank you for your concern for me," she said to Charles. "I am not at all nervous, for what I have to say is but the truth. However, I *am* angry, for my father was greatly worried by my abduction, and his friends and mine were put to immense effort to find and rescue me. Most of all, I am outraged that these two men seated here before you should have plotted treason against so fine a king.

"It was on the morning of the hunt that Clodion forced me to the side of the field and took my horse's reins from me. Clodion believed, and rightly, that those near to us would be so occupied with following the hunt that they would not notice what he was doing." She went on to recount everything she had seen and heard, including the plot Autichar had revealed to her, the plan to draw Charles into

238

battle with Duke Tassilo after making certain
that he would have to divide the Frankish army
in two in order to fend off a prearranged Saxon
uprising. She ended with the tale of her escape
from Autichar and how Michel, Redmond, and
Guntram had found her, rescued her from her
pursuers, then done battle with Autichar and
his men.

"Of the battle itself I will let Redmond and
his companions tell you, since I was not there
to see it," Danise said. "I have no word to say
in defense of either of the accused men, save
that Autichar did prevent Clodion from taking
me into the forest and raping me on that first
night. He and Clodion quarreled about it. I
am grateful to Autichar for that one act of
kindness."

"Danise," said Charles when she fell silent,
"I would hear the confirmation of this scheme
from your own lips once more and have everyone else present hear it also. Autichar did tell
you that his private army was camped near
the Rhine, awaiting his arrival there? And that
this army would be among those placed at my
cousin Tassilo's disposal when the time came
to fight against me and my men?"

"That is so," Danise replied.

"Again, I must applaud your courage during
this ordeal," Charles said, "and your wit in
talking Autichar into revealing his scheme."

"It was not entirely his own plan," Danise
said. "Clodion claimed credit for devising part
of it, including the way in which he would be
found. And Autichar was very ready to boast

of how easily he would destroy your Frankish warriors." This statement drew a murmur from those same Fankish warriors that boded no good for Autichar's future.

"I may want to ask you more questions later," Charles said to Danise. "For now, you may join Hildegarde on the dais."

Charles next called Savarec to tell how he had been tricked into leaving the hunt so he could not see Clodion taking Danise away. Guntram followed, to give his view of Savarec's story. Then Michel and Redmond each spoke. Several other men who had taken part in the search for Danise and in the battle with Autichar also gave their evidence.

"I do thank you all," Charles said. "Has anyone else aught to say against these men or Lady Ingeborg in this matter before I give the accused leave to defend themselves?"

Again there were a few angry murmurs and fierce looks cast at Clodion and Autichar, but no one else came forward.

"Very well," Charles went on. "Lady Ingeborg, since the charge against you is of lesser importance, I will have you speak for yourself first."

Lady Ingeborg rose from her stool and stepped forward. On this day she was clothed in a loose gown of dark blue. She wore no jewelry, her face was unpainted, and her hair was gathered into a simple knot atop her head. She looked frightened as she took her position before Charles.

"I do swear to you, Charles, that I did not know of Clodion's connection with Autichar,"

Lady Ingeborg declared. "Had I known of it, I would have gone to you at once and told you of it. Clodion led me to believe that he and Danise wished to spend a day alone, without interference from Savarec or Sister Gertrude. That is why I invited Savarec to my tent at Clodion's suggestion. As to putting sleeping herbs in Savarec's wine—I did not wish to lie with him, but only to keep him occupied for a time, as a favor to my old friend Clodion. It appears now that Clodion was not my true friend. He tricked me, as he has apparently tricked everyone else he knew." Sniffling and dabbing at her eyes, Lady Ingeborg stepped aside at Charles's command and resumed her place on the stool set next to Sister Gertrude. The nun regarded her with an expression that plainly said she did not believe a word of Lady Ingeborg's story.

"Clodion," Charles invited, "have you anything to say in your defense?"

"It is all lies," Clodion declared, standing and strutting boldly forward, "a scheme concocted by that foolish girl, Danise. She agreed to spend a day with me while I courted her, for we could find no time when we were not interrupted by Count Redmond or that foreign scoundrel, Michel. How can a man convince a girl to marry him when he cannot have two words alone with her? Perhaps something I said in the forest offended Danise. You know how skittish girls can be. I do not know her reasoning, but Danise changed her mind, said she would never marry me, and then, after we were captured

241

by Autichar, she devised this scandalous tale linking me to that criminal. For all I know, Danise is in league with Autichar to bring me down and ruin my reputation. You will remember, Charles, that Autichar was one of her original suitors. Perhaps she had favored him all along without my knowing it."

"This is an amazing tale you tell." Charles's voice was silky smooth. "And you yourself laid no scheme against me?"

"I have been your loyal servant during the eleven years of your reign," Clodion answered. "Before that, I was your father Pepin's friend as well."

"I do not forget it," Charles said. "You may sit down, Clodion. Autichar, what have you to tell us?"

"Unlike these other cowards, Ingeborg and Clodion," Autichar announced, rising in his turn and taking his place before Charles, "I will not place the blame on anyone else, nor claim a mere girl has misled me. The scheme was mine in its origin. Save for one or two minor details conceived by Clodion, the plan was all my doing."

"I am glad to hear you don't deny it," Charles said, admiration for Autichar's courage creeping into his voice, though Danise could tell he was very angry.

"Why should I deny it? I am proud of it," Autichar responded. "I do admit it was foolish of me to reveal so much of the plan to Danise. Boasting was ever a fault of mine. Still, I believed at the time that she would not live to tell what she knew. I misjudged her. She was—and is—braver and more resourceful than I realized."

"Then you have nothing to say in your own defense?" Charles prompted.

"What I did, I did because I was angry with you for sending me away from Duren," Autichar said. "You wounded my pride, Charles. But my first loyalty is always to Duke Tassilo, whose pride you have also tried to humble."

"I do wonder," mused Charles, "just how much of this scheme was made known to Tassilo?"

"He knew enough of it," cried Clodion from where he sat, "to offer me a Bavarian heiress for a bride as reward for my part in it." At these impetuous words, Charles looked toward Clodion and seemed to be repressing a smile. Clodion did not appear to notice that he had just betrayed himself.

"I remind you, Count Clodion," said Alcuin from his place behind Charles's chair, "that you have had your time to speak. You may not interrupt now."

"Autichar," asked Charles, "have you anything more to say?"

"Only to thank Danise for her words of appreciation to me," Autichar said, looking at her. "Girl, I am glad I did not let Clodion have you. You deserve a better man than he is. My only regret regarding you is that you did not choose me as your husband. I would have greatly enjoyed getting sons on so brave a woman. For the rest, Charles, I make no

243

defense of what I did. None is necessary. I did what I felt was needed to show you that a nobleman cannot be treated as you treated me." Autichar's red hair blazed in the sunlight as he proudly raised his chin and looked challengingly at Charles.

"I do remember," Charles said mildly, "that the decision to leave this Mayfield was yours. You were not sent away."

Autichar made no answer to that. Charles signaled to him to take his seat again.

The king of the Franks sat for a few minutes, chin in hand, considering all he had heard, both before and during that morning. Then he beckoned to Alcuin, and when the cleric bent his head to his king, the two conferred. Alcuin nodded once or twice at something Charles said. A smile crossed Charles's face and faded away. Charles lifted a finger and Duke Bernard leaned down on his other side to answer a question.

Meanwhile, the Franks waited to hear their king's judgment. Some of the men talked among themselves, expressing their anger that anyone would defy Charles as Autichar had done. Others voiced concern that their own daughters might be treated as Clodion had treated Danise if he were not severely punished as an example.

"These are my decisions," Charles announced in a loud voice, and all fell silent to hear him.

"First," Charles said, "I make Count Redmond my deputy to Autichar's army which, as I understand the case, is still encamped near the Rhine awaiting Autichar's arrival. Redmond, you are to disperse that army. The men belonging to it may freely return to Bavaria if they wish. If so, you will escort them to the border, making certain they arrive there without injury to themselves or to any Franks they meet along their way. Some of the men may not be Bavarians, and they are welcome to come to me and place themselves under my direct command.

"Secondly, I will put a stop here and now to the raising of private armies, whose purpose is not to make the Franks stronger, but to increase the power of the owners of those armies. Henceforth, no nobleman may maintain a fighting force larger than the number of men he is required to send to me for my use in time of war. Write it down, Adelbert. This is a new law. Every nobleman in Francia is to receive a formal notice of it within a week.

"Autichar," Charles went on, "it seems to me that you are the person most at fault in all these plottings, for you intended to use your army against your chosen king. For that disloyalty, the lands you hold in Francia that caused you to divide your interests between Tassilo and me are forfeited to the Frankish crown.

"You dangled a captive Danise before me and my friends, hoping thus to lure us to our deaths for her sake. But we are wise fish and will not take the bait. I will send no army against my cousin Tassilo. What I will do is send you, Autichar, in chains and accompanied by an emissary from me who will

tell the entire sorry tale to Tassilo. I believe my
Uncle Bernard, who is also related to Tassilo,
will be the perfect man to send. Uncle Bernard
can assure Tassilo that I believe he had nothing
to do with your schemes, and that Tassilo can
prove his good faith by punishing you as you
ought to be punished."

There were loud cries of approval at this
decision, though a few did voice their disappointment that Autichar was not to be publicly
executed at once.

"Wonderful!" Redmond said to Michel.
"What a joke on Tassilo, to lay upon him
the burden of punishing his own man. Charles
knows that Tassilo is not innocent in all of
this, but he's too wise to say so publicly and
thus provoke the war Autichar and Tassilo
wanted."

"Listen," Michel replied. "He's about to pass
judgment on Clodion."

"Count Clodion," Charles said, "you are
hereby banished from my presence and
stripped of all your titles and all your lands
save for the smallest of your many estates,
the land you hold west of Mainz, safely within
Frankish borders. That one place I allow you to
keep in recognition of your years of service to
me and to my father. In it you are to live in the
company of your current concubines and all of
your children, who are also to be confined on
that estate for as long as you live."

"Hah!" exclaimed Guntram, openly delighted
by this decision. "I've heard stories about some
of Clodion's brats. They are said to be much like

their father. One or another of them will likely put herbs in the old man's wine to send him permanently to sleep, just so the children can get free of living with him and his endless lust."

"Lady Ingeborg," said Charles, "you deserve a milder form of justice for your part in drugging Savarec. As you know, my mother is living in retirement at the convent at Prum. You will join her there, to live under her instruction for the rest of your life—and may it be a long and healthy life. I strongly suggest that you donate all the lands you inherited from your late husband to Prum, to assure your good treatment there."

Now it was Michel's turn to laugh. He knew about Charles's formidable mother, Queen Bertha, whom Charles had sent to live at Prum when she tried once too often to dominate him. Lady Ingeborg would have no easy time living under Bertha's rule.

"What think you of these rulings?" asked Redmond, half choked with laughter.

"I think the king of the Franks is a genius at punishing criminals while appearing to show mercy to them," Michel answered. "He lets others do the real punishing for him. Savarec looks happy."

"So he should," Redmond said. "With everyone laughing at the punishments meted out to Clodion and Lady Ingeborg, Savarec does not look as foolish as he otherwise might."

"There is still more business to be attended to this day," Charles said, raising a hand to quiet the laughing, cheering Franks. "I must now decide what to do with the lands that until an hour ago belonged to Clodion and Autichar. Redmond, come forward. I give to you Autichar's former Frankish lands. Guard them well."

"For this gift I thank you." Redmond went down on his knees, placed his hands between Charles's and swore an oath of loyalty to his king for these new lands.

"Guntram," said Charles, "you also deserve a reward. One of Clodion's former estates is near to Savarec's lands just east of the Rhine. Its location will make it possible for you to continue your valuable service to Savarec, and to me, at Deutz. This land I give to you." He named the estate and Guntram went forward to fall on his knees and speak his oath. Guntram's fierce, black-bearded face shone with joy and pride. Michel saw Danise wiping away a happy tear as she watched her father's loyal man being so handsomely rewarded.

Charles then made several other awards, disposing of Clodion's lands to men who had helped in the search for Danise or who had performed valiantly in the battle with Autichar. A few of those men had been wounded, but none seriously. Only one had to be helped forward by a friend.

"Savarec," said Charles, "I'll add to your holdings a piece of land west of the Rhine, in recompense for what you have suffered over the abduction of your daughter, and in case you occasionally wish for a rest from dealing with Saxons."

"Now there is but one portion of Clodion's lands left, the estate of Elhein," Charles went on after Savarec had made his formal oath for his new lands. "Michel, come here. You came to Duren a stranger, with no memory of your past. In only a few weeks you have proven your worth to us. In reward for your service to me and to Savarec, I give you this land that once was Clodion's."

"Sir, I thank you," Michel responded. "But I cannot accept the gift."

The entire company fell instantly silent. No one had ever before refused a gift offered by a king. Michel knew he was taking a risk, because what he said might so insult Charles that the king would not forgive him. It was a chance Michel had to take. He had a greater prize by far in mind.

"There is only one reward I want," he said to Charles. "The sweetest gift in all the world. I would have the hand of the lady Danise in marriage. I love her as you love Hildegarde. I cannot be happy with any other woman."

Now people gasped, and whispered to each other. Michel's attention was on Charles, and on Hildegarde, who had not spoken during all the long proceedings, though she had listened with open sympathy while Danise told her story of abduction and fear. Michel saw Hildegarde look from him to Danise. He saw the queen lean toward Charles and whisper something. Charles's eyes began to sparkle. He smiled and nodded at Hildegarde's comments, and Michel knew he had not misjudged the royal couple.

"If you would have a wife," Charles said to Michel, "then you will need to provide a home for her. Therefore, I will link lady and lands together. Win Danise, and you also win the rich estate of Elhein. What say you to that?"

"I thank you for your generosity," Michel said, "and for your understanding."

"I know what it is to love well and truly," Charles said. "Savarec, have you any objection to this arrangement?"

"Michel has no title," Savarec said, stepping forward, "and I hoped once to wed my daughter to a count. Nor do we know aught of Michel's family. Still, Sister Gertrude has pointed out to me many times that Clodion and Autichar were not good choices as sons-in-law, though I knew all about their ancestors and both of them were counts.

"Charles, I have learned a valuable lesson from these last few days. I have been too easily dazzled by a man's earthly possessions and by high-sounding titles. The worth of a man ought to be judged by other standards."

"Then you have learned wisdom," said Charles.

"You are too harsh with yourself, Savarec," Michel told him. "In spite of my lack of name, title, or wealth, you have always been a friend to me."

"By your recent actions, Michel, you have proven your loyalty to Charles, and to me, and your devotion to Danise. I cannot in friendship refuse what you ask, nor do I want to refuse you. However, when we first came

250

to Duren I gave the choice of her husband to Danise," Savarec now reminded them. "She must decide, not I."

"Danise." Michel looked at her, seeing love and hope in her eyes. "I did not plan to ask you before so many witnesses, but will you marry me?"

"Yes," Danise cried. "Oh, yes. I never want to be parted from you. Michel, I am so proud of you, and so happy." With that, she fairly flew off the dais and into his arms. The assembled Franks cheered her on and Hildegarde burst into delighted laughter.

"You see," Hildegarde said to Charles, "I was right." Charles took his wife's hand and pressed it to his lips.

Danise and Michel barely noticed the queen's words or the king's action, for they quickly lost themselves in a tender kiss. They did not have long to revel in their private joy. Friends began to crowd about them, congratulating them, until Danise found herself separated from Michel and standing next to Redmond.

"I had planned to tell you tonight that I could not wed you," she said to him, a little embarrassed by the situation. "I am sorry if you were hurt by the way this was done. I never guessed what Michel would say to Charles."

"I believe you and I could have been content together, Danise," Redmond told her. "But if you feel Michel is the man you should wed, then let us be friends. Nor will your choice ever change my friendship with Michel."

"You have a generous heart, Redmond. I

think of you as more than a friend. To me, you are like a dear brother."

"It's not what I hoped for," Redmond said with a wry little smile, "but I'll gladly accept what you offer."

When Redmond moved on to speak to Michel, Sister Gertrude pushed her way through the throng to where Danise was standing.

"So, your choice is made," she said to Danise. "Now you will have to live with it until your last day of life."

"Do not be angry with me because I could not do what you wished for me," Danise begged. "I love Michel as much as he loves me."

"I hope you do not regret it," Sister Gertrude responded. Then, brightening, she added, "I do approve of Charles's decision about Lady Ingeborg, though I doubt if the nuns at Prum will thank him for it. At least this ordeal of a trial is over, and we can forget about Clodion and Autichar and their wicked plans."

However, as they were to learn in the course of time, they had not heard the last of Autichar or his plot.

Chapter 12

New Mexico
October 1992

"If you ask me, it was a stroke of luck having him disappear like that. Why do you want to mess everything up now?" Alice shook her head in bewilderment. "Hank Marsh, you are an idiot to do this. Just leave the guy where he is and forget about him."

"I can't do that." Hank spoke absently because he was working on the computer, checking the electrical connections, moving components around, and then calling up long mathematical equations on the screen.

"Why not?" Alice stuck her hands on her hips and glared at the back of Hank's head. "You're just asking for trouble."

"Yeah, I know." Hank cleared the screen before swinging around to face Alice. "You really don't understand, do you? O.K., I'll explain."

"First," Hank began ticking off the reasons on his fingers. "If I don't get him back, I'm as bad as any murderer, because Mike Bailey went into *my* computer, on a program *I* invented.

"Second, sending someone back in time is only half of the experiment. For me to prove beyond a doubt that my theories about the space-time continuum are correct, I have to be able to bring the object or the person back to this time and this place in one piece and in good health."

"What happens if what you get back isn't a person any more, but just a lump of bleeding protoplasm?" Alice demanded. "How would you dispose of it? Send it back in time again? Or into outer space? And what are you going to tell the authorities if someone finds out what you've done?"

"That's reason number three," Hank told her. "This Bailey guy is not some unimportant nobody. If half of what he said is true, there are important people who know he has been looking for me. I bet he told somebody he was coming here today. Where do you think that leaves me if I can't get him back?

"Fourth, and most important of all," Hank said, "if I want to call myself a scientist, and I do, then I have a moral obligation to make certain that no one gets hurt because of my theories and my experiments."

"I never would have picked you to have a conscience," Alice said.

"You don't know much about me," Hank replied. "You know, India Baldwin told me once that I didn't have any right to fool around with time and space, and I'm beginning to think she may have had a point. Every time I try this experiment, something goes wrong. Maybe I've been breaking some cosmic law I don't even know about."

"You're going soft," Alice said. "I warned you about hiking in the desert every morning at sunrise. Or maybe it's just too much Mexican food that's interfering with your mind."

"Call it whatever you want," Hank said, "but I am going to do my damnedest to bring Mike Bailey back here in one piece. Wherever—or whenever—he is, he doesn't belong there. He belongs here."

Chapter 13

With Clodion sent off under heavy guard to his one remaining estate, Redmond preparing to leave on the morrow to deal with Autichar's army, and Autichar himself about to return to Bavaria to face Duke Tassilo, Michel assumed that the rest of the Franks would spend the remainder of that last day of Mayfield packing up their belongings. Many of them did, but a few had other duties to see to before taking leave of Duren.

"We cannot in good conscience linger much longer," Charles said to Michel and Savarec. "We have already been at Duren days beyond the time we originally intended to spend here, and because there are so many of us, we have eaten most of the food available in the area. It would be unfair to the good folk of Duren for us to stay until a suitable and dignified wedding feast for Danise and Michel can be arranged."

"I have no desire for an elaborate celebration," Michel said. "A simple wedding will do." He thought he saw Savarec breathe a sigh of relief at hearing he would not be expected to provide a festive meal for everyone at Mayfield. Michel reflected that in his concern over the wedding feast Savarec was not much different from many a twentieth century father of a bride. The thought startled him. Michel did not often dwell on memories of his former life, which seemed to him more distant and more uninteresting with each day that passed for him in the eighth century. Now that his future with Danise was a certainty, he was perfectly content to remain in Francia.

"What we can do," Charles went on, "is hold the formal betrothal ceremony late this afternoon, just before our final meal together, the feast that ends Mayfield. If you can come to agreement on the terms of the contract, I'll have my clerics write it out for you."

"That ought to be easy enough to do," Michel said. "If anything happens to me, I want my new lands to go directly to Danise, and then to our children." Michel paused on that thought. His eyes met Savarec's. They smiled at the same time.

"I should like to see grandchildren," Savarec said.

"I will be happy to provide you with them," Michel responded. "I believe Danise and I are of one mind on the matter."

"Danise's dowry is respectable, but not large."

"I don't care. It's Danise I love, not her land or some pile of gold coins. Now, I understand from Redmond that in Francia it is customary for the bridegroom to settle a third of his possessions on his new wife."

Michel estimated that it took them less than ten minutes to come to an agreement. They shook hands on it, and Charles called in one of his secretaries, ordering the contract prepared in time to be signed and sealed before the evening meal.

"Now," Charles said to Michel, "I know you have no wish to be parted from your love, but it is necessary for you to travel at once to Clodion's former lands, to take possession of Elhein. There may be some difficulty if Clodion's relatives are unwilling to leave it. Savarec, can you spare a few of your men to go with Michel? He may need a show of force to convince the present occupants that he means business, and I want all of those confiscated lands firmly in the hands of my own good friends as soon as possible."

"Of course," Savarec agreed. "It's best if Michel puts Elhein into order before he takes Danise there."

"From what I know of Clodion," Michel said, "I'll want to have all the buildings scrubbed and fumigated before I let her set one foot in the place."

While the men conferred Danise searched for Alcuin. She found him among the clerics, directing them in writing out the account of the morning's trial.

"Several copies must be made for the royal records," he said to her. "Then, the new law Charles made today will have to be copied over and over until we have a parchment for every noble in the land. The royal messengers will be kept busy if all the copies are to be delivered within a week as Charles has ordered."

"My father says the royal messenger service is most reliable," Danise remarked. "When he is at Deutz, he receives letters and instructions from Charles every few days."

"Letters will also go out informing everyone of the land gifts made today, and of your betrothal," Alcuin said. "I was glad to see you so happy when Michel asked you to marry him. I have not forgotten how saddened you were last year by Hugo's death."

"Master Alcuin, may I speak with you about that?"

"You look troubled. Are you uncertain about your decision to marry Michel? Do you want the betrothal ceremony stopped? If so, we must speak to Charles at once. It will be difficult for you, there will be gossip and whispers, but a betrothal can be broken if you so wish it."

"I have no doubt at all about marrying Michel," Danise said. "I would like to talk with you about who, and what, he is."

"Ah, yes," murmured Alcuin. "The matter of

Michel's recovery of his memory. Has he told you about it yet?"

"He told me, but he asked me not to discuss the circumstances of his coming to Duren with anyone else. Master Alcuin, something strange has happened. I need your advice."

"Then let us walk apart to a quiet place where we can speak in private."

"That always seems to mean the forest," she said, smiling a little. "Or else the riverbank."

"Since many folk are bathing in the river today in anticipation of their homeward journeys, it will be quieter in the forest," Alcuin noted.

"I'll take you to the place where first I found Michel," Danise decided. "Perhaps we'll find some answers there."

When they reached the spot, Alcuin looked around with considerable interest.

"It seems an ordinary enough place." Gathering his black cleric's robe about him, he lowered his tall frame downward to the ground, inviting Danise to sit beside him. "Surely, we will not be disturbed here," he said.

"I must start by begging you not to judge me too harshly," Danise said. "I am forced to make a personal confession before I can begin my story, because I believe two events are deeply connected, one to the other."

"I am not an ordained priest," Alcuin warned her. "I cannot give you absolution from your sins or impose a penance on you. I can, however, promise not to reveal anything you tell me."

"I don't believe this involves a sin," Danise said. "Master Alcuin, after Michel rescued me and took me upon his horse, Redmond ordered him to remove me from the scene of the battle with Autichar."

"So much I heard from you yesterday and again in the tale told to Charles this morning," Alcuin remarked quietly, "but naught has been said of what transpired during the night when you and Michel were alone together. Is it of that time you wish to speak?"

"When it began to rain we took shelter in a charcoal maker's hut," she said, "and there we lay together. There was no wicked lust in our actions. I knew then, as I know now, that Michel loves me and I love him."

"Your confession does not shock me," Alcuin told her. "Nor does it surprise me. It is but the way of young men and women when the desire is present and the opportunity occurs. Since love is present between you, and since you are now to wed, I find no great harm in what you did."

"Neither did I, either then or now." Recalling her night with Michel, Danise looked at Alcuin with shining eyes. "It is what happened afterward that disturbs my thoughts. During the night the door of the hut blew open in the storm. Michel went to close it, and as he stood in the open doorway, there came a great flash of lightning. At that moment, I saw Hugo. He and Michel were the same person."

"It would seem to me quite natural for you to be thinking of Hugo at such a time,"

Flora Speer

Alcuin mused, "since what you never knew with Hugo, you had that very night enjoyed with Michel. Perhaps you cast your thoughts backward briefly, and in that moment you saw in your mind's eye the image of Hugo."

"No, it wasn't my imagination, or a dream," Danise cried. "Hugo was *there*, Master Alcuin! His form and his face enveloped Michel. And I *knew*, not in my thoughts but in my heart and—yes, it was so and still is—in my very soul I knew that part of Hugo, the best and dearest part of him, lives on in Michel."

Alcuin's eyes grew wide. He looked at Danise for so long a time that she began to be afraid he would speak of blasphemy or heresy. He did not, and when he spoke again his words brought comfort to her troubled thoughts.

"So strange a mystery defies mere human comprehension," Alcuin said. "I do not doubt what you have told me, Danise. It is well known that a deep and true love transcends time and place. It can even conquer death."

"When I first began to care for Michel, I felt guilty," she said. "I feared I was being disloyal to Hugo's memory. But no more. I will never forget Hugo—some part of me will always love the Hugo I once knew—but I love Michel now, and in him, Hugo also."

"Perhaps Hugo's spirit drew Michel here to Duren, to find you," Alcuin suggested.

"A love beyond time," Danise murmured, half to herself. "It would be just like Hugo to want me to be happy again. Michel said something like that soon after we met. But Hugo would not arrange; he would never insist. Hugo would simply put happiness in my path and let me stumble upon it in my own way. Master Alcuin, is it wrong for me to think like this?"

"The ways of heaven are beyond the understanding of any mortal," Alcuin replied. "Who in this land would dare to say why Michel so suddenly appeared at Duren? Or by what means?"

When Danise looked sharply at him, he raised a hand, silencing her before she could speak.

"Do not say anything more on this subject, Danise. I have my suspicions, but I think it best if they are not confirmed. If I were to learn something definite, I might then feel obligated to take action. What you and I have said here, I will never repeat. 'Tis better so."

"I understand your scruples, Master Alcuin. I will not burden you with a terrifying, an almost unbelievable, truth. I will only tell you that Michel has information about our friend, India. He says she is well and happy and has married a good man."

"I am glad to hear it. I will always remember India with affection. And you, my dear." His words and his tone of voice startled her. It was almost as though Alcuin were saying a final farewell to her. When he smiled at her, Danise shrugged off this impression and returned to her original request.

"I have not spoken to Michel of what I saw on that night. Do you think I should tell him? He did trust me with his truth. I ought to reciprocate. Master Alcuin, you are older and wiser than I, and you think more deeply than I could ever hope to do. What advice will you give me about all of this?"

Alcuin rose, and so did Danise. He took both of her hands in his and stood looking into her eyes.

"I do not find any wrongdoing in you, or in Michel in regard to your love for each other. I cannot explain what you saw or what you now believe about Hugo. As for telling Michel, do what your heart urges you to do. I do not think I have been able to help you much, Danise, and for that I am sorry."

"Your willingness to listen has helped me more than you know," she said. "I will tell Michel, when the time is right for him to hear what I have to say."

They remained as they were, standing with linked hands until Alcuin bent forward to kiss Danise upon both cheeks. Once again she had the odd feeling that he was saying farewell.

"Go in peace and be happy," he said, and released her.

After Alcuin left her to return to his work for Charles, Danise wandered slowly back toward her tent, thinking about their conversation until her meditations were suddenly interrupted.

"Where have you been?" Michel caught her around the waist, lifting her off her feet and twirling her around and around until she shrieked with laughter and commanded him to put her down. He obeyed, but only to kiss her.

"Have you heard about the betrothal?" he asked, still with his arms around her waist.

"Do you mean ours?" she responded, laughing at him. "Of course I have. I was there. Or have you forgotten my presence so quickly?"

"How could I ever forget anything about you?" His eyes crinkled in answer to her laughter. "I was talking about the formal reading of the contract and the feast. It's set for this evening. Didn't anyone tell you?"

"I have not seen my father since the trial this morning. Nor Sister Gertrude nor Clothilde, either. I was talking to Alcuin, in private." Noting his surprised expression, she said, "I'll tell you all about it soon. I promise I will. Now, what is this about a formal ceremony?"

"It's true." Clothilde came around the corner of the tent. "Danise, do you mean no one told you about your own betrothal ceremony? For shame, Michel!" But the maidservant's eyes were sparkling with mischief.

"Who told you, Clothilde?" Michel teased her. "Guntram, perhaps?"

"Did everyone at Duren know except me?" cried Danise, feigning annoyance.

"How could we tell you what Charles has decided if you were off somewhere with Master Alcuin, discussing philosophy or the motions of the wandering stars?" Clothilde demanded. "I have unpacked your best gown and it is airing now. I'll help you with your hair. Michel, do go away and let her get ready. I believe Redmond has a silk tunic for you to borrow for the ceremony."

"Clothilde," said Michel, "you have been taking lessons from Sister Gertrude in how to order people around." After stealing another kiss from Danise, he went off to find Redmond.

"I am so happy for both of you," Clothilde said. "And, have you heard? Charles has given land to Guntram, too."

"I was there when he announced it," Danise reminded her.

While the two women were inside their tent preparing Danise for the ceremony, Sister Gertrude appeared. With pursed lips and a sour expression she surveyed Danise's deep green silk gown and the gold jewelry that had once belonged to Danise's mother. As custom required for this ceremony, Danise's hair was left loose. Clothilde brushed it until it flowed in a pale silver-gold river over her shoulders and down her back almost to her knees. Danise's eyes were wide, and whether from excitement or from the reflection of her gown, they appeared more green than gray.

"Doesn't she look lovely?" cried Clothilde. "Oh, I must hurry and put on my own best dress."

"Hummph," said Sister Gertrude, frowning.

"Can't you be glad for me?" Danise begged. "You are still my friend and teacher. I do not love you less because I will marry Michel."

"Under the circumstances, it is probably best that you do wed him," Sister Gertrude conceded. "I only hope your decision does not prove to be a mistake."

"I am sure it is not," Danise said. "Dear Sister Gertrude, travel to Deutz with us."

"Of course I will," the nun responded. "It is my duty to stay with you until you are married. After that, you won't need me anymore."

"I will always need your friendship, and your love," Danise said.

"If ever you come to grief, if you need a refuge, you know you will find it at Chelles as you did once before. You will always be welcome there."

A chill touched Danise's heart, making her fearful for a moment. She recovered quickly, telling herself it was only a memory from the previous unhappy year. Her grief was over now, and only happiness lay ahead.

"Thank you for your kind words," she said, daring to hug Sister Gertrude. "Certainly, I will visit you at Chelles, but it will be a time of joy, not of sorrow. Michel and I will carry each of our children to Chelles for your blessing. Clothilde, are you ready? I hear my father talking to Guntram. Hurry now, don't make me late for my own betrothal."

The late afternoon light was gold and green, the tree leaves glowing in clear, rain-washed air and bright sunshine. Beside the Frankish encampment the Rur flowed deep blue on its way to join the River Maas and then the Rhine.

Hand-in-hand with her father, with Clothilde

and Sister Gertrude behind her, Danise walked from Savarec's tents to the dais that had been used earlier in the day for a less joyful purpose. As she stepped upon the dais she was met by Hildegarde and her ladies. Charles already stood upon the dais with his special chaplain and Alcuin. Just as Danise arrived, Michel also appeared. Redmond and Guntram were his companions.

Danise caught her breath at the sight of the man she loved. The tunic lent to him by Redmond was of blue silk almost as brilliant as his eyes. She recognized the gilded leather belt he wore. It belonged to Savarec. She cared not that he came to her in borrowed finery. Michel had proven himself, he was a noble of Francia now, a friend of Charles and of many other nobles. Soon he would have his own tunics and belts and a sword forged for him alone.

The happiness radiating from Danise on that afternoon did not depend upon promises of rich garments or accoutrements, nor upon rewards expected in the future. Her joy was born of love. She saw her own happiness reflected in Michel's face. He took her hand and held it while Alcuin read out the betrothal contract. He held it still when Charles's chaplain blessed their betrothal and urged them to keep themselves pure until they were properly wed.

Since the contract Michel and Savarec had made was brief, the entire ceremony took only a few moments. Then Charles swept her into his bear hug of an embrace to wish her happiness and long life. Her father was next to kiss her, followed by Sister Gertrude, Clothilde, Redmond, and Guntram. A host of others crowded about Danise.

"Am I never to be allowed to kiss her?" asked Michel, himself the recipient of many embraces, especially from the ladies.

"Time enough for that, later," Charles laughed, slapping him on the back. "You heard the chaplain, my friend."

But Michel took Danise by the shoulders and bestowed such a lengthy kiss on her ready lips that their friends began to laugh at them. The newly betrothed couple sat together at the feast that followed, secretly holding hands beneath the table.

"It was a bit like a wedding ceremony," Michel said, giving Danise a passionate look that made her grow so warm she feared she must be blushing. "The only thing I didn't like was that line about keeping ourselves pure. After the other night, you and I are going to be together again as soon as possible."

"I wish it could be so, but do not imagine for a moment that Sister Gertrude or even Clothilde will allow me to be with you without a chaperon until we are truly and finally wed," she informed him. "Nor my father, either."

The final feast at Duren was scarcely over before Michel's friends led him away to a tent shared by several unmarried men, where they planned to continue their private celebrations. Even Savarec and Guntram went with them.

"You see," noted Sister Gertrude, openly annoyed, "this is the way of men. At heart they care little for women."

"Not true," cried Hildegarde. "They are but saying farewell to each other in their own way. Charles will join them in a little while. Let Michel go, Danise, and don't be jealous of the friends he has made. Michel will not see most of them again until next Mayfield, and soon he will be entirely yours."

By the look on Sister Gertrude's face, Danise knew she was not pacified by the queen's comments. However, there was little time left for discussion of the matter. Charles had announced that he intended to be gone from Duren at dawn, which meant the women would have to make haste to say their own farewells. Danise embraced Hildegarde with some misgiving. The queen did not look well enough to make even the short journey to Aachen, but she would not admit to ill health. For Hildegarde, her place must always be at her husband's side, and she would not complain that Charles wanted her there.

"Charles has decided that after the autumn hunting season is over we will move to Worms for the winter," Hildegarde said to Danise. "Savarec has been summoned to the winter council meeting there. If you and Michel would like to travel with him, you would be most welcome among my ladies. And, Sister Gertrude, I am always glad to see you."

"Poor lady," Sister Gertrude muttered to Danise as they returned to their own tents. "You see what happens when a man loves his wife too well and will not keep himself from her bed. Hildegarde will not cease to have children until Charles's devotion kills her. Do not allow the same thing to happen to you, Danise."

While not unaware of the dangers inherent in childbearing, Danise privately thought it would be wonderful to give Michel several children. And the getting of them would be a joy. She spent a busy hour helping Clothilde and Sister Gertrude pack clothes and other belongings into the wooden chests in which they would be transported to Deutz, but though her fingers were nimble in her task and she answered the questions and comments of the two other women, her thoughts were all on Michel and the life they were going to have together.

Chapter 14

Danise was not looking forward to the journey from Duren to Deutz. Not only would she have to part from Hildegarde, Charles, Alcuin, Redmond, and a host of other friends on the morning after her betrothal, she would be separated from Michel, too, and that was worse than all the other losses put together.

"I will be at Deutz in a little more than three weeks," Michel promised her. "I have told Savarec I want to marry you the day after I arrive there."

Still unwilling to let him go Danise clung to him until, after one last kiss, he gently set her aside. She understood why Charles wanted Michel to make haste to secure his new estate from Clodion and Clodion's grasping family, but during the next weeks his absence was a constant ache in her heart. She wished she could ride through the springtime landscape of Francia with him and show him the wide and sparkling Rhine, the little village of Koln and, when they finally crossed the river, the fortress of Deutz where her father acted as Charles's commander. Most of all, she missed Michel's compelling presence at her side. She arrived at Deutz in a dispirited state.

"The time will fly faster than you expect," said Clothilde. In recent days the maidservant was the only person in whom Danise could confide, since Sister Gertrude was still unreconciled to the idea of her marriage. "There is so much to do, Danise. There are clothes to be sewn, household goods to be collected—sheets and quilts, dishes and pans. And furniture. Does anyone know how well Clodion had furnished his house at Elhein?"

"Whatever was Clodion's, I would want removed and burned," Danise responded. "I will have in my home no object that once belonged to him."

"Give it to the poor," suggested Sister Gertrude. "Clodion was so miserly that there must be many living on his land who could use a bed or a table."

Clothilde was right when she said they would be busy. Savarec left word in Koln that he wanted to be notified of any peddlers who came through the town with goods a bride might use, so several times the women boarded the ferry that plied the Rhine, crossed to the western shore, and there investigated some itinerant merchant's wares. Savarec set aside a room where the items thus collected could be stored, and he gave Danise furniture and linens that had once belonged to her mother.

There was also the bridal chamber to be prepared, for the tiny room Danise usually shared with Sister Gertrude and Clothilde when they were at Deutz was not suitable. Savarec chose the best guestroom, a large, airy chamber on the second floor, with a double window that looked out over the garden. He ordered the walls freshly whitewashed, the floor and windows scrubbed, and then he left it to Danise to furnish it as she wanted.

She took a typical Frankish bed from one of the other guestrooms. The wooden frame was made with carved railings at head and foot and a long rail down the side that was placed next to the wall. The mattress she stuffed with fresh straw and covered it with a feathered quilt so the straw would not scratch the occupants. New linen sheets, freshly stuffed feather pillows, and a blue quilt from her mother's belongings completed the bed. Danise added to the decor blue curtains, a carved wooden clothes chest, a table with basin and ewer, and a chamber pot tucked under the table.

While all of this was being prepared, she continued to sew on her clothing. With Clothilde to help her and unknown to Sister Gertrude, whom she felt certain would have been shocked, Danise made a nightrobe of sheer linen with delicate white embroidery at the round neck and short sleeves. Clothilde sewed several rows of narrow pleats around the hem of the garment.

"Michel will love to see you in this," Clothilde said.

"I'll wear it for my first night with him. Oh, Clothilde, when I think of it, I cannot breathe for excitement. I love him so much. I can't wait to be his wife, to have our own home and all of our lives together to look forward to. It will be so wonderful."

While Danise busied herself with bridal preparations and dreamed of the future, Michel was dealing with the unbelievably ramshackle estate that now belonged to him. Located several days' ride due west of Aachen and set in a heavily forested area, Elhein had been used by Clodion mainly as a hunting lodge.

"How can I bring Danise to such a place?" Michel asked Guntram. "The main building needs massive repairs. From the looks of the fields I have seen, there won't be much in the way of crops to harvest and store for the winter. The servants are sullen, and since they are all free people, they are likely to leave at any time." He paused, looking around his great hall in consternation.

"If they have not run away under Clodion's rule," Guntram said, "then they are too disheartened to fend for themselves. They will stay, Michel. Your task will be to convince them to work."

Michel stared at the simple warrior who had tended him when he was ill and weak,

who embodied courage and everyday common
sense. Guntram had his own new estate to see
to, yet at Charles's request he had come willingly to help his friend. Michel made a silent
vow not to fail either Guntram or Charles. Most
of all, he would not fail Danise.

"I have with me fifteen good men, including
you," he said to Guntram. "I plan to use all
of you. Send some people out to round up
everyone who lives at Elhein. I want every
single person—man, woman, and child—to
appear in front of this building at midday.
I am going to give them a feast to celebrate
my arrival. Then I'm going to put them to
work." He was not sure how Guntram would
take these orders, but that dependable man
grinned his approval and went off to carry them
out. Michel breathed a sigh of relief. Having no
practical experience in managing a large estate,
and knowing he would have access to nothing
more than hand tools, he did not know if he
could succeed in what he wanted to do, but
he wasn't going to give up. He was going to
prove to himself that he could turn Elhein into
a self-supporting and profitable estate, and at
the same time he would make Danise proud
of him.

He soon ran into trouble. The two women
who worked in the kitchen did not have
Guntram's faith in him. They argued and
complained when Michel told them what he
wanted of them on that day, saying they did
not have time to prepare a feast, and not
enough food or drink. Feeling very much the

tyrannical medieval baron, Michel refused to listen to their objections.

"It is midsummer, a time of abundance," he said. "I have just sent a group of my men out to hunt birds and rabbits for you to cook. I want you to start making bread at once. When the women I have ordered to attend this feast arrive, I will send them to you. Put them to work. Give the older children baskets and tell them to go into the forest and fields to collect berries. There are wheels of cheese in the coldhouse. I know, because I just saw them. Bring some of them out and serve them. At least Clodion left plenty of wine in the cellars. We'll broach a few casks, but not too many. I want everyone sober enough to understand what I am going to say."

"Kitchen work is women's work, not men's," cried the slovenly woman who claimed to be the cook, "and Count Clodion never let anyone but himself touch the wine, nor drink it, neither."

"It's not Clodion's wine anymore," he reminded her. "It's mine now and today I intend to share it with the folk who work for me."

Both kitchen women gaped at him as if they could not believe what they were hearing.

"Before you do anything," Michel directed, "heat some water and wash your hands and faces. There's not much else you can do today except get the food on the table, but tomorrow I want this kitchen scrubbed from top to bottom. From its condition right now, I'm surprised you people haven't all died from food poisoning.

Do you have any other clothes?" he ended, frowning at the filthy, tattered garments the two women were wearing.

"This here's all we got," said the so-called cook.

"I'll do something about that as soon as I can. While you are cleaning tomorrow, make a list in your head of the supplies you'll need for the kitchen. When I go to Deutz in a couple of weeks, I'll stop in Koln and get as much as I can and send it to you. I'll also see that you get cloth for new dresses. What are you staring at?"

"I be needin' a new kettle," said the cook. "Th' old one's cracked. Clodion never cared 'bout that."

"Ain't no soap left." Her companion eyed Michel with cautious hope. "Can't clean wi' no soap."

"Right." Encouraged that they were at least paying attention to his wishes, Michel made a fast decision. "Tomorrow you make soap. The following day you clean. I'll tell the other women to help you. As for the new kettle, you shall have two of them. In the meantime, do the best you can with what you have here now."

He knew they did not quite believe him. Neither did the rest of the folk whom Guntram and his men rounded up, who came reluctantly and sullenly to the midday feast he had ordered and who listened to his speech as if they had heard it all many times in the past.

"You can't expect them to change all at once,"

278

Guntram said later when Michel voiced his disappointment at the general lack of enthusiasm for the changes he proposed to make. "From what I've heard, Clodion was cruel but he was also lax. He'd beat a few peasants on each of his visits, kill one now and then just to show he could, and take the prettiest girls for his own entertainment. But he didn't care a bit what they did when he wasn't here. These people aren't used to working regularly, and they aren't used to an honest master, either."

"They'll have to get used to both, and fast," Michel replied. "I intend to whip this place into shape before Danise comes here."

She was the reason for everything he did. He wanted to write to her, but there was no parchment or ink available, not even a wax tablet. No one at Elhein knew how to read or write. Michel quickly learned how to keep lists in his head as his companions did. He learned a lot in those few weeks before his marriage to Danise, and most of it depressed him, for he soon realized he was far out of his depth.

He was overwhelmed by the sheer volume of work that had to be done using the simplest technology. For all his training and archaeological experience, he did not know enough about the details of daily life in the eighth century. He would have been lost without Guntram's help. By the time he departed Elhein for Deutz and his wedding to Danise, Michel was deeply discouraged.

*   *   *

It was raining when Michel first saw Koln. He had been there several times in the twentieth century, when he and his English-speaking colleagues referred to it as Cologne, and when it was a large and prosperous city. Michel's principal interest in it at that time was for its twin-towered Gothic cathedral and for the excavated remains of a Roman villa that had a splendid mosaic floor in the banqueting hall. He had once spent an interesting morning in the museum built over and around this villa.

What he saw on this present visit was a village set within the boundaries of the rebuilt Roman walls, with the Rhine providing extra protection along its eastern side. Long forgotten by the inhabitants of Koln, the Roman villa lay beneath half a millenium of dirt and rubble, and while the town was served by a church built in the Romanesque style, the cornerstone of the great cathedral would not be mortared into place for another three centuries. Michel regarded Koln with a dizzying sense of discrepancy, before reminding himself that he was the one out of proper time and place.

Directly across the fog-shrouded river from Koln lay Deutz, the fortress Savarec commanded. There was a flat-bottomed ferry, little more than a raft with railings, to carry them across the river.

After helping to load their horses onto the ferry, Michel and the men with him stepped aboard and the ferryman poled them slowly across the Rhine. As they drew nearer, Michel

could see the sentries patrolling the walls of
Deutz. To his archaeologist's trained eye it was
obvious that, like Koln, Deutz had once been a
Roman outpost, built to protect this convenient
crossing place from the depredations of the
wild tribes who, even in those distant Roman
times, lived in the eastern forests. Plainly, the
Franks had the same sort of defense in mind
when they added to and refortified Deutz, using
mellow old blocks of Roman-cut stone for their
additions.

Outside the fortress walls there were a few
dwellings near the ferry landing, probably for
the families of the men who worked the ferry.
Beyond these houses, some fields were under
cultivation. A dozen or so peddlers had set up
awnings or wooden booths along the short,
muddy road that led from the ferry to the
fortress. Comparing the organized simplicity
of Deutz to his own estate, Michel wondered
what Danise would think when she first beheld
Elhein.

He did not have long to engage in dour
misgivings. Just as the ferry reached the shore,
bumping gently against the wooden wharf,
Michel saw two mounted figures emerge from
the fortress gate and head toward the ferry.

"Danise," he breathed, recognizing the smaller of the riders despite the concealing hooded
brown cloak that shielded her from the rain.

"Did you doubt she would meet you?" asked
Guntram. "And Savarec with her. What have
they done with Clothilde, do you suppose? Or
with Sister Gertrude?"

Flora Speer

Michel wasn't listening. He leapt ashore and hurried toward the two who were now almost at the ferry landing. Seeing him, Danise slid off her horse with a cry of welcome. She ran no more than two or three steps before she was swept into Michel's arms.

He could not get enough of her sweet mouth, could not hold her close enough. He kissed her again and again, neglecting to greet Savarec, forgetting everything and everyone else in his delight at holding Danise once more.

"I've missed you so," she gasped between hungry kisses. "I feared you would be delayed, or not come at all."

"Nothing could keep me away from you," he told her. "Nothing." His desire to kiss her yet again was forestalled by Savarec's deep chuckle.

"Michel," Savarec said, "you will be happy to know that all the preparations are made. You and Danise will be married tomorrow. That is, unless you have changed your mind?" This dry question was followed by a wink and another chuckle.

Michel released Danise long enough to put out one hand to Savarec, but he kept his other arm firmly around his love's waist.

"It's good to see you again, sir," he said, "and, no, I have not changed my mind. Nor would I. Not in a thousand years."

"Come along," Savarec invited. "Don't stand here in the rain. There is a fire in the great hall, and food and drink awaiting us."

With the horses quickly unloaded, they

remounted and all rode the short distance to the fortress.

A firepit ran down the center of the great hall and Savarec had ordered fires lit there to stave off the damp chill. Tables were being set for the garrison's evening meal and several dozen men stood about the hall talking while they awaited the call to table. The men who had come with Michel and Guntram greeted their friends and, after a final word of thanks from Michel for all their help, they disappeared upon their own business, leaving only Michel, Savarec, and Guntram in the group about Danise.

"It is not right for you to be the only woman in this hall with so many men here," Savarec said to Danise. "Leave us now."

"I want to stay with Michel," she protested, taking his arm.

"I allowed you to greet him. Now, go to Sister Gertrude," Savarec ordered. "We will join you shortly."

"Father, you no longer need to be so protective of me," Danise said, shaking her head and smiling at him. "I am as good as married and every man here knows it." But she did leave, sending an inviting look in Michel's direction as she went out of the hall.

"Now," said Savarec to Michel, "I want to hear about Elhein. What kind of place is it? Did you have trouble with Clodion's people there?"

"No real trouble, but I couldn't have managed without Guntram," Michel said. He went on to give Savarec a carefully edited version of what he had found at Elhein, what he hoped to do there, and how the work was progressing. Guntram added his bit, but neither of them revealed to Savarec the true state of disrepair or uninterested servants they had found there.

"It will take a lot of hard work," Guntram summed up the situation, "but once Michel's changes are put into effect, Elhein will be a productive estate, with a very nice house for Danise and Michel."

"I am relieved to hear it," Savarec said. "I wasn't sure what sort of place it would prove to be, or if Clodion had some of his concubines living there. I did not want Danise sent to a house that would forever remind her of Clodion and what he did to her."

"By the time Danise sees Elhein, there will be no trace of Clodion left," Michel promised. But his conscience pricked him. He knew Savarec wanted something better for Danise than Michel would be able to provide for her at Elhein. Michel wanted something better for Danise, too.

The small but clean guestroom to which he was soon conducted, the pitcher of hot water, wooden bowl of soap, and clean linen towel provided by a polite maidservant, all were lacking at Elhein. How could he take Danise there and subject her to such a rough existance? Yet he did not want to postpone their wedding for fear of losing her. In this miserable state of indecision he washed, put on a clean tunic, and went to join Savarec, Danise, and Sister

Gertrude for a light evening meal in Savarec's private chambers.

Danise noticed Michel's distraction at once. She did not think he was angry with her, nor did she believe her father had said anything to upset him. She sat through the strangely quiet meal, during which each of the four people at table was preoccupied with personal thoughts. Danise decided she would have to get Michel alone if she was to convince him to tell her what was weighing so heavily on his mind.

"The rain has stopped," she said, a little too brightly, into the silence at meal's end. "Michel, you have not seen the garden. Let me show it to you. If it's a fair day tomorrow, the ceremony will be held there. I teased Father until he agreed to let me have my way on that."

"It is too damp for you to walk there." Sister Gertrude's expected protest was halfhearted, as if she spoke only out of habit, knowing perfectly well that her years of control over Danise's actions had already ended.

"Let them go," said Savarec. "There is no harm in allowing them time alone now. By this hour tomorrow, they will be wed, and Danise no longer our concern."

"I know you well enough to believe I will always be your concern," Danise responded, putting her arms around his neck and resting her cheek against his. "Father, I will not stop loving you because I am married to Michel. We will see each other as often as before, since most of the last few years I have spent away from you at Chelles."

"That's true enough." Savarec kissed her. As she left the room with Michel, Danise momentarily rested a hand on Sister Gertrude's shoulder. Sighing, the nun lifted her own hand to pat Danise's.

"You must not think they don't like you," Danise said to Michel, leading him down the stairs and toward a narrow door in the stone wall. "It's just that they both love me and it's hard for them to let me go."

"I can understand their feelings," Michel replied. "I wouldn't want to let you go, either."

Danise went through the door first, then paused, trying to see the garden through Michel's eyes. It was an oblong, walled space, and not as well kept as in the days when Danise's mother had been alive to tend it. Yet, protected from the wind as the garden was, with high walls on all four sides, the herbs and flowers planted there grew well without much attention. A second door in one long wall opened directly into the kitchen, and near to this door the herbs were planted so they would be readily available to the cook. Elsewhere in the garden, since it was early July, late roses still bloomed on the bushes planted by Danise's mother. The white lilies had grown profusely, doubling and redoubling over the years, and their sweet fragrance permeated the moist, still air.

Danise and Michel walked along the gravel path from one end of the garden to the other while Danise explained where Michel was to stand on the following morning, where Savarec's secretary and his chaplain would be, how she and Savarec would enter through the door Danise and Michel had just used. She could tell Michel wasn't really seeing the garden or listening to her description of the plans for their wedding day. Her eager words failed and she stopped speaking, watching him for some sign as to what was wrong. When he did not break the silence that lay between them, she felt forced to speak.

"I have talked too much," she said. "It's your turn now. I want to hear what you have been doing during these past weeks."

For a while he regarded her with a bleak expression, until she began to wonder if he would ever speak to her again. He did, after taking a deep breath. She thought he was steeling himself to give her bad news and she stiffened her backbone and set her face to hear it without weeping or otherwise behaving in a cowardly fashion.

"Danise, I have to be fair to you," he said. "When I tell you about Elhein, you may decide that you want to back out of this marriage."

"Why would I?" she cried. Fearing for an instant that Sister Gertrude's dire predictions about men leaving women they professed to love might be at least partly true, she asked, "Have you decided that you don't want to marry me after all?" Even as she spoke she knew it could not be so. She and Michel were meant to be together. There must be some other reason for his talk about their not marrying. He confirmed her belief.

"There is nothing I want more than to marry you," he protested. Again he hesitated before bursting into speech. "It's Elhein. The place is a disaster. The house isn't fit for you to live in, I don't know if the few crops they've planted there will feed everyone through next winter, there isn't enough livestock. I hate the thought of taking you there. The worst thing about it all is that though I can issue orders, and I think after the last couple of weeks the people there will obey me, still, I don't really know what I'm doing. I haven't had the right training for this job. I know what the end result of my efforts should be, but I'm not sure how to attain them. I am an archaeologist, not a farmer, or a hunter-gamekeeper, or an architect and builder. I should be all of those things. Thank heaven Charles sent Guntram with me, or I would have made a complete mess of things."

"And this is why you think I should not marry you?" she asked.

"It's why I think you will regret it if you do," he replied.

"Oh, Michel." She started to laugh, until she saw the regret and the pain in his face. Then she sobered to speak earnestly. "If we had married at once instead of waiting, this would not have happened. You are so clever at disguising your foreign origin that I sometimes forget you were not born a Frank. Let me tell you that in most noble Frankish marriages, it is the woman who manages the land, because the husband is so often away from home." She laid one hand on his chest and her voice took on a lighter note. "Who do you think has charge of the royal treasury? Or control of the crops from Charles's own lands?"

"I don't know," he said. "I suppose he has a treasurer, and a steward."

"No," she said. "Hildegarde. Who can a man trust more completely than his wife?"

"She does all that work? No wonder she's always sick. After the last couple of weeks at Elhein, I can appreciate how much work she must do every day, that I never noticed."

"Hildegarde doesn't count every single coin or golden dish in the treasury, or each sheaf of wheat or cow or goat on Charles's land and her own," Danise said. "There are stewards and secretaries to help her, as you guessed. But the final responsibility is hers, and if it were necessary, Hildegarde could walk into the most dilapidated estate and begin restoring it to good condition within an hour. So could any other well-trained Frankish noblewoman."

"Are you telling me that you know how to do those things that I have been having so much difficulty with?" he asked.

"I have known how to do those things since I was ten years old," she replied. "I haven't had much opportunity here, where fortification is the primary reason for the existence of Deutz, nor very much chance to show what I can do at Chelles, either. But I believe that you and I together can turn Elhein into a fine and happy place."

"And I thought late twentieth century marriages were supposed to be liberated and equal." He put his arms around her. "Danise, what you are talking about is a real partnership. But tell me, while you do all that work what am I supposed to be doing?"

"You, my dearest Michel, are meant to be the great warrior, the one who meets in council with Charles and the other nobles to decide if we are to go to war in a particular year, or to keep the peace. He may send you on a mission to some distant land, such as Lombardy across the Alps, or Northumbria beyond the Narrow Sea, where Alcuin was born. Or Charles might assign you to travel about Francia to make certain that his laws are carried out and the people treated justly. Those are the duties of a Frankish noble."

"I don't think I'm going to like that last part of the deal," he said. "Not if it means leaving you behind."

"I will be with you as often as I can," she promised.

"I want you with me all the time," he whispered, his face in her hair.

"Perhaps you were not treated fairly when we were betrothed," she murmured. "No one troubled to tell you what would be expected of you."

"Why should they?" he asked. "No one but you and I knew that I had no idea what I was getting into. It's my own fault, Danise. In my previous life I spent too much time digging up ruins and not enough studying social customs."

"Now that you do know what is expected of you, do you still want to marry me?"

"I will never marry anyone else," he promised.

"Nor will I." At that moment it occurred to Danise that there must be Frankish men who found their lives as warriors frightening or perhaps, at least occasionally, not to their liking. She could not imagine such a man revealing his innermost concerns in the way Michel had done. Redmond certainly never would, nor Guntram, nor her own father. That Michel trusted her enough to speak so openly endeared him to her all the more. She promised herself she would see to it that they would always talk to each other in this way. There would be no secrets between them.

No secrets at all. She would tell him at once about her vision of Hugo and what she believed it meant.

"Michel," she began.

"What are you two thinking of?" Sister Gertrude hurried through the doorway and along the garden path to confront Danise and Michel. "It is raining again, and you stand here embracing while you are being soaked, and what's more, where you can be seen by anyone glancing out a window. Do you want to spend your wedding day coughing and sneezing?"

"You are right, Sister Gertrude." Michel released Danise from his arms and took her hand instead. "After tomorrow, it will be my happy duty to protect Danise. I hope I can do the job as well as you have done. I'll start by

291

taking her out of the rain at once."

"I am glad to know one of you still has some sense left," snapped Sister Gertrude. As she shooed the lovers indoors like a hen with her chicks, Michel sent Danise a twinkling glance and her heart constricted with love and happiness.

Danise knew she would have no other chance to tell Michel about Hugo on that night. They would not be allowed to be alone together again until after they were married. And on the next night . . . she grew warm and trembled at the thought of Michel making love to her again.

There was no real need for haste in telling him about Hugo. She would do it later, after the wedding celebrations were over, after they had enjoyed a night or two of tender pleasure. It would be easier to tell him then.

The rain stopped during the night and the morning sun dried the path and the plants in the garden so dampness no longer threatened the shoes and the clothing, or the comfort, of the wedding guests. But the air was still heavily loaded with moisture that drew the scent from all the plants, so the fragrances of lilies and roses and herbs added a delightful note to the freshly clipped greenery and the neatly swept path. Sister Gertrude had seen to these preparations shortly after sunrise, and had inspected the garden twice since that time to be certain all was in readiness.

Just before noon Michel and Guntram along with Savarec's secretary and chaplain all stepped to the bare wooden table set at the far end of the garden. Upon the table the secretary placed the parchment copies of the marriage contract and then stood back, waiting.

Guntram, who was to act as Michel's witness, wore his best dark green woolen tunic and had his black beard and hair newly cut. For this occasion Michel wore again the blue silk tunic that Redmond had lent to him at Duren and then insisted he keep.

There were only about twenty-five or thirty guests. The commander of Koln, his wife, and son, along with a few important officials had come across the Rhine on the ferry. Savarec's chief officers, three or four distant cousins with their families, and Danise's aunt on her mother's side, made up the guest list. The subject of their concentrated interest, Michel waited in nervous expectation until the door at the far end of the garden opened to admit Sister Gertrude and Clothilde, who moved forward to take their places among the guests who stood awaiting the bride.

Savarec came into the garden through the same door, his portly figure clothed in a dark red tunic, his short green cloak thrown back to reveal the gold chain and medallion that marked his office of fort commander. Michel spared his future father-in-law only the quickest of glances, for Danise appeared and took her father's arm and Michel could see nothing else but the woman he loved.

She wore a new gown for the occasion,

made of thinly woven cream wool, decorated at neck and sleeve edges with narrow bands of embroidery in Danise's favorite bright green. Her hair was loose, brushed until it shone, and rippled as she moved. Her jewelry was simple, just a gold bracelet on each wrist. To Michel she was the most beautiful creature he had ever seen. She never took her eyes away from his. She came toward him on Savarec's arm, her face glowing with happiness, her lips softly parted.

Michel would make other vows in a few minutes, spoken before the witnesses gathered in the garden and made legal by his signature on the parchment of their marriage contract, but in the instant when Danise put her hand in his and moved to stand beside him facing the priest and secretary, Michel made the sincerest vow of all, silently swearing to his Maker and to Danise that he would love her forever and protect her to the end of his life.

They looked only at each other while the contract was read. It was little different from their betrothal contract, only the clause citing their agreement to wed within one year being eliminated. When the secretary was done, Danise and Michel knelt with clasped hands to receive the chaplain's blessing.

Michel was allowed to kiss her then, and he did so lightly and quickly, still holding her hand, just bending his face down to hers. He did not dare to embrace her. So strong was the love he felt for her, so deep his gratitude that she had consented to be his, that he knew if he put his arms around her then, he would not be able to let her go until he had embarrassed both of them as well as Savarec and all his guests with brazen evidence of the passion and tenderness he was experiencing.

For Danise, from the instant when she entered the garden Michel's eyes were magical lodestars, drawing her to him. The touch of his hand sent a surge of heat through the veins of her arm and up to her heart. Every hope or dream she had ever cherished was centered now in Michel. She understood the chaste kiss he bestowed on her at the close of the ceremony. If he had put his arms around her at that moment she knew she could not have separated from him when the kiss was ended.

He had to release her hand so she could sign the contract, but by then it did not matter. By then they were bound together in heart and spirit and she knew they could never be parted. Later, in private, they would become one body, but Danise knew that however exquisite the delights of physical passion, the love between herself and Michel transcended the constraints of his time or her own, for had he not been sent to her so that they could love and be together?

Danise moved serenely through all the congratulations and the feast that lasted until late afternoon. When the clouds closed in again and rain threatened once more, she went with her father and Michel to the fortress gate to wave farewell to those guests who wanted to return to Koln while it was still dry. The rest of the guests remained congregated in the great hall, eating and talking. They were joined by Savarec's men who came off duty and whom Savarec made welcome.

Eventually, Sister Gertrude and Clothilde quietly took Danise out of the hall and escorted her to the bridal chamber. Clothilde ordered a small tub of hot water prepared. The two women undressed Danise and helped her to climb into the tub, where she stood while Clothilde soaped and rinsed her. Then Sister Gertrude wrapped her in a towel.

"I will pray for your happiness," the nun said.

"Pray for Michel's happiness, too." Danise suddenly felt shy in front of Sister Gertrude, so she held the damp linen towel close around her body.

"I will pray that you will not be proven mistaken in him." Sister Gertrude pursed her lips.

"I love him with so much of my heart that I would die without him," Danise cried, eager to make this dear friend and substitute mother understand what she was feeling.

"Then you truly need my prayers, child."

"Ah, don't!" Tears stood in Danise's eyes. "I know you love me. Wish me well. Wish me happy. Be glad for me."

"I am." With one thin hand Sister Gertrude touched Danise's cheek. "Because I love you, I fear for you. I do not want anything—or anyone—to hurt you. I tried to keep you safe, but you would have none of my way of safety.

Now you will have to find your own way."
Sister Gertrude headed for the chamber door.
With one hand on the latch she stopped, not
looking back when she spoke again. "I do wish
you happy, Danise. And I wish you joy of him.
'Tis a delight I was never fortunate enough to
know."

"Poor soul," Clothilde whispered after her.
"I do believe, for all her hard words about
men, that she still grieves for the young warrior she loved so long ago, who died before
Sister Gertrude could enjoy what you will
know tonight. Now hurry, Danise, put on your
nightrobe before Michel comes."

Chapter 15

Danise should not have been nervous, yet she was. The memory of making love with Michel on the night after he had rescued her from Autichar was still vivid in her mind. But what they did on this night, in this freshly white-washed room, was a sacred duty. Were it left undone, theirs would not be a true marriage.

She stood alone in the center of the bridal chamber, clad only in the gown made by herself and Clothilde from a linen so soft and sheer that it appeared to veil each line of her body in wisps of flowing smoke. When Michel came into the room she tried to still the sudden quaking that revealed how little real courage she possessed. The effort did not help. Her breasts lifted with her sharp intake of breath, the rosy nipples straining against the soft fabric. She knew Michel saw it. He was looking at her as if he wanted to devour her. He said nothing, he just turned to bolt the chamber door. Danise wet her lips and waited.

"You look like a sacrificial lamb," he said. "You shouldn't be afraid of me. What will happen is not unknown to you." He smiled at her as if he, too, were remembering the charcoal makers' cottage.

"It is—" Danise gulped, trying to control her cracking voice. "It is the occasion."

"I know. I've felt it all day." He touched her cheek, then took his hand away. "I never realized before that marriage is exactly what the church says it is. A mystical union."

"Yes." She could not look anywhere but into his dazzling blue eyes.

"I am going to undress." His hands worked at the buckle of his belt. "Don't look away from me, Danise. You weren't ashamed to look at me the last time. Don't hide now. I want us to experience everything together, from this day onward."

"Shall I help you?" She gestured as if to lift his tunic.

"Just stand there," he said. "Just let me look at you. This night is for you, Danise. Tonight I am going to show you how much I love you."

He removed his garments without haste, laying them on the clothes chest, and then he came toward her, fine-boned, well-made, his straight black hair newly trimmed, his face clean-shaven. His remarkable eyes drew and held her. So strong was the emotion shaking her that she put up her hands, laying them on his chest to hold him off until she could absorb the reality of his naked presence.

"No one will intrude on us," she murmured, half to herself. "What we do here is acceptable in earth and heaven."

"Not even Sister Gertrude would dare to stop us." His mouth lifted in a quick little smile, and then he was entirely sober once more, as solemn as Danise. He put his hands on her waist, pulling her forward. Her arms slid up around his neck.

"Michel." His name was a breath of sound, scarcely uttered before his lips descended to hers. In this, the first kiss they exchanged since the chaste touching of lips to lips at the end of their marriage ceremony, Danise found an end to all nervousness. Michel's mouth and his body pressing against hers were familiar to her and beloved, yet strange, too, because they had been separated for nearly a month. His tongue gently pushed her lips apart so he could enter her mouth, and at the moment he did, she felt him harden against her.

She quickly lost herself in the warmth and growing passion of his embrace. With one arm around her waist and the other beneath her hips he raised her onto her toes, and then off her feet entirely, holding her along the length of his body from shoulder to thigh, making her drunk with kisses beyond counting, with love that soon would demand fulfillment. Danise threw back her head, arching against him so he could kiss her throat and shoulders. But almost immediately she grabbed at his hair, pulling his head up to kiss his mouth once more. She hungered for his mouth, for his lips on hers.

"Michel," she gasped, "oh, my love, for all the time when we have been apart, I have dreamed of this night, and prayed for it to come."

"No more than I have." He shifted his hold on her. She was not at all surprised a moment later to find herself lying upon the lavender-scented sheets of their bed. Michel stretched out beside her.

"Did you make this?" He was tugging at the hem of her gown. "All that embroidery must have taken weeks to finish."

"Clothilde helped me. We did it for you, to please you."

"I'll be careful not to tear it, since it was a labor of love. But then, everything that happens in this room tonight is a labor of love." He was still trying to remove the gown. Danise wriggled a little so he could pull the delicate linen higher, until her thighs were revealed to him. She no longer felt shy when he looked at her, or when he stroked a tender hand across her soft skin.

"Sit up, Danise." When she obeyed his whispered order, he drew the nightrobe over her head and tossed it aside. She lay back against the pillows, smiling slightly, fascinated by her own reaction to his unabashed approval of her. She knew he loved her, but she had not fully understood how much her pale beauty could excite him. Indeed, in a land where many women were blondes, Danise had never

301

considered herself unusual or special. Now that she was the object of Michel's rapturous admiration, she discovered how easily her own desire could be ignited by the knowledge that he wanted her—more than that, he was eager to have her. She saw his manhood rising tall and proud and felt a surge of power and delicious anticipation at the sight.

"I cannot believe how beautiful you are." Michel sounded almost awestruck. He continued in a low, emotional voice, "I was beginning to wonder if the last time we were together was only a figment of my imagination, but here you are, just as I remember you, and so incredibly lovely that mortal men should be forbidden to look at you, for if once a man looks, he will be fated to gaze at you until he dies from feasting on too much beauty." As if to know her in some way other than by painful sight, he touched her face with sensitive fingertips, then moved on to caress her throat and shoulders and breasts in the same way, all the time smiling in delight at her gasped exclamations of mounting pleasure. His hands moved lower, over hip and thigh and knees, before he returned to her throat to begin the delicate motions all over again.

She touched him, too, her boldness growing in response to his evident enjoyment of what she was doing. The tension building between them increased until it threatened to destroy them before they were ready for it to end. As a moist, aching heat spread throughout Danise's body, she began to writhe under his caressing hands.

"Danise, my love." Michel rose above her, his eyes locked on hers. Her breasts felt hot and heavy, her thighs trembled and fell apart without her willing it. Even her fingertips tingled.

"In all the world," Michel whispered, "through all time to the very end of eternity, you are the only one I love."

"Michel, I want—I need—oh, please!" She saw in his eyes that he understood her desperate plea, for it matched his own need. He delayed no longer, but pushed hard against her. Danise opened to him, taking him deep inside her in one sweet, moist rush.

"Danise, Danise." Michel's voice in her ear was harsh and strained with his effort at self-control. But why should he exert control any longer, when she could not?

"Michel, I love—love—" She broke off, unable to speak with ecstasy overtaking her.

She knew Michel was moving hard in her, knew she moved in response to him, but there was no more thought in what she did, there was only the desire to be as close to him as she possibly could, to be one with him and never be separated again. A strangled cry tore from her throat. She heard Michel groan and sensed that he had stopped his stroking motions at the point where he was pressed so tightly into her that his presence was almost painful. Danise stopped moving, too, stopped breathing, believed her very heart had stopped beating. For a long, tense moment she and Michel clung together, straining against each other until, in a devastating burst of emotional and physical joy, Danise's fervent wish was granted. In that instant she and Michel were made one, were bound together beyond all breaking asunder, were truly and for all eternity made one flesh, one heart—were, finally and irrevocably, married.

Long after the tremors stopped, after her sobs of release had ended, Michel held her, stroking her tangled hair and kissing her brow. At last he tilted her chin upward and she saw that he was smiling at her.

"I love you," he said, repeating the words he had used over and over again during the past hour. "After what just happened, those words seem inadequate, but I can't think of any others to use."

"They are enough," she sighed. "They are the best words to use when one has been moved beyond the most distant spheres of heaven and then returned safely to earth once more."

Happy tears choked her. She could not speak again, she could only curl into the safety of his arms and rest her head against his shoulder while she silently thanked all the powers of heaven and earth for bringing them together.

Two days after Danise and Michel were married, Sister Gertrude departed Deutz to return to the convent at Chelles. The leave-taking was a tearful one on Danise's part. For all her stern and difficult ways, Sister Gertrude was genuinely concerned with Danise's welfare, and Danise knew the nun loved her. She was a bit surprised, however, to discover Clothilde weeping as Sister Gertrude made her last farewells at the ferry wharf.

"Clothilde, you are still welcome to go with me," Sister Gertrude said, fending off an emotional embrace from the maidservant.

"I cannot." Clothilde wiped her streaming eyes. "My place is with Danise, and you know full well I am not made for the cloister."

"Foolish woman." Sister Gertrude scowled at Clothilde. "Nevertheless, the doors of Chelles will always be open to you. Do not forget the place where you will be welcome. Nor you, Danise. Remember what I have said to you on the subject."

Danise could not reply. Trying not to break down and weep aloud, she hugged Sister Gertrude.

"Enough of that," said the nun in her sternest voice. Turning from Danise, she spoke again. "Savarec, I thank you for the donation you are making to Chelles, and for the men-at-arms you are sending to guard it until we reach the convent."

"They are meant to guard you, too," Savarec said. "Your friendship is more precious than gold, your value above that of fine rubies."

Sister Gertrude actually smiled, acknowledging Savarec's paraphrase of a lesson from the Bible.

"I value your friendship, too," she told him. "It's a rare man who has no malice in him, but you are such a man. Of course, you are not always as wise as you ought to be." Savarec

305

took no offense at these last words, but only smiled and clasped her hand.

"Farewell, Michel." Sister Gertrude turned brisk. She swept past Michel to board the ferry.

"I will take good care of Danise," he promised her. "I'll guard her with my life."

"If you do not, you will answer to me." Sister Gertrude stepped onto the ferry unaided, scorning the helping hands of the men-at-arms who accompanied her. She moved at once to the far side of the ferry, and there she stood, facing the western shore, not once looking back, a tall, thin, rigidly erect figure.

"Where I come from," Michel murmured, looking after her, "we'd call her one tough lady. And it would be a compliment."

They all remained on the wharf, watching the ferry move slowly across the Rhine.

"I suppose you will be the next to leave me," said Savarec to Danise. He heaved a long, dramatic sigh. "Soon, I will be all alone here."

"We can stay for a day or two more," Michel responded. "We'll see Guntram off to his own estate tomorrow, and then the next day or the day after, Danise and I will head for Elhein."

"And Guntram gone, too, after all these years with me. I shall truly be alone then." Savarec looked so forlorn that Danise laughed, hoping to cheer him up.

"Father, you know perfectly well that I have seldom been at Deutz since I began school at Chelles," she reminded him.

"That's so. Perhaps my sense of disquiet is

only the result of weariness after a too-exciting Mayfield followed by the marriage of my only child. I will soon recover, I am sure, once we at Deutz return to our usual routines."

Neither Deutz nor its inhabitants were destined for routine peacefulness, nor were Guntram or Danise and Michel able to leave for their respective estates as they had planned. When the ferry that had taken Sister Gertrude to the opposite side of the Rhine returned to Deutz it was crowded with men and horses. The ferryman made two more trips across the Rhine after that first one, and his counterpart who was based at Koln did the same. On the very last crossing of the ferry, having seen all his men safely over the river first, came Redmond. The news he brought was distressing. At least, Danise found it so. The men seemed to think it was exciting.

"There is new trouble in Saxony," Redmond told them, "and Autichar is behind it."

"I suppose you are going to tell us," said Savarec, "that the Saxons are angry about the failure of Autichar's plot against Charles. What have those heathen tribesmen done now? Burned Frankish villages? Raped and slaughtered innocent women and children? Or have they been murdering Christian missionaries again as revenge for the end of their wicked scheme?"

"I do believe Charles wishes that isolated acts of vengeance were all he has to deal with," said Redmond. "No, Savarec, the news is worse than you could have imagined. Autichar was taken to Bavaria by Duke Bernard and there delivered up to Duke Tassilo, just as Charles ordered. Tassilo said he would keep Autichar imprisoned while he considered exactly what terrible punishment to lay on that traitor, but he delayed his decision until past the time when Duke Bernard was bound to leave Bavaria to rejoin Charles."

"Don't tell me," Michel put in, "let me guess what happened next. Once Duke Bernard was back in Francia proper, Tassilo released Autichar."

"Not exactly." Redmond sent his friend an approving look. "Though I believe you have come close to the truth of the matter. Tassilo claims that Autichar escaped from his prison. Autichar is now rumored to be in Saxony, where he is expected to stir up violence against the Franks."

"You mean, he was *permitted* to escape?" exclaimed Savarec. "If this is true, then Tassilo is as much a traitor to Charles as Autichar is."

"We may never know the whole truth of it," Redmond said. "Tassilo sent word to Charles that he has executed the guards who let Autichar escape."

"Of course he'd kill them," said Michel. "Dead henchmen can't talk and implicate their master."

"That's what I think, too," Redmond agreed. "Tassilo also sent his most profound apologies to Charles, along with word that he has moved men into Saxony in search of Autichar."

"That would be a neat way to cover up troop

308

movements," Michel noted.

"No one ever said Tassilo was a fool," muttered Savarec. "Cunning, concerned only with his own interests, consumed with jealous hatred of Charles, a despicable traitor—all of these things Tassilo is, but he is not stupid enough to challenge Charles directly unless he is absolutely certain he can win a contest between them. Redmond, from the story you've just told us, I assume that Charles is sending you into Saxony to add your men to the troops already there."

"I am to ask you to add a contingent of your own men to mine. Here is the order." Redmond handed Savarec a rolled parchment containing Charles's signature as he always wrote it, in the shape of a cross. "Charles told me to warn you that his spies report the Saxons are greatly inflamed by the collapse of Autichar's plan to rid Saxony of Frankish rule. On their own, in retaliation against us for Charles's punishment of Autichar, the Saxons have begun attacking Frankish settlements not only on the border but well into Frankish lands. Now, with Autichar on hand to urge them onward, Charles expects more serious attacks."

"They will not strike as far west as Deutz," Savarec said. "We are too far away. But if they cross the River Weser, they could attack Paderborn."

"That's what we are to prevent," Redmond told him. "Since Paderborn is a royal seat, Charles does not want the Saxons to take it."

"If they did," said Michel, "it would be bad for

309

Frankish morale and for Charles's reputation."

"Exactly so." Redmond nodded. "That is why we are ordered to stop the Saxons while they are still well east of Paderborn. Savarec, may I impose upon your hospitality for a night or two? When Charles summoned me to Aachen, I pushed my men hard to reach there as quickly as I could, and stayed at Aachen only a few hours before setting out again to bring the news to you. As a result, my men and their horses all need to rest. At any rate, you will require time to prepare your own troops. If we stop here at Deutz, we can travel together."

"Of course, Redmond." That Savarec was thinking hard could be heard in his abstracted answer. "I am overstaffed at the moment. Since we are in no serious danger here, I can spare half my garrison. I'll leave my lieutenant, Hubert, in charge. Michel, you may want to send Danise across the river to Koln, or even on to Elhein while you are away with us."

When she heard of this plan in the privacy of the chamber she shared with Michel, Danise objected vigorously to her father's continuing parental protectiveness.

"Deutz is perfectly safe," she said to Michel. "Saxon uprisings occur all the time, and not in years has the disorder reached this far from the present border of Francia. I will not leave, Michel." She did not ask him to remain with her. She knew he would have to go with her father and Redmond. For him to do otherwise would be cowardly, and she did not want anyone to question Michel's courage.

"I could order you to go," he said.

"If you do, I will not obey," she informed him. "You or my father may need me here. I will not leave Deutz. When I see Elhein, it will be with you, or I will not see it at all."

"Rebellion in the ranks," he muttered, but he did not look annoyed. He caught her hands, pulling them around his waist with rough tenderness, forcing her to step closer so he could hold her in his arms. He began to nibble at her bare shoulder. "It will take me a few minutes to think of an appropriate punishment for this particular mutiny. Bear with me while I consider the subject."

"Your absence from my side will be punishment enough," she whispered, her blood warming to the touch of his lips. "But you will return safely to me. I know it as surely as I know the sun will rise when morning comes."

"Do I love you because you are an optimist?" he asked, gently ravaging her earlobe. "Or is it because you have such confidence in me?" Swinging her off her feet, he headed toward their bed.

"You love me because you were meant to love me," she murmured. "You could not do anything else."

"Sweetheart, I love you because you are you." He laid her upon the bed and got in beside her. "With all my heart, for all time . . . Danise . . . Danise—"

His hands on her, his mouth and tongue, all unleashed the passion Danise had come to expect from him, but never to take for granted.

311

She knew how precious Michel's love was. She reveled in his desire for her, returning it in full measure. They joined together in a heated rush and she did not think again for a long time, not until she lay relaxed in his arms, in the sweet contentment of passion temporarily spent.

"So, you think I couldn't do anything else but love you?" he teased. With one finger he traced her lips before kissing them. "My lady, were you hinting that you won my heart with a magic potion? You sounded remarkably sure of your power over me."

"It was not my power," she murmured, nestling closer to him. "It was heaven's will. It was our fate."

"Predestination?" His fingers strayed downward toward her breasts. "That idea doesn't leave much room for free choice on my part. Or on yours."

"You once suggested as much yourself, that you might have been sent to keep me from living a lonely life. Have you forgotten?" Lulled as she was by their just completed lovemaking and by the way his fingertips were tracing patterns of renewed warmth across her skin, Danise said what she should have waited to reveal until she was fully awake and thinking more clearly.

"It was because of Hugo," she said. His fingers, which had reached the very tip of one breast and were playing there in a most delightful way, stopped their tantalizing motions.

"Hugo," he said in a tight voice. "Would you like to explain that statement? Do you imagine that I am some kind of consolation prize, sent to you because Hugo died?"

"You were not meant to replace Hugo," she said.

"I am damned glad to hear it." Forsaking her tender embrace he rose to his knees, glowering down at her until Danise got up on her knees, too. And there, kneeling and facing each other in an unhappy travesty of the positions in which they had once begun to make love while in the charcoal makers' hut, they fought their first bitter quarrel.

"Go on, Danise." Michel sounded as though he was determined to goad her into a damaging admission. "Tell me exactly what you meant about Hugo, and why you were thinking about him while you and I were lying naked together."

"Hugo is in you." His truculent attitude did not deter her from speaking what she believed was truth. "I saw him, Michel. After we made love for the first time, in a flash of lightning, I saw Hugo's face and form imposed upon yours. In that moment I knew that some part of Hugo survives in you, and that very part of him is what first drew me to you. It is also what made you want me so insistently."

"That's crazy!" he shouted at her. "You are wrong, Danise. Dead wrong."

"I know what I saw," she insisted. "Though you were born in different times, you and Hugo are each part of the other."

"No! I am *myself*, Bradford Michael Bailey, in the wrong century and the wrong place, but

I am not someone else, and don't ever think that I am."

"I have pondered long upon what I saw that night." In response to his anger Danise tried to keep her own voice quiet and to choose her words sensibly. "Hugo had a younger sister, and after he died, Charles arranged a marriage for her. Did she—will she in a few years when she is old enough—marry and bear children? Could you be her descendant? Is the remnant of Hugo's bloodline what I recognized in you when first I saw you?"

"How the hell should I know the answer to that?" he demanded, apparently only made more furious by her attempt at reasonableness. "There are more than twelve hundred years between now and my own time, generations and generations of people. I have thousands of ancestors. How could I know if a particular woman was one of them?"

"I do not really think it is a matter of the flesh," she said. "Rather, it is a spiritual matter. Michel, there is no reason for you to be jealous of Hugo. I love you now. *You.*"

"Do you?" He looked at her as if she were a stranger to him.

Danise refused to lower her eyes. She was sorry she had been foolish enough to raise the subject of Hugo, but she was not going to back down. She knew what she believed, and she was not going to change her mind about it, so Michel would just have to lay aside his indignation and accept the fact that contained within his being was some small part of Hugo. To Danise, it did not seem such a terrible thing, but apparently a man—a twentieth century man, she reminded herself—saw it differently.

"Is that all I am to you?" he demanded. "All I've ever been in spite of everything we've said to each other and the promises we've made? Am I just a crummy substitute for a dead man?"

"I do not know what that word *crummy* means, but you are no substitute," she cried. "Michel, I love you."

"No." He glared at her, injured masculine vanity and plain jealous rage showing in his posture and his expression. "You love Hugo. You always have. But I am *me!* I can't take Hugo's place. I can't be what he was. I wouldn't want to if I could."

"I know you are Michel. I love you *because* you are Michel. Why can't you understand what I am trying to explain?" Danise stopped, choking back her own irritation before it could take fire from Michel's wrath and flame up out of control, scorching them both beyond repair.

"I don't belong here, in this time," he told her, his face and voice hard, "and from what you've just said, I don't think I belong with you, either."

"But I love you." Irrational fear caught at her. "You said you loved me and would forever. All those beautiful words that lay between us—did they mean nothing?"

"I do love you. That's why this crazy idea of yours hurts so much. If I didn't love you, it wouldn't matter that when you go to bed with me, you think you are making love with someone else, or that you fell in love with me because you mistook me for your precious Hugo." He got off the bed and reached for his tunic.

"Don't leave me," she begged. "Stay and talk to me until we settle this difference."

"I'm going downstairs to the great hall. Redmond may still be there, or Guntram. I feel the need to talk to someone about practical concerns, someone who won't try to convince me that I am a twentieth century reincarnation of an eighth century warrior, who has been sent back to the eighth century to make you happy." He paused, shaking his head. "Do you hear how ridiculous that sounds? How completely insane?"

"Even Alcuin could not explain it," she said.

"You talked to Alcuin about this?" He was shouting again. "Before you ever said a word to me?"

"Alcuin believes there is no sensible explanation," she told him.

"Well, he was damned right about that!"

"He said some things are beyond human comprehension, and ought simply to be accepted."

"Now that sounds like something I'd expect to hear from an eighth century scholar," he said scornfully. "Don't ask questions, just accept the wildest possible ideas on faith alone."

"Do not insult Alcuin!" she cried, her own temper igniting. "Nor me, either. I have told you truthfully what is in my heart and what

I believe. I think what has happened is a beautiful thing, for it proves that love does not die when our bodies do. Yes, I love Hugo in you, but that does not detract from the Bradford Michael Bailey I have learned to love, and into whose keeping I have given my life, my heart, and my future. I will not take back what I have said here tonight. Nor will I ever stop loving you. *You*, Michel. If your manly pride is injured, I am sorry, but it does not change what I feel."

She saw the anger go out of him, saw it replaced by a weary sadness, and she wondered if he would ever forgive her for what she had revealed.

"Get some sleep," he told her. "I am going below to talk to my friends."

In the great hall Michel poured himself a cup of wine. Redmond was nowhere to be seen, nor was Guntram, but Savarec sat at the long table talking to one of his men-at-arms. Michel slammed his cup down on the table, then dropped onto the bench near his father-in-law. Savarec finished what he was saying to his man and dismissed him. He sat quietly while Michel swallowed most of the wine in one gulp and refilled his cup.

"I know that look," said Savarec. "I've seen it before on other men's faces, and I have no doubt I wore it often enough myself while my wife lived. So, you and Danise have enjoyed your first quarrel."

" 'Enjoyed' is not the correct word," Michel

Flora Speer

replied, draining his cup a second time.

"The wine won't help," Savarec told him. "It will only give you a sore head in the morning and in the meantime, it will annoy Danise still more if you join her in bed in a drunken condition. Believe me, Michel, I know this from my own experiences."

Michel did not answer. He sat staring into his empty wine cup and Savarec sat watching him.

"Danise's mother was the only woman I have ever loved in all my life," Savarec said after a while. "Since her death I have bedded a few women, for I am not without male desires, but never again have I loved as I loved her. She loved me, too. And yet, we quarreled frequently, on many subjects. It is difficult for men and women to live together without differences arising between them."

"I'd be willing to bet you and your wife never quarreled on the subject Danise and I just discussed," Michel said.

"I do not want you to tell me about it," Savarec cautioned. "It's best if you settle your problems between the two of you, and best if I don't take sides, which I might if I know what your disagreement is. But I will give you some advice, Michel. It is unwise for a man to go to war leaving behind a wife with whom he is at odds. If you never see each other again, Danise's grief will be all the greater if the two of you have parted in anger."

"I'm not sure this quarrel can ever be settled," Michel said glumly. He wasn't thinking only of his quarrel with Danise. He was also recalling a night centuries in the future, the painful sorrow of love betrayed, a woman's mocking laughter, his own vow never to trust or love another. . . . He had broken that promise to himself, and as a result his past seemed to be repeating in the saddest and most intimate of ways. "Savarec, did you know Hugo well?"

"Not really. He came through Deutz occasionally on business for Charles. I know that Charles valued his friendship, as did many other nobles. Is that what's troubling you? Michel, Danise would not have wanted to marry you unless she was sure in her heart that she has recovered from her love for Hugo. There is no need for you to be jealous of her old affection for him."

"That's what she says," Michel told him, "but I'm not so sure."

"The man is dead. Danise loves you, and only you."

"I wish I could believe that." Michel could not say aloud what he was thinking. *I wonder how you would have reacted, Savarec, if your beloved wife had ever informed you that she thought you were the reincarnation of her old love. How could you ever again be certain that when she looked at you, or put her arms around you, that it was really you she was seeing? How could you know that she was making love to you and not to him?*

Chapter 16

Deutz was a place founded upon military preparedness, so it took less than a day for Savarec to make the necessary arrangements to lead a troop of men-at-arms into Saxony. Under his direction baggage carts were quickly filled with the equipment of a campaign—tents, folding tables, beds, chairs and maps for the officers to use. The barber-surgeon who was to go along piled his cart high with bandages, medicinal herbs, skins of wine, leeches in jars, and a collection of surgical tools every bit as terrifying to look upon as the weapons the men-at-arms would carry. Meanwhile, those same men-at-arms packed their saddlebags with extra clothing and food for themselves and their horses. So many of his men were eager to march through eastern Francia and into Saxony that Savarec was forced to order a dozen would-be volunteers to remain behind lest his men at Deutz be depleted to a dangerous level.

Michel worked as hard as any of the other men, assisting Savarec where he could be of use, and Redmond when Redmond needed an extra hand. Having brought no warriors with him from Elhein except for those whom Savarec had lent to him, Michel would ride and fight under the command of his father-in-law.

Danise knew Michel was avoiding her. He had not returned to their bed on the night of their quarrel. Now the long, busy day was drawing to its close and still he had not spoken one word to her. The coming night would be the last one before he left for Saxony, and she did not know if he would spend it with her or continue to stay as far away from her as he could without actually leaving the confines of Deutz.

Standing in the courtyard watching Michel talk with her father, Danise was consumed with apprehension. She still believed that everything she had said to him was the truth, but all the same, she bitterly regretted telling him about Hugo. She had spoken without careful forethought, expecting her words to bind them still more closely together. Instead, those words had driven them apart. With that emotional separation came fears for his life. Because she believed he had been specially sent to her, she had assumed that he could go into battle and emerge unscathed. Now her confidence was shaken. No man was safe in battle. No one knew that sad truth better than she.

"Michel has found his rightful place with us." Redmond paused beside her, having approached while her eyes were on her husband. "He's a good man, and a good friend. You chose well, Danise."

I wish Michel would believe that, Danise thought. Aloud she said, "I pray you will all return unharmed after driving the Saxons into a defeat so disastrous that they never rise against us again."

"The Saxons always seem to rise again," Redmond said. "I do wonder whence comes their resilient spirit. As for returning safely, not all of us will. We know the risks. So do you."

"My father is growing too old for battle," she said, seeing anew Savarec's portly figure and graying hair.

"He may not be involved in the actual fighting," Redmond said, "but I for one would not be without him. Savarec is able to understand a battlefield at a glance. He always knows when and exactly where to send in fresh troops, when to press forward, when to pull back. For years he has studied how the Saxons fight. It is my hope that on this campaign he will stand upon some nearby vantage point and direct the fighting, letting younger men like myself and Michel and Guntram plough into the thick of it."

"God keep you safe, dear Redmond," she cried. "You and all your men. And Guntram.

And Michel. If Michel—if Michel—" She swallowed the rising tide of fear and went on, saying to Redmond her friend what she could not say to Michel her love. "If Michel were killed, I would retreat to Chelles and never leave it again. Nor would I live long without him, not even in that safe and blessed place. My heart was broken once before when Hugo died. I could not survive a second such blow."

"I'll do what I can, Danise, but in battle—" Redmond broke off when Michel and Savarec approached.

"All is ready," Savarec announced. "Now for a hearty meal and a good night's sleep. We will be up before dawn tomorrow and away from Deutz ere the sun tops those trees over there."

"You sound happy," Danise reproached him.

"Excited," Savarec corrected. "The start of a new campaign always makes me feel like a boy again."

"Savarec," said Redmond with a glance at Danise, "may I ask your advice?" He drew the older man aside, leaving Danise and Michel alone.

"Wait," Danise cried when Michel would have left her to join them. "You have not spoken one word to me since last evening."

"What do you want me to say, Danise?" He looked as fierce and forbidding as any Frankish warrior whose thoughts were on war and not on love.

"Say that you love me in spite of our differences, that you forgive me for hurting you so badly. I wish I had not spoken."

"Whether you spoke or not, what you believe would still be the same," he said.

"Let us not part in anger, for we know not what the coming days will bring. Say you will not stay away from me tonight."

"I do plan to join you," he said, speaking coldly and deliberately. The look he gave her, raking her from head to toe, was chilling. "Every soldier wants a woman before he goes off to war. Funny thing about women—they are interchangeable. Any convenient one will do. And you are convenient to me, aren't you?" He spun on his heel and walked away, leaving Danise gasping in shock.

Hurt, anger, and damaged pride warred within her. She wanted to lash out at Michel, to say to him words as cruel as those he had just tossed at her like the sharpest of spears. And then she realized that she had already used words as weapons against him. What Michel had said to her was causing her only a taste of the pain he must have felt when she had told him about Hugo.

"What has happened to us?" she cried after him. "How have we so quickly destroyed the beautiful, perfect love that was going to last until time and the world ended? Oh, Michel, what have I done? And what have you done?" He did not answer her. He just continued to walk farther and farther away until he disappeared into a group of men who were loading up the last of the baggage carts.

*   *   *

Danise sat beside Michel at the farewell feast that evening. Though it was as lavish as Deutz could provide, and ample proof of Savarec's claim to set the best table east of the Rhine, the meal did not last long. Savarec was insistent that all the men leaving on the morrow must be in bed early. Those who had women at the fort did not complain. The others obeyed their commander in good humor, knowing he was right.

It was not yet dark on that midsummer night when Michel appeared in the bedchamber he shared with Danise. Early as it still was, she was waiting for him with her hair loose and wearing the nightrobe she and Clothilde had made for her wedding night.

"I do not want to continue our quarrel," she said, not waiting for him to speak or even to bolt the door. "We have done terrible damage to the love we share. We must repair it this night, before you go away."

"What do you propose to do?" he asked, regarding her with unchanged coldness. "Do you plan to dump me out of a tree, or perhaps that window over there, to see if you can induce a fresh bout of amnesia? If I can't remember who I am, I could just be whoever you want me to be. That might be easier for both of us."

"You are so angry with me because I hurt you so badly," she said, "which only proves the depth of your love."

He did not answer her. He stripped off his clothing, letting the garments fall where they would. When he approached her, Danise backed away. This was a Michel devoid of the tenderness she had come to expect of him. She saw the pain and the rage he was trying to control, and she feared what he might do if some word or action of hers were to set that rage free.

"Yes, that's right," he said, coming toward her as though he were some powerful beast of the forest and she the prey he was stalking. "Get onto the bed."

"Michel, please, wait."

"The pleading should come later," he snarled. "In the meantime, if you don't want it damaged, take off that nightgown. Tell me, Danise, was it part of the bridal clothes you made for Hugo?"

"No! It was made for your delight. I thought of you and dreamed of your lovemaking with every stitch I put into it. You are being unfair, Michel."

"I am unfair? I don't think so." His voice was like the low growl of an animal about to pounce. "I am just the poor fool who fell for you. That's a good one, isn't it? I *fell* all right— fell out of a tree, into love, into a situation I can't begin to understand. Do you have any idea what you did to me last night?"

"I am sorry."

"You damned well ought to be sorry."

He moved so quickly that Danise did not see what was coming. She was standing near the bed. Michel grabbed her left arm, spun her around, and flipped her onto the mattress. She landed face down, with her arm twisted behind her. He did not hurt her, but surprise made her cry out when she realized he was straddling her thighs, his stiff manhood prodding at the cleft between her buttocks.

"Michel, what are you doing?"

"Tonight I am going to teach you who I am. When I leave this room tomorrow morning you will be convinced, completely and for all time, that I am not Hugo."

"I know you are not. I know you are Michel, and you are the one I love. How many times do I have to say it before you understand that what I believe does not detract from *you*, from who and what you are?"

"It is possible," he purred into her ear, "that you could prove to me during the course of this night that you do have some small degree of sincere feeling for me. Or is it just the physical part you enjoy?"

"Don't make me ashamed to love you!" She jerked her head around so she could see him better. She couldn't do much more than move her head. He still had a tight grip on her left arm, and now he lowered himself until he was lying along her back, his weight pressing her down into the mattress. His muscular thighs were clamped over hers, holding her legs together so she couldn't use her knees to lever herself out from under him. When she tried, he simply tightened his thighs around hers, and as he moved his manhood rubbed hard against her.

Suddenly she was glad she was unable to turn

Flora Speer

over, for if she could do so, he would be inside her in an instant, and in his present mood he would not stop until . . . until . . . She groaned, acknowledging what she would have preferred to deny. If he were to take her in that way, hard and angry and unloving, still she would welcome him, for her own growing anger at the way he was treating her was fueling her desire for him. Even if he should take her without bothering to turn her over first, still she wanted him. She had to fight her own inclination to move against him in an inviting manner.

"Don't you think I'm the one who ought to be insulted?" he demanded. "I fell head over heels for you, but you didn't want me at all. You were looking for Hugo."

"If you could lay aside your jealousy for one moment," she yelled at him, "if you could forget your injured pride long enough to think about what I said last night, you might begin to understand that I was talking about something strange and wonderful and beautiful. Something supernatural, Michel, a circumstance so amazing and incomprehensible that it ought to enhance our love instead of destroying it."

"You're not going to blame me for this. You're the one who ruined what we had." Releasing her arm at last, he rolled off her, but when Danise tried to push herself up into a sitting position he wrapped a hand around each of her wrists and pulled. Before she could catch her breath she was on her back and he

328

was once more positioned across her thighs, facing her this time.

"How did you do that?" she gasped.

"Martial arts. A twentieth century skill." His face and his eyes were cold.

"You have become like a Frankish warrior," she whispered, "hard and tough, ready to go into battle, there to kill or be killed. But I am not your enemy."

"That is something you are going to have to prove to me," he told her.

"How can I hope to prove anything to you when you are holding me prisoner? I won't run away from you, Michel. I want to love you, not do battle with you."

"Do you?" He lowered his body until his lips were almost upon hers. His flat belly pressed on her own, and when he drew in a breath of air, his chest rubbed against her breasts. For a moment his eyes softened. "God, how I wish I could believe you."

"I mean it. I love you, Michel. I love *you*."

"Sure you do." His eyes were cold again. His kiss was a brutal assault on her senses.

Though fully aware of his simmering fury against her, Danise heard in his cry of distrust all the love she knew he still felt for her. If she could reach that love beneath the layers of pride and jealousy, of anger and disbelief that cloaked his heart, then she might be able to draw forth the tender emotion she cherished yet had lost by her own words and actions. Nor could she deny that his newly harsh attitude was stirring an answering fire in her.

With his mouth still grinding upon hers she wrenched her wrists out of his grasp so she could wrap her arms around his shoulders, meanwhile returning his demanding kiss with matching passion. She raked her nails across his back, she bit and scratched and pretended to fight so he could have the pleasure of subduing her—until she was not pretending anymore, she was wild with passion, desperate to hold him inside her yet struggling against him. They wrestled like warriors in the ring at Mayfield until, with a growl worthy of the beast she had earlier imagined him to be, he rammed himself into her, thrust following hot thrust. Danise screamed and screamed again, still struggling, still fighting for her love, until their joined bodies erupted into a throbbing, pounding climax that stopped the next scream before it left her lips—that stopped her breath and his.

There followed a gentler time of warmer kisses and kinder caresses. They did not speak. Danise feared if she said one word they would begin to quarrel once more and all Michel's pain and her regret would pour out of them to taint their last night together. For these few hours their bodies would have to tell of the love their tongues might have ruined forever. When he became hard again and came at her with a driving desire equal to their first joining, she responded in kind, knowing it was what he needed from her, knowing, too, that his ferocity would not hurt her.

She thought he might well fear that if he

were tender and gentle with her they would both dissolve into tears and remorse for what they had done to themselves and to each other. She would not cry, not during that night or on the morning to come. She would give him whatever she thought he required of her until it was time for him to leave her. Only in that way could she prove her love to him. And it seemed to her as the night wore on and he made love to her again and again, that he was trying to prove his own love to her. His kisses and the way in which he took possession of her body became less forceful. It might have been the result of simple weariness, or perhaps the slaking of a violent passion. Or it might have been—please God, it was!—his realization that no matter what he demanded of her, she would not deny him.

She dozed off once, and wakened later to the touch of his fingertips on her face, brushing back her hair and caressing the margin of her lower lip. His glance was tender while he looked at her hair and her mouth, until he saw that she was awake. Then his face became closed and tight and he put her hand on him and made her rub until he was hard, while he stroked her into trembling acquiescence. He rose above her once more to take her with renewed fury, groaning and biting his lip at the end as if he would conceal any indication of softer feelings. Danise, gasping and shaking beneath him, cried out her love repeatedly, but received no answer from him, though she believed he felt the same despairing affection that she did.

She had not known there were so many different ways to make love. Nor had she dreamed how much tenderness or how much grief her heart could hold. When the notes of a trumpet being blown in the courtyard called Michel from their bed, Danise lay a little longer, sore, exhausted, her body sated and her heart near to breaking, for not once during any of their couplings had Michel said he loved her.

She sat up, sliding to the side of the bed, looking down at the linen sheet all wrinkled and stained with the evidence of Michel's passion, and she warned herself once more not to weep. She stood on somewhat unsteady legs and went to the table to pour out water so she could wash.

"You'd better hurry," he said. "Savarec is eager to be gone before sunrise."

"So are you, I think. You look forward to leaving me." She turned from the water basin, a towel in her hands. "Shall I help you arm?"

"No, thanks." His voice was cool, as if he spoke to a complete stranger. "There's a boy coming to help with the chain mail. I suggest you dress before he gets here. No, wait a minute." He caught her around the waist, pulling her toward him. He was wearing his tunic and breeches and the rough wool scratched at her bare skin. "Who am I, Danise? Don't stare at me like that. Answer me."

She flung back her head, shaking a river of silver-gilt hair off her shoulders, meeting his glare with her own brave look, refusing to be cowed by him.

"I said, who am I?"

"You are Michel of Elhein," she said, matching his cold tone. "You are the man I love and will love until I die. If you do not know it now, I don't know what else I can do to show you that you are everything to me." How terrible to say such heartfelt, binding words in such a cold voice, with defiance in her face and posture. She kept her back rigid against the forward pressure of his hands.

She had her reward, small though it was. She saw a glimmer of warmth in his eyes, a faint softening in his features, before he pulled control over himself once more.

"We shall see," he said. "Only time will prove the truth of your claim, and today we have no more time. That's the boy knocking at the door. Put on your dress so I can let him in."

Their final leave-taking, in the courtyard where Savarec's men were gathering, was cool. Michel stood before her, looking deep into her eyes as if he wanted to read her soul, as if he had not had the chance to do so during the night. He did not touch or kiss her.

"See you later," was all he said before he turned from her to mount his horse.

Danise's farewell to her father was much warmer. She put her arms around him and kissed him several times, and her affection was fully returned.

"Come now," Savarec said at last. "You'll

make an old man weep. We won't be gone long, Danise. A few weeks at most and then those Saxons will be begging us to show mercy." Another kiss, a pat on her shoulder, and Savarec was off to see to his men.

From Redmond Danise had a quick embrace and a kiss on the cheek, to which she gladly responded.

"Take care of yourself," she begged.

"Ah, no," he told her, laughing. "The warrior who tries to be cautious on the battlefield leaves himself vulnerable to great dangers. I intend to fight like a madman."

"Aye," said Guntram, coming up to them in time to hear Redmond's words. "That's the best way to come out of a battle whole. Fare you well, Danise, until we meet again." Guntram clasped both of her hands.

"Fare you well, Guntram."

Then they were all mounted and gone, riding through the gate, leaving Danise alone.

Chapter 17

Michel knew his skill with Frankish weapons was less than proficient in spite of his constant effort and practice, but he had more than a few things to prove to himself and to others. Never did he want Danise to have cause to say or to think that he was a lesser man in battle than Hugo had been.

Damn Hugo! And damn his own stupidity, for flying off the handle when Danise had revealed her reincarnation theory. She had sounded like some New Age guru and Michel, whose interests ran to more practical and scientific concerns, had reacted like the besotted lunatic he was, jealous of his wife's first love.

He would not have much longer to think about his monumental idiocy. He might not have time to think about anything at all, ever. He, Savarec, Redmond, and Guntram stood together with a few others of Savarec's men on a little rise overlooking a Saxon village. Guntram had just returned from reconnaissance.

"They are all there," Guntram reported. "All the leaders of the uprising. I saw Autichar, too."

"He's here? Good." Savarec grinned. "Let's try to take him prisoner. We'll put him in heavy chains, shackle his wrists and ankles, and send him to Charles for a present."

"Better to kill him and be done with the trouble he causes wherever he goes," advised Guntram.

The men paused in their discussion while Redmond listened to a report from one of his scouts.

"Our men are in place," Redmond said. "The village is surrounded and we've taken care of the sentries. My man says the Saxons are completely unaware of our presence. I trust they will be surprised to see us."

"Michel," said Savarec, "you are to go with Redmond and fight with his men."

Throughout this conversation Michel had been wondering if his companions were really as calm as they appeared to be, or if they were just good actors. Personally, he was terrified by what lay ahead, but he wasn't going to show it.

"I still think we should charge on horseback," he said. "That would really surprise the hell out of them."

"The object is to creep up on them in silence," Redmond admonished. "Horses make noise."

"I've heard the Saracens in Spain and the Holy Land charge into battle on horseback," Savarec said. "It must be a splendid sight to see. Perhaps one day Charles will take a lesson from the Saracens and have his own armies trained to fight that way instead of dismounting first."

"He'll do it in just a few years," Michel said, adding with dark humor, "I hope we all live long enough to see it happen."

"We must believe that we will." Redmond clapped Michel on the back. "Come along, my friend, it's time to move into position. Guntram, good luck to you. God willing, we'll meet again at this same place when the battle is over."

The men all shook hands before they moved into battle positions, leaving Savarec on the higher ground where he could see what was happening and if necessary send one of the men who remained with him onto the field with new orders.

The Saxons were indeed surprised by the swift and unexpected attack, but they were not in disarray for long. Within moments they had their swords and battle-axes in hand and were cheerfully hacking away at their Frankish opponents.

Michel had never been in battle before, and in any case the wars of his time were far different in dimension and weaponry from eighth century warfare. As for the men involved in ground fighting, he thought the screams, the stench, the blood and the fear must be the same in any battle. Nor did the need to kill an enemy before being killed oneself change from century to century. But how terrible it was to cut down one man and, before the light had gone out of his eyes, to be pressed to move on to serve another man in the same cruel way. Through a growing sickness of spirit Michel did the best he could, blotting out such unnerving thoughts so he could concentrate on physical action.

Because he was neither as strong nor as well-trained as his Frankish companions, it was inevitable that soon his sword arm would begin to tire. Ignoring the ache in his arm and shoulder, Michel slogged on, doggedly doing what must be done. His weakness was quickly perceived by a tall Saxon with golden hair and beard, who bore down on him with battle-ax raised for a death stroke. Clearly this man did not suffer from the same qualms about taking life that afflicted Michel. Michel's arm felt like lead, but he lifted it slowly in response to the Saxon's approach. If he was going to die here in the bloody mud of a Saxon village, then he would go down fighting. No one would be able to call him a coward.

The grinning Saxon roared out a long string of unintelligible words then stopped short, an amazed look on his face as Redmond leapt between Michel and the Saxon. An instant later Redmond's sword found its mark. But the Saxon still had a bit of life left in him.

He brought his battle-ax down onto Redmond's shoulder, slicing through chain mail and muscle and bone. Then the Saxon toppled forward on his face to lie in the mud.

Michel caught Redmond as he fell. Sinking to his knees Michel eased Redmond downward, cradling him with his head upon Michel's chest. At some level of his mind Michel perceived that the sounds of battle were moving away from where they were, leaving the two friends in an area of relative quiet dominated by the awful noise of Redmond's struggling breaths. Michel wasn't thinking about the battle anymore.

"Damn it, Redmond! What do you mean, saving my life like that? Now look what you've done!" Michel yelled in mingled grief and horror as he realized the full extent of the damage inflicted by the Saxon's final stroke.

"My friend." Redmond's eyes were open and he was fully conscious, but there could be no question that he would die in a matter of moments. Blood gushed from his wound, soaking Michel's arm and chest. "Danise— Danise loves you."

"I know. I love her, too. I'll take care of her. Oh, God, Redmond, this shouldn't have happened! Not to you. Hang on, I'll try to find the surgeon." But before the words were out of Michel's mouth Redmond had gone to a place where wounds and pain and bloodshed did not exist. Gently Michel laid his friend down on the ground and closed his eyes. "Stay there, Redmond. Wait for me. I'll come back for you. I won't leave you in this hellhole. I'll take you out of here. I promise."

Michel rose, sword in aching hand once more. The fighting had moved off to one side of the village, but he could see that the combatants were edging slowly toward the spot where Savarec still stood directing the battle with a few of his men around him. The Saxons were trying to push the Franks backward so they could get to Savarec. It looked as if they might succeed.

"Tell him about Redmond." Michel was finding his thought processes oddly slow and disjointed, but he instinctively knew what he had to do next. Stumbling and wavering on his feet, he started toward Savarec. "Needs to know—needs reinforcements there. Where's Guntram? Help Savarec. Must help." The slight rise in the land seemed like a mountain to him, but he trudged onward until he stood within a few paces of his father-in-law.

"Savarec," he said, noting with some astonishment that his voice was hoarse, as if he had been shouting all day long. "I have—have a report to make."

Savarec turned toward him, recognizing him and just beginning to smile in greeting. Savarec's lips opened to say something, but no sound came out. Instead, there was a whistling noise unlike anything Michel had ever heard. Before his disbelieving eyes the source of the noise, a long spear, flew through the air and imbedded itself so deep in Savarec's back that he was dead on the instant. Immediately a shout went up from the men surrounding Savarec, a rising howl of grief and outrage.

"A cowardly stroke!"

"Who? Who did this?"

"Autichar! There—see—it's Autichar!" That last cry came from Michel, who raised his sword to point toward the unmistakable figure wearing a fancifully decorated helmet and a dark red cloak.

"Damn you—traitor, kidnapper, villain! *Damn you!*" New strength flowed into Michel's aching, weary body. With the rush of adrenaline his confused mind cleared. Now he had one purpose and one purpose only, and he knew the men would follow him. Every last one of them was as furious as he was at the manner of Savarec's death.

"For Savarec!" Michel shouted at the top of his lungs. "For Redmond! Stop Autichar!" At the head of Savarec's men he charged down the little hill and into the fray, leading them into the midst of the Saxon defenders. He fought like one gone berserk, not caring what happened to him, intent only on avenging his fallen friends and capturing Autichar, whose fault it all was. Enraged by the cowardly killing of their commander, the Franks followed Michel's lead as he had known they would. They fell upon the Saxons in a frenzy, forcing them back toward the edge of the surrounding forest . . . backward . . . and still back . . . and back again. . . .

"It's over," Guntram said, taking the sword out of Michel's numb hand. "You can rest now.

You are a hero, Michel. Men will tell of your deeds on this day for years to come."

"No." There was moisture on Michel's face. He thought at first it was blood, until he realized he was crying, and had been crying for a long time. "Redmond was the hero, not me. Redmond saved my life."

"Every man here knows you saved the day when we were beginning to falter," Guntram told him.

"Any other man would have . . . all furious . . . Savarec's death." Once again he could not seem to put his thoughts together into a coherent sentence.

"You'd best let the barber-surgeon wash that wound out with wine and bind it up. You don't want to lose so good a sword arm to infection." Guntram touched his arm and Michel looked down to see blood welling out of a cut just below his elbow.

"Didn't notice before." His tongue was thick, his mouth dry. He felt as if he was going to vomit. "Thought it was someone else's blood.

"Redmond. Savarec." Michel made himself look around at what remained of the burned-out Saxon houses. "Have to . . . to take them back." Remembering their deaths—remembering all the deaths that had occurred on that day, friend and foe alike—he bent over, emptying his stomach onto the ground.

"It's all right." Guntram's hand rested on his shoulder for a moment. "It happens when a man is overtired. Get to the surgeon, Michel.

Ask him to give you some of his wine to rinse your mouth."

"The dead." Michel refused to move from where he stood.

"The Saxons we'll bury here. Our own we'll put into the baggage carts and take them to Paderborn," Guntram said. "It's not far, only half a day's journey. We can get coffins there, and bury them properly, with a priest in attendance."

"Not Savarec." Michel's head was reeling, but he had to be certain that Guntram understood what was to be done. "Not Redmond, either. Not at Paderborn. They have to go to Deutz."

"Yes, you're right. I'll see to it. Now, will you get to the surgeon before I have to carry you?"

"I'm going." He barely made it to the medical cart before he collapsed. The surgeon examined his wound, proclaimed it but a minor one, and gave Michel herb-infused wine to drink. Michel spent the night wrapped in his stained cloak, lying on the ground with the other wounded men, slipping into and out of terrifying dreams. In the morning he was weak but his head was clear. His arm ached badly, but the surgeon assured him it would soon heal. It was then, while he ate a bit of bread and drank some wine the surgeon gave him, that Guntram came to tell him Autichar's body could not be found.

"He must have escaped again, but not for long," Guntram said. "We will hunt him down and either kill him or take him to Charles for justice. One way or another, Autichar will pay for his evil deeds. Not only is he a traitor to Charles, but he is responsible for Savarec's death, and for Redmond's."

They rode to Paderborn that day, taking with them in the baggage carts the dead and those too badly wounded to mount their horses. They traveled so slowly that it took them until late afternoon to reach their destination. The royal residence at Paderborn was a large wooden building. There Serle, the nobleman who was in charge in Charles's absence, made them welcome and saw to it that they were given baths and fresh clothing. Later, he listened to their reports while secretaries wrote down all that was said.

"The messengers will leave before dark and ride hard," Serle promised. "Charles should have the reports in less than three days. The present commander at Deutz will have his by tomorrow evening."

"I have to be the one to tell Danise about her father, not Hubert," Michel protested. "I will go with them."

"You could not keep up with the royal messengers," Serle responded. "The reports are in sealed packets, which are passed from rider to rider along the way. Thus, while men and horses must stop to rest, the packets never do. And the riders travel as fast as their horses are able. But, surely you know this without my telling you."

"Michel has only recently come to Francia," Guntram said.

"We're glad to have you here," said Serle.

"From what I've heard of you this day, you are a great hero."

"I am *not* a hero!" Michel exclaimed.

"And modest, too." Serle nodded his approval.

"Come and rest," Guntram urged when Michel would have lost his temper. Later, in the room they were sharing, Guntram said, "You may as well enjoy your new fame, Michel, because everyone who was there on that day knows how valiantly you fought. Danise will be proud of you when she hears of it."

"Danise will be too heartbroken by Savarec's death to care whether I fought well or not," Michel said. "Anyway, I can't remember what I did after the fighting started. It's all a blurry horror."

"So is any battle, once it's over," Guntram agreed. "Michel, Savarec's death leaves me as commander of the men he led into Saxony. I am going to give you an order and as your commander, I warn you, I don't want any argument about it. Our surgeon tells me your arm will require a week or so of rest before you can fight again. Therefore, I am sending you with an armed escort to take Savarec and Redmond back to Deutz. I will give you a message for the commander there. I am going to need more men to finish the task Redmond and Savarec set out to do. Spend a day or two with Danise. Comfort her as best you can. Then, when the fresh troops are ready, lead them back here to Paderborn. I will send regular messages to Serle, telling him where I can be found."

"And where will you be, Guntram?"

"Tracking Autichar." Guntram's expression was fierce at the best of times. Michel had never seen him look the way he looked at that moment. If there had been any compassion left in Michel's heart for Autichar, he might have felt a twinge of pity for the man. But Autichar did not deserve pity. He deserved whatever Guntram might do to him.

They buried their dead in the morning and then ate a simple funeral feast. At dawn on the next day Michel and the men assigned to him left Paderborn for Deutz.

Since the beginning of the battle with the Saxons Michel had tried to think only about what was actually happening at any given moment. Now, riding through the forest with men who for the most part were preoccupied with their own thoughts, he discovered that though he wanted to wipe the memory of the past week out of his mind, he could not do it. Over and over during the first days of that sad journey he relived the scenes of battle and the deaths of his friends, which seemed to him to be meaningless, since Autichar was still alive and free and the Saxons would continue to defy Frankish rule. In military terms the battle would change little in Saxony or Francia, but in Michel an enormous change had occurred. Having seen the horror of war firsthand and having faced his own death, he was no longer the same man.

Time, even the passage of a few days, can

work wonders upon a shocked and sorrowful mind. So can distance change a man's perspective upon terrible events. Gradually, as he and his companions left Paderborn farther and farther behind while they moved ever closer to Deutz, Michel began to think less often of the battle and more about what lay ahead.

His quarrel with Danise now appeared to him as mere foolishness, the result of his own intractable ego. If Danise wanted to believe that there was something of Hugo living on in Bradford Michael Bailey, what harm could that belief do? All his former jealousy of Hugo had been washed away by the same kind of blood and pain and fear and grief that Hugo must once have experienced, until now Michel felt an odd kinship with that fellow warrior.

Hugo, poor devil, had never known the part of Danise that Michel knew—not the passion or the sweet, tender womanliness, nor, surely, the determined female protecting her right to think as she wanted to think. Hugo had known only the innocent young girl. Why, then, should Bradford Michael Bailey find Danise's belief about Hugo threatening when she had told him over and over again that she loved him, and only him?

Because he was an arrogant idiot, who didn't deserve her love. He vowed that he would find a way to make it up to her for all the rotten things he had said to her, because he knew after the last terrifying week that nothing in the eighth century or the twentieth, or in any other time, was worth the losing of her love. No, not even his damned pride was worth such a loss.

Traveling slowly because of the cart with the coffins, from Paderborn southwestward to Deutz Michel and the escort sent by Guntram plodded along through forests, across rivers and streams until, finally, they found themselves within sight of the Rhine.

When they arrived at Deutz itself, the sentries upon the walls challenged them but did not delay their entry. On hearing who they were, one of the sentries called down to his cohorts within and immediately the main gate swung open. Michel and his men rode into the courtyard, there to be welcomed by Savarec's lieutenant in charge, Hubert, who had ordered the men-at-arms drawn up into two rows on either side of the entrance as a tribute to their fallen commander. Between these rows of men the cart with the coffins slowly rolled.

Danise came through the door of the main garrison building just as Michel finished speaking to Hubert. Seeing her sad-faced and solemn, looking from him to the two coffins in the baggage cart, Michel knew she would not have to be told that he had brought her father home to her.

She did not weep or wail. She stood quietly, drooping a little, hands loose at her sides, not moving until Michel approached her. Then, all the anger between them swept away by tragedy, she went into his arms without a word, so he could hold and comfort her. She stayed silent in his embrace until men came to take the coffins off the cart.

"Let me see my father," she pleaded, "and Redmond, too. If I am to say a last farewell to them, I must see what has happened to them."

"You can't." Michel held her more tightly, feeling the quivering of her smaller frame against his strength. He knew that a gentle kind of cruelty was necessary against her, to prevent a worse cruelty if she should see the wounds that had caused the deaths of father and of friend. "I wouldn't have wanted you to see them immediately after they died, let alone now, when their bodies have been carted across Francia for more than a week in damp summer weather."

He felt her revulsion then, felt her retching in his arms, and though he had made his point and no longer feared she would insist on viewing what she ought not to see—what he could never forget no matter how long he lived—still, her reaction to what he had said made the wounds in his own heart even deeper. He asked only a few brief questions of her as to how and where she wanted her father buried, before he handed her over to the weeping Clothilde.

"I am going to make the arrangements," he said. "We'll do as you want and bury Savarec first thing tomorrow, and have prayers said for Redmond at the same time. Redmond's body is to be sent on to his own home for burial. Guntram suggested I notify the governor of Koln, who is a distant cousin of Redmond's, and let him decide what to do about sending the coffin on from there. I will take care of everything, Danise. When I finish, I'll join you and tell you anything you want to know. For now, go with Clothilde."

"I have put food and wine in your room." Clothilde met Michel at the chamber door. "Please coax Danise to eat. She has barely swallowed a crumb since the first news came of Savarec's death."

"I'll do what I can. Thanks, Clothilde." It was difficult to smile. Michel feared he had probably only twisted his face into an unpleasant grimace. Clothilde did not appear to notice.

"You look as if you have not eaten recently, either," she said. She touched his wounded forearm. "I left clean bandages on the table next to the food. If you are wise, you will ask Danise to change the linen on that wound. Oh, and there's hot water for washing, too."

When Michel put his hand on the door latch, Clothilde stopped him.

"What word of Guntram?" she asked. "Is he well? Was he wounded, too? Why did he not return with you?"

"He took only a minor wound on one cheek," Michel said. "He claims his beard will hide it when it heals."

"Where is he now?"

"Somewhere in the eastern forests, trying to track down Autichar."

"If anyone can find that traitor, Guntram can. I will pray for his safety. Thank you for telling me, Michel. Guntram is a valued friend.

I feared he might have died with Savarec."

"If he had, I'd have brought him home with the others."

Clothilde nodded, looking at the bedroom door.

"Danise needs your love," she said, and went quietly away.

He found Danise sitting on the side of the bed with her hands folded in her lap and her eyes lowered. In her undyed woolen gown, with her pale hair bound into a single braid hanging down her back, she appeared to be no more than a wraith who might vanish at any moment. She did not move when Michel entered the room. He did not know what to say to her, so he spared her only a glance before he began to remove his clothing.

"I can leave, if you would prefer to be alone," she said, her voice just above a whisper.

"The one thing I do not want is for you to leave me," he said. When she looked upward, he saw the frightened, wary emotion in her eyes and decided to defuse the situation as much as he could. "I will need help bathing, and I can't put on a new bandage by myself. Will you help me?"

"Of course." There was no change in her voice or her manner. Michel had the impression that she was not really with him, that her thoughts were far away.

Clothilde had left a wooden tub along with a pitcher and two buckets full of hot water. After soaping himself using part of the hot water,

Michel climbed into the tub and crouched down so Danise could rinse him with the remaining hot water. Draped in a linen towel he then sat on the bed and let her unwind the old bandage.

"It doesn't look too bad, does it?" Michel regarded his wound as if his forearm and the red slash on it belonged to someone else. "I thought it would become infected, but it hasn't."

"Wounds that bleed heavily often clean themselves." Using cool water mixed with wine Danise washed the wound before wrapping it in a strip of clean linen.

"I'm hungry," he said when she was finished. "Let's eat."

"I'll wait until later, but I will be pleased to serve you."

"No, you won't." He caught her lightly by the wrist. "Clothilde tells me you haven't been eating. I am going to feed you."

"Please don't."

This was not the Danise he knew. This quiet, withdrawn creature bore little resemblance to her former vital, sparkling self. Now that he looked at her more closely Michel could see that Clothilde was right. Danise looked as if she had not eaten a decent meal since the day when he and her father had ridden away from Deutz. She had attempted to do something similar after escaping from Autichar. When she was afraid or worried, or grieving as she was doing now, Danise stopped eating. Michel scooped her off her feet and into his arms, the linen towel dropping away from his waist when he moved.

"You see? My wound is as good as healed already."

She did not respond to his light tone. In fact, when he laid her down on their bed she flinched away from him. It dawned on him that she might imagine he was going to force himself on her. She probably thought immediate sex was what a man would want when he had been away from his wife for several weeks. To show her he had other things on his mind he left her on the bed while he searched through his clothing chest for a fresh linen undershirt and a lightweight woolen tunic. Once he was decently clad he took up the tray of food and carried it to the bed.

"Move over," he said. "Scrunch up against the wall so I have some room to put this thing down. Now, what has Clothilde left for us under this linen cloth?"

"Cold chicken," Danise said without enthusiasm. "Bread and some of the cheese you like. Plums."

"Cut a slice of cheese for me, will you? And a slice for yourself. I'll pour the wine."

He sat on the outer side of the bed, positioning himself and the tray so that if she wanted to get away from him she would have to spill both food and wine. He ate the cheese she gave him, but when she offered a second slice he shook his head.

"Not until you've eaten a piece," he said. "I'm half starving, but I won't eat until you do. That chicken looks delicious. My mouth is watering." Sipping at his wine he watched her reaction. She stared at the food on the tray, then looked up at him.

"Truly, I am not hungry," she said.

"Truly, you are going to eat," he countered. "For myself, I am aching to sink my teeth into that chicken, but I can't until you have a piece first."

"Don't talk to me in that way." Her voice remained oddly lifeless and unlike his Danise, but there was a momentary flash of spirit in her eyes. "I am not a child."

"Then don't act like one. *Eat*, Danise."

Slowly she stretched out her hand to pick up the knife and carve a slice off the breast of the chicken. She nibbled at the edge of the meat she held.

"Eat all of it. Chew it and swallow it down. Then drink some wine." He kept his eyes on her until she did as he ordered. "That's better. I've seen too many people die recently. I don't want to add you to the tally."

"Would it really matter to you?" Her voice was still low, but it had a bit more life to it. Her eyes were on the tray of food rather than on his face.

"It would kill me. Here, have some cheese."

"You haven't said—"

"I haven't said a lot of things," he interrupted, pushing the slice of cheese between her open lips. He refilled her wine cup and handed it to her. "We'll eat and drink first, then we'll talk." Slowly, bit by piece by sip, he convinced her to eat what he considered to be a small meal. It was not as much food and drink as he would have liked her to consume, but it was a start. When they were both finished, he set the tray aside and sat back against the headrails of the bed, resting his head on the wall behind it, stretching out his legs. Danise curled up in the corner next to him.

"Tell me about my father's death," she said. "And about Redmond's, too."

"I'd rather not."

"I need to know, and the telling may help you." There was a little color in her pale face now, and she didn't look quite so much like a lost and lonely ghost.

"Perhaps you're right." He decided he would give her just the outline of events, but when he began to talk it all spilled out, every gory detail. She listened, wincing now and then until he had told her all about the days of searching through the forest until they found the village where the leaders of the Saxon bands that had been causing so much trouble were gathered, and how they had surprised and done battle with the Saxons. She did not weep, not even when he described Redmond's brave death and her father's end.

"Thank you," she said when he was finished.

"There is more I want to tell you, but it's not about tracking Saxons or fighting them, it's about me. Danise, I know I have treated you badly. Can you forgive me? Can we try to get back some of the feeling we've lost? You have no idea how much your love means to me."

She presented him with the same wary, troubled gaze with which she had regarded him on his entry into their bedchamber.

"If you wish to couple now," she said after a few tense minutes, "of course I am amenable. It is my duty, after all."

"That's not what I meant. Danise, I love you with all my heart and soul, and making love with you is part of it. However, at this moment I am so damned tired I'm not sure I could manage it. What I want is just what I said, for you to forgive me. I also want to tell you something about myself that I never tell anyone. It's not meant as an excuse for my despicable behavior toward you, but it may help you to understand why I acted the way I did. Now, I know you are worn-out, too. You've had a rough time of it in the last couple of months, and probably just about all you can take of emotional stress, so if you want me to shut up until later when you feel better, or if you want me to keep quiet altogether, just say so." He deliberately sprinkled this speech with words she would have to translate into Frankish. She usually smiled when he did this and he knew she enjoyed exercising her intelligence to make sense of what he was saying. He wasn't sure the gambit would work this time, until her expression lightened and he thought he detected a momentary flash of humor in the gray-green depths of her eyes.

"I will listen, Michel. Say what you want."

"All right," he said, wishing he could put his arms around her and draw her head down onto his chest, so he could make his promised explanation without having her eyes on his face with such burning intensity.

"You know I was divorced from my first wife," he began.

"Yes, you told me. It was good of you to be so honest about a part of your previous life that can have no meaning here in Francia."

"Well, that's just it. My divorce still has meaning for me. That's why I've never talked about it, not in either century." He stopped, thinking how to say what had to be told. Deciding it was wisest just to state the facts, he continued. "She cheated on me. I walked in on her one day and found her in bed with someone else. Then, later, I learned she had been involved with several other men as well as the one I caught her with."

"You divorced her because she committed adultery? Michel, I am sorry."

"In the twentieth century, you don't go into court and shout 'adultery,'" Michel said. "We call it 'irreconcilable differences.'"

"Whatever you called it, it was still a dreadful wrong against you." She put out her hand to touch his with ready sympathy. Michel caught her fingers, to hold on to them while he made the rest of his explanation. Somehow, the warmth of her hand in his made the telling easier.

"What mattered to me was not just the physical act that she had committed with other men, though that was bad enough," he said. "It was the breaking of the bond of trust between husband and wife that destroyed everything I had ever felt for her. After the divorce, I swore I'd never trust another woman. But when I first came here to Francia, I didn't know who I was or anything about my past, so I neglected to put up all those defensive barriers I had been using to keep myself from being hurt again. By the time I regained my memory, I was so deep in love with you that my sordid marriage was irrelevant."

"You knew you loved me even then? So quickly?" He could not tell what she was feeling, he could only look into her soft eyes and marvel that they were together in the same room and that she was still listening to him.

"There's something else I have to confess," he said. "From the very beginning you were special to me. It was as though we belonged together, but I couldn't figure out why."

"Ah." A faint smile trembled at the corners of her mouth.

"Don't get all excited," he continued. "I know what you're thinking, but I have been taught to disregard the supernatural in favor of a scientific explanation. I put my peculiar feelings down to a confused state of mind."

"What nonsense," she said. "What foolishness, not to accept that there is more to life than what you can see or hear or hold in your hands."

"Can you understand now why I reacted so badly when you told me that you thought I was at least a partial reincarnation of Hugo? I felt as if I had been betrayed by a woman for a second time, as though it was Hugo you were loving and wanting instead of me. I guess you could say I saw it as a kind of cosmic adultery. And then you refused to back down in what you believed, and I just got more and more angry and more and more hurt because I thought you didn't love me anymore—or that you had never loved me at all. That last night when we were together, all I could think about was how to make you forget Hugo, how to make you love *me* and not him. I was trying to force you to love me. I did that to you, knowing full well that love can't be forced. It must be freely given."

"What I understand from this explanation," she said, "is that while Hugo's ghost has been in my mind and heart, your adulterous wife has been in yours."

"Can ghosts be exorcised?" he asked.

"Devils are exorcised," she told him with great seriousness. "Ghosts must be laid to rest, gently and with love, by fulfilling what they have left undone in this world. Hugo has been laid to rest because I love you, and in you, whatever remains of him. I do not understand this, I only accept it. As Alcuin would say, it is beyond human comprehension."

"I can't think of a single thing my ex-wife left undone in this world," he said. "But I think I know what you mean. She's in my past, and that relationship is over and finished because I love you now. She doesn't haunt me anymore, not after the last few weeks."

"I love you," Danise said. "I will never betray you."

"I know. I think I've always known it, in my heart. It's my brain and my overactive ego that foul things up from time to time."

"From time to time," she repeated, smiling more openly.

"Come here." He slid down in the bed until his head was resting on the pillow. He pulled her down beside him where he had wanted her all along, with her head on his shoulder and his arms around her. "It doesn't matter what you believe about this mystery, Danise. You can think I'm Hugo, or Attila the Hun, or Santa Claus, just as long as you love me. Believe what you want. Who am I to say what's truth and what's falsehood or even just imagination? All that really matters is that we love each other, in this or any life. Danise? Danise?" When he lifted his head so he could see her face, he realized that she was fast asleep and probably had not heard his last, impassioned words. He brushed his lips across her forehead before settling back against the pillow. Within moments his own eyes closed and he, too, fell asleep.

The coffins of Savarec and Redmond were carried to the garrison chapel as soon as they reached Deutz, there to rest overnight under the eyes of an honor guard chosen by Hubert. It was late morning when the folk of Deutz gathered for the funeral service. Savarec was buried in the graveyard just outside the fortress walls. At Hubert's order he was placed so that he was facing eastward toward Saxony, where he had fought so bravely during many campaigns. Throughout the service and the burial Danise stood tight-lipped and dry-eyed with Michel on one side of her and Clothilde on the other. The governor of Koln and his wife were there to pay their respects to Savarec and to accompany Redmond when he left Deutz for the last time.

In midafternoon Michel and the men who had come with him from Saxony carried Redmond's coffin onto the ferry. During the crossing they remained standing at attention around it. Danise, at her own insistence, went aboard with the governor and his wife, to be with them while they were all poled across the Rhine to Koln. It was evening before Danise, Michel, and the men with them returned to Deutz. Hubert greeted them in the great hall.

"All is in readiness, Michel," Hubert said. "I have assigned eighteen men to your command. You will be able to leave before dawn to return to the eastern forests. May you and Guntram be successful and quickly bring to justice the traitor responsible for the deaths of Savarec and Redmond."

By the time she and Michel reached their room, Danise was in tears.

"I was wondering when you would finally break down," Michel said, taking her into his arms. "My darling, I swear to you, when this fighting is over, I will never leave you again. You and I will go home to Elhein and live there for the rest of our lives. If ever I have to leave Elhein, even for a short time, you will go with me."

"It's the fighting that frightens me," Danise whispered. "I cannot pretend to be brave anymore, or to believe that because you were sent to me, you will be safe. If so many good men can die in battle, if Father and Redmond are gone, then why not—?"

He did not let her finish. Seized by superstitious dread at the thought of what she might say, he covered her mouth with his fingers and then with his lips, effectively silencing her.

What started as a kiss meant to quiet her gained in depth and sweetness until Danise was murmuring and sighing in his arms and Michel, denied expression of his love for her for too many weeks, could barely restrain himself. He took her to their bed and there, with aching tenderness, with repeated vows of undying love, he tried to erase the memory of the last time he had taken her, when he had been relentlessly determined to prove his manhood and his claim on her.

With gentle fingers on throat and breast and thigh, with prolonged kisses and fierce restraint of his own passion so as not to rush her, he wooed Danise anew until she blossomed into a creature of warmth and welcoming desire. Sheathed in her sweetness he told her again of his love, just before they shimmered together into a fulfillment so delicate and perfect that when it was over he hesitated to move or speak until she took the initiative.

"I could not bear to lose you," she whispered.

"You won't. Danise, I swear to you, I will come back to you when this campaign against Autichar is over. No matter what rumors you hear, or who tells you I am dead, don't believe it unless you actually see my body. But you won't see my body," he added hastily when she cried out and clutched at him in fear. "Before I reach Paderborn again, I fully expect to meet Guntram along the way, marching Autichar toward Aachen in chains."

"All the same, I will pray for you constantly," she said. "I'll do it not just for my sake, for that would be selfishness. After all you have endured in your lifetime, you deserve to live for many long and fruitful years."

"I will," he said. "*We* will. Together. I'm certain of it."

He was never so proud of her as on the next morning, when she stood with Clothilde, waving farewell to him as once more he rode away from Deutz into Saxony. She shed not a single tear, at any rate not in public. He suspected that she would spend most of the rest of the day weeping in her own room, but at least she did not cry in public. If she had, he might have broken down, too, because he was not as certain of his safe return as he pretended to her. He lived in terror of the battles ahead of him. One battle had been more than enough. He did not think he could face more bloodshed.

Leaving Danise was the hardest thing he had ever had to do. Looking back at her as he rode out of the gate, raising his hand for one last wave, he wondered if he would ever see her again. And then he swore to himself, as he had sworn to her during the night, that no matter what happened, he would find a way to return to her.

Chapter 18

"It didn't take me long to find Autichar," Guntram said to Michel. "He lost most of his allies near Paderborn in that battle with us. I knew he would have to take shelter with a friend until he can think of a way to stir up yet more trouble for Charles."

"I expected him to flee into Saxony," Michel said, "or else head for Bavaria."

"Duke Tassilo would not be happy to see him again, not while he's a fugitive," Guntram replied. "Let Autichar win a battle or two against Charles, and Tassilo might be willing to renew their friendship, but for now Autichar knows better than to set foot in Bavaria."

"What about those of his Saxon allies who are still alive?"

"The Saxons are used to failure in their

constant uprisings against Charles. They might be inclined to receive Autichar as a friend, but only if he appears in Saxony at the head of his own warband. Autichar needs to recruit more men. That's why I'm not surprised by what he has done. When he escaped us near Paderborn, he fled south. I believe he hopes to cross the Rhine somewhere north of Mainz and then head west into Francia proper."

"Thus hiding out under Charles's very nose? Yes, I think Autichar would relish that idea. But, wait a minute. Isn't Clodion exiled to an estate west of Mainz?" Seeing Guntram's grin, Michel knew he had guessed aright. "Autichar and Clodion, together again and stirring up more mischief for Charles to put down. What a pair. But will Clodion be glad to see his old partner in crime or not?"

"We aren't going to give Autichar the chance to find out the answer to that question," Guntram said. "We are going to stop him before he crosses the Rhine, so he never gets anywhere near Clodion's estate."

"How many men does Autichar have at the moment?"

"Six," Guntram replied, "while I have a dozen and now the eighteen men you brought from Deutz. I must remember to thank Hubert for his generosity. We far outnumber Autichar's resources."

"Do they know we're here? Can we plan another surprise attack?"

"I thought we might pay them a visit this very evening," Guntram said. "Preferably an hour or two after they've settled down for the night. My men have been reconnoitering the land, and report that a nighttime attack shouldn't be too difficult."

Guntram was right. It was not difficult at all, and to Michel's vast relief it was neither a long nor a bloody encounter.

"Two are wounded, all six are taken prisoner," Guntram said less than an hour after the fighting started. "But in the confusion Autichar escaped once more."

"He can't have gone far," Michel said. "We have all of their horses. I bet he's skulking in the woods nearby." Turning slowly about he eyed the forest surrounding Autichar's camp, looking for some sign that the man was there.

"As soon as we have the camp secured, I'll send out a search party," Guntram decided, "though I doubt if they will find a trace of him before daylight."

While Guntram was giving orders to his lieutenants, Michel thought he detected a furtive movement among the trees. He could not tell if it was Autichar or some nocturnal animal. A quick glance around the camp told Michel that Guntram had all of his men well occupied in cleaning up after their brief skirmish and in making certain the prisoners were well tied and guarded, and the horses brought into a makeshift corral so Autichar could not steal one for himself. With a shout to let Guntram know in which direction he was heading, Michel plunged into the forest in pursuit of whatever creature he had just seen.

He had not gone far before he became aware of a deep and unnatural silence pervading the forest. The light of the campfire he had left did not extend more than a few yards into the trees and though there was a full moon high overhead much of its glow was shaded by dense leaves. On a warm early August night the forest should have been alive with the noises of insects and the rustlings made by animals. The stillness indicated to Michel the presence of someone who did not belong there. His own presence could have acounted for quiet in his immediate vicinity, but not for such a vast, echoing silence. Something about the dark emptiness made the hair stand up on Michel's arms and along the back of his neck.

Then a twig crackled behind him and he heard an indrawn breath. Whirling, he looked through the trees, squinting until he discerned a broad-shouldered figure.

"You came on too fast," said Autichar. "You rushed right past me. I'm here, Michel, waiting for you."

In the dim light Michel could see the gleam of Autichar's sword blade. He lifted his own sword, waiting for Autichar's attack.

"I haven't heard the latest gossip," Autichar said in a conversational tone. "Have you wed the lovely Danise yet? And bedded her? If so, I vow you will not have her again. In fact, when my new plan has succeeded, I shall take Danise for my own, and get my future sons on her."

"Over my dead body," Michel snarled.

"As you wish." Autichar chuckled, a man sure

of his own prowess in battle and with women. "Draw nearer to me, Michel, so we can cross swords. Otherwise, how can I kill you and take your wife to my bed?"

Even though he knew his reaction was exactly what Autichar wanted, the image of Danise struggling in Autichar's arms was enough to send Michel forward in a direct attack on the man. Autichar was a brilliant swordsman, handling the long Frankish broadsword with practiced skill and ease. It took but a moment or two for Michel to realize he had no hope of winning this contest. Not only was Autichar an expert, he was apparently able to see in the dark and he took full advantage of Michel's unequal experience.

Michel refused to give up or to call for help from Guntram and his men. He wanted to return to Deutz and tell Danise that he was the one who had brought down her father's killer. Thinking of his love, Michel redoubled his efforts.

Yet while he fought Autichar, Michel was constantly aware of a sensation of being pulled backward, as though a magnet was drawing him away from Autichar and into the dark, silent forest. He tried to ignore the feeling. His life depended on noticing Autichar's every movement, but in the darkness that was almost impossible to do. Autichar's sword touched his side, and then an instant later nicked his forehead, barely missing his left eye and drawing blood from both strikes. Sticky wetness dripped into his eye and oozed down his left cheek. Reduced to flailing at the spot where he thought Autichar was, Michel fought on.

And then it began to grow light. It wasn't daylight. It was much too early for dawn, but nonetheless the forest began to take on an orange-gold glow. Except for the clash and slide of their two swords and the heavy breathing of Michel and Autichar, the eerie silence around them deepened.

At first Michel was grateful for the light because it enabled him to see his opponent more clearly. In those initial moments he imagined that Guntram and his men had made torches and were moving into position behind him so that he could see Autichar while Autichar would have to look directly into the flames of the torches. But soon the light was brighter than any assembly of torch-bearing men could have produced, and now Autichar stopped slashing at Michel to stare openmouthed at something behind him. And then, unbelievably, Autichar dropped his sword and fell onto his knees. His eyes were fixed and staring.

"What the devil?" Michel turned to see what had so amazed Autichar.

There, pulsating among the trees, was a globe of orange-gold light so brilliant that it lit up the forest for acres around its center. The silence of the forest was broken, for Michel could hear shouts coming from the direction of Guntram's warband. And there was another sound.

"Mike. Mike." The disembodied voice came out of the globe of light. "Come on. Hurry up."

"Who are you?" Michel felt the pulling sensation again. It was almost irresistible.

"Who the hell do you think I am? Do you want to get home again or not?" The center of the globe moved nearer.

"Home?" Michel could not stop staring into the light. Its pulsations had a hypnotic effect on him. He could not move, he could only stand where he was while the globe came nearer and nearer.

"O. K., now," said the voice. "Just stay put for a minute. Don't move."

Michel could do nothing but obey. He was immobilized within the sphere of light now enveloping him. He heard a whimpering sound and knew it was Autichar. He recognized Guntram's voice, calling to him. And then he was encased in silence once more, suspended in orange light.

"Bingo!" The voice in the light shouted in triumph, and the light went out.

Michel was lost in darkness and silence so absolute that he was not even aware of the beating of his heart. He tried to scream and could not. No sound came, though his mouth was open. He could not breathe, and he was falling . . . falling. . . .

"What have you done with Michel?" Guntram hauled Autichar to his feet. In the torchlight Autichar's eyes were glazed and his mouth hung open and slack.

"What's wrong with him?" asked Uland, one of Guntram's men. "Has he gone mad?"

"Where is Michel?" Guntram shook Autichar. It did not help. Autichar stared at Guntram unseeing until Guntram flung him away. Autichar fell to the ground and lay there, breathing but not moving.

"He might have seen something that terrified him," Uland suggested. "A huge beast, perhaps."

"No beast would frighten Autichar into such a state," Guntram declared. "He's a great hunter. He's killed more boars than you or I ever will."

"If it was a beast," remarked one of the other men, "it might have dragged Michel away with it."

"In that case, we should have heard screams or a call for help." Guntram scratched his head. "And what about that light we saw? What made it and what doused it? Autichar, damn you, speak to me. What did you see?"

Autichar could not, or would not, speak.

"If there is a man-eating beast in here, we can't hope to search the woodland until daylight, or someone else could be killed," Uland said. "If the beast took Michel away, he's dead already."

"Aye." Guntram heaved a long sigh. "That does seem to be the only possibility. Take Autichar back to camp. We'll set double sentries for the rest of the night. At dawn we'll begin searching for Michel—or for his body."

"Poor Lady Danise," said Uland. "First her father was killed, now her husband. And I've heard she was friends with Count Redmond, too. Three tragic losses for so sweet a lady."

"And I'm the one who will have to tell her." Guntram shook his head sadly. "And I've lost another good friend, too. I liked Michel."

Since they held Autichar captive and since he did not look to be in any condition to attempt an escape, Guntram felt free to spend as much time as he thought necessary in looking for Michel. He and his men searched for three days. Never did they find any trace of Michel, not a scrap of fabric from his clothes, nor so much as a single drop of blood, nor any evidence of a struggle.

"Autichar knows what happened," Uland said on the third night. "He could tell us if he would only speak."

"I am beginning to think Autichar will never speak again." Guntram regarded his captive as if he were some unfamiliar and fascinating form of animal life from the fabled lands beyond the sunrise. "Look at him, Uland. He has to be told to eat and drink or, as far as we can tell, he would starve to death and never know he was hungry. He fouls himself unless he is instructed to tend to his own needs. He takes no notice of what is happening around him. All he does is stare unceasingly at something that isn't there."

"He has gone mad," Uland insisted. "I've said it all along. What shall we do now, Guntram?"

"I see no reason to continue to search for a man who has vanished as if he never existed. We may never learn what has happened to

Michel. But I have a duty to Charles to report what has occurred here and to send Autichar to him as soon as possible. We leave for home at dawn."

"You'll want a good rider to take the reports to Deutz and to Aachen," Uland said.

"No." Guntram was thoughtful. "No reports yet. I'll dictate them when we reach Deutz."

"But," Uland began, then stopped at the look in Guntram's eyes.

"No one is going to tell Danise about this except me," Guntram said. "Nor are we going to Paderborn. It's out of our way. We ride northward, directly to Deutz. And when we get there, I'll make sure Clothilde is with Danise when I give her the news. I'm only a rough warrior, but Clothilde will know what to do and say."

"It cannot be," Danise said. "I will not believe it."

"I'm sorry." Guntram spread his hands in a helpless gesture. "Danise, you ought to cry. It would relieve your feelings."

"I have nothing to cry about," she said. "Michel is not dead, for I have not seen his body."

"I've been dealing with a madman for a week," Guntram told her. "Don't you go glassy-eyed and silent, too, like Autichar." He looked around Danise's bedchamber as if he were still searching for Michel.

"I am not mad," she assured him. "Michel is out there, lost in the forest. We must find him."

"Oh, no, Danise." Clothilde caught her hands and held them tightly. "You cannot think to go to that place yourself?"

"The first thing I am going to do is talk to Autichar," she said. "And then, Guntram, you are going to repeat the entire story to me, just in case you forgot something the first time. I want to know every detail."

Danise felt as though an iron band had been wrapped around her chest, constricting her so she could not breathe properly. But that same band kept her upright instead of allowing her to fall upon her bed and weep. The iron band kept her talking and thinking and trying to find a way to discover what had happened to Michel.

At first Autichar was no help to her. After consulting with Guntram, Hubert had confined Autichar in a ground level room and set two men-at-arms to watch him at all times until he could be sent on to Charles at Aachen. So far as anyone could tell, Autichar did not know he had been imprisoned. During the daylight hours he sat upon the side of his bed and stared into nothingness. When night fell, someone had to order him to lie down or he would continue to sit on the bed, not knowing he ought to sleep. He had degenerated into a pitiful creature, but Danise would not be deterred from trying to get information out of him.

"Please," she begged him, "tell me what has happened to my husband. You were kind to me once, Autichar, when I was your captive. Be kind to me once more and tell me what you know. Please, Autichar. Do you remember how I spoke in your behalf to Charles? If you will but talk to me now, I swear I will go with you to Aachen and I'll beg Charles to spare your life. Autichar—*please!*"

Whether she coaxed or threatened him, Autichar gave no indication that he was aware of her presence. After an hour with him, Danise gave up. Telling the guards to notify her at once if there was any change in Autichar's condition, she left him. Seeing him withdrawn into his own private world had suggested a possibility to Danise, but it was a possibility she was not ready to consider. Not yet, not until she had investigated all other explanations for Michel's disappearance.

"Find Guntram," Danise said to Clothilde. "Ask him to join me in the garden."

"I believe he is with Hubert," Clothilde answered. "Now that Savarec is gone, Guntram will be leaving Deutz soon for his own estate, and he will have some final duties to complete before he goes."

"Yes, I remember he was planning to leave Deutz soon after my marriage," Danise remarked.

"Guntram has risen far above his original position as a simple man-at-arms. It says much for his courage and intelligence that Charles awarded him those lands."

At any other time Danise would have noticed Clothilde's carefully unemotional voice and seen how downcast she was, but at the moment Danise was trying to think of a way to convince

Guntram to go along with what she wanted to do. By the time Clothilde brought Guntram to her in the garden, Danise had concluded that the best way to deal with him was by being direct. Guntram was a straightforward warrior, so more subtle methods of persuasion would be lost on him. He was also an honest and openhearted man who would do anything for his friends.

"Guntram," she said to him, "in the name of the friendship you held for my father and for Michel, I ask for your aid."

"You have it," Guntram said at once. "Tell me what you want."

"Your attendance," she replied, "along with that of perhaps two or three men who also knew Michel."

"Since there's no coffin we can escort to a gravesite," Guntram said, "do you want us to stand as an honor guard instead, during a mass for Michel's soul? You will have no difficulty finding men for such a duty. Michel was well liked."

"It's not a religious duty I require of you," Danise said. "I want you and the men you choose to act as my escort, and perhaps as my guards, if it proves necessary."

"On your way to Elhein?" Guntram began to look a bit wary. "It's a rough place, Danise, and you know no one there. I'd far rather see you safe at court under Hildegarde's protection. Charles will find you another husband to hold Elhein."

"I do not need another husband while my

own husband is still alive," Danise snapped with unaccustomed sharpness. "I have no intention of going to Elhein just yet, nor to court. Guntram, I want you to take me to the place where Michel vanished."

"Why?" Guntram asked. "I've told you how we searched the area for three days and found no trace of him. It has been raining again. All footprints will be washed away. Danise, if there were a thread of Michel's clothing, a strand of his hair, any sign at all of him, we would have found it and continued searching. But there was nothing. Nothing," he concluded.

"I believe everything you say," Danise told him. "I know you did all anyone could to find Michel. But, Guntram, I have been thinking that he might have lost his memory again and simply wandered off into the forest. Perhaps Autichar struck him hard on the head and thus rattled Michel's wits." Danise paused to let Guntram think over this idea.

"It could be so," Guntram said, "though we should still have found some sign of Michel's passage through the forest. If you are right and he is wandering lost and unaware of his own name, how can we hope to find him?"

"I have a small likeness of him, that was in his purse when first he came to Francia," Danise said. "Did you ever see it, Guntram? Michel gave it to me as a keepsake."

"Now that you mention it, I have seen it." Guntram's worried expression lightened. "Do you mean to show it to any folk we meet in the area where he was lost? Now, that is a good idea. Someone may recognize him. But I and my men could take the likeness with us and do as much as you might. There's no need for you to go, Danise."

"If Michel has lost his memory again, he will need me by his side as soon as you find him," Danise said. "Furthermore, I will not give that likeness of him into anyone else's hands. If we do not find him, it will be all I have left of him. But we *will* find him, Guntram. We *must* find him."

Although he expressed continuing doubts about the probability of locating Michel, Guntram agreed to act as Danise's escort.

"But only if you go, too, Clothilde," Guntram said. "It's not right for a young woman to spend days and nights in the company of warriors without a female companion."

"I could not let you leave Deutz without me," Clothilde responded.

"Then we will go tomorrow," Guntram said. "I'll speak to Hubert about this plan. I'm sure I can convince him to release Uland from duty temporarily along with two or three of the other men who were with Michel and me and who know that area well by now. But, Danise, you must understand that we may not find him alive. We may find his body—or find nothing at all, as happened before."

"If we find his body, at least we will know what happened to him, and we can bring him home for a Christian burial," she replied. "I have considered that possibility." She did not add that it was a possibility she refused to accept.

"What would you do then?" Guntram asked.

"If we do not find Michel," she said, "I will turn Elhein over to Charles and retire from the world. I will go to Chelles and die there, for I cannot live without Michel."

At this, Guntram and Clothilde exchanged a look of understanding.

"We will do our best to find Michel," Guntram promised.

Danise, Clothilde, Guntram, and four other men set out early the next day. In her scrip, the small purse she wore at her belt, Danise carried the stiff little card that bore Michel's likeness. Whenever they met other travelers, or passed peasants farming the land or, as happened twice, encountered king's messengers heading toward Aachen with reports for Charles, Danise pulled out the card and, saying it was painted by a foreign craftsman, she asked if the man depicted had been seen. The answer was always negative.

They traveled inland from the Rhine, avoiding the riverside cliffs and promontories that rose upstream south of Deutz. Their errand was too urgent to allow them time to view the scenery. Instead, they took a track Guntram knew through the deep forest. For the most part they slept under the stars and ate the food they brought with them. It was three and a half long days after leaving Deutz before they came to the clearing and the dead ashes of the site of Autichar's camp.

"This is where we last saw Michel," Guntram said. "We'll stop here again and begin our search from this spot."

"I want you to show me where you found Autichar after he was struck dumb," Danise told him as soon as she had dismounted.

"There's little to see except trees," Guntram said. "I've looked at that place a dozen times, but perhaps you will notice something I have missed.

"It's here," Guntram said a few minutes later, having led Danise through a grove of trees. "I marked this tree with my ax so we could find it again while we were searching the first time. This is exactly where we discovered Autichar kneeling on the ground, unable to speak."

"We must examine every bit of this area," Danise said, looking around at tree trunks and heavy underbrush.

"We already have, many times over, but we'll do it again for you," Guntram said.

The men worked until dark, nor did Danise spare herself or Clothilde from the effort. They discovered nothing that might tell them what had become of Michel. When evening came Danise sat by the campfire, only half listening to the men talking. She felt a little guilty because she had not told Guntram what she feared had really happened to Michel, what she hoped and prayed had not happened.

She was the only one in Francia who knew that Michel had come to her time from the future. Guntram's insistence that all his searching, and his men's, had produced no sign of Michel made Danise believe that her husband might have been returned to his own time. The thought that Michel might be living more than a thousand years in the future and unable to contact her, the fear that she would never see him again, was enough to drive her close to madness. She thought it was possible that Autichar had seen Michel leave the present time, and the sight had stricken him dumb with terror.

This was why Danise had been so set upon making another search for Michel. She had to *know* where he was. Even if they discovered his mangled body, it would be better—or would it? Did she want him dead rather than alive and well in a time and place so far removed from her? Was she that selfish?

"No. Not dead," she whispered. "Not Michel." At once Clothilde's arm was across her shoulders.

"We should not have come," Clothilde said. "This unhappy search is breaking your heart."

"I could not stay at Deutz. We may still find him. He might be here yet, injured or without his memory. Whatever force made Autichar speechless may have sent Michel wandering through the wilderness. Oh, Clothilde, if we do not discover *something* to tell us where he is, I think I will die! I must know! I must!"

But the morrow brought no new evidence, and by nightfall Danise could sense that the men believed all their efforts were meaningless.

Still, she could not stop searching. Again and again she returned to the tree Guntram had marked, there to stand gazing about her as if by sheer longing she could bring Michel back to her side.

On the fourth morning of their stay at Autichar's camp, with the men grumbling that there was no sense in remaining where they were, with Guntram declaring that this must be their last day in that place if nothing were found, Danise went once more to the marked tree. Looking around her, she admitted that there was little chance that she would ever see Michel again.

"Michel. Oh, my love, where are you?" She turned slowly around in a complete circle, the skirts of her worn and stained green woolen gown swirling about her ankles. She was so tired of holding back tears she did not want to shed, fearing that weeping would be an admission that Michel was lost to her forever. She knew that out of respect for her father and affection for her, Guntram and his men had done far more than any other men would have cared to do, continuing to look for Michel when all hope of finding him was gone. She had to let them stop searching. She had to put an end to her time with Michel.

She could not do it. Before he left Deutz to rejoin Guntram, Michel had told her not to believe in his death until she saw his body. She had not seen so much as a fingernail.

But she could not make the men keep looking. If she did not stop the search, they would stop it without her permission. They would tell her it was over. Clothilde would be sympathetic and weep with her. Guntram would pat her on the shoulder and say he was deeply sorry and he would mean the words he spoke. Uland and the other men would look solemn and sad. Not one of them would understand how uncertainty gnawed at her.

The tears came at last, pouring down her cheeks. Danise leaned back against the marked tree, unable to stand without its support. Slowly she slid down the trunk of the tree until she was crouching at its base, hands over her face, sobbing aloud.

" 'Ere now, what's this I see?" came a rough, unfamiliar voice.

Danise looked up to see half a dozen men watching her. Their clothing was ragged and worn, but their weapons were in the best of repair and they all looked as if they would use those weapons at a moment's provocation. Wiping her damp cheeks, Danise got to her feet.

"What are you doing here crying, wench?" asked the man who had spoken to her before. He took a step toward her. "Isn't this Autichar's camp?"

"The camp is that way." Danise, still wiping tears away, spoke without thinking. "But Autichar isn't—"

"Never mind," said the man. "We'll just have some food and drink while we wait for him. Are you one of his women?"

"Why do you ask?" A dreadful suspicion

occurred to Danise, making her regret her
ready response to this man's previous question.
"Are you friends of Autichar?"

"That we are," said the man. "We're part of
the contingent he took into Saxony and left
there while he made a foray back to Francia.
Autichar sent word to us to join him here."

"Aren't there more of you?" Danise asked, as
if she thought there should be many more.

"Those heathen Saxons killed some of us,"
came the answer. "We're all that's left. Come
along to the campfire, girl, and let me enjoy
your company. I haven't seen a pretty wench
like you for weeks. Saxon women are too tough
for my taste."

He caught Danise's hand, pulling her in the
direction of the camp. Danise hung back,
tugging on her hand, trying to get free. She
was afraid of what these men might do when
they discovered that Autichar's camp was no
longer Autichar's. From the looks of them, they
would protest the change with their weapons.
Danise knew that even if all of Guntram's men
were at the camp and not out searching for
traces of Michel, there would only be five
of them to these six ruffians, each of whom
looked as if he could take on any number of
warriors and defeat them. There was Clothilde
to consider, too.

Danise believed if she tried to give the alarm
these men would kill her at once without
compunction.

But if Michel were gone and would not
return, what did her own life matter? And

what chance would she and Clothilde have if Guntram and his men went down to defeat?

Danise stood still, refusing to move when Autichar's henchman yanked on her hand again. She drew a deep breath, opened her mouth, and screamed as loud as she could.

"Guntram! Attack! To arms! It's an attack!"

Chapter 19

"All right! I told you I could do it."

"You're going to regret this, Hank." Alice scowled at Hank before she turned her attention to Mike. "Put down that stupid sword. And if you're planning to be sick, get into the bathroom first. It's there, through that door."

Mike heard her and saw her pointing arm, but he couldn't believe what he was seeing and hearing. Nor could he speak for a couple of minutes. Alice was right, he was choking with nausea. At least the wound over his eye wasn't bleeding anymore.

Slowly his stomach settled down and the back bedroom of Alice's little house came into clearer focus. Alice herself was looking at him as if she expected him to be sick all over the floor, and Hank—Hank was grinning almost literally from ear to ear.

"What did you do?" Mike said to Hank as soon as he could speak.

"I just proved my theory for a second time," Hank crowed. Mike wouldn't have thought it possible, but Hank's grin became even broader. "I've been told over and over that it couldn't be done, but I did it!"

"Did what?" Mike demanded.

"I have now sent two people into the past at different times and brought both of them back safely," Hank said. "I want to debrief you right away. Where did I put that notebook?" He turned aside, riffling through some papers on a nearby table.

"Hank, look out!"

"You don't have to yell, Alice," Mike said with deadly calm. "Hank knows exactly what kind of danger he is in, up against the wall with a Frankish broadsword pointed at his jugular vein. Alice, get over here and stand next to Hank so I can keep an eye on you, too. If either of you make a wrong move, Hank is a dead man, and Alice, you'll be next in line for execution. Don't think I can't do it. My reflexes are a lot faster than they were when I left here three months ago."

"Three *hours* ago," Hank corrected, then fell silent when the point of Mike's sword pressed a little more deeply into his neck.

"You wouldn't dare hurt us," Alice began.

"Try me and Hank's blood will be all over your bedroom floor," Mike threatened.

"Do what he says, Alice," Hank begged. "Jeez, Mike, what are you so upset about? You just had a terrific adventure, and you are part of a world-changing experiment. Why, when word of this gets out, we'll all be famous—and rich."

"You amaze me," Mike said. "How can anyone who is a certifiable genius be so appallingly stupid? Don't you know what you've done? Or how dangerous it is to move people around in time? Where's your common sense, man? Or don't you care? What are you going to do, Hank, sell tickets and send people back in time so they can change the past and in changing it, destroy the world we know?"

"Hey," Hank broke into this tirade, "the world we know isn't so great. Maybe a bit of tinkering with the past would help to improve the present."

"Maybe tinkering with the past would prevent you from being born," Mike told him. "Ever think about that, boy genius?" He was sorely tempted to drive the tip of his sword blade through Hank's throat. Murder might well be the only way to stop a lunatic like Hank from continuing his experiments. It took only an instant's reflection to make Mike realize he couldn't kill Hank. Not yet, anyway. First he needed a favor from Hank, and he knew just how to convince him to do what he wanted. "Hank, I'm going to make a bargain with you."

"What kind of bargain?" Hank looked down the length of Mike's sword and gulped. "Do you think you could move that thing a little to the left? It's pretty uncomfortable where it is."

"I'll take it away altogether if you agree to do what I want," Mike said. "In fact, I know a way to make your fortune while at the same time proving beyond any dispute that your theory is true and your experiments are a huge success."

"How?" asked Hank. "Hey, come on, put the sword away. I'm willing to listen to any proposition you've got."

Mike lowered the sword and stepped back one pace. Hank let out a relieved breath. Alice looked as if she might faint.

"O.K.," Hank said. "What's your idea?"

"You are going to send me back to exactly the time and place from which you just removed me."

"That's not going to prove the validity of my theory to anyone in the twentieth century," Hank objected. "You won't be here to back me up."

"I will be here," Mike told him, "because on my prearranged signal, you are going to retransport me back here again."

"I don't get it." Alice pushed herself away from the wall. She was still pale, but the angry intensity Mike had noticed in her on their first meeting was flaring anew. "Why do you want to go back and forth like that? What's the point?"

"The point is," Mike answered her, "that when I come back here for the second time, I won't be alone."

"You want to bring someone with you, out of the past?" Hank stared at him. "Jeez, Mike, I don't know about this."

"Well," Mike responded, shrugging his shoulders as if it really didn't matter, "if you think the problem is beyond your intellectual capabilities, then forget it."

"I didn't say that." Hank chewed his lower lip, thinking. "You make a good point. Somebody from another time, swearing that I brought him here, and with firsthand information about the past to back up his claim, would prove conclusively that my theory is right. It's a great idea, Mike, but I'm not sure this computer can do it. Not without serious modification, I mean."

"How long would the modifications take?" Mike asked.

"A couple of days. I'd have to bring in some more equipment." Hank walked across the room to stand looking down at his computer. "You know, it could work, but it would be dangerous. You could be left there permanently. Or you could get stuck somewhere between the two times—in transit, so to speak—and never get out again. You'd die in there."

"It's worth the chance." Mike met Hank's eyes squarely, praying that Hank couldn't see how many lies he was telling, or how afraid he really was.

"It would mean you'd have to trust me," Hank said.

"You got me back once. I'm betting you can do it again, especially since it would be to your benefit to have two people claiming to be participants in your experiments."

"Who is this person you want to bring into the twentieth century with you?" Alice demanded. "How do we know it's not someone dangerous, who'll go crazy in this time and start chopping people up with a sword like that one?" She sent a fearful glance toward the weapon still in Mike's right hand.

"It's not a warrior," Mike said. "It's my wife. I can't live without her, and after all the grief she's been through recently, I'm pretty sure she won't last long without me, either."

"Your wife?" exclaimed Hank. "Hey, you really did have an adventure, didn't you, old buddy? I'll have to hear all about it sometime." He socked Mike on the arm in a playful way.

Mike nearly did kill him then. He restrained himself, knowing that without Hank's help he would never see Danise again.

"Well?" he said to Hank. "Can you do it, or not? And if you can, are you willing to risk everything on one grand experiment?"

"The whole idea is crazy," Alice said. "Hank, you know it can't be done. You barely got Mike back, so how can you imagine you could retrieve two people at once?"

"It's a challenge, I admit, but hey, I like a tough puzzle. Now look, Alice, you are going to have to help me."

"I'll do anything I can," Mike offered.

"Yeah, sure." Hank's attention was on his computer. "Hey Alice, you know that old computer you stashed in the dining room closet? Show Mike where it is, will you? And help him move it in here while I write out a list of stuff for you to buy over at Electronics Discount Mart. I've just had a brainstorm."

It took them four days to modify the computer to Hank's satisfaction. Mike curbed his impatience with the intricate, tedious work. He wanted everything to be just right before Hank attempted to move him to the eighth century and back to the twentieth again. After listening to Hank's explanation of the process they were going to try, Mike knew he would only have the one chance to reach Danise. He also thought the passage of a few days would mean little to Danise, because if his plan worked out, to people in the eighth century it would be as though he had never been absent.

"Don't be too sure of that," Hank cautioned when Mike voiced this belief. "We're talking about an experimental effort here. After years of moving people around I may fine-tune the computer to within a second or two, but not yet. You'll be lucky if I can send you back to a week or so after you left."

"If that's the best you can do, I'll have to live with it," Mike said. "Just be sure you don't make me materialize in thin air or the top of a tree the way you did the last time. And send me to the right place. I can make my way home from there and claim I got lost in the woods."

"Hummph," said the ever-unpleasant Alice. "Wandering in the woods for weeks? I'd never believe an excuse like that."

"You've never seen an eighth century forest," Mike responded.

"We're all set," Hank said. "Mike, do you have any last minute details to attend to before you leave on this trip? Want to eat, drink, go to the bathroom?"

"No, thanks." Mike would not admit to the trepidation he felt about the whole enterprise. His feelings didn't matter. Danise's did, and it was worth any risk to have her with him. "Let's get on with it."

"Now, remember, when you're ready to come back, press on this gadget I've fastened to your belt, and keep your wife right next to you. Jeez, will you look at this, Alice? An eighth century Frankish sword and the latest electronic invention, both hanging from the same belt. Is that a sight, or what?"

"Don't congratulate yourself yet," Alice said in her sourest voice. "It may not work."

"It has to work," Mike told her. "I'm betting my life on it. And my wife's life, too. Hank, when I give the signal, get Danise and me back right away. No delay, understand? I plan to choose exactly the right minute and I don't want any foul-ups from this end."

"Yeah, yeah." Despite his claim that all was in readiness, Hank was still fiddling with switches and with the dial on a mysterious gauge installed only that morning. "Jeez, Mike, you make me feel like the mad scientist in some way-out science fiction movie. Give me a break. You said you'd trust me."

"Right." Mike sincerely hoped Hank would

not discover just how little he was trusted until Mike and Danise were safely in the twentieth century. By then, it wouldn't matter that Mike had secretly made several telephone calls while Hank was busy with the computer and Alice wasn't there. "What do you want me to do, Hank?"

"Just come over here," Hank instructed, "and put your hand on the screen. Yes, like that. O.K., here we go."

Hank threw a switch on the computer. Mike heard a humming noise followed by the appearance of the familiar pulsating orange-gold light. Then came the blackness and the sensation of falling. This time there was a difference. This time he welcomed the feelings of dizziness and nausea. Nor did the black silence terrify him. Now that he was on his way to find Danise, his earlier concerns about the experiment vanished. He was excited and yet perfectly serene about what he was attempting to do.

Until he heard Danise screaming. . . .

Chapter 20

"It's an attack! Guntram, help!" Even as she screamed out her warning, Danise was surrounded by Autichar's men, all of them with drawn swords or battle-axes in hand. They closed in around her with relentless purpose written clear upon their faces.

Danise knew she would be dead before Guntram reached her, but at least he and Clothilde and the others would be warned. Her sacrifice might enable her friends to live. The only thing left for her to do in these last moments of her life was say her prayers.

Clasping her hands at her bosom, Danise closed her eyes, thinking of Michel, praying for his well-being and happiness, wherever he was. A quick prayer for the safety of Guntram and Clothilde and the rest of their group followed.

Before she finished it, rough hands pulled the linen scarf off her hair and grabbed at her braids, jerking her head backward, baring her throat to her killer's blade. Something— sword or ax, she knew not which—slashed across her cheek, drawing blood. This was the moment, then. Waiting for the final, death-dealing stroke, Danise gathered all her strength and courage to withstand it without flinching.

Her next and final prayer ought to be for herself, but suddenly her willingness to die vanished and Danise was filled with a blazing anger and a resurgence of her desire to live. She, the daughter and wife and friend of brave warriors, was not going to allow herself to be cut down like a willing victim! Whether she ever saw Michel again or not, she was going to make him proud of her. She was going to die fighting and until her last breath she was going to continue to shout out her warning to Guntram.

When she opened her eyes she looked right into the face of the man who had first accosted her, the leader of the warrior band. Unclasping her fingers from their prayerful position she pushed hard against the man with both hands, forcing him backward. He was not expecting her sudden movement. He stumbled, collapsing against two of his fellows, who were crowding around her. They caught his arms, pulling him away from her.

Surprised by their action, and by an unusual glare, Danise blinked. The sunlight was unnaturally bright here in the deep woods where it ought to be shady. The men around her were all falling back now, staring at something she had not yet seen, and leaving Danise standing alone.

No one spoke. There was a strange silence filling the forest glade. The unusual light grew stronger, and Danise began to wonder if she were already dead. She looked in the direction in which all the men were gazing, and saw a globe of orange-gold light. Caught in amazement she stared at it, unable to move. A human figure stepped out of the light and came toward her.

"Danise!" She recognized that beloved voice.

"Michel? *Michel!*" She was in his arms and she knew he was no ghost and no dream, either. He was alive and so was she. "You came back for me!"

"What are you doing here?" he demanded. "You should be safe at Deutz. Never mind, you can tell me later. Actually, this is a stroke of wonderful luck."

"Michel, where have you been? What is that light? It hurts my eyes, and look at Autichar's men, how they are standing so still, staring at it."

"Hush, darling. Don't talk, just listen. Those fellows will probably recover from their shock in a minute or two. Danise, I have found a way to take you with me into the twentieth century. At least, I think I have. I have to warn you, it is dangerous. Will you take the risk? Will you go with me?"

"You cannot stay in Francia any longer?"

Danise held on to his hands, unwilling to release him even for an instant.

"I have to return to the twentieth century," he said. "If I don't, Hank will never stop his experiments. Who knows how far he will go or how much damage he'll succeed in doing? Once I've fixed things so he can't move people around in time anymore, I won't be able to come back here. Danise, I hear Guntram, and he sounds as if he's coming closer."

"I shouted to warn him of the attack. But, Michel—"

"There's no time for any explanation," he interrupted. "Right now, Danise—this instant—you have to decide. I know this demand is unfair to you, but it can't be helped. Are you going with me, or are you staying?"

"I will go anywhere with you. I cannot live without you."

"Be absolutely sure. Once we go, there's no turning back."

"I am with you, Michel, to the very end of time." There was no doubt in her heart, only joy.

"Then hold on to me and try not to be too frightened. I love you, Danise." He pulled her toward the waiting light.

"And I love you. Oh, what is that box on your belt?"

His hand was on the box, pressing it hard. It began to emit a strange humming sound. Danise would have jumped away from it, but Michel caught her with his free arm, holding her tight against his side.

"Don't let go," he said. "Stay right here with me."

The humming noise grew louder, and suddenly they were drenched in light so brilliant that Danise pressed her face into Michel's shoulder to shield her eyes from it. Then, in the next moment, all was empty blackness. All things familiar fell away from her, leaving her completely alone except for Michel, who still held her close.

She was not afraid. Whatever was happening, she was with her love. If they were dying, they would die together, and she had been prepared for a death far worse than this. She was not even afraid when they began to fall.

"It is beyond my understanding." Guntram shook his head. "So many men, all discovered in the same unexplainable condition. First Autichar, and now these men, all of them found on their knees in the same location, every one staring at nothing with expressions of horror on their faces."

"I can explain it." Uland crossed himself, then made the sign a second time. "There is a dreadful monster living somewhere in this forest, a creature that snatches away people without a trace. Autichar saw it when Michel was taken. Now these men have seen Danise carried off in the same manner."

"Who are they?" Guntram gazed down at the six pitiable figures, then looked around. "They were heavily armed. See, Uland, there are two battle-axes and here is a sword someone has dropped, but every man of them still has a weapon in hand." Bending down, Guntram removed the sword from the unresisting fingers of one man. "All armed and yet stricken dumb and immobilized. Never have I dealt with so great a mystery."

"Guntram?" Clothilde hurried through the trees. "Your men tried to stop me, but I must know. Where is Danise?"

His eyes suddenly full of tears, Guntram picked up a bloodstained linen cloth. He held it out to Clothilde. Smothering a cry of anguish, she took the cloth from him.

"What has happened here?" Clothilde recoiled from the unmoving men kneeling in silence before her.

"Whatever creature took Michel away has also taken Danise," Guntram said. "Perhaps the intent of these men was as evil as Autichar's intent. Perhaps that is why they have been punished as he was."

"Oh, no! Danise! Danise." Clothilde paid no heed to Guntram's suppositions. She heard only his words about her mistress. "Danise!" Guntram caught her, stopping her from plunging into the trees in search of Danise, holding her in place by embracing her with an unbreakable grip.

"We should leave here at once," Uland advised. "This is a dangerous and unnatural place."

"We cannot leave," Clothilde cried, struggling against the restraint of Guntram's arms. "We must find Danise. Guntram, begin a search."

"You sound now the way Danise sounded when she heard of Michel's disappearance," Guntram said. "I do not want to be unkind to you, Clothilde, and you know I loved Danise as if she were my own daughter, but I will not risk the life of any other person in a fruitless search. We have from Danise's loss the proof we were seeking for Michel's death. That bloody headcloth tells us she was badly injured or killed at once, and her body carried off by the beast. There can be no chance for her survival. Surely, the same fate also befell Michel. That is what I will report to Charles."

"I have been with her since she was a baby," Clothilde sobbed. "How can you ask me to give up so easily?"

"You will do it because there is nothing else you can do," Guntram said, though not unkindly. "I am convinced that Uland is right. There is a monster lurking in this forest, which you must agree is dense enough to conceal any number of large beasts. I believe we will never find Danise or Michel, or any trace of their bodies, and I wish I had never agreed to bring Danise to this terrible place. If I had refused her, she would still be alive. I blame myself for her death."

"Don't say that. If you had refused her, she would have come here alone." Clothilde was calm enough by now to consider what Guntram was saying, and to appreciate the depth of his grief. "Danise would never have believed that Michel was gone without seeing for herself. Now she knows the truth of his disappearance, and we shall never see her again. We must pray that they are together and happy in heaven."

"Come back to camp with me, Clothilde," Guntram said, "and there pack up your belongings and Danise's. Uland, get the other men to help you move those poor lost souls. We'll take all of them with us, mounted on our extra horses. We leave for Deutz within the hour."

With a last, sorrowful glance around the forest glade, Guntram turned toward the camp. Looking at him as she walked beside him, Clothilde saw the tears coursing down his fierce warrior's face.

Chapter 21

"Come on, come on," Hank urged. "We can do this."

"There is absolutely no point in talking to a machine," Alice muttered. "I told you it would never work."

"Get out of the way. You're no help to me at all." With his left arm Hank pushed Alice aside. He moved her just in time. Where she had been standing, right next to the computer, two figures materialized.

"Gotcha! Yeeow!" Hank's yell of delight was cut off when sparks began to fly from under the table where the computer was. "Alice, cut the power!" Alice raced out of the bedroom.

"Jeez." Hank shook his head in disgust. "I think we just blew all the circuits."

"Michel," said Danise, "this is the man for

whom you mistook Adelbert, isn't it? They are much alike, but I do see a difference. Adelbert is taller, and much more neat in his appearance."

Hank had been paying more attention to his computer than to his newly material-ized guests. Now he stared in fascination at the lovely eighth century apparition who was speaking to Mike in a soft voice, using a completely unfamiliar language. Except for one word.

"Why didn't you tell her to call me Hank?" he demanded. "I never use my middle name."

"Never mind that. You did it!" Mike stuck out his hand. "Hank, I have to admit, I wasn't sure you could handle two people at once, but you are something else when it comes to computers. Congratulations."

"Yeah." Hank neglected to shake hands with Mike. His eyes were still on Danise. "I can hardly believe it myself. Aren't you going to introduce me?"

"You bet I am. This is my wife, Danise." Putting his arm around her, Mike switched to Frankish for the rest of the introduction. "Danise, this is the man who made it possible for you to come with me."

Smiling at the unkempt young man, Danise put out her hand in the same way as Mike. This time Hank paid attention. He raised her hand, examined her fingers to make certain they were solid, and then raised them to his lips in what he obviously imagined was a gracious gesture of welcome to this living relic of an ancient and heroic age. His bemused contemplation of Danise's features was interrupted by the reappearance of the owner of the house.

"What the hell are you doing?" Alice demanded. "You've never chewed on *my* fingers!"

"I am kissing her hand," said Hank in his most dignified manner. "It is a continental custom. Perhaps if you were more ladylike, I'd do the same for you."

"You are a real wacko," Alice responded.

"Danise," Michel asked, seeing her sway and put a hand to her head, "are you all right? We ought to find a bandage for that cut on your cheek."

"I am a little dizzy," she said, "and I'm very glad that I did not break my fast this morning, for my stomach is most uneasy. I think it will pass before long. Michel, are we safely where you wanted to go? Is the movement in time completed now?"

"It is. There's no returning for either of us. Have you any regrets?"

"None, so long as I am with you." She put her arms around him and Michel bent his head for a quick kiss.

"Welcome to the twentieth century, my love," he said.

"I want to see everything." Danise was so excited by the prospects before her that she could hardly speak. "Your cities, your schools. Have you horses in this time?"

"You are going to have to teach her to speak English," said Alice in her sour way.

"She'll never make it if she insists on using that gibberish."

"I plan to teach her myself." Turning his attention to Hank, Mike gently set Danise aside and went to the computer. "What happened to it, Hank?"

"You know the new component, the one I added to boost the power so I could move two people instead of just one person at a time?"

"Yes." Knowing he was going to have to stop Hank from repairing the computer, Mike closely watched every move Hank made. "What about that component?"

"I pulled in extra power to feed it. As a result, there was a short circuit. The wiring in this house is pretty old and couldn't take the extra juice. I got you here just in the nick of time. Another few seconds and you wouldn't have made it."

"The fuse for the computer circuits has burned out," Alice informed them, "and two other fuses besides."

"What does that mean for your computer?" Mike asked Hank, hoping it meant the computer was irreparably damaged.

"It's going to take a lot of work to fix it," Hank said. "If the fuse didn't blow soon enough, it could take weeks, maybe months, to repair. But that doesn't matter now. I've proved my theory, and you and Danise are here to back me up, just as we planned."

"What about repeating the experiment in the future?" Mike regarded the computer with intense interest.

"As long as I have the disk that's in there now, and the notebook, I can replicate the experiment at any time. You put the second disk in your jacket pocket just before you left here the first time. I don't suppose you brought it back with you?"

"It's lost in the eighth century, along with my other personal belongings."

"That's a shame," Hank said. "I really would like to have both disks, but at least I have the remaining one." He got to his knees and began looking under the computer table.

"What are you doing?" Mike asked.

"Unplugging the whole system." Hank's voice was muffled. "Hey, Alice, go put in a fresh fuse. I'm going to try something. If I can get this baby humming again, I won't have as much work as I expected."

Alice obediently left the room. Hank remained beneath the table. Looking toward Danise, Mike put a finger on his lips, cautioning silence. She nodded. Mike picked up the notebook that lay open next to the computer keyboard. A quick glance at it told him it was the right notebook, the one Hank had stolen from India Baldwin. Mike handed the notebook to Danise.

"Hang on to this," he said softly. "Don't give any sign that I'm doing anything more than explaining to you what is happening. Move slowly toward the door and be ready to leave at my signal. Hank may try to make trouble when he sees what I am going to do."

"Please don't kill him," she begged. "Were it

not for him, we would never have met. I am grateful to him for that."

"No one is going to be seriously hurt," Mike assured her. "But I have to stop Hank from continuing this insane work of his. If he can get that computer going again, he'll be right back at it within the hour."

When Danise stepped out of range, Mike drew the sword that still hung from his belt. Down at floor level, Hank began to slide out from under the table.

"Is everything unplugged?" Mike asked.

"Yeah, it's safe to work on it now," Hank replied.

"Good." Holding his sword in both hands, Mike swung back his arms and aimed a mighty slash at the computer.

"Hey, what are you doing?" Hank scrambled to his feet. "Cut that out! You're ruining my computer."

"I know." Mike hacked at the machine again.

"Stop it!" Hank made a move toward Mike, then jumped out of the way of the flashing blade. "My computer!"

Mike did not stop until the computer and all its special components lay in pieces. Then, after sheathing his sword and while Hank stood shaking his head in trembling, speechless rage, Mike lifted the floppy disk out of the ruins and gave it to Danise to hold.

"I've wrecked the edge of my blade, probably permanently," he noted to Hank, "but it was worth it to stop you."

At this point Alice returned to the bedroom.

"What do you think you're doing?" she shouted at Mike. "Just look at this mess!"

"Hank's career in organizing time-travel tours has just ended," Mike announced.

"You promised to back up my claims," Hank cried. "How am I going to prove the truth of my theory if I can't replicate the experiments? Mike, we could have been rich! I could have won a Nobel Prize." Hank's heartbroken litany of complaints ended only when Mike seized him by the shirtfront, lifting him off his feet.

"Listen to me, Hank," Mike ground out. "Any promise you think I made to you is overridden by the moral imperative to keep you from destroying the present-day world. Your experiments with the space-time continuum are over. Get that? Done. Finished. *Finito. Kaput.*" With a gesture of supreme disdain he set Hank back on his feet.

"What about my work?" Hank was close to tears. "You talk about me destroying the world when you don't know for a fact that it would happen, but you have just destroyed *my* world. Everything I hoped to accomplish was tied up in that computer." He broke off, regarding the ruined computer with swimming eyes and a tragic expression.

"Oh, I am so sorry." Danise could not understand what Mike and Hank were arguing about, but her ready sympathies were stirred by the pathetic sight of a man in tears over the destruction of a treasured possession. Hands outstretched, she moved toward Hank, intending to comfort him and to thank him

410

for saving her from a lifelong separation from Michel.

She never reached Hank. Alice stepped between them, snatching at the disk and notebook Danise was holding. At once Danise whipped her hand behind her back. She could not understand what Alice said, but the woman's anger was obvious to her.

"Leave Hank alone. You and your precious Mike have just about killed him. His work was all he cared about," Alice said. Turning to Mike, she went on, "You get out of here, both of you. *I* will take care of Hank."

"The situation is not as bad as you think, Alice," Mike informed her. "I'm not completely ungrateful for Hank's help in bringing Danise into the twentieth century to live. But just in case his last experiment failed and I never returned, I made a couple of phone calls yesterday, while you were at the electronics store and while Hank was too busy in here to keep an eye on my activities."

"What do you mean?" Alice took a menacing step toward Mike.

"Stop!" Danise put up a hand to keep Alice away from her love. "Michel, beware. I cannot understand her words, but I can tell this woman's intent is malicious."

"Keep her away from me and from Hank," Alice ordered, glaring at Danise, who looked back at her with no trace of fear.

"I plan to do just that," Mike replied, smiling at Danise. "Far away from both of you."

"What did you mean, you made phone calls?"

Alice now demanded. "To whom? And why?"

"At any time now you are going to have some interested visitors," Mike said.

"Who?" Alice went white. "Did you turn us in to the Feds? You bastard! After all we did for you! I warned Hank he should leave you there in the past, and good riddance to you, but he wouldn't listen."

"Not exactly the Feds," Mike told her. "There is nothing to be frightened about. I told you when I first came here that there are people who are extremely interested in Hank's work. I think by the time the sun sets today he should receive an absolutely fascinating job offer in a slightly different and much less dangerous line of work."

"Oh, yeah?" sneered Alice. "And what about me? Am I going to end up paying for what happened here?"

"I daresay, if you could bring yourself to try a little tact and just a smidgen of graciousness, you might talk yourself into a new line of work, too," Mike said. "After all, you have been Hank's assistant for some time, haven't you?"

"A job? Fat chance." Alice stared at him, openly disbelieving. "I haven't worked for months. I'm practically bankrupt after supporting Hank with my savings. He said when his experiments were finished, we'd both be rich. But you ended those dreams. Are you telling me someone is going to offer me work, just like that? Out of thin air?"

"Stick around and find out," Mike said. "I think you'll be pleasantly surprised." He took

Danise's hand. "Come on, my love, it's time for us to leave. Oh, by the way, Alice, I would appreciate it if you and Hank would keep quiet about Danise's sudden appearance."

"You don't have to worry about us talking," Alice said in a slightly more agreeable tone than she ordinarily took when speaking to Mike. "Nobody would believe us if we said where Danise has come from, or how she got here. We'd be locked up for nut cases."

"I knew you'd understand. Good-bye, Alice. Hank." With his wife's hand clasped firmly in his, Bradford Michael Bailey walked outside, into the bright sunshine of a New Mexico morning. His car was still parked beside Alice's house, where it had been for the better part of a week. Mike looked at his car and then at Danise.

"I know I have asked a lot of you today," he said to her. "I am going to ask more now. I want you to trust me completely, and not be frightened by what is going to happen. Just remember that this time is very different from your own."

"I trust you with my life," she said, stepping away from the house with him. "Haven't I proven as much?"

"Indeed you have. Danise, you and I are going to climb into that dusty red chariot you see just in front of us. I am going to fasten belts across your shoulders and around your hips so you can't fall out, and then we are going to move faster than you have ever moved before. I don't want you to be frightened."

Flora Speer

"I have come across twelve centuries to be with you," she replied. "Nothing can frighten me."

"I'm not so sure about that."

"Where is the stable?" Danise asked, looking around. "I will help you with the horses."

"This chariot doesn't use horses." Mike stopped walking to regard Danise with a smile. "Although we do have a unit of measurement that we use to describe how many horses would be required to do the work of the engine in this car."

"*Car,*" she repeated, trying to make sense of what he was telling her. "*Engine.* Oh, a machine. Yes, I have watched builders with their machinery, the ropes fitted around little wheels that they use to lift heavy stones."

"The engine in this car is much more complicated than that," Mike said.

"There is so much I need to learn. May I see your machinery?"

"There isn't time right now, but later I'll be glad to explain it to you. I want to get you out of here before Hank's visitors arrive." He was running his fingers beneath the car. Danise watched him, expecting some wondrous thing to occur.

"Michel, what are you doing?"

"As far as I can remember," he said, "my keys are lost in the eighth century. But I have an extra car key hidden here, in case the other is lost." Retrieving the key, he opened the car door. "You sit down in there, Danise. I'll fasten the safety belts for you."

414

Danise stood where she was, pulling on the drawstring of the scrip that was fastened at her waist.

"Your belongings," she murmured, tugging loose a knot and reaching into the little purse. "I almost forgot that I have this. Will it be of any use to you?" She handed him a stiff little card.

"You brought my driver's license with you?" Mike took the card, then flung his arms around her. "You wonderful woman. God, how I love you. My darling, you have saved me endless hours at the Motor Vehicle Department, not to mention saving me from possible arrest if we're stopped and I don't have it."

"You are pleased, then?" Danise paused to let him kiss her before she got into the car. After Mike fastened the belts around her and climbed into his own seat, she looked at the panel in front of him and at the wheel he was apparently going to use to maneuver the machine. "Michel, how many *horsepowers* are there in this chariot—this *car?*"

"If I told you," he said, "it would terrify you. Perhaps you ought to close your eyes until we are moving."

"No. I must face these challenges so that I can live my life as any woman of your time would do."

"All right. You asked for it. But, please, Danise, don't scream while I'm driving. What I am going to do now is perfectly normal for this time and place."

"I am not afraid," she said again.

"Maybe you ought to be." He put the car into gear and began to back out of the driveway. Danise went white and bit her lip, but she uttered no sound as he eased into the street and shifted gears. Out of the rearview mirror he saw two long, black limousines approaching from several blocks away. "Just in time," he muttered, and floored the gas pedal.

Danise did not scream. She clenched her hands together until her nails cut into her palms, but she kept her mouth shut and her eyes open. Michel handled his strange chariot with such ease and sureness that she felt certain this means of travel must be safe. Surely she would soon grow used to it.

"How are you doing?" His hand was on top of hers. She wished he would put it back on the wheel.

"We are traveling so rapidly that everything passes in a blur," she said.

"You'll get used to it. Here we are." He pulled into a space in front of a long, two-storied building. "This is called a motel. It's the best accommodation in town, though admittedly, that's not saying much. Wait here in the car, till I pick up the key to my room."

He strode away from the car to a building faced with the most enormous windows Danise had ever seen. While she looked eagerly at every object she could see and at each oddly dressed person who walked past Michel's car, Danise began to practice the new words she had learned.

"Motel," she said aloud. "Town. Car. Computer. Driver's license. *Horsepowers*." The last word made her laugh. She imagined a team of miniature horses, galloping as fast as they could inside the part of Michel's car where the engine was. And then she thought of Francia, and the friends she would never see again, and her laughter ceased.

"What's wrong?" Michel opened the car door to help her out of the safety belts and the low seat.

"I was thinking of Clothilde and Guntram," she said. "Of Sister Gertrude, and Alcuin, of Charles and Hildegarde, Uland and Hubert. I will miss all of them sorely.

"But I am not sorry to leave them behind, Michel. My place is with you, and I will make new friends. It's just that it's difficult to say farewell to the old ones."

"I know," he said. "I will miss them, too. Danise, it is going to take you a while to get used to all of this. I'll help you as much as I can, but please, be patient with yourself.

"Now, while we were at Alice's house you mentioned that you haven't eaten today. There is a coffee shop here at the motel, on the other side of the office. We can eat there and they'll put the charge on my bill. I won't have any cash until my new credit card arrives, which ought to be some time later this afternoon, since that was one of several calls I made yesterday. I told the company my old card was lost and I would need a replacement. Luckily, I didn't have to tell them *where* it was lost." He stopped, grinning at the perplexed look she gave him. "You don't have the faintest idea what I'm talking about, have you? Just come with me."

"In Francia, hungry travelers are given a meal without regard to their ability to pay," she said. "Michel, what about your sword, and my clothing and yours?"

"Believe me, we'll be better off if I leave the sword in the car, though it will be safer hidden in the trunk. As for what we are wearing, I don't think anyone will notice. That purse at your belt is the very latest style."

The sword would not fit in the trunk. He wedged it into the back seat, after wrapping it in an old sweater he found in the trunk. After satisfying Danise's curiosity with a hasty explanation about the necessity for a spare tire, Mike took her hand and led her to the coffee shop.

She tried to act as though everything she saw was not amazing to her, but it was difficult not to clutch at Michel's arm and inquire about the smallest object. The dining hall into which they were ushered by a woman in a scanty outfit and with a most outrageously painted face contained many small tables, each in its own alcove fitted with padded benches.

"Waddaya have, hon?" Another skimpily gowned, painted young woman loomed over them. Danise looked helplessly at Michel.

"I'll order the food," he said to her, and proceeded to talk to the young woman in his own language while Danise looked out the window. There, on the road beside the motel, cars similar to Michel's rushed by.

"Where are they all going?" she asked. When Michel and the maidservant both stared at her, Danise said, "The cars. There are so many. And so much *horsepowers*. They go so fast."

"You'll get used to it," Michel said, laughing. "I just realized that you don't know what a fork is. I'll have to teach you to use one."

While the maidservant was gone he showed her the implements on their table, explaining the use of each, as well as of the jars of condiments and napkins made out of extremely thin, parchment-like material. When the food came, on shiny white pottery platters, Danise repeated the name of each item Michel had ordered.

"Steak," she said. "Scrambled eggs. Toasted bread. These are very thin slices. Butter. Why so little of it, and why isn't it in a bowl? What is this strange little packet? Jelly? What is jelly? Oh, it is much too sweet. If I eat it, it will make me ill, the way too much honey does. Michel, what is this dreadful brew in my cup? Why are you laughing now?"

"Because you are right," he said. "It's called coffee, and it is a dreadful brew. In other restaurants, it is made in a better way, so that it tastes delicious, especially with lots of cream."

They made a game of the meal, laughing at Danise's attempts to convey food to her mouth with the four-pronged instrument Michel called a fork.

"I can see you are going to learn quickly," he

said when they were finished.

"Since you tell me it is rude to eat with my fingers, I will have to learn, or starve." She gave him a contented smile.

After leaving word at the motel desk that the messenger with his new credit card could find him in his room, Michel took Danise there and listened in amusement to a new series of comments from her.

"How clever to place the bed in the middle of the room instead of in the corner against the wall," she said. "You can get in or out from either side, though you would have more room for your friends to sit if it were against the wall. There is no trestle bed beneath it for guests. What is this box?"

"Television," he said. "An invention that will teach you a lot about this world. At the moment, I would like to show you a modern bathroom."

"I can scarcely believe it," she cried a few minutes later. "You have only to turn a handle and hot water comes pouring into the basin. How Clothilde would enjoy this. Michel, you bathed in the River Rur and never complained. How uncivilized you must have thought us in Francia."

"Never uncivilized," he replied. "In some ways, your people were far beyond mine. Besides, it was worth taking a few cold baths to find you. Would you like to be introduced to another twentieth century invention?"

"Oh, yes. This is all so exciting. My thoughts are spinning."

"Take off your clothes," he ordered. He was pulling at his own tunic, so Danise complied without further question.

"Ah," she said when she saw him naked. "You have been teasing me. This is no twentieth century invention. You want to make love with me." He waited until she had pulled down the coverlet to prepare the bed before he took her by the shoulders and pushed her back into the bathroom. There he turned on the shower.

"Step in," he said, and Danise obeyed. Michel followed her, pulling the curtain across the opening. Then, beneath the pounding water, with clouds of steam rising into the cool air of the room, he began to wash her. He started with her face, and when he was done and had kissed her eyes, her nose and mouth, he invited Danise to wash his face. Next he unbraided her hair and rubbed into it a pleasant-smelling concoction that foamed into a thousand bubbles and left each strand as smooth as silk after the bubbles were washed away. When he was done with her, Danise washed his hair in return. Turning off the water, he soaped her body with his hands, not missing a single spot, fondling every curve and crevice from her earlobes to her fingertips to her toes.

"Now it's your turn," he breathed, handing the bar of soap to her.

She thought she knew his body, but now she discovered there were parts of him that she had never seen or touched before. There was, for instance, a sensitive spot just behind his left ear. He begged her to stop when her tongue lingered there too long, and he told her she was supposed to use the soap instead. She saw the effect her attentions were having on him. Never had he been so large and hard. She wondered if he would take her right there in the slippery shower, but he urged her to wash his back instead. She traced her fingers over rippling muscles and down his spine to the enticing cleft between his buttocks. Slowly she let her soapy fingers slide within. With a groan, he caught her hand and pulled her around to face him.

"I have not finished here," she murmured. "There is so much more that requires a thorough soaping."

"That can wait until later."

"See how eagerly it rises to meet my cleansing hand," she persisted, stroking him, reaching between his legs.

She should have remembered how strong he was. Within the blink of an eye he pulled her arms around his neck and pressed himself full against her body. His rigid manhood slid between her moist thighs. Sighing with happiness, she offered herself to him.

"Not yet," he whispered into her ear. "Wash the soap off first."

They stood beneath the cascading water, locked in a fiery kiss.

"Never have I been so clean," she murmured. "I could remain here, like this, all day."

"I can't let you do that. We have other plans." He turned the handle and the water stopped abruptly.

Then Danise was out of the shower and her hair was wrapped in a thick pink towel. Another towel enfolded her body. Michel, still dripping wet, lifted her into his arms to carry her to the next room and deposit her on the bed. The towel around her fell away. Michel covered her.

"This does not change," she whispered. "Not in twelve centuries. Not in a thousand centuries."

"Not in all eternity," he agreed, and made her his in his own century.

Michel was in the bathroom shaving and Danise lay on the bed half asleep, dreaming of his lovemaking, when the unknown noise began. Danise sat up, looking around to discover the source of the noise. It seemed to be coming from a pale brown object that sat on the table beside the bed.

"Michel?" No answer came from the bathroom, but then, Michel was making a fair amount of noise with the instrument he was using, which he had told her would remove his beard. So many objects in this time made noise. People were noisier, too, Danise thought, recalling the shouting maidservants—no, the *waitresses*, she reminded herself. *The waitresses in the coffee shop.* Now it sounded as if the instrument beside the bed would never stop its buzzing-ringing noise.

Danise put out a tentative hand to touch the instrument. It came apart in two sections and the noise stopped.

"Hello?" The voice came from inside the instrument.

"Michel!" Danise leapt from the bed to the bathroom in one great swoop. "Michel, help me!"

"What's the matter?" The rough beard was gone from his face, but she was too frightened to notice its absence. "Danise, what is it?"

"It spoke," she quavered, waving toward the instrument now lying on the floor. "Will it take me back to Francia? I don't want to leave you. I don't!"

Bravely Michel strode forward to pick up the section of the instrument that Danise had dropped. To her astonishment he spoke to it before putting the two sections together and replacing them on the bedside table.

"Michel, what was that?" She was shaking so hard that he drew her down onto the bed where he sat holding her until she was calmer.

"I'm sorry. I forgot how much you still have to learn. The perfectly innocent instrument that terrified you is called a telephone. It will not send you back to Francia. The voice was the messenger from the credit card company. I am going to the office to get my new card. Where is my driver's license? I may need it for identification." Leaving her side he pulled on clean breeches and a short-sleeved blue shirt. He picked up the license and stuck it into the breeches. To Danise's eyes he was now dressed in much the same way as on the first day she had seen him in Francia.

"Why don't you get dressed, too?" he suggested. "With the new credit card I can get cash, so we can buy gas for the car. Then we'll be able to leave this town, which I think would be a good idea. I'd like to put a few miles between us and Hank before nightfall. I don't think there's going to be any trouble, but just in case someone comes looking for us and asking questions about you, let's bid a fond farewell to New Mexico."

But when he returned to the room a short time later, Danise was still sitting on the bed, looking so dejected that he began to be seriously worried about her.

"Talk to me," he said. "Tell me what's wrong and don't be shy about it."

"I am just beginning to realize how difficult my future will be," she said. "There is too much I do not understand. I am afraid, Michel— afraid I cannot learn everything I ought to know in order to be a good wife to you. I am completely lost in this time. Details that you consider ordinary, such as the arrival of a message on a telephone, are miraculous or frightening to me."

"You already are exactly the wife I want, and you are intelligent enough to learn quickly," he said. When she shook her head, unable to respond because she was trying not to cry, he put his hand beneath her chin, lifting it till she was forced to meet his eyes. "Do you remember that day before we were married, and the conversation we had about what would be expected of me as a landed, married, Frankish noble? I was as upset then as you are now."

"I do remember. But this is different," she said. "At least you knew a little about Frankish life. I know nothing."

"What you described to me on that day was a true partnership," he said, choosing to ignore her claim to know nothing. "That is still what I want with you, Danise. I'll help you over the rough spots until you get used to living in this time."

"What can I contribute in return?" she cried. "You were a warrior, a wise councillor to my father, as you would have been to Charles. You knew how to do those things. I do not know how to be a twentieth century woman."

"You are *my* woman. All I want from you is for you to love me for the rest of my life. As a matter of fact, I don't think you will have as much trouble living in the twentieth century as you imagine," he informed her. "Furthermore, I know of someone who can help you, who can even speak to you in your own language if that is what you still want to do when you finally meet her."

"Who is this person?" If Michel believed in her, then perhaps her fears were groundless after all.

"Your old friend, India Baldwin," Michel said. "I have to return her disk and notebook to her. They are the reasons why I came to New Mexico in the first place."

"India?" Danise's face lit with pleasure. "You told me once that you don't know her."

"That's right. I've never met her. It was her

brother-in-law who sent me on this chase after Hank Marsh. But I have a feeling that India will be glad to see both of us. So, my love, arise and attire yourself in that old green dress of yours, and let us be on our way."

"The gown is well worn," she said, taking it off the coat hanger, "but if I wash it carefully, I can still wear it."

"You do have a lot to learn." She could tell he was teasing her, and she began to smile in response to the laughter in his blue eyes. "At the first large city we reach, I am going to take you shopping for a new wardrobe. And that, my dearest love, is one twentieth century custom you are going to enjoy from the very start."

Chapter 22

Guntram found Clothilde in the room that had once belonged to Danise and Michel. She was packing up her late mistress's belongings.

"What will you do with them?" he asked, stopping just inside the door. Clothilde looked up from the gown she was folding.

"The wife of the governor of Koln distributes clothing to the poor. I'll send them across the river to her. It's what Danise would have wanted."

"And what will you do now, Clothilde?"

Before she answered Clothilde finished her work, putting down the lid on the clothes chest with a gesture of finality and a long sigh.

"There, that's done. I suppose I could offer my services to the governor's wife. She is a kind lady. Or I could go to Chelles. Sister Gertrude has promised there will always be a place for me there."

"Do you want to spend the rest of your life with Sister Gertrude?" Guntram grimaced in a way that would have been comical were Clothilde's situation not so grim. "Is that really what you want to do?"

"I haven't much choice, have I?" Clothilde ran her fingers over the lid of the wooden chest, not looking at Guntram.

"Well, now," said Guntram, "there is another opportunity that you may not have considered. I am leaving tomorrow for my own estate. You could go with me."

"What can you want with me, Guntram?" Clothilde asked with a deprecating laugh and a gesture to indicate her sturdy figure. "I am at least five or six years older than you, and I have never been a beauty. You could easily find a younger, prettier woman to perform whatever the duties are that you were thinking of asking of me."

"I care nothing for your age, nor should you," Guntram said. "You and I have seen two young lovers die, while we live on. Nor have I ever had a taste for silly young girls. I have always preferred an older, more sensible woman. Clothilde, we have been on friendly terms for years, have we not?"

"Yes, but—"

"I have never married." Guntram spoke right over Clothilde's objections. "Nor have I any female relatives. I saw at Elhein what can happen when there is no competent woman on hand to manage a man's home for him. I fear I will find something similar when I reach my own new home.

"I know you, Clothilde. I have watched you over the years. You are a capable, honest woman, and for all you think you are no beauty, your plumpness and your sweet face are pleasing to me. So is your quiet voice. I would like to give the running of my household to you. As for anything more, well, I know you will want time to recover from the loss of Danise. I will not press you for more than you are willing to give. But if, after a while, you find me pleasing, too, then you have but to let me know of your feelings. Would you call that a fair bargain?"

"It's more than fair to me, Guntram, but not so fair to you." Clothilde bestowed a wistful smile upon him. "I did not really want to live at Chelles. And the thought of being a servant to someone whose ways I do not know . . . you are right, I do need some allotment of time to recover from so many deaths."

"Then you will go with me?"

"Once I have discharged my last duties to Danise, I am free to do as I wish."

Guntram made no motion toward Clothilde, nor she toward him, but there was a happier light in Guntram's eyes than there had been for weeks, while on Clothilde's face the lines of grief and worry began to ease.

"I'll have someone carry Danise's chests down to the ferry," Guntram said. "If you like, I'll ride across the river with you and wait while you take them to the governor's lady."

"That would be kind of you."

After a moment Guntram put out his hand. At once Clothilde placed her own into it and stood looking into his dark, fierce eyes.

Chapter 23

Cheswick, Connecticut
Early November 1992

"What a pretty house.' Danise swung her elegantly shod feet to the pavement and got out of the car.

"It's Victorian. Remember, I told you about Queen Victoria?" Michel closed the car door behind her and together they walked through drifting autumn leaves up the path to the front door. It was opened by a tall, dark-haired man who carried about him a remarkable air of authority.

"I'm Theo Brant," the man said to Danise. "My wife has been waiting eagerly to see you again."

"Danise?" There was a movement behind the

man. He stepped aside and a slender young woman with soft brown hair appeared.

"India!" Danise threw herself into her old friend's arms for a long and tearful embrace.

"Look at you," India cried when she could speak again. "Danise, you are so beautifully dressed. You look quite the twentieth century woman. Of course your coat would be dark green. As I recall, you wore green as often as possible."

"Michel has given me excellent advice about fashion." Danise's reply made India laugh.

"Why don't we go into the study?" Theo Brant suggested, shepherding them through an arch into a room lined with bookshelves. A cat lay sleeping in the sun that streamed in through a bay window, and a fire burned beneath an ornate mantel.

"So many books." Danise gazed at the filled shelves with shining eyes. "Michel is teaching me to read your language at the same time I learn to speak it." She broke off to reach down and scratch the cat's ears.

"That's Charlemagne. He's named for Charles," India said. "Disgraceful, isn't it, to name a cat for a great king? But he was christened long before I met Charles, and he's too old for me to change his name now."

"Does your husband know, then?"

"Indeed I do." Theo Brant heard Danise's whispered question. He sent a meaningful look in Michel's direction. "You and I should have a long talk sometime soon. I understand we have a lot in common."

"I had a rough time coming to terms with Danise's ideas about the same people cropping up again from time to time throughout history," Michel responded. "From something your brother said to me, I gather you dealt with a similar problem when India told you what had happened to her."

Danise could tell that Michel liked Theo Brant immediately. He should. They had been friends once, long ago. They would be friends again.

"I have a present for you," Michel said to India. He handed her the notebook and the floppy disk he had taken from Hank's computer room. "The other disk is in a wooden clothes chest at Elhein, along with a pair of jeans, a denim jacket, a wallet with a few credit cards, and a set of keys. I can only hope to heaven that I'm the archaeologist who finally digs up that chest. Otherwise, there are going to be a lot of historians hustling to rewrite the past."

"Does anyone else know about these remarkable events?" Danise asked.

"Madame," said Theo Brant, "your command of English is excellent for someone who has been in this country for such a short time. To answer your question, aside from Hank Marsh and his assistant, whom we hope will both have sense enough to keep quiet about what Hank has done, the four of us and my younger brother Mark and his wife are the only ones who know. I assume there are also certain people at high levels of our government who have at least a suspicion as to what happened, because Michel called them in to do something to stop Hank. He has been stopped, hasn't he, Michel? Or are you *Mike* now?" Theo finished with a smile for the other man.

"Either is fine with me. Let's just say that Hank has been guided into a different career path," Michel replied. "I don't see how he can cause any more trouble. But just in case, India, I think you ought to destroy both the disk and the notebook."

"You are absolutely right." India began to tear the pages out of the notebook and toss them into the fireplace. "My first husband made these notes. I know he would be horrified by the use Hank has made of them. He would give me the same advice you have, Michel. Now the disk." It followed the notebook into the fireplace, and all of them watched it burn and melt.

"Now," India said, turning from the hearth, "will you stay to dinner? We have a lot of catching up to do, and I am longing to show Danise how food is cooked in the twentieth century."

When the women returned to the study from the kitchen some time later, they found Michel agreeing to consider a position as a faculty member at Cheswick University, where Theo Brant was chairman of the history department.

"If you do that," Danise said, "then I can live near to my oldest and dearest friend."

"I could only accept with certain conditions," Michel said to Theo. "I want to go back to

435

Francia, to work on the dig I started last year before all this business with Hank began. That's where Danise will be invaluable to me, since she has firsthand knowledge of the Franks. She thought at first there was nothing useful she could do in this time, but I have convinced her otherwise. She will have to be careful what she says about the eighth century, though."

"You may talk freely to us, Danise," said Theo. "Just don't say anything about your origins outside this house or your own home."

"Of course," Danise responded demurely. "I do understand, Theo. None of us would want to be locked up for nut cases."

"A fine command of English, indeed," Theo said in a dry voice. When the laughter had died away, India looked at Michel.

"From what my brother-in-law Mark has told me, I'm sure you know people who can provide the passport Danise will need if you are planning to travel to Europe," she said, "but I would like to make a suggestion of my own."

"What's that?"

"Remarry Danise in this century. If some formality arises in the future, for which you have to produce an original marriage certificate, you are going to have one awful time contacting the priest who blessed your first ceremony to ask him to delve into his records!"

"Danise," said Michel, turning to her, "will you marry me again?"

"Yes," she said. "In this or any time."

"I'll be happy to help with the arrangements." India embraced her friend.

"Danise." Theo's eyes were twinkling. "I think we ought to introduce you to a marvelous invention created by your own people just a few centuries after your era. Michel, will you help me with the glasses? It's time to break out the champagne."

Author's Notes

In the year 779, Charles did actually promulgate a law forbidding the raising of private armies in Francia, for the reasons he notes in this book.

Later in that same year, Hildegarde gave birth to a daughter, who was named Bertha in honor of Charles's mother.

The plot against Charles devised by Autichar, Clodion, and Duke Tassilo of Bavaria is entirely fictional, but the spirit of it is true to history. Duke Tassilo was a problem to his cousin for decades, backing many schemes to unseat Charles from the Frankish throne.

In A.D. 788, this most disloyal of his nobles finally exhausted even Charles's legendary patience by making an agreement with the pagan Avars, wild nomadic horsemen who lived on the eastern borders of Bavaria, to make war together against Charles. Charles sent the Frankish army into Bavaria and defeated Tassilo, who was then taken to the royal seat at Inglesheim and there tried for treason. He was found guilty. The penalty was death but, "for the love of God and because Tassilo is a kinsman," Charles commuted the sentence.

Tassilo, his wife, whom many believed had inflamed his hatred of Charles, their sons and daughters were all sent to various monasteries and convents to live out their lives in enforced peace and in contemplation of their past crimes. Tassilo's only request was that he not be forcibly tonsured in front of the other Frankish nobles. To this Charles consented, and the barbers did their work in private.

Love Just in Time

Flora Speer

After discovering her husband's infidelity, Clarissa Cummings thinks she will never trust another man. Then a freak accident sends her into another century—and the most handsome stranger imaginable saves her from drowning in the canal. But he is all wet if he thinks he has a lock on Clarissa's heart. After scandal forces Jack Martin to flee to the wilds of America, the dashing young Englishman has to give up the pleasures of a rake and earn his keep with a plow and a hoe. Yet to his surprise, he learns to enjoy the simple life of a farmer, and he yearns to take Clarissa as his bride. But after Jack has sown the seeds of desire, secrets from his past threaten to destroy his harvest of love.

___52289-6 $5.50 US/$6.50 CAN

Love ONCE & FOREVER
FLORA SPEER

Laura has traveled here, to this time before the moon has come to circle the earth, to embrace Kentir beneath the violet-and-ochre brilliance of the Northern Lights. In his gray-blue gaze, she sees the longing he cannot hide. His lips seek hers and find them. In his kiss she tastes the warmth of amber wine and the urgency of manly desire. She drinks deeply, forgetting that for them there can be no past, no future; for he is of a time that is ending, while she belongs to one that has yet to begin. Closing her eyes to the soft shadows of the lantern lights, she gives herself to him, determined to live out her destiny in this one precious night.

___52291-8 $5.99 US/$6.99 CAN

Determined to locate his friend who disappeared during a
spell gone awry, Warrick petitions a dying stargazer to help
find him. But the astronomer will only assist Warrick if he
promises to escort his daughter Sophia and a priceless
crystal ball safely to Byzantium. Sharp-tongued and
argumentative, Sophia meets her match in the powerful and
intelligent Warrick. Try as she will to deny it, he holds her
spellbound, longing to be the magician's lover.

___52263-2 $5.99 US/$6.99 CAN
Dorchester Publishing Co., Inc.
P.O. Box 6640
Wayne, PA 19087-8640

Please add $1.75 for shipping and handling for the first book and
$.50 for each book thereafter. NY, NYC, and PA residents,
please add appropriate sales tax. No cash, stamps, or C.O.D.s. All
orders shipped within 6 weeks via postal service book rate.
Canadian orders require $2.00 extra postage and must be paid in
U.S. dollars through a U.S. banking facility.

Name_____
Address_____
City_____State_____Zip_____
I have enclosed $_____ in payment for the checked book(s).
Payment <u>must</u> accompany all orders. ❏ Please send a free catalog.
      CHECK OUT OUR WEBSITE! www.dorchesterpub.com

FOR LOVE AND HONOR

FLORA SPEER

Bestselling Author Of *Love Just In Time*

Falsely accused of murder, Sir Alain vows to move heaven and earth to clear his name and claim the sweet rose named Joanna. But in a world of deception and intrigue, the virile knight faces enemies who will do anything to thwart his quest of the heart.

From the sceptered isle of England to the sun-drenched shores of Sicily, the star-crossed lovers will weather a winter of discontent. And before they can share a glorious summer of passion, they will have to risk their reputations, their happiness, and their lives for love and honor.

__3816-1 $4.99 US/$5.99 CAN

"Flora Speer opens up new vistas for the romance reader!"

—Romantic Times

A valiant admiral felled by stellar pirates, Halvo Gibal fears he is doomed to a bleak future. Then an enchanting vision of shimmering red hair and stunning green eyes takes him captive, and he burns to taste the wildfire smoldering beneath her cool charm.

But feisty and defiant Perri will not be an easy conquest. Hers is a mission of the heart: She must deliver Halvo to his enemies or her betrothed will be put to death. Blinded by duty, Perri is ready to betray her prisoner—until he steals a kiss that awakens her desire and plunges them into a web of treachery that will test the very limits of their love.

_52072-9 $5.99 US/$7.99 CAN

Destiny's Lovers
FLORA SPEER

She is utterly forbidden, a maiden whose golden purity must remain untouched. Shunned by the villagers because she is different, Janina lives with loneliness until she has the vision—a vision of the man who will come to change everything. His life spared so that he can improve the blood lines of the village, the stranger is expected to mate with any woman who wants him. But Reid desires only one—the virginal beauty who heralds his mysterious appearance among them. Irresistibly drawn to one another, Reid and Janina break every taboo as they lie tangled together by the sacred pool.

___52281-0 $5.50 US/$6.50 CAN

REFLECTIONS IN TIME

ELIZABETH CRANE

Bestselling Author Of *Time Remembered*

When practical-minded Renata O'Neal submits to hypnosis to cure her insomnia, she never expects to wake up in 1880s Louisiana—or in love with fiery Nathan Blue. But vicious secrets and Victorian sensibilities threaten to keep Renata and Nathan apart...until Renata vows that nothing will separate her from the most deliciously alluring man of any century.

_52089-3 $4.99 US/$6.99 CAN

DESPERADO
SANDRA HILL

Major Helen Prescott has always played by the rules. That's why Rafe Santiago nicknamed her ''Prissy'' at the military academy years before. Rafe's teasing made her life miserable back then, and with his irresistible good looks, he is the man responsible for her one momentary lapse in self control. When a routine skydive goes awry, the two parachute straight into the 1850 California Gold Rush. Mistaken for a notorious bandit and his infamously sensuous mistress, they find themselves on the wrong side of the law. In a time and place where rules have no meaning, Helen finds Rafe's hard, bronzed body strangely comforting, and his piercing blue eyes leave her all too willing to share his bedroll. Suddenly, his teasing remarks make her feel all woman, and she is ready to throw caution to the wind if she can spend every night in the arms of her very own desperado.

_52182-2 $5.99 US/$6.99 CAN